Praise for *Friends in High Places*

"The sybaritic middle-aged heroine assumes one of her many fake identities, grabs her Louis Vuitton luggage with the secret compartments, and roars off in a Maserati Quattroporte to an ultra-glam location. . . . Don't you wish you were going along? I know I do!"

—*The Seattle Times*

"In her fourth go-around (after *Perfect*, 2005, etc.), Kick Keswick, bling-burglar extraordinaire, 'rocks' again. . . . Kick's unapologetic joie de vivre, unhampered by qualms about age, weight, or fleecing philistines, will thrill the Red Hat jet set."

—*Kirkus Reviews*

"Just in time for beach season is *Friends in High Places*, Marne Davis Kellogg's tenth novel, and the fourth in the Kick Keswick series. It's fun [and] fast paced . . . Kick comes up with solutions for the necklace embarrassment, solves the nun's survival, wraps up a major criminal investigation, and even makes some friends for the first time in her life. She has fun, and so do we."

—*The Denver Post*

"A sumptuous Kick Keswick mystery is the latest in a series, but can easily stand alone. She's a reformed jewel thief with an expensive taste in food (especially white truffles) and clothes—and a Scotland Yard detective for her husband."

—*The Decatur Daily*

FRIENDS in HIGH PLACES

Marne Davis Kellogg

ST. MARTIN'S GRIFFIN

New York

FRIENDS IN HIGH PLACES. Copyright © 2007 by Marne Davis Kellogg. All rights reserved. Printed in the United States of America. No part of this book may be used or reproduced in any manner whatsoever without written permission except in the case of brief quotations embodied in critical articles or reviews. For information, address St. Martin's Press, 175 Fifth Avenue, New York, N.Y. 10010.

www.stmartins.com

Library of Congress Cataloging-in-Publication Data

Kellogg, Marne Davis.
    Friends in high places / Marne Davis Kellogg.
        p. cm.
    ISBN-13: 978-0-312-33731-5
    ISBN-10: 0-312-33731-0
    1. Keswick, Kick (Fictitious character)—Fiction. 2. Jewel thieves—Fiction. 3. Auctioneers—Fiction. 4. Nuns—Fiction. 5. Americans—Europe—Fiction. 6. Provence (France)—Fiction. 7. Italy—Fiction.
    I. Title.

PS3561.E39253 F75 2007
813'.54—dc22

                                                                    2006048099

First St. Martin's Griffin Edition: March 2008

10 9 8 7 6 5 4 3 2 1

For Peter,
my dearest darling

ACKNOWLEDGMENTS

The publication of my fourth Kick Keswick adventure, and tenth novel, brings only thank-yous.

I thank God first, for everything.

In this business agents, publishers, and editors are similar to God, and I have landed in a very fine place, indeed. This outstanding team of professionals is dedicated to the goal of making each novel the best it possibly can be. At St. Martin's Press: Sally Richardson, publisher; Matthew Shear, vice president and publisher, St. Martin's paperbacks; and especially my editor, Jennifer Enderlin, associate publisher. Working with Jennifer, one of the industry's most admired editors, is rich and rewarding—her vision, creative input, and knowledge are amazing. Thank you, Jen. I also thank associate editor Kimberly Cardascia, who is as solid as a rock—responsive, organized, unflappable, and positive.

At Trident Media Group: Robert Gottlieb, president and CEO, and

Kimberly Whalen, vice president and agent, are top professionals at the top of their game—accessible, thinking, working, and selling. They are awesome.

Many, many thanks to Suzanne and Blair Taylor, owners of Barolo Grill and Enotec Imports. In October 2005, Peter and I were in Piemonte for a few days and they flew over to take us on a tour of Gianni Gagliardo's vineyard in Barolo, followed by an astonishing lunch at Il Belvedere. We had white truffles with each course and two magnums of wine—one Barbaresco and one Barolo. Oh, *Dio*. It was one of the most memorable, and by far the most expensive, meals we've ever had, and we can't wait to do it again! Thank God we had a driver. The Taylors, along with Chuck and Barbara Gray, introduced us to Lago d'Orta, Villa Gippini at the San Rocco Hotel, and Villa Crespi.

Blair also advised on the Italian wines, and Hal Logan, president of the Colorado Chapître of the Confrérie des Chaveliers du Tastevin, advised on the French—their selections are ideal and we all benefit from their willingness to share their extensive knowledge and expertise.

In August 2006, I held a contest for Chocolate-Cherry Cupcakes—the response was gratifying and fattening. Thanks to all who participated, and congratulations to Betsy Schrott of New York City, whose recipe became the inspiration for the molten chocolate-cherry cakes in this book. They are heavenly. Without the culinary expertise and recipe-testing assistance of Susan Coe Weiss and our daughter-in-law, Courtney Kellogg, I don't know what I would have done. They made countless batches of chocolate-cherry cupcakes, and we all agreed that Betsy's were the best—her recipe appears in its entirety on my Web site.

Thanks to Leslie Carlson, general manager of the Garden of the Gods Club; she and her staff took beautiful care of me and the dog during my writing sojourn there.

As always, any mistakes are mine.

Love and undying thanks to: Mary and Richard who still take my calls but don't invite me over very often any more; Mary Lou and Randy who continue, selflessly, to head-up my Paris research department; Margaret and Mike Wilfley for a spectacular launch party in their garden; Marcy and Bruce who never say no—to me, at least; Pam and Bill for their friendship; Mita Vail; our next-door neighbor, Judith; my best customer, Sally; McKenna and David for reading an early draft; Kate and Jill for holding things down on the homefronts, and Shannon and Miriam for holding things down at headquarters; and the cowgirls of the National Western—I am so proud to be a member of that team.

I am grateful for the Connecticut Kelloggs and the Colorado Davises; for my darling mother's grace, courage, and sense of adventure; for Major Hunter R. Kellogg, USMC, his elegant, remarkable wife, Courtney, and their Duncan and Delaney; Peter and his fiancée, Bede; our wire fox terrier, Kick, who makes me laugh all the time but is bored out of her mind living in the silent world of a working writer, and, of course, for my beloved Peter. Thanks to his generosity, support, patience, and sense of humor, he's let my writing become a priority. Plus, he's somehow able to pretend that it's always a pleasure to live with me. It is, in fact, always a wild and hearty pleasure living with him.

MARNE DAVIS KELLOGG
Denver, Colorado

FRIENDS
in
HIGH
PLACES

CHAPTER *1*

Éygalières, Provence

"You're looking particularly elegant this evening, Kick," Thomas said as we turned onto the road from Éygalières to St. Rémy on our way to a dinner party at the Balfours' farm in Les Baux. "Very calm. Serene, in fact."

"What a lovely compliment." I smiled over at my husband. "You know, in the last few months, since we got home from that extraordinary trip to Switzerland and I retired for good, I have been feeling secure. It's silly, I know, because the statute on my crimes doesn't expire for who knows how many years and, to my knowledge, Interpol hasn't suspended the international dragnet for me."

"No. But at least I can keep you out of their sights."

"And there isn't a bounty?"

Thomas laughed. "No. No bounty. And listen, if worse came to worst, and you were somehow identified and apprehended, you've done such outstanding service to the crown over the past couple of years, I'm sure Her Majesty's courts would look upon you with compassion."

"Oh, wonderful—you mean only ten years' hard labor instead of life?"

"Something like that," Thomas teased. "But I'll come visit you every day." He turned serious. "Kick, believe me, you're in no danger. I'd tell you if you were. I love seeing a contented smile on your face—you've earned a little peace in your life, a little serenity. Enjoy it."

Maybe Thomas was right. Maybe it was time for me to let up a bit, move down from my normal state of high-alert. But I've never been relaxed or complacent—after all, you don't get to be the most elusive and successful jewel thief in history by being, to use the vernacular, laid-back. My journey from an impoverished girl born to a destitute mother on the fringes of the Oklahoma oil fields to the sunlit existence of a millionairess well-settled in the legendary lavender fields of Provence had been arduous, dangerous, and meticulously planned.

And when I decided it was time to leave the game, I simply disappeared, and immersed myself in the luxury gleaned from decades of solitary, anonymous work. I vanished into the gauzy fairytale world of the super rich who spend their days bathed in golden light and Premier Cru Burgundy. And, as if that weren't enough, a short time after returning to my Provencale farmhouse hideout, La Petite Pomme, I crowned my notorious career by becoming the wife of Sir Thomas Curtis, Scotland Yard's revered Inspector Emeritus. So now, when I was called to duty—occasional assignments that I accepted reluctantly—I worked for the good guys, on the side of the law.

Some may say I'm lucky—they'd be wrong. I don't believe in luck and I didn't get where I am by wishing it so. I've always believed in cautious, considered, controlled advancement, leaving as little as possible to life's inevitable vagaries. But it was true, I had earned time off for good behavior. Maybe I would lighten up a bit.

I leaned back and watched the beautiful countryside fly by, a slight smile played about my lips. "If you want to know, Thomas, sometimes I do feel as though I've quite swallowed the proverbial canary." I laughed.

What a silly, stupid thing to say.

CHAPTER 2

Thomas squealed, practically on two wheels, around the corner onto the D-27, the steep curvy road to Les Baux. He couldn't resist revving the big engine of his brand-new Porsche 911 Turbo S Cabriolet and downshifting as loudly as possible as we approached each S-curve and then flooring it so the g's forced us back into the molded seats. (Occasionally, he'd miss the correct gear and shift into one too high or too low, which invariably brought on a whispered epithet. I bit the inside of my lip and didn't say a word.)

Oh, dear, I thought. Here comes trouble. A large convertible appeared ahead. A stately conveyance with the temerity to be going only double the speed limit, instead of three times. Thomas charged up on their tail and gunned the engine impatiently while I silently hoped the offenders weren't going to the Balfours'. But of course they would be. What else would a lovely, shiny, brand-new, meteor blue Bentley Azure—I mean really, there were only a few of them in the world, they were as rare as hen's teeth—be doing on this road at this hour?

Thomas stuck the nose of his car practically beneath the Bentley's rear end and revved again. It was unseemly.

"What shall we do, darling?" I said. "Just go ahead and ram him?"

"Don't be a backseat driver," he snapped.

I looked out the window, trying to keep from laughing.

Thomas was full of contradictions, and that's why I loved him. For instance, he claimed to be retired. It was a ruse. Retired people don't wear pagers or carry BlackBerries, particularly in Provence. In reality, he'd become head of Europe's elite international anticrime task force and had frequent hush-hush conversations and unexpected, unexplained absences. He was a genius, an intellectual snob—brilliant, professorial brain, occasionally absentminded. But, for all his cerebral superiority, he should never be behind the wheel of a high-performance, ridiculously expensive machine like this—the color was sizzling: *Rouge Indiene*—because he was an exceptionally poor driver. He simply didn't pay attention to what he was doing. It takes a certain type of brain—thoughtful and analytical—to be a chief inspector, not the gee-whiz, showboat, zip-zoom, tight leather pants mentality one typically associates with the owner of a machine like a Porsche Turbo.

"Thomas!" I screamed. I couldn't help it.

The two vehicles arrived at the Balfours' drive at the same moment, but theirs stopped just inside the front gate. And when Thomas finally woke up, he had to slam on the brakes and swerve sharply to avoid smashing into them. Gravel sprayed through the air, peppering the side of the expensive convertible like machine gun bullets and making the passengers duck to avoid being pelted by the stones. I even heard one of the ladies cry out. The driver frowned over at Thomas. "Easy. Easy," he patted the air with his hands. His accent was American.

"Sorry, old chap," Thomas called over jovially through my window. "Expected you to go on up to the front." We continued around to the foot of the walk. "Stupid bastard," he muttered once we were well past them.

"Nicely done." I patted his thigh when we rolled to a stop. I untied my scarf and shook the dust away.

"Thanks," Thomas said and patted the dashboard. "This is a great car."

"Hmm," I agreed. In my side mirror I watched the Bentley's owner bend down and run his hand over the mirror-like finish of his $200,000 vehicle, which was no doubt lacquered with one hundred hand-rubbed coats of something very rare. I think I even saw his chin quiver a bit.

"Kick!" Flaminia, my Persian-Parisian friend with the world's most exotic appearance and the accent to go with it, ran to greet us. Her coal black hair was pulled into a chignon to which she'd added an enormous shocking pink rose from her garden. She had on slim pumpkin-colored silk slacks, a billowy black silk top, and a torsade of amethysts. "What a gorgeous suit," she said to me. "And I'm so glad you've worn that brooch. One day, if you wake up and find it missing—you'll know where to look."

I glanced down at my lapel—the brooch really was exceptional, part of my jewelry collection that was centered around grapes and wine, all basically the same design but with varying stones and precious metals. This particular piece had nine rare golden South Sea pearls—ranging in size from twelve millimeters to eighteen—gathered into a stunning cluster of glistening grapes with garnet pavé leaves. They gleamed from the bronze silk of my jacket—looking luscious and almost edible. The earrings matched, single glowing grapes with garnet leaves and a gold twist of vine.

"Thank you, Flaminia," I said. "I never get tired of looking at it either. Tell me, who all is here this evening?" I slid a slight glance to the glamorous quartet that had emerged from the convertible.

"Oh, you know. Old friends, new friends—summer's last good-bye. Excuse me, will you?" She moved toward the new arrivals and extended her hand while Thomas and I stepped through the gate into her garden where, as Flaminia had said, old and new friends were already well into the swing of the evening.

The sound of the piano could be heard in the background, and white-jacketed waiters moved gracefully among the guests with cocktails in crystal tumblers and flutes of champagne. For some guests, this had been their first residential summer in Provence—such as the now somewhat defensive Americans from the Bentley—and for others, it was where they spent June through the end of September and then returned to their busy lives in Paris or Brussels or New York. Flaminia was considered to be the most gracious hostess in all of St. Rémy, her invitations were certainly the most sought after, and tonight as we gathered around her hilltop pool—a classic art nouveau aquamarine rectangle—the light of the setting sun bathed our faces in its clean, pure light.

Thomas and I were chatting with a small group along the stone wall where the terrain fell away spectacularly, vanishing from sight until it reappeared on the valley floor hundreds of feet below. When I say "Thomas and I were chatting" with them, that's not entirely correct. Thomas was. He was, after all, Scotland Yard's celebrity Inspector Emeritus. I, on the other hand, was looking around for the waiter with the bottle of champagne to come our way for refills, nibbling on a Beluga canapé, and eavesdropping on the "Bentley American" men on the opposite side of the pool. The water magnified the sound of their voices as it ricocheted across.

"I understand from Keesling Fowler that Ballantine's is going to settle rather than have this situation go public," said the man who'd been driving the car. He had on a dark green sport coat and tan linen slacks. "Apparently, Sir Bertram acknowledged that the jewels are fakes—and not even very good ones, at that. Someone changed the stones between when the Fowlers bought the necklace at the auction and received it in registered post."

Sir Bertram. Fake jewels. My skin was instantly cold. Chills ran up my spine and I think I stopped breathing.

The other man, who was bald and wore glasses with heavy black rims, didn't respond.

"You know as well as I do this is the sort of bad publicity that could put an auction house out of business," he continued. "Switching goods on the buyers. Didn't you just join the Ballantine Board, Logan? What the hell's going on?"

"The firm is definitely facing a number of challenges at the moment," Logan shrugged and answered casually. "A lot of it is just business as usual in an auction house. Nothing that can't be handled."

The man in the green jacket studied him for a moment before speaking. "You can't B.S. me, Logan. We've been good friends for too many years. Our kids grew up together. We've vacationed together. We've bailed each other out a few times. I want to know what's happening—you know you can trust me, it will not leave this place. I've got my eye on a couple of pieces at the fall sales but I'm not sure I want to bid on them if there's a chance they or their provenances are false."

Logan nodded again, and absentmindedly rotated his cocktail glass between his hands before answering. "If you want to know the truth, just between us? It's a hell of a mess. Fake jewelry is just one of the issues. The house has had a few irregularities in the paintings department, as well. At the third-quarter Board meeting last week we gave Sir Bertram till the end of the year to get the place cleaned up. He's let Andrew Gardner go—the director of the jewelry department who's always been considered a genius—he's the one who put Ballantine's on the map in the jewelry world."

Fake jewelry? Fake paintings? Andrew Gardner fired? For those in the know in the world of Magnificent Jewelry auctions, Andrew Gardner was considered the ultimate authority worldwide, and to lose him just a matter of weeks before the major autumn auction season opened was suicide.

I'm not the fainting type, but suddenly I was dizzy. I saw lightning and heard thunder—although there wasn't a cloud in the sky—and then the world started to spin. The next thing I knew, I was under water. Bill Balfour had a hold of one of my hands, my champagne glass was still firmly clenched in the other. The serene, secure expression had been washed off my face.

CHAPTER 3

Bartlesville, Oklahoma—1965

You might be wondering why the mention of fake jewels, fake paintings, Andrew Gardner, and Ballantine & Company would make me faint. Well, it all began in Bartlesville, what seems like a hundred years ago. It certainly was a different world. I was a different person and my life bore virtually no resemblance to what it has become.

I remember the day as clearly as if it were yesterday, the day the wheels for change ground into motion.

I hung the padlock over the hasp on my bedroom door and snapped it shut, although the trailer—which at the moment smelled of buttered popcorn and L'Air du Temps perfume—and everything in it was so flimsy, the Big Bad Wolf could have huffed and puffed and blown the entire affair over and open.

"Where're you going, Kathleen?" Mother asked, her words already a bit slurred, as I passed through the narrow galley that served as our living and dining room. She was sitting on the couch watching *Mission Impossible* on television with one of what she referred to as "her gentlemen callers," although since I was a seven-year-old I'd known the men may or may not have been gentlemen, and that they more properly should have been referred to as clients. Open bottles of Four Roses bourbon and Seven Up sat on the coffee table between the bowl of popcorn and the man's stockinged feet. The clients never looked at me beyond a quick, embarrassed glance, because I always glowered at them as though they should have been ashamed.

"Out with Ray," I answered.

"Ray Thompson?" She emphasized his last name.

"Yes."

"Don't be out too late, Kathleen. You hear? Even if his daddy is the president of the bank." She was trying to impress the client and give the impression that she was a good, caring, and competent mother. She was none of those things. And the client could have cared less—he wasn't there to try to borrow money or get into the country club.

I draped my sweater over my arm, put on my baby blue heart-shaped sunglasses, which matched my sun dress, which was a cheap knock-off of a Lanz Original, and my flats, which were cheap knock-offs of Capezios, and went outside where Ray was waiting in the gleaming jet black pickup his dad had given him for his eighteenth birthday. I've always been a sucker for cars—the faster and shinier the better—so now, with Ray in these beautiful new wheels, I was inclined to smile on him with a great deal more favor than if he'd been a poor boy in a lesser ride.

I had a reputation at school for being stuck-up but the fact was, I had standards, and plans for myself. I saw myself as discriminating. I had no intention of living my mother's life, just as I had no intention of spending my days in Bartlesville, Oklahoma, headquarters of Phillips Petroleum. Here's what I liked about the oil business: the money. The rest of it was just minor aggravating details.

Ray jumped out of the cab and ran around and opened the door for me. "Hi, Kathleen," he said. "You look beautiful. That's a beautiful scarf."

"Thanks, Ray. It's French. It's from Lanvin." It wasn't French and it wasn't from Lanvin. It was a little nylon pocket scarf from Beck's mark-down bin but Ray wouldn't know the difference. I'd tied it around my neck where I knew the tail ends would flutter in the breeze just as Grace Kelly's had in *To Catch a Thief.* "I love your new truck." I climbed into the cab and stroked the red leatherette padded dashboard and the bench seat that was specially covered in a Southwestern blanketlike fabric.

"You really like it?"

"I do."

He gave me a quick kiss, put the vehicle into first gear, popped the clutch, and we pulled away from the trailer court in a cloud of dust and took off down the highway at about a hundred miles an hour. I sat next to him and put my hand on his thigh, and he put his hand on mine when he wasn't busy shifting.

Ray and I were a couple. We were going steady. He'd given me a little heart-shaped gold charm with a tiny pearl that I wore on a chain around my neck. We were the coolest couple at Bartlesville High. I was in love with him and he was in love with me. Everyone wanted to be us—I was so pretty and he was so handsome and we both got straight As. Ray was going to attend Harvard and then wanted to move to Washington, D.C., to be a lawyer and make a difference in the world. And I was going with him.

"Thought we'd grab a burger," he said as he maneuvered the pickup into a stall at Big John's Drive-In. "And then—just because I promised—we'll go to the Cherokee and see that sob-sister Russian movie you've been carrying on about."

"You mean *Doctor Zhivago?*"

He nodded and rolled his eyes. "Women," he said.

"Oh, Ray, thank you so much." I threw my arms around him. "I love you."

"I love you, too, babe." And then he kissed me, right there in front of the carhop.

I loved the idea of everyone seeing me at Big John's Drive-In with Ray. I also loved the idea of having one of Big John's Double Cheese Burgers—two patties of prime Oklahoma beef grilled to perfection with two thick slices of melted Velveeta, shredded lettuce, and a secret sauce that combined the irresistible tang of vinegar and the sweetness of sugar, with ketchup, grated onion, mayonnaise, a dash of cayenne, and that one other special secret ingredient that I've never been able to identify. The base of the sauce, as I would discern years later, was similar to a Louis without the pimento, or Thousand Island Dressing without the chopped egg. Whatever was in Big John's Secret Sauce— no one could get enough of it.

"You know one of the things I love about you, Kathleen?" Ray said between bites. "You aren't like the other girls who just pick at their food. They're just a bunch of skinny runts. You like to eat. A man wants a woman he can hold on to."

A man. A woman. Ray was eighteen, a senior. I was fifteen, a sophomore. But there it was. I guess between Lara and Zhivago and the new truck, I didn't stand a chance. That, and Ray's promise that nothing would happen. Two months later, I dropped off a urine specimen at the office of a doctor a hundred miles away in Tulsa and told the nurse I'd call in a few days to find out if the rabbit had died or not.

It had.

"It's not mine," Ray said.

"But Ray," I cried. "That was the first time I ever did it."

"It's not mine. Besides, I'm in love with someone else."

I watched all my dreams fly out the window.

The next day, I skipped school and took the bus back to Tulsa. I stared at the doctor. "What am I going to do?"

"What about the father? Don't you want to tell him? Don't you want to get married?"

"I already told him. He won't marry me."

The doctor studied me quietly across his desk where a picture of his wife and daughters smiled at him. He was a kind-looking man with beautiful blue eyes and a burr haircut.

"How old are you?"

"Eighteen."

He didn't challenge my answer, and now as I look back on it, it was because he didn't want to hear the truth—the last thing he wanted was a pregnant minor on his hands.

"Are you familiar with the Florence Crittenden Homes?"

"I've heard the name. What are they?"

"Homes for girls in trouble where you can go and stay until you have your baby and then, if you don't want to keep the baby, they put it up for adoption."

"Where is this place?"

"There's one in Omaha."

I just sat there and stared at him. I had no idea what to do. How to place a long distance call. How to get to Omaha. I had no money. Panic rose in me like water coming to a boil.

If that wonderful man hadn't picked up the phone and dialed Omaha and made arrangements for me to be picked up that afternoon, I hate to think what would have become of me.

As it was, there was still a lot of water that had to pass under the bridge for me to become what I had in mind. But this is where it all started.

⟍◎ ◎⟋

In those days, delivering mothers were knocked out for the ordeal, which makes eminently more sense to me than all the pain and suffering girls are forced to endure these days, so when I came to from the anesthetic, the nurse asked, "Do you want to see . . ."

"No." I cut her off and shook my head. "I don't want to hear any more about it."

"I understand," she said quietly, and put her hand on my forehead and smoothed my hair into place. It was an act of incredible maternal kindness and I wanted to grab her and hold on for dear life. "A lot of girls feel the same way."

I looked at her gratefully and for the first time through this entire affair, since I told Ray, I almost cried. But something had changed in me, frozen solid. There was no softness anywhere in me anymore.

"Mrs. Kelly, the woman from the adoption agency, is waiting with the paperwork. Are you ready?"

"Yes."

"Let me help you sit up." She raised the head of the bed, put a pillow behind my back, and neatened the covers. "This will just take a minute."

I looked at her and nodded. "Will you stay?"

"Yes, if you'd like me to."

I don't remember anything about Mrs. Kelly. I only remember that she had a clipboard and asked me if I was sure of what I was doing and did I have the legal right to do so. I said yes and signed a sheaf of papers and she was gone. And that was that. I never even asked her if it was a girl or a boy. I just wanted it over.

The following ten days I spent in the hospital were like living in Fairyland. I'd never been pampered and I loved it. I had sponge baths, backrubs with sweet-smelling Jergens lotion, sitz baths, bed jackets, and sleeping pills. My sheets were changed every day and the food was amazingly well-balanced, nutritious, and delicious. My body regained its shape quickly, as any teenage girl's would, with all that lovely young skin that's strung tight as a drum top. By the time I was recovered enough to go, I had a new wardrobe, thanks to a generous donor, and the home had made arrangements for me to live in a rooming house in Tulsa and lined up a job for me in a department store. I was on my own. I never went back to Bartlesville and I never saw my mother again.

CHAPTER 4

I was almost seventeen and things were going so, so well.
I still had my job at the department store but my wage—a measly
dollar sixty-five an hour—scarcely covered my lipstick, linens, and
earrings. To supplement my income, I was on my way to becoming a
very successful thief. Stealing was so easy to do, so unexpected of a
girl like me, that no mark ever cast a suspicious eye in my direction. I
took to burglary like a duck to water.

I'd just follow a man or woman or couple into a jewelry store—we
had many mid- to high-end retailers in Tulsa at that time due to the oil
boom—and sulk around in their distant wake as their shy, slightly
overweight daughter. Then, while the proprietor was busy showing his
wares, I'd casually drop all manner of trinkets down my white cotton
schoolgirl blouse into my well-developed cleavage. When the grown-
ups were done, I'd trail them out and immediately head down to the
bus station where I'd lock myself in a stall in the ladies room, change

my clothes, and pull on a wig and dark glasses. Then, I'd go around the corner to the pawn shop where the proprietor was only too happy to convert my swag into quick cash. We had an excellent professional relationship: he never asked me where I'd gotten the loot and I never asked him why he paid me so little for it, because in truth, it was more than I'd ever had and seemed like a fortune to me.

I got caught twice, and each time the judge had let me go with a stern warning and a teary promise from me that it had been an accident, a misunderstanding, and I'd never do it again.

I flourished.

When I rented it, the walls in my tiny garden apartment were beige. I painted them seashell pink and installed pure white carpeting and loaded the bathroom with every possible luxury I could imagine—sweet-smelling soaps, bath oils, almond lotion, and soft robes. I'd even been successful enough to buy a bright yellow Corvair convertible. I kept completely to myself. I had no friends, and I wasn't interested in making any.

One afternoon, I applied for a job at Mallory's Fine Jewelry Store, but he and his skinny secretary—who he was probably fooling around with as well, because he had a picture of his wife on his desk and thanks to my mother's chosen profession, I could spot a cheater a hundred miles away and, believe me, Mr. Mallory had all the earmarks—had practically laughed in my face. They waited until I was out of the door, but not out of earshot before calling me fat. And pimply. I've never been pimply. I had beautiful skin, pale and smooth. And I wasn't what you could call fat. I just had a few extra pounds. And they said I had no class. That particular remark really hurt because class was the one thing I wanted most of all.

That night back in my apartment, as I ate dinner—a bowl of minestrone soup sprinkled with parmesan cheese, a plate of toasted, buttered saltines, and a Dr Pepper—no matter how much I tried to tell myself that Mr. Mallory was nothing but a lowlife, his cruel remarks still stung. I couldn't help it. I felt completely defeated, swallowed up by embarrassment and anger. The way you feel when you can't even bear to look at yourself in the mirror. Drenched.

I made more saltines, such a simple thing to do: brush a saltine with melted butter, add a little salt, and put it in the oven at 350 for about ten minutes. Sometimes if I was feeling fancy, I'd sprinkle them with a little Worcestershire sauce. While I was waiting for the crackers to toast, I flipped through an issue of *TIME* magazine and saw an article that practically made my eyes jump out of my head. It was about a very rich woman in Texas who had ordered her groom to drug her injured racehorse so he could run in a big race, which he lost, and then they had to destroy him. I couldn't believe my eyes. The groom testified against her, but she claimed it was all simply a big misunderstanding, and because she was rich and married to a powerful man, her lawyer dug up a mountain of dirt on the groom and destroyed his life. The judge dismissed the case.

It all came together for me right then. All the wrong that had been done to me that was completely out of my control—my mother and her clients who made me wait outside the trailer, Ray Thompson and his lies, the abandoned baby, Mr. Mallory and his cruel mouth. All it takes is one act of kindness to change a person's life and other than the people at the Florence Crittenden Home who had to let me go, no one had ever taken the time to hold out a hand. I got mad as hell and I decided, even if it took my whole life, I'd get even. I'd succeed in spite of them and I'd make them pay for their success. I'd get even with rich people who mistreat or make fun of poor people, or fat people, or people who are subservient to them, or animals which are totally dependent on them; people who doped their racehorses or humiliated their children or docked their housekeeper a day's pay when she couldn't come because she or her children were sick or made fun of someone who wasn't as smart. These were bad people who deserved to lose the things they loved—these would be my targets from now on. They would have to pay. They would not get to enjoy the things they loved if they were acquired through the pain and suffering of someone else.

"You're in a lot of trouble, Mr. Mallory," I said out loud.

I would only rob the people who deserved it. I became a one-woman crime wave—I was the talk of Tulsa. And I caused Mr. Mallory quite a lot of pain for quite a while. I robbed one of his stores every chance I got. I also let my notoriety go to my head, began to believe my own publicity, and finally my ego and my indignation let me get too big for my britches.

*

"Name?" the matron said.

"Kathleen," I answered.

The Juvenile Court room was cold and smelled like cigarettes. It was packed with youngsters—fear, tears, and regret on many of their faces, rebellion on others. Most of them were with their parents or their attorneys.

The matron was a mean-looking old biddy. She frowned at me over the top of her glasses like she wanted to pinch me. "Oh, yes. I know you." She picked up a stack of files and rifled through them. "You're next up to see the judge. I imagine he'll send you away this time."

"Kathleen," the judge intoned. Now here was a man who wanted to make a difference, who wanted to help children, keep them out of trouble, help them turn from their lives of crime—mostly little mischiefs and misdemeanors like joyriding and petty theft—and get them back on the right road to a good life. When he looked at me, I could see disappointment written all over his face.

"It pains me to have to do this, but this is the third time you've appeared before me, and now I'm bound by the law to take harsh action. Do you have anything to say for yourself before I pass sentence?"

"I'm sorry, Your Honor," I said. "I'd really appreciate another chance."

"Can't do it. Six months in the Oklahoma State Reformatory for Girls." He banged his gavel and the crabby matron took a rough hold of my upper arm and yanked me away. It was the only time I ever saw her smile.

I made the most of my time in reform school. All the other girls took sewing and Home Ec classes because all they wanted to do was get out and get married. I took jewelry-making classes and read books on famous diamonds. I intended to be somebody. I intended to be the greatest jewel thief in the world.

When I "graduated" from reform school, I had gained the wisdom to know I had so much more to learn.

I buckled down.

CHAPTER 5

London—1969

I'd become a popular coed on a full scholarship at Oklahoma State University: a straight-A student, a glamorous Kappa, and a geology major. I signed up for the summer trip to Europe. After ten cities in ten days, or some equally grueling, gruesome schedule, we finally arrived in London. I loved the weather, the people, the food, the river, the clothes, and the history. I loved it all. Seeing the jewelry stores on New Bond Street pushed me over the edge. This would be where I would leave the tour and begin my life.

I got a Mary Quant makeover—including blue eye shadow, platinum pink lipstick, and wooly false eyelashes—and spent the last of my money on a psychedelic minidress and pink vinyl go-go boots. All that was left in my purse were the tools of my secret trade: lock-picking sticks, a pair of jeweler's needle-nosed pliers, and a jeweler's loupe. It didn't matter—I would find a job and be back in business in no time at all.

"Oh, my," the shop girl said. "You look just like Twiggy! Good luck, dear, and mind the rain."

And there I was, out on Carnaby Street, without a penny to my name and without a plan, when it started to pour. My rayon minidress dress stuck to me like plastic wrap to a bowl of ripe plums, and I stood there, clueless as to what to do next, which way to turn.

And just at that moment—like the chariot that came down in the whirlwind and took Elijah to heaven—a Rolls-Royce Silver Cloud splashed out of the storm and sixty-five-year-old Sir Cramner Ballantine invited me in, draped his cashmere scarf around my neck and his Burberry raincoat around my shoulders, and took me to a sumptuous suite at Claridge's which, as those who have been there know, is similar to heaven.

"What is your name, young lady?" We sat at opposite ends of a coffee table in the sitting room of the suite—I'd never seen anything so richly appointed or sophisticated except in Joan Fontaine and Doris Day movies. A butler arranged tea.

"Kick," I replied.

"Kick? What an interesting name."

I nodded, very pleased with my choice. "Kick Keswick."

"Where are you from?"

I looked him straight in the eye. "As of today, Sir Cramner, I'm from London."

He understood what I'd done without my saying another word. "Then I say let's have some champagne."

That was the day my life began. I owe everything to my beloved Cramner, presumably up there now, possibly smoking cigars, with Elijah.

He hired me as his Executive Assistant at Ballantine & Company Auctioneers, which had been in his family since 1740. He secured a ninety-nine-year lease on a roomy flat on leafy, exclusive Eaton Terrace, a flat I still maintain. He taught me discernment—how to recognize and appreciate the finest in art, furniture, jewelry, food, and wine. He turned me into a lady.

Cramner always felt a little guilty he couldn't marry me, so he showered me with gifts, including the Pasha of St. Petersburg, a thirty-five carat perfect diamond I wear on a long, thin, almost invisible platinum chain around my neck. And even more generously: he gave me an 8 percent share of Ballantine & Company in the name of the KDK Trust. K–D–K being my initials, Kathleen Day (for Doris) Keswick, to be specific. No one, except for Mr. Beauchamp, the trustee at the Private Bank of London, knew who was behind the KDK Trust, and he represented my interests on the Ballantine & Company Board of Directors.

During the evenings when Cramner was not at my flat, I went to work in earnest to pursue my chosen vocation—always sticking to my moral standard of stealing from those who should not be entitled to enjoy their treasures, and believe me, there was never any shortage of marks. It always amazed me how rich people liked to brag about how they'd been able to trick people out of receiving their due. My victims were as easy to spot as the noses on their faces—sometimes all I had to do was pick up the morning paper.

I stole in two ways—one of which leads directly back to why I fainted and fell into Flaminia and Bill Balfour's swimming pool in Provence.

For decades I was London's notorious Shamrock Burglar, which required a great deal of technical knowledge and nerves of steel. In addition to being able to disarm the most modern security systems and crack the most crack-proof of safes, I was a master of disguise, criss-crossing London dressed one moment as a gray-haired housekeeper, another as a prim schoolteacher. I had a discerning and well-educated eye and stole only the finest.

"Well," one dowager told the morning paper philosophically, "If someone was going to steal all my jewelry, at least I have the satisfaction of knowing my collection was good enough for the Shamrock Burglar."

The implication being that I'd cleaned her out. She knew as well as I did that some of her pieces were up to standards and some weren't. Much of it was junk and I left it behind.

And then, more to the point of why I fell in the Balfours' swimming pool: thanks to the jewelry-making classes I took, as you will recall, at reform school, and my geology major in college, the second way I stole was by making perfect, undetectable duplicates of pieces that came through the auction house using highly detailed photographic blow-ups of the originals taken by the in-house photographer for the experts' use in describing the pieces and for publication in the sale catalogs. My duplicates were indistinguishable from the real things. I worked quietly and very happily in the small, well-equipped jewelry-manufacturing studio hidden behind a secret door in the closet of my London flat. I even had the very satisfying opportunity to replace an entire pink diamond necklace that was purchased at auction by the woman in Texas who doped and then shot her horse, or rather, had it shot.

To my knowledge, none of my copies had ever been detected.

And now? Listening to those gentlemen converse across the pool? This could be a disaster. It was enough to make anyone faint.

CHAPTER 6

Éygalières, Provence—Today

"Are you sure you're all right?" Thomas asked as we drove slowly down the hill. Flaminia had loaned me one of the terry cloth robes from her pool house and I had a towel wrapped around my head. Even so, I was freezing. He put his hand on my forehead. "You're burning up."

I nodded. My teeth wouldn't stop chattering and I couldn't stop shaking. I'd never been so undone. "It's Bertram," I said. "I'm afraid he's in trouble."

"Oh?"

I told Thomas what I'd heard. "If a scandal like this is allowed to spread, it could destroy Bertram, as well as the house's credibility. It could put him out of business."

"Mmm. I see your point. But I must say, I'm a little surprised. I had no idea you felt so strongly about Ballantine and Company that hearing about a scandal would make you lose consciousness."

"Oh, well," I tried to gloss it over. "You know. It just gets back to Sir Cramner's legacy. Bertram's got the place back where it rightfully belongs, I'd hate to see the whole thing disappear. Actually, I think I fainted because I was a little lightheaded—too much champagne too quickly."

Thomas looked over at me and I knew he knew I was lying.

He didn't know it but, because of me, many, many Ballantine & Company customers had spent millions on fakes. Very fine fakes, to be sure, but fakes nevertheless. And while it may seem an impossibility, detective work being what it is today, the beam of a powerful spotlight can fall on faraway places. It's conceivable that with enough innovative elbow grease, the light could fall on me and even Thomas wouldn't be able to protect me.

Thomas knew I'd been the Shamrock Burglar, and he'd come to terms with that because while he'd been London's superstar Chief Inspector, he'd also been secretly operating as the Samaritan Burglar, a do-gooder who stole unprotected, highly valuable works of art from VIPs' homes. While I left shamrocks in an emptied safe, he would leave a note where the painting used to be, warning the victims to take better care of their possessions. And then he'd unobtrusively leave the work at a police station so the somewhat humiliated owner could reclaim his property and upgrade his security system. We'd met in London, each unaware of the other's avocation, and it was only months after I'd retired and moved to Provence that he reappeared and presented me with a Renoir that I'd watched him steal from the darkened bedroom where I was cleaning out the safe in the owner's pitch black closet, breathless for fear of discovery.

Love was a new experience to me. After I was let down by Ray Thompson following the formative evening on the front seat of his pickup truck, I'd learned only to trust the hard, cold beauty of precious stones, never to put my trust in a human being. From that day forward—until I decided to take a chance on Thomas Curtis—I never considered real, true love to be an option because it was a human condition I'd never given or received. It was just one of those things I didn't expect ever to know—like flying a spaceship. And it's been a challenging road for me to travel. I've always had a problem with the truth—I still haven't told Thomas anything close to the whole truth about myself. But I'm trying, particularly because I do love him. He is the dessert of my life.

The drive home seemed to take forever. Finally, the red Porsche rolled to a quiet stop at the front door of our farmhouse. Thomas helped me out of the car and put his arm around me. He guided me in and settled me on the sofa and tucked two blankets around me. He poured us each a cognac from the drinks table in the living room. Across the valley, the moonlight bleached the rocky cliffs on Les Alpilles—the Little Alps—so white they looked as though they were covered with snow.

"What else can I get you?" His eyebrows were tented with concern and his bright blue eyes searched my face.

"Sit down, darling," I said. "I need to tell you a few things."

I came close to telling him everything. I told him about the jewelry fabrication and switching pieces at Ballantine & Company. I told him approximately how much money I really had, but I admit I didn't tell him exactly where it all was.

"That answers a lot of questions," he said.

"What do you mean?"

"I've added up in my mind the approximate value of all the pieces you'd taken as the Shamrock Burglar and even putting top dollar on all the goods, they still didn't seem to me to be able to support your lifestyle—the London flat, the farm, the exquisite haute couture clothes and jewelry, the Jag convertible and the Mercedes wagon. The wines, alone, that you purchase would put a serious dent in most budgets. And you never bat an eye."

I nodded. "You're right. I'm sorry I didn't tell you sooner. I don't know if you can even begin to imagine, Thomas, how hard telling the truth is for me. I've never done it before."

We sat side by side on the sofa, our feet resting on the tufted ottoman coffee table. He turned and put his hand on my cheek. It was a warm, comforting gesture. I put my hand over his and drew it to my lips and kissed his palm.

He didn't say anything.

"Is this how you crack all your suspects?" I asked. "Kill them with kindness?"

"I've loved you from the moment I met you, Kick, when I thought you were an executive secretary. And since then, I've seen you in operation—as the Shamrock Burglar . . . as Priscilla Pennington in Portofino when you retrieved the Millennium Star for me . . . and as Princess Margaret of Romania in Switzerland when you took an incredible risk and retrieved the jewels for Her Majesty. You are an unbelievably gifted and talented individual and I know a lot of that skill comes from your ice-cold nerve and your ability to disguise yourself, to dissemble, and to stare down your most worthy opponents without flinching. And it doesn't take Sigmund Freud to figure out that those characteristics came from somewhere that does not bespeak a normal background. So, tonight, if you feel like talking, tell me as much or as little as you like. I won't love you less for any of it."

I sat quietly for a moment. I know my face was calm but inside I was churning. I could feel the truth boiling in me, scalding me like lava. I could easily swallow it as I had for my entire lifetime. I had to choose. If I were going to live an honest life, have a truly happy, committed marriage and partnership with my husband, none of it could be based on lies anymore. I had to tell the truth.

"There's one more thing."

He looked in my eyes, waiting for me to come to him.

"There was a baby."

"I know."

I didn't think I'd heard him properly. "Excuse me?"

"I said, 'I know.'"

I was shocked. "What do you mean, 'you know'? How could you?"

"Kick," he said. "I'm a detective. I've known for years."

"Why didn't you say something?"

"What was there to say? I knew sooner or later if you wanted to tell me, you would."

"I don't even know if it was a boy or a girl."

"I can find out if you like."

I shook my head. "It doesn't make any difference. I'm registered on all the Internet adoption sites, so if he or she wants or needs to find me, they can."

Thomas nodded, understanding. "That's the right decision. It's up to the child if he wants to be found or not."

"I don't want to foul up his life twice," I said, still amazed by the fact that Thomas had known all along. It wasn't a subject I cared to dwell on. "Back to the point at hand. Now do you understand why I want, correction, why I *need* to help Bertram?"

"Somewhat clearer. What do you have in mind?"

"I'm not sure. I'll come up with something."

He poured us another cognac and then we sat there, holding hands and watching the moon move across the valley. Not talking. Just completely content to be in each other's presence. I felt a sort of lightness, a freedom. I'd told him more of the truth about myself than I thought I could ever tell anyone. Truth was a good thing—perhaps I'd tell him everything next time.

As I drifted off to sleep, my last thoughts were, why *didn't* I just go ahead and tell him everything? Why didn't I tell him I suspected Owen was involved?

CHAPTER 7

Owen Brace. A name out of the past. Where to begin.

After Sir Cramner's death, when his son had almost completely run the revered old company into the ground, the newly formed luxury goods conglomerate, Brace International, acquired Ballantine & Company in a tax sale. The merging of the corporate cultures—one wore dark suits, the other dark T-shirts—failed miserably. Longtime employees bailed out like rats from a sinking ship. My letter of resignation was prepared.

It was a day like any other. I watched a well-dressed couple leave Owen's—formerly Sir Cramner's—office as quickly as they could without going at a dead run, looks of incredulity, indignation even, on their faces, heads shaking. Without the slightest glance at my desk, where I sat properly clad in my black Chanel suit and pearls, they charged down the two-story-long staircase to the main foyer and out the front door.

One more prospective seller delivered into the hands of our arch-rivals, Sotheby's or Christies.

This would be the time to tell him. I picked up the envelope that contained my letter.

"Miss Keswick," Owen's voice boomed from his office. "Come in here."

I stayed put.

"Please."

I picked up the envelope and my stenography book and went in. I still couldn't quite believe it. The office looked basically the same as it had for centuries, since Sir Cramner's ancestor had founded the house in 1740. It was still furnished with the oversized desk with two Chippendale armchairs in front and the uncomfortable settee on the opposite wall with the delicate coffee table and the two tiny side chairs that would collapse if anyone were to actually sit in one of them, which, in the thirty-plus years I'd been at Ballantine & Company, to my knowledge no one had. Hunting prints hung on the paneled walls and reference books sat on the credenza. Nothing had really changed except the man who sat behind the desk and oh, my, what a difference.

Owen Brace stood there, one hand in his pocket, impatiently rapping a pencil on the leather writing pad with the other. He was impossibly handsome—blue-black eyes, dark hair, superb physique. He was dressed in tan gabardine slacks, slipper-soft black leather Italian loafers, a black cashmere sport coat, and a black T-shirt. He was the epitome of international, jet-set elegance. In some circles. Not ours. He represented everything I thought was wrong with the world—loose morals and a disrespectful, arrogant and vulgar attitude. He was repugnant. In fact, I absolutely loathed him.

He had appeared on the scene out of nowhere and gobbled up some of the world's most visible luxury brands, including leather goods, automobile manufacturers, fashion houses, wines and liquors and put them all under the umbrella of Brace International. Ballantine & Company was his newest takeover target, and he'd decided to make it his corporate headquarters as well. Our venerable auction house was suddenly surrounded with movie stars, fancy cars, high-stakes games of corporate chicken over Brace International's eye-popping debt, and wall-to-wall girls wanting to get a little piece of the man himself, who seemed to thrive on nonstop sex. It was shocking.

I was the residual executive assistant. I came with the territory. I could scarcely bear to be in his presence.

"What in the hell is wrong with these people?" he asked rhetorically. "I offered them a great deal and they said they were going to take Sotheby's offer."

"I'm not surprised."

"What do you mean by that?"

"Mr. Brace, the auction business is based on trust. We're similar to undertakers and that's the way we need to appear and behave. We don't have senses of humor. We don't tell dirty jokes and we don't live our lives on the front pages. You look and act like a playboy."

His eyes twinkled and his lips curved into a lopsided, boyish, self-satisfied grin. "I am a playboy."

"Really, Mr. Brace. You're going to run this company into the ground and I won't stay to watch." I held the envelope toward him but he refused to take it. I placed it on the desk in front of him. "This is my letter of resignation, effective immediately."

"I won't accept it."

"Fortunately for me, that's not an option you enjoy."

"I hate to admit it, but I need your help, Miss Keswick. What in the hell is your name anyway?"

"Miss Keswick will do just fine."

"Well, I need a few pointers. I need to know how to connect with these stuck-up snobs."

"Well, you could begin by not calling them stuck-up snobs, which they aren't. They're, for the most part, people of refinement and taste, and they look at someone like you with utter horror. To put it in a way you and your crowd would understand: They don't want your grubby paws all over their great-great-great-grandmother's tea set."

He stared, nonplussed. "What do I do?"

By the time I was done with him, he dressed like a banker instead of a bookie. He stopped shooting his cuffs, cracking his knuckles, and chewing gum, and started ordering the proper wines. He began to be able to tell the difference between a Peter Max and a Pieter Bruegel.

And unfortunately, by the time I was done with him, my contempt and hatred had turned to passion. I replaced the hard settee in his office with a long, soft, comfortable sofa loaded with down cushions.

With my encouragement, he hired the legendary auctioneer Sir Bertram Taylor away from Sotheby's and slowly, like a big ship changing course, Ballantine's began to turn a profit. It seemed the dawn of a new and golden age for Ballantine & Company.

We were all high on the success, hot with desire. Owen said he was in love with me and I said I was in love with him. He proposed. I accepted. Oh, God. It was fun. It was a giddy, steamy freefall into an exotic, erotic world full of forbidden promises and pleasures. It was more fun than I'd ever had in my life.

It was in the midst of all of this euphoria that two unfortunate, unrelated events—a murder and a bombing—occurred at Ballantine & Company. That was when I met Chief Inspector Thomas Curtis. He was kind, refined, rumpled, intelligent, and charming, just the sort of man I would have been attracted to in my former life. But now, thanks to Owen, I was a babe. I was hot. And instead of being the younger woman, I was the older, mature, experienced woman who had swept the notorious, elusive, bad boy Owen Brace off his feet. I'd scored a big one for women of a certain age, putting all the naysayers who say we don't have it anymore in their place. I didn't give Thomas Curtis a second look. He was the old Kick Keswick. Owen Brace had stripped away all my fuddy-duddiness and voilà! The newer, hipper, very cool version had emerged.

The only fly in the Ballantine & Company ointment, for Owen at any rate, was the outstanding, unidentified 8 percent owned by the KDK Trust. He couldn't identify the owner of it, much less get his hands on it. In spite of the fact that I thought I loved Owen and was going to marry him, I didn't trust him. I would never tell him I was the KDK Trust and I would never sell my position in the company. It became the relentless, digging, twisting burr under his saddle. It drove him wild.

As with all things that seem too good to be true, this was. He began a flagrant affair with Odessa Niandros, the billionairess, and people began to look at me and whisper about me behind my back as though I were a pathetic creature. Which, it turns out, I almost was.

You'll note I said: almost. Thanks to a serious misstep on Owen's part—attributable to his chronic tendency to underestimate me—I discovered he had known all along that I owned the KDK Trust. He intended to marry me to get his hands on my stock so he could not only sell Ballantine & Company, but also, when—not if—his financial house of cards of ill-gotten gains collapsed, which seemed imminent and inevitable, his wife could not be made to testify against him.

Owen Brace, I discovered just in the nick of time, was a con man and a son-of-a-bitch.

I was horrified and humiliated.

I never let on. But behind the scenes, I quietly implemented my exit strategy and planned my revenge. Just before I left the country with my mega-million stash of stones and cash, I launched a dazzling series of parting shots, if I do say so myself.

I met privately with Sir Bertram and gave him my shares of Ballantine & Company. He was a gentleman of the old school, like Sir Cramner and Thomas Curtis, and if the house had any future at all, it would be with him.

I set Owen up. I framed him, and I called the police. The scandal caused his teetering empire to collapse and him to vanish off the global playing field.

And now? As Thomas dozed peacefully beside me and starlight filled the valley with a silvery glow, I could intuitively feel Owen's fingerprints all over the new troubles at Ballantine & Company.

And if I were right, what on earth was he up to? Well, whatever it was, he wouldn't get away with it.

CHAPTER 8

The incessant beep of Thomas's pager awakened us. He, the dog, and I had fallen fast asleep in the living room and we all leapt in different directions when the thing went off. Dawn was just breaking.

Thomas went to his study to return the call, and by the time he was off the phone, I'd put myself together, more or less. My hair was gathered into some semblance of order, I'd washed my face, dressed in pink silk slacks, a white cotton blouse, and ballet slippers, and started the coffee.

He came into the kitchen looking harried.

"What's up?"

"I can't tell you."

"You'll need to do better than that, Thomas." I poured us each a steaming cup of strong coffee.

"Shall we take the dog for a walk?"

I nodded.

"You'd better put on a wrap," he said. "It's chilly." He held one of my quilted velvet Hermès riding jackets—not that I did any actual riding. I mean, truly, who would go riding in a pink quilted jacket? I slipped in my arms and traded my slippers for walking shoes. We clipped on Bijou's leash and stepped into the clear morning, neither one of us saying a word.

"There's been an extraordinary robbery," he said after a moment. "Top, top secret, of course."

I felt his eyes glance quickly at me, as though he were wondering whether or not he could trust me.

"Thomas," I said.

"I know you'd never open your mouth to anyone about anything, Kick, but I want you to appreciate how serious this is. The international consequences are as complicated as it gets."

My arm was tucked through his and I gave it a squeeze. "Tell me."

"Someone, more accurately some ones—it was clearly a very well-equipped, well-organized team of professionals—have broken into the Markazi Bank in Tehran. That's the Central Bank of Iran. Killed the guards and made off with a few of the Iranian crown jewels."

"You're not serious." I came to a dead stop.

Thomas nodded. "Can you believe it?"

"No. It's impossible."

Bank Markazi Iran was the repository of what was considered to be the most vast collection of jewels known in the world. No person, no country, is believed to possess a treasury the size and quality of Iran's, nor fabrications of stones as mind-boggling as theirs, such as the Nadir Throne—commonly (and erroneously) referred to as the Peacock Throne—which, alone, is said to have over 26,000 precious gems.

"I'm not sure what's missing," Thomas said, and began walking again. "They'll tell me when I get to London. The task force's job will be to retrieve them and return them to the Iranian government. Hopefully without anyone ever finding out."

"And you want my help?" Now there it is. I have said I was retired but when a heist as grand as this one is mentioned, I lose all my rehabilitation. My lifelong passion for stealing jewelry always seemed to lurk just beneath my skin like an electrical current, a fire I couldn't put out. Confetti flies through my head and then my focus becomes refined until it is a laser beam lighting up its target. I'd give just about anything to see the Iranian crown jewels.

Silence.

"Thomas?"

He always needed my help in repossessing stolen gems, whether it was the Millennium Star or Empress Josephine's Emerald or Queen Elizabeth's Cambridge and Delhi Durbar parure. Thomas wouldn't know how to go about stealing a piece of jewelry if his life depended on it. As he himself said: I was his secret weapon. He started walking again.

"Well, that's just it, Kick," he answered, and turned us back toward the house. "I can't involve you in this."

"What do you mean?"

"It's a dangerous, emergency assignment. These are bad people who've pulled this off—they play by a set of rules that has nothing to do with what we consider civilized. These are the sort of people who steal enriched uranium to build bombs and blow up governments. It's a bad situation."

"But, Thomas . . ." I began.

"I'm leaving this morning. They've sent a plane for me. A car should be here any minute to take me to the airport."

"But, Thomas . . ." I said again.

He held the kitchen door while I stepped through. Once inside, my darling husband put his hands on my shoulders and looked at me quietly. His eyes were the pure sky blue of Kashmir sapphires. The flash of sunlight on shiny chrome glinted through the trees at the end of the lane.

"Make sure you let me know where you are and what you're doing. Don't do anything silly. Helping Bertram is one thing, putting yourself in danger is another."

"Don't worry."

"I love you, Kick Keswick."

"I love you, Thomas Curtis."

He scrawled an emergency phone number on the kitchen note-pad and walked out the door. I watched the car go down the lane until all that remained was a fine settling of dust.

Well.

Hell.

CHAPTER 9

I made a café au lait and carried my bowl of blueberries and warm pain au chocolat into the garden. I read the paper and tried to have a normal morning, but Bertram and his predicament kept intruding. I knew I could help him in a heartbeat, and it would be something to do, something to break my inertia.

Oh, let me be truthful for a change: I wanted to help because I didn't want Bertram's predicament to become mine.

Finally, after an hour or so of quietly watching the bees get to work in the lavender beds, and the apples seeming to grow pinker by the second—they'd already begun to fall—a plan began to take shape and I knew once I got myself suitably put together, everything would come into place.

This may sound a little compulsive but it's the way I'm made: I cannot do anything properly—particularly plan a major heist—until I am completely at my best: shampooed, made-up, and in a decent outfit. The conditions must be ideal. This is along the same lines as, I believe you cannot paint a lasting masterpiece on a stained canvas or cook a lovely dinner in a messy kitchen or rob a bank if your nail polish is chipped.

I put away my breakfast dishes and stopped off in the laundry room to check on my bronze silk suit, which drooped from its hangers so tragically it looked as though its heart had been broken. It had been such an exquisite ensemble—a couture Louis Féraud, cut and made to fit my figure perfectly. At least the dripping had stopped. When it was dry, I'd box it up and ship it back to Paris to see if they could salvage it.

I dropped my blouse and slacks in the hamper, and while the shower warmed up, I examined myself in the floor-to-ceiling boudoir mirrors. They had a slight pinkish cast to them, which can do wonders for even the tiredest face and saggiest body. I wasn't alarmed by what I saw, just amazed. I felt so young and energetic—well I've never been exactly what you could call energetic. In fact, I loathe exercise. But I felt young and good, healthy. So I was always slightly startled by the sight of my body. Somewhere along the line there had been a seismic shift. Almost overnight, everything that had been up, went down. And there it would stay. Oh, well. I love my body, and have ever since Sir Cramner taught me not to be ashamed of my physical assets, not to try to hide them in white spinnaker-sized bras, white cotton panties, and unflattering caftans and muumuus, but to turn them into assets and wear nothing under my clothes but beautiful, lacy lingerie.

I let the hot water pour over me for a long time while I laid out my next steps. I wasn't sure exactly where they would lead—there was always the possibility Bertram wouldn't be glad to hear from me, that he wouldn't admit to any problems or scandals, that he would tell me to mind my own business, but I had to make the first move, otherwise nothing would happen at all. I dried my hair—I spend an absolutely insane amount of money to keep it the same warm, honey blond as Catherine Deneuve's and the late Princess Grace's coiffures. In fact, I'm often mistaken for Miss Deneuve, which I take as an enormous compliment. Once I secured my tresses into a smooth French Twist, I tucked a fresh gardenia along the side, applied my makeup, and dressed in a pair of lightweight taupe silk slacks, a cool tunic top, and black ballet slippers, daubed a touch of Bal à Versailles behind my ears, and hooked a string of oversized, graduated Afghani turquoise stones around my neck. The two remaining squares of a small Santander espresso-chocolate bar sat in their wrapper next to my sink. These little Columbian chocolate bars—known as The Chocolate Jet—are a genius and jolting combination of high-octane, caffeinated cocoa that is at once tangy, semisweet, a little peppery, and very powerful. One square is the equivalent of one shot of espresso. I ate them both. Now I was set, ready to get to work.

I pushed aside the pale yellow rug in the center of the white tile bathroom floor and then pressed a small, invisible button hidden flush with the bottom of the window sill. A large rectangular section of the floor rose with a slight hydraulic hiss. I knelt down, and with the slightest touch the well-balanced panel swung away easily to reveal a satiny blue-black steel safe. A small screen at the bottom left-hand corner of the steel plate front changed from a steady red glow to a regular blink. In thirty seconds, if the correct sequence weren't followed, a deafening alarm would sound and the safe would seal itself up for six hours. I keyed in the electronic combination, placed my index finger on a digital scanner, and then leaned down and put my eye next to an optical scanner. Seconds later, the blinking red turned to green and the sound of impenetrable steel mesh could be heard retracting.

This particular safe contains a dozen 14" × 6" × 36" safe deposit boxes, lined up vertically, packed primarily with perfect diamonds. There was always a market for perfect diamonds, they seldom lost value. I kept the colored stones in Zurich and Geneva, with a few particularly fine exceptions. This safe also contained precious metals, passports, drivers licenses and credit cards, a variety of electronic scanners no larger than garage door openers but able to crack the most complicated encryptions and disable the most advanced alarm systems, and hundreds of thousands in cash: dollars, euros, and British pounds.

When Thomas referenced my background of disguise and dissembling, I didn't take it as an insult. It was the truth. I was blessed with the sort of looks that could render me wallpaper as easily as they could set me center stage. And those abilities had rescued me from dangerous and compromising positions many times. I had developed a number of identities over the years and I kept them up-to-date. A few of them even had dossiers on Google and Yahoo.

This morning, it took about an hour to select enough identities, cash, credit cards, and gizmos to cover every contingency I could envision. I placed them all in the false bottom of one of my canvas and leather Hermès travel satchels. Then, I picked up the phone.

CHAPTER 10

"Ballantine and Company." The man's voice bespoke an upper-class background.

"Good morning," I said. "Sir Bertram's office, please."

"May I ask who's calling?"

"Miss Keswick."

There was the briefest pause. "One moment, please, Miss Keswick."

I felt a stab of disappointment that there was no discernable warmth or recognition in his voice. No, welcome home. No, where have you been? No, I've heard so much about you. Had my entire thirty years at Ballantine & Company been institutionally eradicated, excised in the same way Stalin axed those on the outs from official photographs?

He put me on hold. I could picture the phone ringing at the top of the main staircase where my old desk sat like a battlement, an intimidating command post for the supreme commander's gatekeeper. I wondered what Bertram's executive assistant was like. I pictured her as being a sophisticated Wallace Simpson-esque type of woman in a trim black crepe sheath dress, pearls, and a smooth coiffure. An iron hand in a velvet glove. Icy or warm as circumstances dictated. An able sentinel for the office of the managing director. A woman who could slice you to ribbons with the slightest glance. A worthy successor.

"One moment, Miss Keswick, while I connect you."

"Kick?" It was Bertram. "Is it really you?"

I was so surprised to hear him personally, it took a second for me to gather myself. "Bertram, how are you?"

"I'm excellent. Better than excellent, in fact. How wonderful to hear your voice. You simply disappeared off the face of the earth, and now here you are back just as quickly. What can I do for you?"

"I've found retirement is awfully dull."

"Oh?"

"I'm thinking of going back to work and thought I'd check in with you first—Ballantine's has become so successful with you at the helm, Bertram, and with the season about to get underway, I thought you might be able to use an extra pair of hands during the fall sales. It doesn't have to be anything fancy."

A long silence ensued. "Well," he finally said, "I think I could find a spot. In fact, I know I could. You've been very hard to replace, Kick— all that expertise and institutional history you carried around in your head. I don't need to tell you that you have attained legendary status around here."

"I doubt that, but I appreciate the compliment."

"Are you interested in any particular field? Paintings, decorative arts, furniture, jewelry? I was always very impressed with your knowledge of eighteenth- and nineteenth-century English furniture, so you would certainly be a welcome addition in that department. Or," he paused, "my assistant, Ruth, is going on vacation shortly, possibly you'd like to sit at her desk and reacquaint yourself with the house and then decide what you'd like to do."

That was an extremely tempting offer because whoever was executive assistant to the managing director knew everything that went on. On the other hand, I didn't want to get bogged down in all the minutia associated with that position. I wanted to be on the fringes, in the background and able to come and go as I pleased, especially if Owen was involved. I needed to follow my own agenda. I didn't want an actual job.

"That's very generous, Bertram, but I was thinking more in terms of an associate spot. I'd love to work with the Jewelry Ladies."

"Let me give it some thought. Are you available for lunch tomorrow?"

"Indeed."

"Good, I'll put Ruth on and she can schedule it. Come by for a quick look-see at elevenish and we'll go from there. See you then." He put me on hold and the next voice I heard was that of Ruth, just what I expected: gracious, distant, and wary.

CHAPTER *11*

London

Bijou and I caught the British Airways afternoon flight from Marseilles to Heathrow, arriving in London in a beautiful, cool drenching rain. What a refreshing break from the Provencal oven. Thank God for England. The car rental service met me at baggage claim with a black Jaguar S-type sedan, which, as far as they knew, they had rented to a Mrs. Lillian Hallaby for a period of three months, certainly more than enough time for my purposes. With some creative loading, the accommodating young man was able to wedge in all my luggage.

"Thank you," I said and handed him a twenty-pound note.

"Thank you, Mrs. Hallaby. Will that be all?"

"Just perfect," I said and pulled away. By five-thirty, I was headed into the City with the rain pelting the windshield and the wipers flapping back and forth. Bijou, back feet on the seat and front paws on the dashboard, kept her little black eyes on the road. I drove cautiously, well-familiar with the Jag's skittishness on wet roads.

Ever since I bought the farm in Provence, early every morning, whether I'm "in residence" or not, my houseman, Pierre, picks up a pain au chocolat, a baguette, a small bottle of milk, and the morning papers and leaves them on the kitchen counter. Sometimes he has repeated the ritual for months at a time to an empty house, replacing the previous day's supply with the fresh one. Some may see this as an extravagance but in fact, the bread, milk, and papers are not costly when they are weighed against the amount of peace and comfort they bring me—they are priceless. The knowledge that I can vanish like smoke to my little farm and close the gate at the road, light the fire, watch the sun rise and set across the valley, and that tomorrow and the next day and the next day, Pierre will appear faithfully every morning with my breakfast and an accompanying note asking if I need anything special—as though this in itself weren't special enough—is all I need.

No matter where I am or what I'm doing, if I'm in danger, disguise, or flight, my ability to envision Pierre's small utility truck rattling to a stop at my pink-apple-colored kitchen door at six o'clock every morning, Pierre stamping the dust off his boots and then carefully arranging my daily provisions on the blue and white tile counter, along with a fresh bouquet of flowers in the yellow crockery pitcher every Friday, checking to make sure the pilot lights hadn't gone out on my stove or hot-water tank, that no rain had blown through my hyacinth blue shutters, no pipe had broken and no mice had attacked my pantry; that no matter what had happened, Pierre was steady and dependable as a rock, that he was always looking out for me and my comfort, afforded me an incalculable sense of security and well-being. If my extravagance were to offend people's sensibilities—which I'm sure it would if they knew about it—well, I would simply have to say that that's their problem.

On the other hand, since I had no idea when, if ever, I'd return to my London flat, I'd simply left it with Mr. Beauchamp at the bank that I'd call him prior to my arrival and he would send over the house-keeper with a load of provisions—fresh flowers for the sitting room; fresh linens on the bed; fresh eggs, milk, Gruyere cheese, whole grain bread, butter in the refrigerator, and a good selection of fine wines and champagne.

So it was with a sense of comfortable homecoming that I turned onto the little side street and splashed to a stop at the security gate at the top of the drive down into the mews of the exclusive Eaton Ter-race flats. Planters of red geraniums punctuated the glossy black garage doors. The guard emerged from his bungalow, approached my window, and held an umbrella over his head and the side of the car, keeping the rain off both of us.

"Good evening, ma'am. How may I help you?"

I pulled out my own driver's license, not Mrs. Hallaby's. "I'm Miss Keswick."

He took the card and examined it. "Very pleased to meet you." He smiled and touched his hat. "I'm Daniel, at your service. May I send the porter to help with your luggage?"

"Please."

He pushed the button on a remote and the black wrought-iron gates swung open and I proceeded down the slope to my garage.

I suppose it should have felt odd or disconcerting to suddenly find myself back in the home where I'd lived for over three decades, but it didn't feel odd, it felt wonderful. Everything was just as I'd left it—my clothes in the closets and drawers, the paintings in their places, including the van Gogh over the fireplace in the sitting room where a large vase of white Casablanca lilies sat on the corner of the Boule desk. I switched on the music and my favorite ballet, Gounod's *Seasons*, added its welcoming note. In the kitchen—cups, glasses, and sets of dishes filled the glass-fronted cabinets; the pantry cabinets were stocked with all the necessities, and the professional appli-ances gleamed in readiness. The wine cabinet was stocked with two bottles each of Dom Pérignon, Le Montrachet, and Alain Michelot's 1999 Nuits Saint-Georges, Les Vaucrains. The refrigerator had the req-uisite fresh eggs, milk, and cheese. I could almost see Cramner sitting at the kitchen table reading the evening paper and sipping a scotch neat, waiting for his tomato soup and cheese soufflé to appear before him.

Gardenia potpourri delicately scented my bedroom where soothing champagne-and-salmon-pink paisley covered the walls and gathered in pleats to a mirrored corona in the center of the ceiling. An antique chandelier with crystal drops the size of hen's eggs cast a warm glow. The Monet—a large oil of a white crockery pitcher overflowing with a decadent arrangement of fully bloomed pink roses—hung above the mantel, and in the mirrored bath, my collection of bubbling bath salts were still arranged as I'd left them on a small glass table next to the gigantic old-fashioned tub.

I couldn't help but smile. All was so regular. Yet it was all really so totally different. That's not actually correct: it was all the same. I was changed.

I stepped to the back of the closet and pushed a hidden button and the wall swung away, revealing my jewelry studio workroom with everything neatly in place. I switched on the lights, which were so intense they left nothing in shadow, and ran my fingers across the familiar tools on my jeweler's bench. I sat down in my chair and twirled around. It was a perfect work space, soundproof, air-conditioned, and linked to the outside world by a series of video screens relaying images from pinhole cameras installed throughout the flat and at the front door. This was the factory. This was the room where, through a life of crime, I had diligently assembled my fortune, my safety net.

A sickening feeling of dread crept in. Was it possible someone—someone like Owen?—had purposely set out to draw me back? No. I was simply being paranoid, giving Owen credit for more brains than he actually had. But that was all right. One of the reasons I stay ahead of most people is that I do overestimate them—I prepare myself for every contingency. It's only by underestimating a person's or a situation's power to affect you that you can find yourself being controlled by circumstances, rather than the other way around. I wasn't a control freak in the strictest sense of the word: I wasn't interested in controlling other people. I was interested in reading people, studying them, finding my way into them and then controlling every possible aspect of my relationship with them, taking what I came for, and then disappearing into the fog. But I didn't want to control them or their lives, per se—I didn't want them to remember anything about me.

I switched off the lights and stepped back into the closet, through the screen of my beautiful Chanel business suits—all black or navy blue—all clean and pressed and ready to get back to work. How bizarre that I could step so effortlessly from one life to another like a game of hopscotch. No wonder I hadn't told Thomas the whole truth, there were so many versions.

The rain had stopped by the time I finished unpacking. I hooked on Bijou's leash and we walked to my old favorite Indian restaurant near Sloane Square where the curry was so hot it could curl your hair and where they greeted me so casually, it was as though I'd had dinner there the night before.

I tried not to keep checking my cell phone to see if Thomas had called but I couldn't help it. He hadn't and it rather irked me. I wondered if he was in London, if we'd run into each other. Probably better if we didn't. He didn't want me to know what he was up to and I felt the same way, mostly because I wasn't too sure exactly where this was going to lead. But I knew I was headed in an important and worthwhile direction. I'd come to think of it as a sort of crusade.

CHAPTER *12*

The next morning, Ballantine & Company fairly sparkled with first-rate maintenance when my Jag rolled to a sedate stop at the venerable façade in St. James Square. The brass gleamed and the black wrought-iron spiked fence and front door shone with fresh paint. Sunlight glittered off the four stories of paned windows. A handful of the last tourists of summer wandered about with their guidebooks out, looking slightly miffed that nothing much actually went on in the famous square where every door required a proper introduction to enter.

"Thank you," I said to the doorman who helped me out of the car. I'd dressed in a moderately conservative black and taupe tweed suit with an ivory satin blouse, pearls, and black suede pumps, a step up from regular business attire—closer to Lady of the Manor come to town to check on her holdings.

Inside, the cavernous foyer was quiet. To the right and left, the doors to the showrooms and sales rooms were closed in preparation for the fall sales that started in just days, kicking off eight months of nonstop activity. Most of the experts were upstairs in their offices, finalizing their goods and exhibits and endeavoring to confirm as many advance bids as possible. And downstairs, in the four levels of basement vaults and storerooms, blue-coated workmen were polishing the lots of fine furniture, while other experts examined and re-examined the Impressionist paintings with magnifying glasses, just to make certain they hadn't missed anything at all in their descriptions.

I knew the schedule and routine as well as I knew my own name.

Once I'd passed through the thorough, airport-style security procedure, a round little bespectacled fireplug of a woman, who could have been Joan Plowright's daughter, stepped forward at the bottom of the stairs. She'd been waiting for me with her hands clasped together on top of her tummy. Her hazel eyes bulged behind large glasses and her lips seemed scarcely up to the task of covering her teeth. She had a lifetime of struggle written on her face. "Miss Keswick?" It was the voice I'd heard on the phone.

"Yes."

"I am Ruth Provender, Sir Bertram's secretary. Sir Bertram is ready to see you if you'll follow me. Although," she paused and added in a clear effort not to seem ungracious, "you no doubt remember the way." I could tell she was trying to not be defensive, or maybe she was insecure.

We ascended the central two-story staircase at a steady pace and I was almost overcome with a sense of possession, of tenure and longing. The cedar-lemon smell of Ballantine's signature furniture polish and floor wax permeated everything and transported me across time and space. The walnut banisters glowed with the patina of their 250 years and the wide Persian runner muffled our footsteps. I'd climbed these stairs for the first time when I was eighteen years old, when I was somehow wise enough to know I didn't know nearly enough about anything. This house had been my home for my entire adult life and I knew every square inch of it. I'd had no idea how much I'd missed it. I wanted to see Sir Cramner waiting for me at the top, hands in his pockets, beaming at me like a proud father, and Alcott, the ancient porter, waiting there beside him with a tray of sticky orange rolls. The climb was full of ghosts. I didn't want it to end.

Ruth pulled slightly ahead, entering my line of vision and terminating my euphoria as effectively as an electric shock. Clearly, she was the antithesis of what I'd expected, but maybe that wasn't such a bad thing. In an attempt at stylishness, her frizzy reddish brown hair was tied back into a sort of a pigtail with an Hermès floral silk scarf that was far too big for so little hair. I placed her age at near forty, but in fact she could have been anywhere between thirty and eighty. It's not entirely fair to say that Ruth trudged in her one-inch, stacked-heel pumps, and while I thought Bertram could have used someone a little zippier, in her defense I will say she was wearing an expensive black gabardine suit that had been skillfully tailored to camouflage multiple lumps and bumps, and her pearls looked to be of good quality. It crossed my mind that she almost seemed to have the heavy, sure-footed tread of a boxer or a bodyguard.

The reception area was unchanged from when I'd last decorated it—the warm cherry paneling showed tender care and the particularly lovely Constable was still on the wall. Bertram stood in the open door of his office, looking rotundly fit—quite a bit rounder in fact than he'd been when I'd last seen him—very relaxed, and very much the lord of the manor. Which he was. The ancient regime was dead, long live the king.

Bertram was a dapper, proper, affable fellow. His bespoke suit was charcoal gray, his shirt white and starched, his tie yellow silk, and his shoes were polished to a fare-thee-well. A thin gold chain looped across the front of his vest. His gray hair was brushed straight back, his cheeks were rosy, and his eyes bright behind rimless glasses. In the auction world, Bertram was considered the king, the ultimate auctioneer, and you could see why. He was so enthusiastic, so positive, he radiated confidence and practically bounced when he walked. He was like a force of nature. No one would ever be able to guess from his chipper demeanor that his board of directors had him on a timer.

No wonder the media loved him so. Like Thomas, Bertram had become a star, a media darling. And now that I looked at him, I realized he and Thomas even looked a little alike, but there the similarities ended.

My Thomas tended to be arrogant and dour, always speaking down to his interviewer and audience as though they were stupid as asses and scarcely worth his time or effort. He'd get a pained expression on his face, brush the white hair back from his brow, and stare into the cameras with those beautiful blue, blue eyes that seemed to say, Why do I bother trying to explain all this complicated stuff to all you pathetic dunderheads? You'll never be able to grasp any of what I'm saying. And then he'd pause as though searching for the right words to put it into the simplest possible form that one or two of the Neanderthals might grasp. Sometimes it wasn't worth the effort, and he'd say something like, "It's far too complicated and would be an utter waste of my time to attempt to explain to your viewers." The viewers loved it, loved him. I think every one of them thought he or she was the only one who was Thomas's intellectual equal. And while he'd never admit it, Thomas thrived on the attention.

Bertram's public persona was the opposite. He was charming, accessible, always happy to explain or educate without seeming arrogant or condescending. And he was available. Because of the nature of his business—part of his job was to be seen at black-tie galas, openings, royal tea parties—he was always circulating, always friendly, always happy to bound up to the camera to say a few good-natured words and explain to the viewers why this painting or that piece of furniture was so rare or valuable. He made everyone feel that if they were to find themselves at a fancy party or an auction, they could hold their own. They'd been educated by Sir Bertram Taylor. He appeared at least bi-weekly on *Upstairs/Downstairs*, the SkyWord celebrity reporter, Giovanna MacDougal's weekly gossip program.

I couldn't imagine what had gone wrong to put the house in such trouble and Bertram, himself, in such jeopardy.

"Kick." He approached with his arms extended. "You look positively smashing."

We embraced, which had the effect of putting Ruth Provender on alert. "I'm so glad to see you. You've met Ruthie."

She and I nodded and smiled at each other, and she bobbed a little curtsey.

"Come in. Come in," Bertram said. "Would you like a quick coffee before we go?"

"That would be lovely. Just black, thank you."

Ruth set her jaw to the task as Bertram held out his arm for me to enter the inner sanctum, formerly Sir Cramner's office and then Owen Brace's lair, scene of numerous bacchanalian encounters—some with starlets. Some with me. The memory of them made my scalp tingle. Thank God, Bertram had completely redecorated the office and that seductive sofa—lovely cranberry silk damask with deep down cushions—was gone. I felt my cheeks grow hot.

I glanced at the paneled wall where a secret staircase led down to the mews and wondered if Bertram knew about it. Sir Cramner had used it often to dodge his wife, Lady Ballantine, and I had used it a handful of times myself to bring counterfeit pieces into the house and, conversely, to take their authentic counterparts out. I wondered if Bertram knew that the entire ancient building was honeycombed with secret passages, entrances and exits.

"I know Ruthie seems an absolute fright," he said once the door was closed. "But she can handle a calendar, a computer, and major clients like no one I've ever met. She is unspeakably kind, hardworking, strong as an ox, she has virtually no life other than Ballantine's and me, and Mrs. Taylor didn't object to her, and that alone was worth it."

I took a seat across the huge desk, which was the only piece to survive his redecoration. It had been the managing partner's desk since the early 1800s and the scene of many monumental, historic deals. And trysts. And sexual calisthenics. And oh, my. If this room could talk. I tried to put an image of Bertram with Ruthie flopped over backward before him out of my mind. Oh, for heaven's sake, Kick. What is wrong with you? Stop it. Sir Cramner and Owen Brace are long gone and you're a very happily married woman. But my thoughts were not unreasonable—after all, there was precedent.

"Bertram," I said. "Are you saying that your wife has passed away?"

He nodded, matter-of-factly. "A year and a half ago."

"I'm so sorry." I recalled the small crush I'd had on him when he joined the firm and my disappointment that he'd been married. Suddenly I was thinking of Bertram with me flopped over backward before him. And I could tell he was thinking the same thing. I read somewhere once that people have a sexual thought every ten seconds or something equally silly. Ridiculous.

"She was a good old girl but sick as a dog. She was ready to move on." He gave me a lopsided grin and changed the subject. "It's wonderful to see you looking so well, Kick. Hard to believe that you've never married and settled down into a lady's town-and-country life."

I opened my mouth to answer but thought better of it. No reason to muddy the waters with Thomas. I wasn't here to cheat, have a fling, or flirt. I had a clear mission and then I'd be gone. Besides, my private life was off-limits. It always has been.

"Well, of course, that's neither here nor there, is it?" He said. "I had Ruthie make us a reservation at Wilton's."

"Wonderful. And it's such a beautiful day, we can walk."

"Actually, I'd prefer us to take the car. I'm embarrassed to admit I'm suffering from a little spot of gout and walking too much is sheer agony."

"I'm so sorry." It's funny how the mention of gout can shoo any sort of even slightly adulterous thought from your mind like snuffing out a candle. The image of an aging gentleman's miscolored, swollen, gouty leg is a real bucket of ice. Poof. It's gone. I took a nice cool, relaxing breath. Things were properly back in perspective.

CHAPTER *13*

There was a sharp, businesslike rap on the door immediately followed by Ruth elbowing her way in with the coffee tray and a small plate of Ballantine's signature miniature orange rolls. As though she'd read my mind, she'd added some fresh lipstick and blusher, which had the effect of masking the fatigue in her face. In fact, she looked quite pretty. She deposited her tray on the corner of the desk and placed a cup and saucer—white porcelain emblazoned in navy with the Ballantine coat-of-arms—in front of each of us and then filled them with steaming coffee poured from a silver pot.

"I know you're on your way to lunch, Sir B, but I thought Miss Keswick would have missed the orange buns." She offered the plate. "Madame," she said with a silly French accent. I took two of the tiny rolls, which were covered with an orange-caramel toffeelike glaze flecked with bits of orange zest.

"Thank you so much, Ruth. I was hoping you'd bring these." I bit into one and the soft, sticky treat filled my mouth with familiar flavors and my heart and head with solace. These buns were like mother's milk to me.

"There's really nothing like them, is there?" She beamed as proudly as if she'd baked them herself.

I shrugged my shoulders a bit. "I suppose not." I could have been much kinder. I could have told her I'd dreamt about these buns and was so happy to be eating one it almost made me cry, but the fact was, I found myself resenting "Ruthie." I resented her harum-scarum looks and I resented having her stand in my place. I knew I was having a childish, jealous little fit, but I didn't care. I found myself wishing Bertram would fire her on the spot.

She gave me a perplexed look over her glasses and then lumbered out without a word, closing the door definitively behind her.

"The house looks beautiful," I said.

"Maintaining a landmark like this never stops—I think Sir Cramner would be pleased."

"I know he would."

"Well, let me see," he paused to think. "As you know, we're in the midst of preparing for the fall sales—Impressionists first and then Magnificent Jewels—so the public side of things is quite down to zero at the moment. But I'll take you around the vaults if you like before we go to lunch—we have some extraordinary pieces coming up."

"That's not necessary, I know how busy the staff is, getting ready. I don't want to disturb them."

"All right then. Let's get down to business." He smiled and rubbed his hands together with relish. "I really put my mind to it after we talked, Kick. And I have a proposition for you."

"Oh?"

"I have hit upon the perfect opportunity. So before we go to lunch, I want to show you your office."

"My office?"

The smile grew larger. "I'd like you to be a director."

"Of?"

He leaned toward me with his hands flat on the desktop. "I thought Director of Continuity would be a fitting title."

"Bertram," I said. "What does that mean?"

"It is quite unusual, but is precisely what its name implies: you, your taste, your expertise, and your style, your, if you will—your cachet, your imprimatur—will provide a link between our past and our future, and a wonderful comfort zone to our long-standing clientele and staff. You're exactly what I've needed to complete the picture— we're poised to dominate the industry, but the single greatest piece I've been lacking is a credible Number Two, who is also possibly a worthy successor in case of emergency."

I opened my mouth to speak, but Bertram held up his hand.

"Now, wait. Just hear me out. I do have a very talented protégé— Roman McIver. He is a super talent behind the auction block but he's not up to par yet on the business side. Everyone in the world knows you were Sir Cramner's most trusted advisor and confidante. You were so savvy in running the business, he could focus on the auctions. Well, this is similar—just a temporary assignment, if you like, to help bring the boy up to speed on the bigger picture. Because, you know, once the season opens, I won't have time to tutor him in all the important corporate ins-and-outs he needs to know if he's to be my ultimate successor." He sat back, knowing he'd delivered a well-thought-out, well-organized, rational, and persuasive argument. "Well, what do you think?"

I swallowed. This was not at all what I had in mind. To be sure, Bertram's plan would provide the open sesame for me to find the troublemakers. But this was an actual full-time job with significant responsibility. It never occurred to me that he'd ask me to be his Number Two. His emergency fall-back. Was this an avenue I was interested in pursuing? No. Not even slightly.

"I think it sounds intriguing," I answered in an attempt not to be rude and reject his offer out-of-hand.

"Good! Not a 'No,' but a good, strong 'Maybe.' I can turn a 'maybe' into a 'yes' in no time!"

"If anybody can, it's you, Bertram. You are the consummate salesman." I smiled at him, but he couldn't miss the 'Not-a-chance expression' in my eyes, which, like all good salesmen, he simply chose to ignore.

"So. Let's take a look in your office—you don't mind if I refer to it as 'your' office, do you? It has a nice, reassuring ring to it. I've had Ruthie working nonstop since your call to get it ready. Perhaps this will give you added incentive to come back home from wherever it is you've been."

"My" new office was Bertram's old one—a wonderfully airy room with a view of St. James Square, a private bath, a large bird's-eye maple desk, comfortable carved walnut fauteuils with cushioned seats, and a portrait of Sir Cramner on the paneled wall above the marble fireplace. I wondered if Bertram knew about the secret entrance that this office had as well.

Ruth stood to the side of the desk and bobbed again in her little nervous curtsey. "We're so glad you're back, Miss Keswick," she said, pulling her lips back enough to show the biting halves of her forward teeth.

"Thank you, Ruth. But I'm still thinking about it."

"Of course you are. I didn't mean to be presumptuous but all of us on the staff are so very pleased you're here."

Indeed, when Bertram and I went back out onto the large landing off the suite of executive offices, there were numerous experts and appraisers milling about—many, many familiar faces. It took almost fifteen minutes to get down the stairs and to the front door, they were greeting me with such warmth.

I had no idea I'd been so missed. In fact, I'm embarrassed to say I'd never given the slightest thought to the effect my disappearance might have had. All the people I'd worked with for so many years, those to whom I'd been mentor, mother, disciplinarian, and arbiter of taste—I'd just left them behind without a glance. I was stunned at their reaction—at their genuine happiness at seeing me again.

And Bertram seemed to know what effect this greeting was having on me. He only smiled and didn't say a work or try to hurry us along. As he'd pointed out, the single biggest element Ballantine's lacked was continuity and I was the only person who could provide it. He was banking on my legendary loyalty to the memory of Sir Cramner to ensure my acceptance.

I was curious if he would bring up the troubles at lunch—the fakes, the phonies, the firing of Andrew Gardner, the ultimatum from his board. I wouldn't be the one to mention them. I had no interest in tipping my hand as to my motives, but if he did bring them up, it would certainly simplify things, enable us to have a more honest, open discussion.

CHAPTER 14

The ride around the corner, up St. James Street to Jermyn Street in the backseat of the navy blue Bentley, reinforced my sense of propriety. The leather seats were soft and fragrant and all the fixtures polished and gleaming, like everything else in Bertram's world. This was the limousine Owen Brace bought but could not afford. The limousine that Owen's thug, Mickey, drove. A thug who Owen insisted be called Michael, as though that could somehow make up for the cauliflower ears and the nose that had been smashed in at least five times, by the looks of it. The limousine in which Owen had frequently put up the privacy screen between Mickey and us.

"Bertram," I said, trying to get Owen off my mind. "I'm glad you kept this car. It's so appropriate for you."

"It makes the right statement," he nodded. "Keeps the house visible."

His driver, Epperson, maneuvered through heavy traffic and pulled to the curb in front of Wilton's, arguably one of the finest restau-

rants on the face of the planet. If you like fancied-up English food, as
I do.

The manager greeted us—this was clearly Bertram's place, just as
the Reading Room at Claridge's had been Sir Cramner's, and Le Caprice
had been Owen's. He guided us to a central booth from which all the
activity in the restaurant could be observed, and from which Bertram
could be observed as well. A successful auction house is built almost
completely on relationships—they are what bring in the private, exclusive, major collections. So the managing director and all the experts
need to keep themselves engaged in the proper circles, on hand and
in place to run into the noblemen and women, the various and
sundry aristocrats, the captains of industry, the individuals of great
wealth who were avid collectors, and those interested in buying and
selling rare pieces, or those simply desperate for cash. Wilton's was
just such a place. Much better than a private club because in fact,
most of the members of the older clubs had run out of money and
relics generations ago.

Heads turned, fingertips wiggled, and air kisses wafted as we criss-
crossed the entire room on the way to our table. Bertram basked in
the notoriety.

"What may I bring you to drink, madam?" The waiter asked as he
whisked a large square yellow napkin into my lap. "A dry martini, or a
Lillet? A glass of champagne, perhaps?"

"What do you recommend, Bertram?" I asked.

"I'll have my usual," he informed me. "A very, very dry Belvedere
vodka martini. The martinis here are even better than those at the
Dukes."

"That's hard to imagine," I said. "I'd better have one, as well."

The chilled stemmed glasses were oversized—almost doubles—
and full to the brim. We clinked.

"Good health," Bertram said and took a long sip. He put down his
glass and regarded me. "I must say, this is quite a surprise to have you
reappear, Kick. The last I saw or heard of you was just before the first
Princess Arianna auction when you came to my office, bowled me
over by giving me eight percent ownership of the firm, and then vanished. That was almost three years ago. What happened?"

"I was exhausted and humiliated. Owen had played me for a fool in a very public way and I couldn't stand around anymore and watch him paw Odessa right under my nose, particularly when I had his engagement ring on my finger and our wedding was days away. It had all become a sickening joke. I had to leave." I sipped my cocktail and the icy vodka sizzled all the way down to my toes.

"He did have a knack of turning anything beautiful into a tawdry situation, didn't he? Where did you go?"

I shrugged. "Oh, you know. Away."

Bertram nodded and finished his drink in a single draw and chewed up his olives. "You were well out of it. He was a scoundrel of the highest order. In fact, the Owen Brace months at Ballantine and Company have been expunged from the company archives. They were simply a black blip on the screen." He signaled for a second round. "Are you ready for another?"

"Not quite yet, thanks." I was trying, not very successfully, to drink slowly. Martinis at any time, but particularly at lunch, are seldom a good idea. As I recall, it was after two or three of them that Owen led me upstairs to the Astor Suite at Cliveden for the first time. Or, maybe that was double Bloody Mary's. I can't recall except that a great deal of vodka followed by a great deal of wine, and a great deal of pleasure, were involved. What a total bastard that man was. "Tell me, how are things at the company? How did you get the firm back on its feet so quickly?"

My question was interrupted by the arrival of the chef de cuisine, a pug-nosed Frenchman in a crisp white jacket and toque. He and Bertram shook hands. They were clearly good friends, and he honored our table with his visit. "The St. Chapelle oysters just arrived. Very, very sweet, the first of the season," he said once Bertram had introduced me. "I insist you have them to start. They are so very delicate."

"Done," said Bertram. "What about the main course?"

"The Scottish lobsters and the sole left the sea this morning. With a bottle of the 2004 Niellon Chassagne Montrachet? Perfection."

Bertram looked at me.

"Sounds lovely," I said.

"Thank you, chef. We accept."

He gave me a little half-bow. "Madame."

A fresh martini replaced my empty one and, thank God, a plate of sliced French bread and soft butter appeared at the same time.

"Now." Bertram swished the olives back and forth in his drink. "Where were we?"

"I was asking you how you got the company back on its feet so quickly because I know Owen had stripped out all the cash."

"Well, first of all, there was a terrific scandal."

"Really?" I spread butter on a crust of bread and took a bite. It was perfect—crunchy, chewy outside and soft inside. A little crunch of sea salt in the butter.

"Didn't you read about it in the papers?"

I shook my head, no. The fact was, I'd orchestrated the entire thing and watched every second unveil itself on television—just as I'd envisioned it—from my kitchen in Provence, while I sipped a glass of 1996 Dom Pérignon and toasted my cunning. But I wanted to hear about it from Bertram, how it looked from his point of view.

"Evidently, Brace had been living on the brink for some time and was getting desperate. He'd had copies—very, very fine copies I might add—of some of Princess Arianna's pieces made and switched them and stashed the real pieces in the trunk of his car."

"You're not serious." I admit I wanted to preen a bit, but naturally, I resisted. I was the one who'd made the copies and stashed the originals in his car. The ideal setup.

Bertram nodded. "Completely. It turned out that was just the tip of all his funny business and his entire conglomerate collapsed practically overnight and he disappeared from the scene as quickly as he'd appeared. Thanks to your gift of the shares, the bank was very amenable to helping me keep the doors open and restructuring, and now we're the preeminent leader in the jewelry world, and a close second in nineteenth- and twentieth-century paintings and furniture. I couldn't be more thrilled with how things have turned out."

I was interested that Bertram still hadn't breathed a word about the company's problems—maybe they weren't quite as serious as the board member had implied.

"I'm so happy for you Bertram," I said. "But not even slightly surprised. I wonder whatever became of Brace?"

Bertram shrugged. "He was let go from jail later that day and simply took off. No one saw him again. But those days are over—let's talk about now. And the future. Let me bring you up to date on the company."

CHAPTER 15

I set my face like stone, ready to feign shock and surprise at the grave state of affairs. But that's not at all where he went.

"As I believe I began to tell you," Bertram continued, "my protégé and successor Roman McIver, is absolutely brilliant. I lured him away from Christie's and, even though he's quite green, he's a breath of fresh air to have in the company—wonderfully well-connected. Travels in a rich, young crowd. His best friend is William Flynn."

"Edgar Flynn's son?"

Bertram nodded, his mouth full of a large piece of bread smeared with an inordinate amount of butter. No wonder he had gout.

Edgar Flynn was a powerful Irishman from Chicago who'd been a good customer of Ballantine & Company and bought dozens of major pieces of jewelry—in which I'd switched most of the stones because he was interested only in size. Quality was not an issue. The bigger and flashier the stone the better, and if he'd ever discovered that he'd bought fakes or inferior stones, he would have absorbed the loss in silence. He was too much of an egomaniac to ever be able to admit publicly that he'd been duped.

His wife, Constance, was as beautiful and charming as he was beastly. They'd been married for decades and were now in the midst of an outrageous, public divorce due to his inability to keep his hands off other women—most recently and famously, supermodel Lauren Cambridge. The tabloids claimed that Edgar had just up and left Constance and planned to marry Lauren. He would probably be pleased to stick Constance with a bunch of phony stones, just to shaft her a little more thoroughly.

"William Flynn's about to marry Alice Vasvar." Bertram swallowed hard; he was so anxious to talk I was afraid he'd choke. "Prince Georg Friedrich Vasvar's daughter. Oh, it's all so delicious. You know that Freddie—that's what everyone's always called him, Georg Friedrich is just too much of a mouthful—is a newlywed himself. He married Marchioness Sylvia Kennington not long ago. I think she's his fourth wife, maybe his fifth, and she is oh-so-very comfortable."

"That's putting it rather mildly," I said, feeling as though this had turned into a surreal encounter with Noël Coward, as though Bertram had moved to another planet. He trumpeted names out of his mouth for all the restaurant to hear, take note of, and marvel at. It was like listening to water gush from a fountain or a Roman herald standing on a box in the square. Edgar Flynn and his wife Constance and their son, William. Prince Freddie and his fifth wife, the rich-beyond-imagination Marchioness Sylvia, and his daughter, the princess bride Alice.

"You know," he proclaimed, "Sylvia's mother is Duchess Mary Margaret Kennington—one of the richest women in the empire."

"What a fortunate windfall for the Vasvars—they've been famously broke for decades."

"Indeed," Bertram galloped along between gulps and bites. "They're sort of a wild and wooly bunch, aren't they? But they always seem to marry well, rescue themselves just in the nick of time. I think Freddie hoped Sylvia would save him—replumb and rewire his family properties and pay for his daughter's wedding—but I've heard on good authority that their marriage is already in trouble. Freddie's been seen here and there with other women. I'm very fond of Sylvia. Do you know her?"

I shook my head. No.

"She's a very charming woman—late forties, maybe even early fifties—and not at all what the tabloids say about her."

"Which is?"

"That she's heartless, a cheapskate, a lightweight, and a dilettante."

"Where are you heading, Bertram?" I asked. "What does all this have to do with Ballantine and Company?"

"Ah," he beamed and held out his hands as though he were a magician holding a beach ball. "Now, I will pull it all together for you. You may or may not recall, but years ago, Edgar Flynn bought the Vasvar rubies here at one of our auctions."

I remembered it very well. The *real* Vasvar rubies were in one of my safe deposit boxes in Geneva.

"And William Flynn is giving them to Alice as a wedding present! Oh, goodness. Isn't it glorious? It's terribly romantic. You do know the story, don't you, about the Vasvar Jewels?"

I knew the story so well, I could have written it myself.

"It's a magnificent ruby and diamond parure," he cooed. "There's a tiara, a necklace, bracelets, earclips, and a stunning brooch with the Vasvar Ruby. Ancient, legendary pieces." Bertram recited them lovingly. "An early Prince Vasvar lost the collection in a poker game in the early nineteen-hundreds and laid a curse on it—saying it would bring terrible misfortune to anyone who owned it until it returned to the control of the family. And now it will. Oh, it's all so terribly romantic." Tears welled in Bertram's eyes. "And thanks to Roman McIver and his friendship with William Flynn, we're moving on to the next generation of collectors that are secure in our house. Oh, the wheel of life, how wonderful it is." He held up a finger to signal for another drink. "Roman's a carbon copy of me when I was his age. The girls go crazy for him. It's like having a young bull around the office." His voice wandered off, presumably to the greener pastures of his youth. Before the gout brought him down. "But he's still young and inexperienced so I've had to carry more of the auction schedule than I anticipated and as a result, to be completely candid, Kick, and this cannot leave this table, the business side is not getting the attention it requires."

Finally, solidly into his third martini—his cheeks and nose growing progressively redder with each sip—he began to come unglued and admit the reality: the company had thrived for a while, but a few months ago problems began to surface when a couple of key experts jumped ship to Sotheby's.

"Then, even worse, a handful of major jewels—which had been verified by Andrew Gardner—were switched during delivery."

"Oh, dear," I said. "That is serious."

"You've no idea what a nightmare this has been. It's been absolute hell. I let Andrew go and I've had to make good on the fakes of course, which is threatening to put us in the red. But, at least it's all remained confidential, and I think, knock on wood, we've weathered the worst of it."

By now, I was seriously alarmed. Bertram was drunk and babbling. And what concerned me even more was that no one in the restaurant batted an eye when he ordered his third double martini, which meant to me that this was something he did every day at lunch.

"I'm so sorry, Bertram." This was the third time I'd told Bertram how sorry I was for him—sorry for his dead wife, sorry for his gout, and now sorry for his bad luck. But the fact is, we make our luck, if such a thing as luck exists, and three-martini lunches were not the way to go if your intent was to flourish.

"Ah well. It's the nature of the beast—fakes are one of the inherent risks in this business. We'll survive this storm just like all the others. But . . ." He ran his hand back across the top of his head, which had the effect of pulling the wrinkles out of his forehead, raising his eyebrows, widening his eyes and, in my opinion, making him look panicked, as though he were about to start screaming. "I'll be the first to admit it: I need some help, and when I heard your voice on the phone saying you wanted to come back to work, it was an answered prayer." With these words, he started to weep. "You can make the difference as to whether we survive or not, Kick. I've got to have some experienced backup or it's going to kill me."

What could I say? I realized things were far worse than the Bentley American men had let on. Bertram had lost control of his company and himself and the whole place could be gone in no time. No wonder the staff was so happy to see me. They were clinging to the decks of the Titanic—Bertram could sell ice cubes to Eskimos but he was obviously drunk most of the time, his eating was out of control, he was probably clinically depressed, and he didn't know the first thing about running a business. I'd already saved the company twice: first *for* Owen Brace and then *from* him. And now here was Bertram, blubbering like a baby. Honestly, what's wrong with these men? Why don't they just act like men anymore?

I wanted to slap him and tell him to grow up.

Although my motives—which were strictly self-protective—weren't what Bertram had in mind, I consented, to an extent. "I'm willing to agree to a practical, short-term arrangement."

"Meaning?"

"Meaning I'll come in, but provisionally. Not as your successor, Bertram, but through the fall sales."

"I have your word?" His face brightened.

"You do."

He extended his hand across the table and we shook.

"That's marvelous. You cannot imagine the relief I feel." His color began to improve immediately. "Excuse me for a moment, will you?" He got up and made his way, very unsteadily, to the men's room.

I passed a little piece of bread to Bijou, who'd been quietly watching the entire saga from her travel bag at my feet.

Several minutes passed. My stomach growled with hunger. The waiter refilled the bread basket. I had another piece. Then, I watched the manager escort what appeared to be paramedics down the side hallway toward the back of the restaurant. A minute or two later, I watched them carry Bertram out on a stretcher.

Oh. My. God. You've got to be kidding.

CHAPTER 16

Giving your word is easy if you lack integrity. Then you can rationalize things to yourself: "Oh, that's what I said, but that's not exactly what I meant." Or, "No one will ever find out." Or, "So what if I never see them again—I couldn't stand those people anyhow." Or, "I know I said I would do it, but now I just don't feel like it."

Although I'd made my living as a thief and a liar and an impostor, I did have a moral compass. And there was no getting around the fact that I'd sat there at lunch and looked Bertram in the eye and given him my word that I'd step in and help. But I certainly didn't have anything like this in mind. That's the problem with life—it comes along and wrecks all your plans.

The entire staff was gathered in the foyer when I returned to the company from the hospital late in the afternoon—they all looked scared to death. Ruth took my wrap and I climbed to the third step on the big staircase so I could see every face. I'd taken special care in the car to repair my makeup and hair, so when I stood before them I would appear confident and in charge. And in fact, I was.

"Bertram has had a relatively mild heart attack," I announced, which was not entirely true. He was close to death but I didn't want to cause any unnecessary hysteria. "And he will need to undergo by-pass surgery, hopefully within the next two or three days as soon as he is stronger. The doctors say he will make a full recovery."

A ruffle of relief passed through the group.

"It's going to take some time—weeks. And I will stand in as acting managing director until I can find a suitable replacement."

"Oh, thank God," someone said. Then another and another. A round of polite applause followed.

"I'll start tomorrow morning with a meeting of department heads. Ten o'clock in the board room. Good evening." With that I turned and climbed the stairs, recalling the brief moment of serenity I'd enjoyed on the way to the Balfours' party. Now my life was completely upside down. I needed to call Thomas and let him know what was going on. Roman McIver and the firm's chief financial officer, Tim Cavendish, both fit and earnest young men, were waiting for me in my office with a stack of papers.

Ruth fluttered around, not sure what to do, until she finally took a seat at the conference table.

"Thank you, Ruth. I'll let you know if I need anything more."

She opened and closed her mouth, trying to muster a defense, a good reason why she should be joining this meeting, but ended up by nodding with a jerk of her head. "Very well," she said, getting to her feet. She closed the door with an abrupt and angry whack.

Early on in my life I'd made it my business to learn to read a financial statement, so that's where I started. Mr. Cavendish sat quietly while I scanned the report. It was worse than I thought. I laid it back on the desk.

"Mr. Cavendish, during Sir Cramner's tenure, the books were kept properly; however, when Mr. Brace bought the company, a minimum of two sets of books were kept, each portraying a vastly different picture. Is this the only set of books you've been instructed to keep for Ballantine and Company?"

Silence.

"You mean it's worse?"

He slid a second sheet across the table and I was stunned at what I saw. "I've never seen so many write-offs. What's going on here?"

"We've gotten stuck with a nasty string of returns."

"*Returns?*" I said. "There are no 'returns' in an auction house."

"It was a new policy Sir Bertram instituted—very hush-hush, but done to attract big bidders. Sort of the way casinos attract big spenders by paying all their expenses. Sadly, a couple of buyers took advantage."

"Who were they?"

"Actually," said Roman, "it was just one."

"And he is?"

"He is vanished, is what he is. He was a con man. The goods he brought back were fakes."

I felt my jaw drop. "You're not serious."

They both nodded.

"We were snookered. Hoodwinked."

"How many times did this person fool you?"

"Twenty million pounds worth."

"Bertram should be ashamed."

The room was silent as both men examined their hands.

"Does the board know how serious this is?"

They both shook their heads. No.

I reexamined the balance sheet. "If I'm reading this correctly, we have enough cash to cover one more payroll."

Tim Cavendish nodded in agreement.

"And all the lines of credit are tapped out?"

He nodded again. "It's quite a pickle, Miss Keswick."

"You're right, Mr. Cavendish." I gave him a brief smile. "It is quite a pickle. When is the next payroll?"

"Friday week."

As the overall picture grew clearer, I saw what Bertram was attempting to do—he was counting on the sales to bring in enough cash to make the subsequent payroll and service the loans. The company was in the worst shape it had ever been in. This was appalling. What had I gotten myself into?

"Is there anything else I need to know?"

"What are you going to do, Miss Keswick?" Roman McIver asked. "We have so much about to get underway." He was an elegant young man. Not handsome in the classical sense, with refined features and sharp edges. His face, with its slightly too-large nose, wide mouth and easy smile, dark, intelligent eyes and thick dark brows, had been put together in a way that made him extremely masculine in a rugged sort of way. Mid-thirties, I'd say. Dark, shiny, somewhat unruly hair. Medium height and well-exercised. Immaculately and expensively clad.

Both men simply stared at me and I could tell they were frightened. They'd been dumped out of their warm, cozy cribs and into the cold rainy street. This was sink or swim time.

"I'm not sure exactly what we're going to do, but I'll tell you the one thing we are *not* going to do is panic, and I'm telling both of you right now, get those wide-eyed expressions off your faces, close your mouths, straighten your backs, straighten your ties, and button your jackets. We're just going to suck it up and shoulder it through."

They both looked shocked and I knew how they felt.

"Now listen to me," I continued, in as kind and direct a manner as possible. "I don't know how old you are but you have now come to one of those major turning points in your life and career when you have to choose. You can either decide to step up to the next level, put all your knowledge and training into action, or you can decide to not deal with the issue head-on and flail around until it controls you, whereupon you will immediately sink out of sight into the overflowing, overcrowded, fetid, stinking pool of mediocrity."

I was glad to note that this remark received a frown and a look of distaste from each of them. Mediocrity was not in their vocabulary.

"This is also not the end of the world," I continued. "We're facing a challenge—it happens in business all the time. You particularly, Roman, have to rise to the situation. In the blink of an eye you—not I—have become the public face of Ballantine and Company. So if either one of you has a brain in his head—which I know you do—when you leave this office, if any of the staff is still here, you tell them that we've had an excellent meeting, we're working on a solid strategy, and not to worry, that everything will be fine. And mean it. Do you have any questions before we call it a day?"

"No, ma'am," they said and shot to their feet. I almost expected them to salute.

"I'll see you both back here for the ten o'clock meetings, but if you're as smart as I think you are, you'll get here by seven-thirty, which is when I'll be arriving. I want you to sit in on the department head conferences, and I want to hear some creative ideas. Good night, gentlemen."

"Good night, ma'am," they said in unison, but I was happy to note that this time when they spoke, their voices were several octaves lower.

I told Ruth good night and left the building. I was surprised to see my car sitting at the bottom of the steps idling quietly, the doorman waiting to see me off. I'd completely forgotten that I'd driven over. It seemed like a hundred years ago that I'd pulled up in front of Ballantine & Company in my rented Jaguar sedan, all done up in a new Chanel suit and looking forward to a little lunch and a possible temporary assignment as an associate in the jewelry department, helping the Jewelry Ladies arrange the exhibits, keeping my hawk-eyes open to spot who was swapping the goods. What a lovely little Miss Marple fantasy that had been.

I went home and poured myself a double scotch and sank into a bathtub filled with steaming water and gardenia-scented bubbles and thought about all the losses the company had suffered. There were always bad debts, uncollectibles, but they were typically few and far between—nothing at this volume. Bertram was very wrongheaded, totally misguided to institute a "returns" policy. But that well-intended, bad judgment aside, someone had set out to take criminal advantage, and the more I examined it, I saw all the earmarks of a vendetta, a conspiracy. An orchestrated attempt to put the company out of business. There was no question about it: It had Owen Brace's fingerprints all over it.

CHAPTER 17

For a number of years—well dozens and dozens, actually, ever since Cramner began to educate me on the finer things in life—I have been able to identify the critical elements that comfort me.

Large, perfect stones have always been at the top of the list, and to have a handful of them in your possession means you have something that can be converted into quick cash to provide for necessities, and that is very comforting knowledge indeed. Pale pink silk quilted bathrobes comfort me as do chocolate, champagne, good scotch, tomato soup, cheese soufflés, and/or grilled cheese sandwiches. Thomas comforts me. But he was off doing his thing and I, evidently, was off doing mine, even though it certainly wasn't what I'd expected to be doing. I used my French cell phone to call Thomas, and if he'd answered, I think I would have said, Let's just go home, disconnect all the phones, open a bottle of bubbly, crawl into our bed, and pull the covers over our heads.

But, he didn't answer.

So after my bath, I put on my pink silk quilted robe, went into the kitchen, and turned on the television. News of Bertram's heart attack had just hit the air and SkyWord's star reporter, Giovanna MacDougal, in a simple black Armani suit—she didn't look as though she'd ever had a proper meal in her life, poor thing—was standing beneath the porte cochère of St. Anne's Hospital with a serious, very intense expression on her thin, taut, angular face as she settled into the first twenty-four hours of her media vigil. I knew inside she was as happy as an old-fashioned busybody snuggling her bottom into a big, plump cushion and settling in for a good long gossip, except in this instance, her bottom was so small it was almost invisible. Poor thing.

This sounds so peevish and paltry of me to say, but I was glad that Thomas was off on a special, top secret assignment because even though I knew he denied it like crazy, he was like a bee to honey around Giovanna. He simply couldn't help himself. She attracted men to her as though she had giant magnets sewn into her clothes—and I just didn't understand it. There was really nothing to hold on to but bones. And while I trusted Thomas not to do anything he would regret, and didn't worry about him jumping into bed with her, in my opinion, nevertheless, she was as available, tempting and destructive as Jezebel.

I freshened my drink, opened a can of cream of tomato soup and scooped it into a saucepan and turned the burner on low. While the soup heated, I neatly arranged a loaf of multigrain bread, jar of mayonnaise, and brick of Gruyère cheese around the breadboard on the counter. I placed a griddle on the stove, melted a few tablespoons of butter in a small saucepan, and grated a nice big pile of cheese and a small pile of shallot. Grated cheese is the secret to a superior grilled cheese sandwich. Then I spread a little mayo on two slices of bread, added the cheese and quite a good helping of the shallot and some chopped pimento, put the top on the affair and brushed it with the melted butter and placed it all—butter side down—on the griddle. Then I brushed the other side with butter.

Out of the corner of my eye, I saw Roman McIver emerge from the front door of the hospital and run headlong into Giovanna.

"Mr. McIver." She thrust the microphone in his direction. "What can you tell us? How is Sir Bertram?"

I was pleased to see Roman's panicked expression had been replaced by that of a mature young man very much in control of a bad situation.

"Good evening, Miss MacDougal," he said. "There's nothing new to report. Sir Bertram will be fine, make a full recovery. Our fall season starts shortly so I've been consulting with him about that. We have some particularly important pieces coming up and we will all carry on as normally as possible."

"So he can talk? Have visitors?"

"Well, I wouldn't go so far as to say he can have visitors—my visit was a special circumstance. After all, he has just suffered a heart attack. But yes, he is able to talk."

"With the fall sales around the corner, who will take the helm at the auction block? Who will bring down the gavel?"

"I will."

"That's quite an exciting step for you, isn't it?" Giovanna said archly.

Roman ignored her tone. "Not really. We have a very strong, experienced team at Ballantine and Company, and Sir Cramner's former assistant, Kathleen Keswick, has come back to manage the business of the firm, so we have the benefit of continuity as well."

My jaw dropped. The air left my body. I staggered to my chair.

"Kathleen Keswick?" Giovanna frowned. "I don't believe I'm familiar with her."

"She was Sir Cramner's Number Two for almost thirty years."

My French cell phone rang.

"Oh, boy." Thomas was so tickled he could hardly talk. "When you decide to take action, you don't waste any time."

"Can you believe your ears?" I said.

"Not really. Where are you?"

"At the flat."

"Can they find you?"

"No."

In fact, unless someone, like Thomas, knew exactly where my flat was, it would be impossible for anyone to locate me through any records. Once I'd given the shares of Ballantine's to Bertram, I'd taken the extra precaution of having Mr. Beauchamp at the bank change the name of my trust from KDK to Auberge. Only Mr. Beauchamp could provide a trail, and he would rather have ground glass for lunch or have his tongue removed than provide any information at all about any of his clients, including acknowledging if they even were clients. So while I knew Giovanna MacDougal would soon have her minions working on locating the mysterious Kathleen Keswick, she'd only run into dead ends, if she were able to develop any leads in the first place.

"Where are you?" I asked.

"In London."

"Have you had dinner?"

"No."

"How soon can you get here?"

"Two minutes."

"Go to the security gate at the mews, and come down to my garage. I'll let them know you're arriving."

I turned the flame off under the griddle, put on a little fresh lipstick, and went downstairs to open the garage door. Moments later, Thomas rolled in driving a dark gray, nondescript official sedan—a much more appropriate conveyance for him than that fancy *Rouge Indien* Porsche. As soon as the garage door was closed, we embraced. Was it only yesterday we'd said good-bye? It seemed ages ago.

Once we were settled, alternately sipping scotch and soup and eating the wonderfully decadent toasted cheese sandwiches, I told him all my concerns about the company, about what a mess it was in, the bad debts and vanishing buyer, the reasons why I thought it was being purposely pushed toward collapse, and why I suspected Owen Brace.

"It may sound crazy or paranoid," I said, "but do you know what ever became of him?"

Thomas shook his head. "No. He left the country as soon as he was released."

"He was run out of Ballantine's with such public disgrace, I have a feeling he's been lying in the weeds for years cooking up a scheme and waiting for the right opportunity to present itself. That would be his style. My intuition tells me he's behind this, pulling the strings."

Thomas considered my comments. "It's certainly possible. He was an insecure, vindictive, egomaniacal, loathsome, short—let me see if I can come up with other terms I could use in mixed company."

"That will do," I laughed.

"I still have trouble believing you almost married him. What were you thinking?" Clearly Thomas was still a little jealous, a little prickly about my affair with Owen. "Oh, all right. I'll see what I can find out."

I placed another sandwich on his plate and ladled more soup into his bowl and added a little dollop of sherry. "Tell me, how is your project going?"

"We've got some good leads. It's a delicate situation, as you can imagine. They made off with a staggering amount of loot and at some point, somewhere, it will emerge as a bargaining chip."

"They didn't get the Darya-i-Nur, did they?" Visions of the immense pink 182-carat table diamond filled my head. The Darya-i-Nur, also known as the Sea of Light, was the preeminent crown jewel of Iran and had been on the world scene since the early 1700s. It frightened me to think of it floating about unprotected, possibly in the possession of someone who didn't appreciate its rich history and rarity. Or, God forbid, broke it up.

Thomas shook his head. "I can't say."

"I understand."

It was so pleasant sitting there in the kitchen, having a relaxed visit. Bijou had curled herself into a tiny ball in Thomas's lap and was sound asleep. I cleaned up the dishes. It was getting late. "Where are you staying?"

"Small hotel near the Yard."

"Do you have to stay there? Or can you stay here?"

"I would love to stay here—I was hoping you'd invite me to spend the night. I've never spent the night here. In fact, I've never been in this flat except on official business. I've never even seen the bedroom."

I started to make a remark about how no one had ever spent the night here, except Owen Brace. Once. And on that occasion, the idea of sharing my bath with someone—something I'd never done in my life and didn't intend to start—practically gave me a nervous breakdown. When we woke up in the morning and he just calmly sauntered in and turned on my shower, I simply couldn't believe my eyes. I realized, if we were really going to go through with our marriage— Well, why would I think we weren't going through with it? We'd only gotten engaged the night before—we'd have to have a serious discussion about how things worked, starting with separate bathrooms. I'd used the guest bath that morning and he never stayed over again and the issue had died a natural death. With Thomas, it had never been an issue. He'd never shared his bath with anyone, either.

"Well," I said. "There's really not much to it." I put a pan of milk on the stove to make hot chocolate. "But it will be my great pleasure to take you on a tour." When the chocolate was ready, I handed him his mug. "Come on, I'll show you around."

The next morning, at about 6:15, I heard a racket in the street, and someone yelling. I peeked through the drawn curtains. It was unbelievable. There was a SkyWord mobile van, with a very tall antenna extending several feet in the air, parked several doors down. I couldn't see who was making the racket, but I knew it was Giovanna Mac-Dougal ringing the wrong bell.

Right church. Wrong pew. Too close for comfort for me.

CHAPTER *18*

It was an unceremonious, inauspicious, and very undigni-fied beginning to my new high-powered position: I slouched down in the seat of Thomas's sedan as he pulled out of the mews. He turned down Eaton Terrace so he could describe to me what was happening. The lovely dark green, grosgrain-ribbon-bound bouclé of my suit skirt rode up most daringly—I could say suggestively but let's be honest. We were on our way to work, our minds filled with more important—dare I say more interesting?—things than sex. Romance was riding in the back seat.

He'd offered to call the Yard to ask them to clear out the media from the quiet residential neighborhood, but I'd told him not to bother. I felt certain everyone else who lived around the square had leapt to the phone and voiced their dismay. And they had.

"The officers have arrived and are making them pack up. Gio-vanna seems to be throwing a fit of some sort."

"She should know better," I said.

He dropped me off a block from St. James Square. The air was brisk so I walked as quickly as I could down King Street, around the corner and down the side steps to the employees' service entrance. I slipped through the door undetected. It was 7:25 on the dot.

Ruth was in my office, fussing about—a small pot of coffee and tray of warm orange rolls sat on the edge of my desk. She was looking particularly put together in a sedate gray suit and pearls. A flat black bow had replaced the giant scarf in her frizzy hair.

"Good morning, Miss Provender." I tucked my black kid gloves in my purse and placed it in the bottom drawer of the desk, placed my briefcase on the surface, and handed her my coat, a black cashmere swing I'd gotten in Paris with a Persian lamb collar and cuffs and black satin frog closures.

"Miss Keswick," she bobbed her little curtsey which, the more I thought about it, seemed more like a boxer dodging a jab. "Messrs. McIver and Cavendish are in their offices if you need them."

"Thank you." I smiled at her and our eyes connected. We both seemed to acknowledge that we were going to make the best of what was a tough situation. We would learn to work together.

"The conference room is ready for the department heads meeting—water, coffee, note pads, pencils. A couple of them worked into the night putting together PowerPoint presentations for you."

I raised my eyebrows. "Impressive."

"These are very dedicated professionals, Miss Keswick. They've just been lacking a firm hand on the tiller."

"Well, I'm happy to oblige. If there's anything I am, it's a firm hand. I haven't taken my eye off the target in my life. Now, if you'd print out the employee roster for me, permanent and part-time, including salaries, and the most recent performance review on each, and ask Mr. McIver to come in."

"Consider it done, madam."

The realization of his new responsibilities had transformed Roman overnight. He entered the room with an attitude of presence and authority. It was as though he'd taken my words to heart and decided to grow up, and I felt a burst of pride. Without warning, I thought of my abandoned child. My son or my daughter who would be just Roman's age, and I hoped that my child had made the decision to walk down the path of his or her life with self-assurance, without fear. And it was a decision, not something that simply happened—like being happy. I knew that Roman had what it took. He was someone I could work with and count on.

I carried a blank pad and pen to the antique conference table. It had formerly graced someone's magnificent dining room and hadn't met its guaranteed minimum at auction, so the house had been forced to buy it—there were a number of such items scattered throughout the building. They represented appraisal errors, or an expert who was anxious to get one part of a collection so he'd made high guarantees on other parts of the lot, or in some cases, the languishing goods simply ran into a lack of interest by any buyers. Ruth had put five miniature red rose bushes in the oblong Edwardian sterling silver cachepot engraved with someone's coat-of-arms and the flora and fauna of their lost estate. The reflection of the roses shone like a Renoir in the gleaming walnut tabletop. I took my place at the head in a comfortable arm chair. The seat was upholstered in millefleurs tapestry.

"Good morning, Roman."

"Miss Keswick." He placed his agenda and a stack of papers on the table adjacent to me. "May I pour you a cup of coffee?"

I smiled. This was another very good sign. This was the sign of a star—someone who would put his ego in his shoe and do whatever it took to make things work smoothly. "Just black, please. Ruth can bring tea for you, if you'd like."

He shook his head. "I prefer coffee, thanks." He placed my cup in front of me and the plate of rolls between us.

"Where are you from, Roman?"

"My family's in Yorkshire."

McIver Steel. McIver Ship Yards.

"Your parents have the Old Masters collection."

He nodded. "Yes."

"Sir Cramner played golf with your grandfather. He was always trying to get him to commit to letting Ballantine's do the sale, if it ever came to that."

Roman laughed. "Well, hopefully that won't ever be necessary but if it is, I think the firm now has the inside track."

"Good."

We covered every imaginable aspect of the business, including the jewelry thefts. It was one thing for buyers to return fakes to us, but for us to be sending fakes out to them was a completely different story.

There was a knock. Ruth entered with the personnel documents I'd requested and Roman excused himself to finish preparing for the staff meeting.

"You know the jewelry girl, Miss Abigail Welsh?" Ruth asked, unsolicited. "Her father owns the Scotch whiskey distillery."

"I know of her, but I've never met her. Why?"

She looked at me over her glasses. "The girl is very bad news."

"Oh?"

"She's a floozy," she declared.

"Really," I said, startled by her description.

"It's disgraceful." Ruth pursed her lips and arched her brows, making her look like a bitter old maid. "She's engaged to be married to a very nice Scottish lad—some young laird or other. Poor thing. He's as cute as can be but very unsophisticated—she's got him on a merry chase. Every time he comes to London to visit, you can just see that he's completely over his head. Oh, my, how she lies to him. She's out every night with the 'smart young set,' Sloane Square's Young Turks. At the clubs till all hours. She's sleeping with Talbot Merrill, and . . ." at this Ruth paused and clenched her mouth in an angry line, her eyes narrowed to slits ". . . and she's completely hoodwinked Sir Bertram."

"Really," I said. "You don't mean to say she's sleeping with him, too?"

Ruth shuddered with disgust. "Oh, good heavens. Worse. Do you know I actually caught them going at it on top of his desk."

"No!" I struggled to keep my face straight.

"Like dogs, they were. She's simply shameless. She has him wrapped around her little finger. I've suspected all along that she's the one stealing the jewelry, but Sir Bertram wouldn't hear of it. Her father's always desperate for money—everyone know there's little money to be made in single malts."

I nodded, unwilling to admit that, in fact, I hadn't known there was little money to be made in single malts. They're so expensive I would have thought there was a great deal of money to be made there, just based on the amount of it Thomas and I consumed.

"Lots of prestige, of course," Ruth sniffed. "But very, very little money." She squared the stack of files and the sound of the hard-covered folders hitting the tabletop sounded like the cracking of a bullwhip, something Ruth no doubt would very much like to take to Miss Abigail Welsh's back. "Well, as I said, Sir Bertram wouldn't hear of it from me about Miss Welsh, but if I were you, that's where I'd start. If you want my opinion," her eyes filled with tears, "if anything happens to Sir Bertram, if he dies from this episode, it'll be Miss Abigail Welsh who's to blame. He's far too old to be undertaking such stressful activities."

I learned four extremely valuable items from this conversation: Ruth was listening in on my calls and at my door. She had her nose in everyone's business. She was in love with Bertram. And everyone at Ballantine & Company was either in love, getting married, sleeping with each other, or all three.

I also saw that Ruth was as devoted to Bertram as I had been to Sir Cramner. And now that Lady Bertram Taylor was dead and buried, Ruth wasn't going to let any fancy little Scottish lass in a kicky little family tartan kilt twirl in and steal her future. I didn't doubt for a second that she would go to the mat over this one if she had to—literally—and based on the breadth of her shoulders and the thickness of her arms that stretched the sleeves of her suit like country hams, I would put my money on her. I suspected she lifted weights or shot puts in her spare time. She would pummel to pieces anyone who said a cross or unkind word about Ballantine & Company in general and Sir Bertram in particular. She'd been covering for him. He was lucky to have her because he needed all the help he could get.

There were other things I discerned about Ruth: she could have used some anger management classes, her aggression was barely disguised. She was from a hard background—every now and then her acquired upper crust accent slid a notch or two back toward Wapping. I knew without asking that she had earned her way through sheer hard work and determination and her emotions were all outside along her skin—she would be an incompetent liar—and so I granted her a bit of credibility.

As soon as she left, I picked up the phone and called security. "Please bring me all the jewelry department tapes for the last twelve months, including those of the jewelry exhibition and client rooms."

"Yes, ma'am," the security chief answered. "I don't think you'll find anything there, though."

"A new set of eyes never hurts."

CHAPTER 19

By the time I returned from the department heads meeting, a chrome file box neatly arranged with colorful DVDs—the jewelry department records for the last twelve months—was on my desk. As was a handful of message slips, three of them from Giovanna McDougal. Ruth was away from her post.

Between the staff meetings and trying to get settled into my office, the day passed quickly. However, it had been on my mind that Giovanna knew approximately where I lived and if I were going to talk to her, which seemed inevitable, I intended to control when and where that happened.

At about five-thirty, I called Thomas.

"How's your day?" He asked.

"Crazy. How about yours?"

"Same." He sounded preoccupied and rushed.

"Thomas, I'm not going to go back to the flat tonight. I'm going to check into a hotel."

"Oh?"

"I'm not interested in bumping into Giovanna MacDougal or one of her scouts. So, if you're looking for me, I think I'll get a room at . . ."

"Hold on, Kick. Something's just come up," he jumped in quickly. "I'll call you back."

"Be safe," I said. "I love you." Just as I rang off, I heard him saying, "Wait! Which hotel?" But it was too late and I didn't want him to assign one of his junior officers to shadow me. I was on my own. It was better that way. I turned off my phone and removed the batteries on the chance that it emitted some constant secret signal.

"Excuse me, Miss Keswick." It was Ruth.

"Yes?" I'd just pulled on my coat.

"There's a nun here to see you."

"A what?"

"A little nun." Ruth's face was expressionless.

"What does she want?"

"She wants to talk to the head of the company."

"Have her see Roman." I pulled on my gloves.

"He's gone for the day. Meeting with a prospective client."

"All right. Give me a couple of minutes. And then show her in."

A little nun. Religious people have always made me uncomfortable. I'm not altogether sure why, but one obvious answer was that I was a thief. Rather, I *used* to be a thief, and that's against one of their laws. I was also an impostor and an inveterate liar—lying being another of my building blocks to success—and I knew that lying was against another of their rules. I also had never depended on anyone but myself, and that was totally the wrong answer where the religious people were concerned. Well, I could go on and on about why religion and I didn't mix but that didn't make any difference. This was business. There was a little nun here to see me and one of the rules of *our* business was "Meet with everyone." You never knew what was going to walk through your door and what package it was going to come in.

As I hung my coat back up, I tried to think if I'd ever actually talked to a nun. I couldn't recall. Of course, I'd seen *The Nun's Story* a hundred times with poor Audrey Hepburn sweating it out in that heavy habit down there in Africa with all those bugs and tropical diseases and getting beaten up by that terrifying lunatic woman in the Belgian asylum. The Arch-Angel they called her. Oh. My. God. When that cell door slammed shut and she chased her around, I thought I was going to die. It was Sister Luke's—Audrey's—own fault. She'd been strictly warned not to open that door. In spite of the Arch-Angel's rational words and beautiful clear eyes, she was a sociopathic murderess. But Sister Luke didn't heed the warnings. That was one of Sister Luke's problems: too much pride and she didn't follow instructions. She was constantly surrounded by a gang of very grouchy older nuns, angry old women in black habits, hating her beauty and her wealthy background and her superior education. They were nothing but a bunch of jealous old crabs—especially when what's his name, the doctor in the African settlement fell in love with her. Poor Sister Luke—drummed out of the corps. I've always wondered if she went back to the Congo and married that doctor.

And of course, there was *The Flying Nun*. Well, naturally they encouraged us to watch it at the reform school where we all thought it was inane. Now, I think we all would love to be able to fly out the window and fix the world.

And now, a nun wanted to see me. I pictured her as my age with short gray hair, wire-rimmed glasses, white blouse, and a plain periwinkle blue suit with a little silver dove pin on the lapel, looking more like a bank teller getting ready for retirement than a Bride of Christ.

Oh, may lightning strike me dead.

I went into my private powder room and repaired my hair and makeup, trying my best to look as crisp as I had at seven-thirty that morning. I was exhausted. The intense schedule I'd thrived on for so many years was about to kill me after one day. All I wanted was a double scotch, a sizzling steak and sliced tomatoes with fresh watercress.

As soon as I hit the intercom buzzer, my office door flew open and in came Ruth. I was beginning to develop a picture of Ruth's behavior when she was on the other side of that door: that she stood right next to it, hands poised before her like a football player ready to scoot in any direction, feet at the ready to leap, rather like a sprinter, ever ready to hurl herself into the fray. She was followed by an absolutely lovely young woman in a black habit. She didn't have Audrey Hepburn's dark, waif-like beauty—just the opposite. She was quite tall, close to six feet—not a "little" nun after all—and had light skin, pink cheeks, and beautiful, clear, sparkling blue eyes the color of the sky. I could tell nothing stronger than a glass of milk had ever passed her lips. She carried a nondescript black leather satchel.

"This is Sister Immaculata, Miss Keswick."

I offered my hand. "Sister. Welcome. Please, make yourself comfortable." I indicated we sit in the small seating area in my office. "May I offer you something to drink? Coffee? Water?"

She shook her head and sat on the benchlike settee. "Nothing. It's late. Thank you for taking the time to see me." Her accent sounded vague, almost American. Her posture was beyond perfect. She laid her hands on her lap across one another. A thin gold wedding band circled her ring finger.

I sat in the side chair. "How may we be of service to you?" I tried not to be abrupt—I didn't want her to get the impression I wasn't glad to see her, that she wasn't welcome, that her goodness and purity put me on edge.

When she raised her eyes and we looked at each other, I got the sudden feeling we'd known each other for years and years.

"I'm a member of a branch of the Hungarian Little Sisters of the Poor, although our particular community no longer exists in Hungary and our convent is in Italy." She smiled at the irony. "Ours is a contemplative order."

Evidently, she discerned I was not entirely certain what that meant.

"We spend our days in prayer, we don't speak aloud to one another, and only the Reverend Mother has contact with the outside world."

"You don't mean you're the Reverend Mother?" I said. "You're practically a child."

Sister Immaculata laughed. "I am the Reverend Mother—this is what Reverend Mothers look like now. For centuries, our community supported itself on the sale of our olive oil and Nebbiolo wine, and through the patronage of members of the royal family in Hungary. In the twenties, Dowager Duchess Shasta Vasvar—our order was founded by one of her ancestors—bequeathed her collection of jeweled Madonnas to us."

"I know exactly who you are," I said, intrigued, my antennae perking up. "The Madonna Illuminata. The murders."

She nodded.

"What an incomprehensible tragedy that was."

I'd been working my way through reform school when it happened but I recalled the international headlines about the cold-blooded murder of an entire community of nuns and the theft of their priceless collection of jeweled Madonnas. I know I said being around religious people makes me uncomfortable, but the fact is, I cannot think of anything lower than murdering a nun. Well, murdering a child is worse, but a nun would be next on my list of too-gruesome-to-contemplate crimes. "Was the killer ever caught?"

Sister Immaculata shook her head. "Never. No suspects were even identified."

"I didn't realize the order had reestablished itself."

"It didn't for decades, but a number of years ago, a small number of sisters, myself included, moved to the property and—thanks to God's grace—we've restored it completely. We rehabituated the vines, which were still alive but had grown wild, and rescued most of the trees, and did an extensive amount of replanting. We no longer enjoy the patronage of the Vasvar family, so we've subsisted on gifts and, as I said, on the sales of the wine and olive oil. The wine sales have been our largest source of support, our vintages are always superior." She shifted in her seat and laced her fingers together. "Unfortunately, last year, the vines were blighted and no amount of prayer or agricultural innovation can save them without a large influx of cash, so we've been forced to take a drastic measure."

"Oh?"

"I need to be assured of your complete discretion and confidence, Miss Keswick. What I'm about to show you—no one can know where it came from."

"You have my word and the word of the house." It occurred to me that my word used to mean nothing—I wouldn't think twice about pledging with my right hand and stealing with my left—and now it did.

She unzipped her carrying case and withdrew a package that was wrapped with string, which she untied and opened. Then she set on the table one of the most remarkable figurines I'd ever seen. A six-inch-tall Madonna made entirely of what looked to be Kashmir sapphires, emeralds, and diamonds.

"We think this is one of our better ones," Sister Immaculata said. "How much do you think it's worth?"

CHAPTER *20*

~~~ I picked up the statuette and held it to the light—it was exquisitely constructed. One sign of a well-made piece of jewelry is if the back is as beautiful as the front. The settings should be precise and show almost the same amount of surface of the stones as the front, although you're looking at the culet—the pointed end—and not the table. The inside of this object was so intricate, it gave me the same sense of awe as standing beneath the Tour Eiffel and looking straight up into its extraordinary framework.

"I've never seen anything like this before," I said. "Is it a part of that original collection? It's my recollection that everything was taken."

"Is it important that you have that information?"

"It is to the extent that I must know you are legally entitled to sell it."

Sister Immaculata nodded emphatically. "Oh, indeed I am. I have the original documentation with me. But it's a rather long, dangerous story."

I looked at my watch. 6:15. "Sister, are you by any chance free to join me for dinner?"

She looked very pleased and not a bit surprised. "I'd love to."

"Good. Let's take care of a little business first." I picked up the phone and asked Ruth to send in Talbot Merrill, the new director of the Jewelry Department.

"He's gone for the evening, Miss Keswick."

I had to make a decision, and it was a big one: no one but Thomas knew of my passion for, and my encyclopedic knowledge of stones. I was more than capable of inventorying this piece before we put it in the safe, but did I want Ruth or Sister Immaculata to know I had that ability? I certainly wouldn't ask one of the Jewelry Girls to assess the object. I trusted the nun, but did I trust Ruth that much? I had no choice.

"Will you come in, please? I need for you to take notes and be a witness."

"Directly." She'd no sooner hung up the extension than she was standing next to me.

I carried the statuette to my desk, turned the lights on bright, opened my desk drawer and withdrew a pair of calipers, a small metal ruler, and a jeweler's loupe which I placed in my eye. Ruth took a chair across from me and held her pen poised to write down my dictation on a triplicate appraisal form—an old-fashioned process from days of yore that will never go out of style. Her expression did not change. She was completely professional as I described each stone, its color, quality, and dimensions. The process took more than an hour, and the whole time, the nun sat on the settee without a word. The only movement was the almost imperceptible snaking of rosary beads through her fingers.

When I was done, I told her my preliminary assessment of the value, pending a thorough appraisal, and she agreed to let us sell the piece. She, Ruth, and I signed the sheet. She slid her copy into the pocket of her habit and I placed the jeweled Madonna in the vault in my office—a wonderfully ornate, huge old thing with a pastoral painting on the front, blue-black steel, seven inches deep of armor on all sides, and a triple combination locking system. It wasn't burglar proof, but the burglar would need to have a great deal of time to work his way through the system to figure out the sequences. The figurine could stay there for safekeeping until the morning when we would move it to the main jewelry vault.

"Is Epperson still on-duty?" I asked Ruth.

"Indeed."

"Would you let him know we'll be out in about five minutes and then call the Stafford and book a table for Sister Immaculata and me?"

"Done."

"I'll see you downstairs," I said to Sister, as she and Ruth left my office. Once they were gone, I quietly changed the combinations on the safe—a simple enough thing to do, if you knew what you were doing; practically impossible if you didn't.

CHAPTER 21

The dining room at The Stafford Hotel was perfect for ladies—slightly fussy and very pretty.

"What may I bring you to drink?" The maître d' asked as he shook out our napkins and let them float into our laps.

"Sister?" I said.

"I would like Chivas on the rocks, please."

"Very well." His expression showed no hint of surprise, and I hoped mine didn't either, but I must say, I was stunned. I never in a million years would have picked her for drinking anything with a drop of alcohol, other than Communion wine. "Would you like a twist with that?"

She nodded. "Please."

"And for you, madam?"

"The same, please."

"Excellent."

"Where are you from originally, Sister?" I asked as I took a nibble of a cheese wafer that was so buttery it melted in my mouth. "I'm trying to place your accent."

"Upstate New York. My father was chairman of the board of Rockford-Rinker."

"And now here you are, the mother superior of a forgotten community of nuns hidden away in the middle of the Italian lake country."

She grinned. "It's wonderful, isn't it?"

"I suppose it would be all right—for a weekend."

She and I both laughed.

"It takes a certain temperament," she said. "From the little I've seen of you, I don't believe you have it. Where did you learn so much about gemstones?"

"In the auction business, you need to know a great deal about a great many things. Jewels have always been one of my specialties, so you just happened to land in the right office at the right time."

"I don't believe in accidents."

Our cocktails arrived and we raised our glasses to one another.

"Here's to a successful sale for the Little Sisters."

"Amen," she replied.

We sipped our scotch in friendly conversation. I had so many questions I wanted to ask her about how she became a nun, how she came to be at Lago d'Orta, how she'd uncovered the statuette when I had the impression that the killers had stripped the entire place, but we got going on the subject of wines and found one of the convent's on the hotel's extensive list.

"Let's order it," I said. "I've never tasted any of your wines."

"It's terribly expensive."

"You're my guest, Sister. I insist."

She smiled and once again, when our eyes met, I felt that wonderful connection, almost as though we were sisters, or co-conspirators. "I know you won't be disappointed," she said.

Our steaks arrived; large dollops of Stilton butter melted across them and ran beneath the puffy duchesse potatoes and wilted spinach. She tasted and signed off on the bottle of Nebbiolo, which was the color of dark red velvet. I sipped it and my mouth was filled

with Italian sun, wisps of fog, and warm ancient earth—it was a gratifying wine to drink, very companionable, enjoyable. There was no
work involved as there could be with, say, a Brunello, a wine that I often had to struggle to love.

"I'm curious, Sister, why you became a nun. If your father was
chairman of Rockford-Rinker, it would seem to me that the whole
world was available to you."

She smiled, not at all put off by the question. "Yes, it was. But I
never felt at ease in that world, never felt as though I truly belonged.
You see, I was adopted when I was just two days old, and although
my parents have done everything for me and I love them, I was always filled with questions and God was the only one who provided
the answers. He's the only one who gave me a home, peace about my
unknown beginnings, and a place I felt I truly belonged."

The noise in my head sounded like horses' hooves thundering
down the track. I studied her face. Our similarities were obvious. Tall,
broad-shouldered, blond, blue-eyed. Adopted. Don't ask her any
more about this, a voice warned in my head, although a million questions forced themselves into my mouth from my heart. "That's lovely,"
I said.

"Your accent is interesting," she said. "Are you an American?"

"I used to be. I moved to England when I was eighteen and became a British subject shortly thereafter." I sipped the wine again—it
had started to grow and was becoming rich, complex, fruity. "It breaks
my heart to think that your vineyard's blighted, this is superb."

"Some even say it's heavenly." She grinned and took a sip.

"Isn't there any way to rescue it?"

Sister Immaculata nodded. "Yes, certainly. But we need the money
to be able to do it—the soil needs to be reconditioned and the entire
vineyard—every single vine—needs to be destroyed and replaced. It's
going to take years."

"How much money?"

"At least two hundred thousand euros to start."

"Isn't that something you could ask your father to help with?"

She burst out laughing. "Oh, dear. Let me see if I can explain. My
vocation is not my father, Jack Lager's, financial responsibility. It is the

responsibility of those who share our faith. If this is supposed to happen, Our Father—that's Father with a capital 'F'—will make sure it does. We are blessed to have the little Madonna to sell and she'll bring us far, far more than we'll need for the entire project. We'll have enough left over to make significant repairs to the convent, such as a new boiler, updated wiring, modern plumbing, a workable kitchen."

"I know there's an incredible, untold story behind this."

Her blue eyes studied mine. "There is," she replied after a moment. I could tell she wanted to tell me.

"If you tell me the story, Sister," I said, "you have my word that it will go no further than this table."

"I believe you." She swirled her glass and watched waves of red dance across the linen and silver. "We know where the Madonna Illuminata and the rest of the stolen collection is, but there's nothing we can do to get them back.

"As I mentioned, our order was founded by a member of the Vasvar family of Hungary and established in the Convento di Santa Maria del Lago on a large property on the shores of Lago d'Orta where the Vasvar family had their summer home. For centuries the family was the order's patron and a family member was always the reverend mother. In 1922, the Dowager Duchess Shasta Vasvar was dying, I'm not sure what of. At that time, the family was very wealthy and powerful, but more and more of their resources were being sold to support the war and the dowager could see that if she didn't make arrangements for some of her own personal possessions, they would be sold as well. Her most prized possession was her collection of jeweled Madonnas, with the Madonna Illuminata as the centerpiece. Are you familiar with it?" Immaculata asked.

"Only to the extent that I've seen a picture or two, but I've never actually seen it, if that's what you mean."

"Well, of course, I've never seen it either, this all happened years and years ago, but we have many paintings and photographs. The Illuminata was two feet tall." She held her hand above the table to demonstrate. "Her face and hands were porcelain, painted so delicately they looked real, and she wore a flared crown of very fine large yellow diamonds; her robe was solid sapphires, her gown diamond pavé with a hem of large pearls and a sash of Burmese rubies. Her arms cradled Baby Jesus, who was made entirely of perfect diamonds—I understand the largest was more than thirty carats."

"How extraordinary."

"Indeed," Immaculata nodded. "The dowager's instructions to the reverend mother, who also happened to be her favorite niece, were to display the Illuminata two or three days a week and she would bring enough revenue that the order would never have to worry about its future." She smiled. "She clearly didn't understand that nuns never worry about their future, but that's neither here nor there. At any rate, all went just as the Dowager Duchess had predicted, until 1963, when two men entered the convent in the middle of the night and murdered all the nuns and stole the collection of Madonnas."

"How do you know it was two men?" I asked.

"Because as far as they knew, they murdered all the nuns. But there was one who survived. Not only did they not get all the pieces, but she saw their faces."

My mouth fell open. "Truly?"

Sister Immaculata nodded. "She's still alive."

When she finished the gruesome, bloody tale, I sat for a time in stunned silence and then felt myself growing offended, even angry. "I'm going to get them back for you," I said.

"How are you going to do that?"

"I'm not sure, but trust me," I said. "I'll find a way."

When the time came for us to say good-bye, I gave her all the cash I had, several hundred pounds. I felt I needed to do whatever I could to delay the sale of the little Madonna for as long as possible, possibly permanently, telling myself it was to save the vineyards because of the superb quality of the wine, but in truth, it was for her. And for me. And maybe for us.

"Please use this to get the project started," I said. "Pay whatever pressing bills you have, and then tomorrow I'll make arrangements to see that you have whatever you need. I'd like to underwrite the whole thing. Anonymously, of course."

"Of course." She studied me very slowly and quietly. "Thank you, Kick. This is the last thing I expected."

We kissed each other on the cheek and I saw her off in the car with Epperson driving her to the Kensington convent where she was staying. I took a cab home to my flat. After spending an evening with this remarkable, calm, self-assured young woman, I was somewhat embarrassed that I'd felt I had to hide from Giovanna MacDougal, that I thought I needed to spend the night at a hotel to avoid her. So, like Ruth, I pulled on my mental boxing gloves and decided to face the music. When the cab turned into Eaton Terrace, all was quiet and normal. There was no one lurking on a corner waiting to thrust a microphone or camera into my face. That's how it works with ego, sometimes. I wasn't as big a fish as I thought I was. Giovanna had moved on.

I put the batteries back in my French cell phone—no messages from Thomas—and went to bed.

CHAPTER 22

The morning was bright, cool, beautiful—heralding a perfect fall day. After a breakfast of grapefruit juice, a toasted English muffin with Fortnum & Mason Citrus Marmalade, a poached egg, and steaming café au lait, Bijou and I walked to the office, a not inconsiderable distance. But the air was bracing and the enormous trees that lined the walls of Buckingham Palace, St. James Park, and The Mall were rich russet and gold; their fallen leaves carpeted the ground and muffled our steps. The dense spices of autumn saturated every breath.

I loved London and as I walked—actually it was a little like a march, something very uncharacteristic for me, even little Bijou kept glancing up at me as though I'd lost my mind, we never went on walks this long at such a pace—I thought about a number of issues, starting with Sister Immaculata. Like her, I didn't believe in accidents, and if it turned out we were in fact mother and daughter, I knew that relationship would find a way to reveal itself. But I couldn't help going over and over the possibilities. How had she gotten from the Florence Crittenden Home in Omaha to upstate New York in two days? Then it dawned on me that her adoptive parents, the Lagers—no doubt a young, attractive, but barren couple with everything else going for them, lots of promise and future—could even have been waiting on the other side of my hospital room door, there in the hall, standing on their toes, unable to breathe for the excitement, praying there would be no hesitation as my hand moved to the paper to sign my baby away. All I remember is that there were so many papers. I signed and signed and signed, and then it was over.

Years later, I'd registered on all the Internet adoption sites, wanting my child to know that if he or she needed a lung or a liver or a kidney, or just had a question or two about where he came from, or wanted to know why it was so hard for her to lose weight, or why they found it so hard to tell the truth, he or she would be able to locate me. But there had never been even a single inquiry. Nothing but silence. Finally, I began to fear that my child—my son, my daughter— most probably was dead. For years, I checked the sites every Saturday morning no matter where I was. But recently, I hadn't. What did it matter if I checked in once a week or once a month—there would never be any contact. And now, what if? What if Sister Immaculata were my daughter? What did that mean to her? What did it mean to me? Then, in spite of myself, I started to laugh. Just imagine—the daughter of the world's greatest jewel thief is a nun. A Little Sister of the Poor? How wonderfully ironic if it were true.

I felt a happiness I'd never felt before, as though some empty place in me began to fill.

Then, I began to think about the story she'd told and to assess how I could help. I'd said I'd get the collection back for her, but frankly, I didn't have a clue as to how I'd go about such a thing, especially with this new position at Ballantine & Company occupying all my time for the foreseeable future. I could, however, send her money. I would tell Ruth not to mention the jeweled Madonna to Talbot Merrill. That I would keep it in my vault for the time being because Sister was having second thoughts. Okay, that was a lie. But, in my opinion, it was an acceptable lie. Or was it? Oh my God, was I getting some sort of conscience? A guilty conscience even? No. I think to lie to protect a nun is in fact a noble deed. I found the explanation reassuring.

I also thought about how I'd been back at Ballantine & Company for three days—counting the day of Sir Bertram's heart attack—and how totally relieved I was it was Friday. I was exhausted! So, as I headed down the homestretch to St. James Square—by now I was carrying Bijou—I began to consider how to spend the weekend.

It used to be that my weekends were generally consumed by quick trips to Zurich or Geneva to deposit stones in one of my various safe-deposit boxes, or to purchase new manufacturing or surveillance equipment, made-to-order synthetic stones—which are virtually indistinguishable from the real thing to the untrained eye— or identities. Occasionally, I'd make a trip to the farm, just to remind myself how fortunate I was and how I couldn't wait until I could retire and live there full time.

But this weekend would be different—it would be a quiet autumn weekend in London. Could there possibly be anything finer? I'd start by sleeping in tomorrow morning and then I'd make some gloriously fluffy, airy, feathery lemon soufflé pancakes brushed with melted butter and warm Fortnum & Mason Orange Marmalade with Rum for breakfast—my mouth began to water at the thought—and read all the papers. And then what? Who knew? That was the pleasure of it all—a completely open agenda, nothing but open highway.

CHAPTER 23

"I saw lights on in the Jewelry Department. Is Mr. Merrill in?"

"I believe he is," Ruth answered.

"Ask him to come up at nine o'clock, please. I have a few calls to make, so I'd like not to be disturbed until he arrives. Oh, and Ruth, please don't mention the jeweled Madonna to him. At dinner last night, I detected that Sister Immaculata was starting to have second thoughts. I won't be surprised if she comes back to collect the piece."

"My lips are sealed. That sort of thing happens all the time."

"Indeed." I went into my office, closed and quietly locked the door behind me, turned the television on to the BBC Morning News, and removed a number of small devices from my purse. The first of these, for all intents and purposes, could have been a garage door opener, but in fact it was a surveillance detector, something used to find electronic audio and video bugs. I wanted to be sure that Ruth only listened through the door, not through the lamp or the telephone receiver, and didn't have holes drilled through Sir Cramner's eyes in his portrait. The room swept clear.

Next, I dragged a straight-backed chair from the conference table to the corner of the room opposite the safe and glued a minuscule camera just on the edge of the canvas of a large oil painting of a clipper ship looking to be in hard straits in a heavy sea. The tiny eye perched invisibly in dark clouds, snugged up next to the thick gilt frame. It was motion-activated and when I stepped into the line of sight, the receiver, which looked like a cell phone, vibrated silently and a clear picture of me returning the chair to the table appeared on its screen.

That key aspect of my business complete, I sat down and slotted the first security CD of the jewelry department into my computer and scanned it quickly. It took only about ten minutes of watching the department's activity, including the ins-and-outs to the private clients' meeting rooms, to find what I was looking for. I understood why the security team had missed it, partly because it was so unthinkable, and also because the changes were so subtle. It took an eye that didn't see the formidable Andrew Gardner on a daily basis to recognize he'd developed a cocaine problem. He always seemed to be rubbing or touching his nose in a telltale manner whenever he was in the back hallways and, over a period of weeks, his demeanor became increasingly manic. This explained not only a need for extra money but also why his mind had grown too frantic to make the switches professionally, thus leaving a stone badly seated or a prong not wholly secured.

As the tapes progressed, although his behavioral changes were subtle and he worked to conceal them because he knew he was being filmed by the security cameras, he became more and more agitated, until he became a frantic mess. It had been Andrew. In my mind there was no question about it.

That still didn't solve the problem of the con man who had returned £20 million of fake paintings, but it reassured me that no more fake jewelry would be leaving the house.

The intercom buzzed. "Mr. Merrill is here whenever you're ready. But," Ruth whispered into the phone, "a word to the wise. Leave the door open. He may try to make a pass at you. He's an extremely aggressive male."

"Thank you for the advice. I'm sure I'll be fine. Unless he's a complete idiot, Mr. Talbot Merrill isn't going to chase his boss around her desk. Please ask him to come in."

I'd met Talbot the day before at the staff meeting, and if he had a little *je ne sais quoi* going for him with the ladies, *je ne sais quoi* it was. It eluded me completely. Over Ruth's glaring objections, I closed the door.

He was well dressed, self-assured, midfifties—this was one business in which age and experience—maturity—were regarded as advantages. He had dark, sparkling eyes, a bald head with a salt and pepper halo, a rather hatchet-shaped, well-weathered, tanned face, as though he'd spent a long time standing at the helm of a sailboat squinting into the North Sea wind in treacherous, stormy conditions, shouting instructions to his mates over the howl. A long upper lip, an easy smile, and impossibly white teeth.

"Good morning, Mr. Merrill," I extended my hand across my desk.

"Please, call me Talbot." I noticed his hand was strong, his nails were professionally manicured—buffed, not polished—and he wore a gold family crest ring on his pinkie finger. "That's a lovely brooch you're wearing. It looks like a Tiffany piece."

"It is. You have a good eye."

"Well," he smiled self-deprecatingly. "It is what I do."

As usual, for work, I was dressed in a dark suit and black suede pumps. I had three graduated strands of sixteen-millimeter ecru pearls around my neck and had pinned to my jacket a brooch that was a cluster of finely realized golden fronds with diamonds and emeralds sprinkled about here and there as though they were raindrops. The earrings matched. They were lovely, not grand, pieces. Just right for work.

"Now," I placed my arms on my desk and leaned toward him a bit. "I know how busy you are getting ready for next week, so I'll only keep you for a couple of minutes. Sir Bertram filled me in on the situation in your department, and I'd like to review your handling processes and procedures. What changes have you made?"

"A number, actually." He answered evenly. "We're encouraging buyers who are present for the sale to take their goods with them and two of us reconfirm each piece in their presence prior to their departure."

"What about telephone and on-line customers?"

"That's a little more complicated," Merrill said. "But the girls and I are doing all our own shipping—nothing goes through the company shipping department. So we reconfirm each piece before it's packaged up and then one of us takes the shipment directly to FedEx personally. I always ask one of the security staff to accompany and make certain it's never the same person twice in a row. I feel confident the problem is stopped because since I took over the department, no one has handled the pieces but us."

"Do you think Andrew was the culprit?"

"I simply cannot picture the great Andrew Gardner stealing from Ballantine and Company."

"It is quite unimaginable, isn't it?" I said.

"Are you going to press charges?" he asked.

I shook my head. "No. We'll just keep this in the family."

"I think that's the right decision. He's done his damage."

"Let me ask you, Mr. Merrill. Why didn't you say anything? How long did you know?"

"Almost from the start, but Sir Bertram wouldn't believe me. As a matter of fact, I don't think he would have taken action except that one of our clients demanded it on the threat of going public."

I let out a small laugh, half disgust, half sadness. "Unfortunately, I'm afraid you're right. Well"—I stood up—"thank you, Mr. Merrill. It sounds as though you have your systems well in place."

"You can be sure of it, Miss Keswick. Now we need to concentrate on repairing our reputation, but the only remedies for that are honest service and time." He stood, smoothed his tie, buttoned his jacket. "I know you've been away for a while—it would be my distinct honor and privilege to take you for coffee or dinner to reacquaint you with London."

"Thank you. I'm well-oriented. But thank you for the invitation. Good day, Mr. Merrill."

I liked him very much—he was a respected professional and he wasn't going to brook any funny business in the running of his department. The subject was closed.

Essentially, I'd accomplished what I'd intended in the first place. There wouldn't be any more fakes sent out and, baring some sort of total disaster, none of the past ones would be able to be traced to me. It wasn't a conspiracy after all. But now I was mired in other issues: such as my promise to run the company until Bertram was back on his feet. And it dawned on me, he may never be back. He was probably so relieved to be out of his quagmire, he would claim his doctor insisted he retire, which would ultimately be in the best interests of the company because I now knew that Bertram, himself, was the problem.

CHAPTER *24*

Almost lunchtime. I was considering returning to Wilton's and having the oysters and lobster I'd missed a few days earlier, when Ruth lumbered in to announce that Mrs. Edgar Flynn was in the reception area and did I have time to see her?

"Of course I do," I answered. "Do you know what she wants?"

"It has to do with jewelry. She originally asked to see Talbot, but he's gone for the day."

"It's only eleven-thirty."

"Mmm," she said, her expression a complete deadpan. "Shacked-up, I imagine."

"Please ask her to come in."

"Righto."

I'd seen Constance Flynn a number of years ago at a number of auctions and recalled that she seemed like a nice and very good-looking woman—wonderful, uniquely Irish coloring with dark hair, blue eyes, and rosy apple cheeks—and when she entered my office, it was as though time had stood still. Her short hair was still dark and shiny, and there was not a wrinkle to be seen anywhere in her face. She wasn't thin by any means but she wasn't what I'd call fat, either. I'd say she tended a bit toward plump. She was dressed simply and expensively in a black pashmina shawl, black cashmere turtleneck, black wool slacks, black socks, black suede loafers, single pearl earrings, black Birkin bag. There was a white line around her ring finger where her wedding and engagement rings used to be and a $125,000 pink gold and diamond Rolex on her wrist.

"What may I offer you to drink, Mrs. Flynn?" I asked once we'd concluded the formalities.

"Do you have any champagne?"

"We do."

"I know it's early, but I'm ready to celebrate." She took a seat across from me and hefted the Birkin bag onto the chair next to her.

"By all means, champagne it is."

Ruth returned with a small ice bucket, a split of Veuve-Clicquot— which she opened and poured with great aplomb—and a small silver salver piled with orange rolls on a lacy dolly. Mrs. Flynn sipped the champagne and glanced at the rolls. I could tell she was having a conversation with herself about not having one.

"How may we be of service to you, Mrs. Flynn?" I asked when we were alone.

"You may or may not be aware of my personal circumstances at the moment," she said. Her voice was melodious and clear and there seemed to be a little glint or glimmer of something behind her direct gaze, but I couldn't tell if it was humor, anger, or defensiveness.

"I'm aware you and Mr. Flynn are getting a divorce, if that's what you mean."

"That's exactly what I mean. But only someone who's dead or can't read or doesn't own a television set could miss the circus we're putting on for the planet. I'm absolutely horrified by it—every day I thank God that my mother's dead—but Edgar set the ground rules by running off with that girl and now, according to the gossip columnists, he intends to marry her. So I've been forced to set a few rules of my own."

She delivered the words evenly but she was clearly angry. Color flared in her face and I could tell that beneath those rosy cheeks lurked a hot Irish temper that it wouldn't take much to ignite and she'd be off and running like a banshee with her hair on fire.

"He's given me an inordinate amount of jewelry over the years and I've decided to sell it all. I'm clearing the son-of-a-bitch out of my life. If he can make a fresh start, so can I. Do you know what I mean?"

Although contained, her fury weighed down every molecule of air. I'd read somewhere before that going through a divorce was similar to dying, that people go through approximately the same five stages as defined in 1969 by Swiss psychiatrist Elisabeth Kübler-Ross: Denial and Isolation, Anger, Bargaining, Depression, and Acceptance, except that in the case of divorce, there's an extra stage between Depression and Acceptance: Revenge. What I'd seen in her eyes were only the remnants of pain, loss, and devastation. Constance Flynn was stalled out at revenge.

I gave her a sympathetic smile and nodded. "Indeed, I do," I said, recalling my revenge on Owen Brace, which had been so exquisitely satisfying.

"Our son, William, is getting married." She refilled her glass.

"So I understand. Congratulations."

She raised her eyebrows and turned her face, chin slightly raised, to the corner of the room, as though she were struggling for the self-control not to say what was at the tip of her tongue, but to reply with what would be the proper response to a total stranger.

"Let's just say that congratulations may be too strong a word," she finally said. "It's open for debate, but that's William's problem. He's a grown man. As he's as enigmatic and cold-blooded as his father. But, William's wedding isn't why I'm here." She studied me openly. "I can tell by looking at you that we're close to the same age, and age does have some compensations, doesn't it? But they're certainly not physical, are they? I mean, you aren't going to be wearing any bikinis around anywhere anytime soon, are you? Or parading about in your lingerie. Of course not! You're too old! Too filled out!"

Well, Mrs. Flynn certainly did look it in the eye and call it as it was. No mincing of words for her.

"And to be run out of my marriage of thirty-five years by a twenty-five-year-old supermodel? Well, there's nothing physical I can do to compete with that. But that doesn't mean I don't have re-sources. Oh, this has been such hell for me, I don't know what I would have done without my friends." She paused and took an unla-dylike gulp of champagne.

"Indeed," I said, surprised she had any friends if she pointed out their physical imperfections as blatantly as she'd pointed out mine. I declined to mention that in fact I do lounge about in my lingerie.

"Oh, forgive me," she laughed. "I apologize. I seem to go off on these tangents—I didn't mean anything personal about you and your bathing suit. Please forgive me—we don't even know each other and here I am talking to you like an old friend or a psychiatrist. You prob-ably have hundreds of bikinis—you might even be a nudist, for all I know."

I started laughing. "There is where I draw the line."

"Oh, me, too. Can you even imagine? Well, it's too scary to con-template. I don't even own a bathing suit anymore, and believe me, putting one on certainly isn't going to get my husband back. Actually, to tell the truth—I don't even want him back. I'm just so damned mad—I just want to kill the bastard. Okay, I'm eating one of these things." She picked up an orange roll and tore into it.

I could tell she wanted him back more than anything.

"Well, obviously, I'm not going to kill him." She paused and patted a dot of caramel syrup off the corner of her lip. "I think this is the best thing I've ever tasted. Where did you get these?"

"We make them here in our kitchen."

"Ambrosia. Especially with the champagne." She took a deep breath, undraped her pashmina and tossed it on the other chair, which seemed to have the effect of calming her down a little bit. "Well, at any rate, as I said, I'm obviously not going to kill him but I am going to cause him pain. I've spent more than half my lifetime as his wife and believe me, I know how to hurt him. He thinks I'm going to show up at this wedding with my head hanging, humiliated by this model-whore of his. He couldn't be more wrong. It's going to be a new me, everything new, starting with the jewelry. I even have a beau who's coming along. Clifton Boatwright." She said the name as though I should know who he was.

"I don't believe I'm familiar with Mr. Boatwright."

Constance nodded, and took a more ladylike bite out of her second roll. "He's an international financier—actually you could say he's sort of like the Warren Buffet of Britain. I'd never heard of him either until a friend introduced us at a dinner party. Major dealmaker and investor, keeps very much in the background. He's practically a hermit, does all his work electronically from his Devonshire country house and spends his free time cultivating roses and orchids. Well, actually, he's a little bit of a nerd—you know, mismatched socks, that sort of thing—but you can't imagine how refreshing it is to be with a man whose ego doesn't require constant public approbation. He gave me this watch." She held up her arm.

"Lovely."

Constance looked at me with a sparkle in her eye. "To tell you the truth, I'm not much of a watch girl; I can take them or leave them. I can look at my cell phone if I want to know what time it is. It's just the fact that it was something he came up with himself. A thoughtful gesture." She regarded the watch with a look of regretful disinterest, as though she'd like to like it better. Then she spun it around on her wrist—trying, unsuccessfully, to pretend it was a diamond bracelet. "It's all right, I suppose. Well, back to the wedding: I intend to land in the middle of this party like an atom bomb. No, like a love bomb! Edgar won't even know what hit the place. And, when he realizes I've sold all the jewelry and have an absolutely divine lover who's richer than he is, he'll be so mad, he'll simply"—she paused—"he'll simply, oh hell, excuse my French, but he'll simply crap."

I should have given a modest acknowledgment but I burst out laughing, a complete no-no in our business. She was truly funny. The behavior of auction house employees around clients must be similar to the behavior of morticians around the bereaved. Straight-faced and sympathetic. People often say things they're ashamed of, or regret later. And, if the employee has participated in the emotion, the clients can come to resent it or be embarrassed by it and the house doesn't get the business. Another Ballantine & Company rule is that employees do not eat orange rolls, or anything else, around clients in the office. I glanced at the Sevres table clock on the mantel opposite my desk and tried to ignore my increasingly empty stomach.

"So." She turned to the bulging Birkin bag and opened it and then paused. "Before we get down to business, do you have another one of these little bottles? This just seems to be hitting the spot."

Once a fresh bottle had been opened and Constance's glass re-filled, she reached into her bag and began stacking velvet boxes and pouches on the desk. "Now, a number of these were bought here at auction in the first place, and I have a story to go with each of them that I think may be useful to put into the catalog with each piece—some are very personal, some are lurid, and some will be just down-right embarrassing. To him. They will provide us with a mountain of publicity angles and help attract top dollar. Oh, how lovely it would be to sell these pieces for double or triple what he paid," she cooed. "Such divine retribution."

"We'll see what we can do. No promises."

She opened a large flat box and I recognized the piece instantly. It was one of the most beautiful necklaces I'd ever seen in my life. De-signed by Cartier in the late 1930s for an Italian movie star, it was a collar of diamond-set rondels fringed with twenty-nine variably shaped cabochon sapphire drops, graduated in size from the central drop of forty-seven carats to seven at the clasp. My mouth went slightly dry—the real sapphires, all twenty-nine of them, were in my safe-deposit box in Geneva.

CHAPTER 25

Remember when I mentioned that—barring some sort of total disaster—no Ballantine & Company fake jewelry could be traced to me? Well, this was just such a disaster—this was a tsunami of chickens coming home to roost. This was my greatest nightmare threatening to come to life.

The real stones from many of her pieces were in my vault at Banque Privée Vilmont in Geneva, and now she wanted Ballantine & Company to resell them for her. You cannot imagine how grateful I was that Talbot Merrill had gone for the day. If he'd been in his office where he was supposed to be, he would have examined Mrs. Flynn's jewelry and pronounced more than half of it to be fake. And then, oh dear, it would have hit the fan in a very big way.

I didn't follow procedure. I quickly cataloged and appraised the pieces myself without a witness, sealing each in its own Ziploc plastic bag. Mrs. Flynn signed the receipt and initialed each of the original bills of sale, which she had the presence of mind to bring along.

"Oh, glory!" She smiled and raised her arms in a gesture of triumph when the last signature was done. "I am liberated. I can't wait to tell Clifton at lunch—he didn't believe I'd do it."

"This is a wonderful collection, Mrs. Flynn." I placed the goods in the safe alongside the jeweled Madonna. "I'm so grateful you thought of Ballantine and Company to handle their sale—there will be a great deal of interest. Now, in terms of the scheduling, it will take us some time to put the sale together, each piece has to be fully appraised and described and photographed. Then the catalog has to be written, printed, and distributed, and we want to be sure to hold it at the most beneficial time, of course. It probably won't be until springtime, but I'll keep you informed of our plans."

"Marvelous." She took another sip of champagne—she was over halfway through the second split, which meant she'd drunk at least two-thirds of a regular bottle. Then she picked up another pastry. "I can't help it. These are the best things I've ever tasted. Just because the sale isn't until spring, that doesn't mean you'll hold off announcing that you're selling them, does it?"

"Not at all—we can put a release out early next week, if you'd like."

She smiled broadly. "Just as long as it's before the wedding."

"When is the wedding?"

"Two weeks. It starts on Thursday, the nineteenth and goes nonstop until Sunday. William's marrying Alice Vasvar—the wedding itself will be at the Vasvar family castle at Lago d'Orta in Italy. It's supposed to be spectacular."

My breath caught. Lago d'Orta, home of the Little Sisters of the Poor. What was it Sister Immaculata had said? "I don't believe in accidents?"

"There are going to be wall-to-wall parties, cocktail parties, luncheons, dinners, wild boar shooting parties, boating parties. Unfortunately, it's become quite a competition, of course, with Edgar and me trying to out-do each other."

"Not very unusual, I'm afraid, considering your circumstances."

"You're right. The whole thing is hideous. And the Vasvars are a big question mark to me—all those Hungarian and Latvian and Bulgarian and Polish and Byelorussian relatives. Those royals from behind the Iron Curtain—it's wonderfully mysterious, isn't it? And they're all poor as church mice."

"I admire you, Mrs. Flynn," I commented. "You're definitely putting the best possible face on what is obviously an extremely difficult and humiliating situation."

"What else can I do? Edgar and Lauren are throwing the welcoming luncheon. Honestly, she might be the most famous model in the world and look like a goddess, but she is as cheap and tough as they come. And manipulative. I can't believe Edgar doesn't see what's going on. She made him hire a friend of hers, a little mouse named Laddie Murphy, to be the wedding planner—God forbid that the bride's family should be in charge of or pay for anything—and she's completely overwhelmed by the entire affair. If you want to know the truth—I've heard that she and Lauren are lovers. That's probably just cheap gossip but I hope it's true. I can't help it. I hate Lauren Cambridge. She's stolen my life. Do you want to hear something wonderful?"

"By all means."

"My daughter, Katie, told me Lauren snores like a freight train. Don't you just love it?!"

Finally, she stopped and took a breath, and when she let it out, she relaxed a little. "The whole thing is a complete joke. Edgar is trying to prove to Freddie Vasvar that he's richer, which is a fact already known to all because, basically, Freddie doesn't have two cents. And Freddie's trying to prove to Edgar that he's classier, which takes virtually no effort. Meantime, Edgar and I are ambushing each other at every turn. I'll admit this divorce isn't bringing out the best in either of us." She stood and began to walk around. "Why am I telling you all this? I haven't stopped talking for five minutes. I don't even know you." She raised her hands in question.

"Because you know it won't leave this room?"

Constance smiled at me. We were the same age and I was sorry for her and I also liked her very much, probably because, in spite of her anger, she seemed to have a sense of humor about the whole thing, not to mention the energy and enthusiasm of a twenty-year-old. She was very real.

"I think you're right. I have to be so careful what I say to anyone, I don't even talk to my friends this way because even though they're standing by me now, I don't trust any of them. You want to know what? When push comes to shove, when Edgar and I are divorced, I won't be a bit surprised to see a number of my 'friends' jump ship and sign up on his team. It's just the way it works."

"Unfortunately, you're right," I agreed.

"Edgar has taken over the best hotel in town and I've rented a villa just up the hill—I haven't seen it yet but the pictures are incredible."

"I've heard that Lago d'Orta is beautiful."

"So they say, although I understand it's a little down at the heels. Certainly not on a par with Lake Como when it comes to glamour and glitz, which I'm sure drives Edgar to distraction, he always has to be at the fanciest places. I must say, even though I may not sound like it, I am quite looking forward to it all—of course, it makes it much easier now that I have Clifton. I just wish he were a better dresser. You know what I mean?"

I smiled, thinking of Thomas and his occasionally rumpled, discombobulated appearance—his wool suits in the summer and linens in the winter. "I do," I answered.

"And I wish I could be happier for William—Alice isn't who I would have picked for my son—I wish he wouldn't go through with it."

Every time she mentioned her son, I got the impression there was a "but" hanging there. Something wasn't right. It was odd.

"I'm sure it will turn out fine," I said blandly. "Tell me, I recall that Mr. Flynn bought the Vasvar ruby parure here at Ballantine and Company several years ago. Does he still own it?"

"You mean do WE still own it?" She exploded.

"I beg your pardon," I smiled. "I meant both of you."

"We do, indeed. In fact, I remember meeting you that day. You were in the jewelry exhibition room putting the pieces in their original cases. You probably don't remember, but Sir Cramner introduced us."

"Of course, I remember perfectly," I answered, chilled at this latest bit of bad news, that she could connect me personally to the Vasvar suite.

"You know the story—that they're cursed until they return to the Vasvar family? I never wore the things. I don't care for rubies that much and I've got enough problems of my own without taking on some Hungarian family's ridiculous voodoo lore. I don't think they've been out of the vault since Edgar brought them home. But William is going to give them to his bride as a wedding present."

"How romantic," I said. "It's like a fairy tale."

"It's part of the deal that Freddie brokered with Edgar. Have you ever met him?"

"No. I've never had the pleasure."

"I haven't either. There haven't been any engagement festivities given by the bride's family, probably because Edgar isn't paying for them, and Freddie wasn't able to attend the party we gave for William and Alice. But I know he's very, very good-looking and quite the ladies' man, and Edgar says that in business, he drives a very hard bargain. That's what this whole marriage is about, in case you're curious: air rights—they're the only thing that the Vasvar family owns anymore. Freddie's sold all the properties but a few. But he had the foresight to maintain ownership of the air rights—I think he owns all the air over the whole Continent. Edgar and William are jockeying to buy the rights because they'll make Flynn Communications the largest wireless company in Europe—eastern, western, and Russia. It's all linked together." She intertwined her fingers and squeezed them into a hard ball. "Well, now you know everything and I'm sorry to have burdened you with all my baggage, but I'll tell you what—I feel much, much better. Like I've been at a fabulous cocktail party."

"Good."

Constance started tucking her empty felt jewel bags and boxes back into the Birkin. "Are you married?"

I opened my mouth to respond, not entirely sure what was going to come out, but she picked up another roll and then put it back down.

"What on earth is wrong with me? If I keep eating these things, I'll never fit into any of my new clothes. Please do me a favor and hide them when I come to visit next time." She smiled and then stood up and so did I. We shook hands across the desktop. "Thank you, Miss Keswick. It's been a pleasure to see you again. I look forward to hearing from you."

I watched her make her way out of the office without the hint of a wobble even though the second bottle was empty.

Most of Constance's jewelry and the Vasvar parure had been purchased at Ballantine & Company and they were now all fake. The connection to the house would be obvious. And if someone really wanted to put his mind to it, it wouldn't be long before a connection was made to me.

CHAPTER 26

"I'm going to step out for a bite of lunch," Ruth said not long after Constance Flynn left. "Can I bring you anything?"

"Nothing, thank you. I'll be going out shortly myself."

I didn't have much time to put things in motion and I had a great deal to accomplish by Monday morning. I watched Ruth fussing about her desk, taking her time about pulling on her coat and scarf. Come on, come on, I thought as I finished one of the rolls Constance had left untouched. Get going.

Finally, with a little ta-ta wave of her fingers, Ruth disappeared down the stairs and I immediately grabbed the phone and called the Berkeley Hotel in Kensington and—using the same identity as the woman who had rented the Jaguar—made a reservation for Lillian Hallaby who would arrive late that night. Then I called the Royal Courier Service and said I had a delivery to go immediately. I filled out a waybill addressed to Mrs. Hallaby, an expected guest at the Berkeley, and by the time I'd finished packing Mrs. Flynn's fake jewelry into a large padded envelope and applied the label, the courier was at my desk. Thankfully, Ruth hadn't returned yet.

As soon as he was gone, I picked up the phone.

"Monarch Aviation," the voice answered.

"Yes," I said. "Mrs. Hallaby here."

"Yes, Mrs. Hallaby. How may we be of service?"

"I need to make a quick trip to Geneva."

"Excellent. When would you like to depart?"

"Can you have a plane ready by two o'clock?"

"Two o'clock this afternoon?"

"Yes."

"Naturally. And when did you wish to return?"

"Tonight."

"Very well. How many in your party, Mrs. Hallaby?"

"Just two—me and my dog."

"So a small jet will be adequate? Or did you wish something larger than a little Lear?"

"A little Lear will be quite enough."

"Excellent. How would you like us to provision your flight?"

My stomach growled at the thought of food. "Hot soup, chicken sandwiches on white bread with mayonnaise and lettuce, crusts removed, and coffee for lunch, please. Then, I think a little champagne and Scottish salmon will be sufficient for the flight back."

"Excellent. Do you need transportation in Geneva?"

"Please. A sedan."

"Very good. We'll see you at two p.m. today, Hangar Four."

"Thank you so much."

"We are at your service."

~~ ~~

An hour after I got home, Lillian Hallaby left the flat, crossing through a series of linked mews and emerging close to Victoria Station. I had put on an expensive chestnut wig, and large dark glasses covered my eyes, which now had lilac contacts in them. I wore a smart Donegal tweed suit and brown suede pumps—I felt I looked quite a lot like

Elizabeth Taylor in her later, more full-figured heyday, post-*Cleopatra* and mid-Richard. Bijou was out of sight in her travel bag, balanced atop my leather-trimmed tan canvas overnight case, which I pulled along behind me.

"Warwick Field, please," I told the cab driver. "Monarch Aviation, Hangar Four."

The armed guard at the gate to the heavily protected private air-field radioed my arrival. After he scrutinized the taxi driver's identifi-cation and my driver's license and passport, he pushed a button. The gate rose and we entered this exclusive wonderland of private execu-tive aviation, familiar only to the extremely wealthy and those fortu-nate enough to be their guests. A number of private jets of all sizes were lined up along the flight-line, some had Land Rovers or Rolls or Bentley sedans or limousines parked alongside, loading or unloading their cargo. Inside the terminal were two counters, each manned with uniformed men and women, most of them talking on telephones with pleasant expressions on their faces. A half-dozen living-room type arrangements of comfortable-looking sofas and chairs, all of which converted to beds, were in the airy lounge area, and a large buffet of fresh fruit, pastries, cheeses, sandwiches, a popcorn ma-chine, and every type of liquid refreshment known to man, ran along one wall. The room was quiet and uninhabited. I went to the Monarch Aviation counter.

"Good afternoon, madam," a man said. His voice was the same as the person I'd talked to on the phone. "We have everything in order for your flight, direct London-Geneva. Your lunch is onboard, as re-quested. As well as some treats for your dog." He offered Bijou a small cookie. "The only item remaining is to complete our business."

"Indeed," I said and handed him Lillian Hallaby's Platinum Ameri-can Express card.

"Your tail number is MAX 59." He handed me my receipt. "And your captain's name is Robert Handley. Here is a list of phone num-bers you should keep with you for your convenience while you're in Geneva. Let me show you the way."

Robert Handley and his copilot were from central casting—retired Royal Marine fighter pilots—trim, square-jawed, totally professional.

"Welcome aboard, Mrs. Hallaby," he said, while the copilot stowed my suitcase in the cabin. "Our flight time will be about an hour and a half. May I get you anything before we take off?"

"I'm perfectly fine, thank you, dear boy." I sat down on the left side of the fuselage and fastened my seat belt. The dog sat on my lap and looked out the window.

"Do you prefer the cockpit door open or closed?"

"Open, please. I love watching you fellows do your work. I don't know how you keep everything straight."

Once we were airborne and had leveled out, I picked up the intercom phone and buzzed the cockpit, where I could see the pilots busy pushing buttons, spinning knobs and talking on their radios.

"Excuse me, young man. If it's not too terribly much trouble, would you fly us by way of the northern Italian lakes?"

"No trouble at all," he replied. "I'll change the flight plan—any lake in particular?"

"Lago d'Orta, please."

"What a beautiful spot that is."

"Thank you," I replied.

The chicken sandwich, hot soup—it turned out to be corn chowder with minced scallions, red peppers, and a hint of sherry—and hot coffee hit the spot. Before long, the copilot came back.

"In about ten minutes we'll descend enough for a close look at Lago d'Orta. We'll circle the area twice—and then please make certain you have your seat belt fastened because we'll need to make a quite steep ascent to get over the hills between us and Geneva." The "hills" being the Alps.

"Thank you, dear." I tightened the seat belt across the heavy tweed of my skirt and prepared to reconnoiter.

CHAPTER 27

I knew quite a lot about Lago d'Orta, of course, because for decades it had been my job to keep myself informed of all the playgrounds of the rich and famous. They were the ones with the best jewelry.

One of the smaller Italian lakes, glacier-fed Lago d'Orta was ringed by steep, rocky Alpine foothills and was best known for its crystal clear water, the beauty of its mild climate and varied vegetation—pines, firs, conifers on the upper reaches; chestnut, beech, and palms on the lower ground—and historic villas and palazzos. There was also an unusual concentration of churches and chapels in its environs, the first built in the early fourth century, when St. Julius—San Giulio—established his church on the island in the middle of the lake. Today, the gigantic, ancient monastery and seminary of the Basilica di San Giulio dominates the Isola di San Giulio, and although it shares the island with a handful of beautiful lakefront villas, the place is said to be quiet and serene. Tourists are welcome but discouraged from speaking.

The plane descended and, as we sped over a mountaintop, suddenly, there it was, glittering in the afternoon sun, like a diamond shining in dark green velvet.

I spotted the Little Sisters' acreage easily, with its mammoth convent, vast grounds, and sloping vineyards from which smoke rose in a steady column. They were burning the vines, sanitizing the earth. I could make out small figures dressed in black tending the fire with what were probably rakes and shovels.

Adjacent to the convent grounds, a number of villas basked in the sun along the bank and up the slopes of the mountains. The lake was small, intimate, almost private, and only forty-five minutes from Milano, so these were primarily weekend and summer homes of wealthy old Milanese families, passed on from generation to generation. Many of the residences were extremely grand, but there were only a few on the mammoth scale of those belonging to the mega-wealthy found at Lake Como or Maggiore. The brand new white limestone Villa Cortina, where Constance and her party would be staying, anchored one end of the tiny town, Orta San Giulio, while the Chiesa di Santa Maria sat like a beautiful yellow wedding cake at the top of a steep cobblestone street, halfway up the hill, just above the central piazza, Piazza Motto. On up the hill sprawled Sacro Monte, an historic and architecturally important complex of twenty-two separate sixteenth-, seventeenth-, and eighteenth-century churches, convents, and chapels. At the opposite end of the Piazza, a line of royal palms fronted the Hotel san Rocco where Edgar Flynn and his party would stay. A beautiful navy blue Chris-Craft lake boat was tied to its dock. A handful of hotel guests sitting at tables on the terrace shaded their eyes with their hands and squinted up at the plane as we circled.

Across the lake, and above it all, atop sheer granite cliffs on a private peninsula, was the enormous Castello Vasvar—a classic, eighteenth-century Italian stone castle with a bell tower and a central courtyard. I thought I spotted a funicular or elevator cage sitting at the top of the cliff, a typical mode of transportation to go back and forth to the lakeshore, hundreds of feet below.

I don't know what I was expecting, but as I considered the scale of the place and the magnitude of the job—well, it was jobs, really, wasn't it? Plural. Replacing all the ersatz rubies in the Vasvar parure plus the gems in Constance Flynn's collection and reclaiming the Madonna Illuminata for Sister Immaculata and the nuns—it occurred to me that for the first time in my life, it was just possible I was going to need some help.

As our little jet turned its nose skyward and shot over the Alps like a silver arrow, it also occurred to me how generous and ingenious it was for the Vasvar and Flynn families to have an autumn wedding in northern Italy at the beginning of white truffle season. Nothing could be more delicious, more decadent, or more expensive. I was so glad I wasn't going to miss it.

CHAPTER 28

Geneva, Switzerland

When the black Mercedes sedan pulled away from the plane, the dog scarcely noticed I was gone. She was sound asleep on the soft leather seat in the airplane cabin. Ten minutes later my car rolled to a stop in front of an anonymous gray building, one of dozens of such edifices in downtown Geneva. A discrete, well-polished brass plaque identified the establishment as the Banque Privée Vilmont. I walked through the lobby and pressed the elevator button to take me to the basement vault, where I stepped into a small beige room that contained two office-type armchairs and a small counter with a heavy grille covering a window. The bright light was harsh, and cold. On the counter sat a ballpoint pen anchored with a thin chain, and a single piece of paper upon which I wrote the number of my account followed by my signature. I slid the sheet under the grille—there was just enough room for the paper to slip through. Then I sat down and waited, and the whole time my mind worked.

This would be a huge job, the largest I'd ever undertaken. I tried not to think about the enormity of the triple-play because I found it quite daunting. I tried, instead, to keep the three elements separate. The first one, replacing Constance Flynn's gemstones in their settings now presumably safely delivered to my suite at the Berkeley in London—had to be done before I went to bed tonight. That was a task that didn't cause me any particular anxiety—it would simply be labor-intensive and require 100 percent of my focus.

But replacing the stones in the Vasvar ruby parure? There was no way I could do it alone, assuming I was even able to locate it before it was presented to the bride. But who could I trust to help me? And would one trustworthy person even be enough to help pull off this switch? The site of Castello Vasvar, itself, was extremely precipitous, and while the physical distance between the hotel and the castle across the lake was not vast, it did require crossing a body of water, which to me was significant since I'd never been much of a water person—quite typical of persons born in Oklahoma. The only other access was driving around the lake to the castle's main entrance on the gentler slope, a circuitous route that could take as long as forty-five minutes.

And finally, what about my promise to Sister Immaculata to rescue the jeweled Madonnas? Whatever made me say such a crazy thing? Don't even start thinking about it now, Kick. Just take care of today's assignment. My head began to ache, and even though I'd just finished lunch, my stomach burned as though I hadn't eaten for days.

Before long, a door opened and a nondescript woman indicated with an extended arm that I should follow her. "Please," she said, and showed me into a comfortably decorated, good-sized private office with a business desk, a credenza, and a conference table. All the surfaces were bare except for a telephone on the desk, which I knew had only an inside line. "Coffee?"

"Please," I answered. "With cream and sugar. And a plate of dark chocolates."

"Kindly make yourself comfortable. You have a number of safe-deposit boxes in your account, would you like for us to bring all of them?" Her English was impeccable and bloodless, flat without accent or inflection.

"Yes. Please. I need three padded FedEx envelopes as well."

"Airbills?"

"Please."

"Kindly make yourself comfortable." She left the room and closed the door behind her. I knew I was locked in.

Several minutes later, a buzzer sounded, the lock clicked, and two porters pushed in carts stacked with safe-deposit boxes almost the size of file drawers, ten of them in all. The woman followed carrying a silver tray with the coffee and chocolates and placed it on the desk.

"How would you like the boxes arranged?"

"On the conference table, please."

Once the men had placed the boxes, the woman asked if there was anything else I needed.

"Nothing, thank you. I'll call you when I'm ready."

They left without a word, securing the door behind them.

I raised the lids on the boxes so they were all standing open, and scanned them thoroughly to reacquaint myself. Four boxes were packed with only one kind of gem each—diamond, emerald, sapphire, ruby. Most people are unaware that rubies and sapphires are both the mineral corundum—the second hardest natural mineral known to science. The hardest, of course, being diamond, which is four times harder than corundum. Ruby is red corundum, and every other color of corundum is called sapphire, which is why sapphires come in a wide range of colors and shades: blue, pink, green, and yellow. The gemstone emerald is the green and most valuable version of the mineral beryl, while aquamarine is its poorer cousin. I could go on and on about stones, their intricacies and geology—my semesters as a geology major at Oklahoma State had given me a good foundation which had turned into encyclopedia knowledge over the years. But at the moment, there was no time to spare.

Two other safe-deposit boxes held varieties of stones sorted by classifications, such as spinels (good stand-ins for rubies); garnets; olivines, including peridot; quartzes, including amethyst and citrine; topaz and tourmalines. One was devoted to pearls, another to platinum ingots, and another to gold.

Each stone was in its own briefke, as the ingeniously folded diamond papers are called, with its exact carat weight, cut, color, and clarity written along the top.

The ninth and tenth boxes held only cash—several million in crisp new bills.

Just to protect myself against this sort of eventuality, i.e. returning stolen stones to their original owners or at least to their original settings—although frankly I'll admit, I never in my wildest dreams thought such a thing would occur—I'd kept sets of scale-sized, high-resolution color photographs of all my pilfered pieces in the document safe at my flat. I placed the stack of photos of Constance Flynn's jewelry in front of me, on the side of the desk facing the conference table, and then removed my jacket, blouse, and Merry Widow-style corset, a foundation I had personally designed for the specific purpose of smuggling gemstones through tight security. It was constructed in a way that could pass a conscientious screener's most intimate frisking—smooth to the touch, inside and out, but thick. It added about twenty pounds to my midsection. I laid the corset out flat above the stack of photos and put my blouse and jacket back on just in case I had to leave in a hurry.

Then, moving quickly, doing one piece of jewelry at a time, I located the appropriate authentic stones and placed them in their proper position on the photos. When each picture was complete, I tucked the stones into Velcroed slots in the corset.

It took an hour to pull the goods for her pieces, and once they were all tucked safely away, and I'd put my clothes back on properly and stretched my back, I treated myself to the dark Swiss chocolate wafers and a cup of steaming hot Columbian coffee with cream.

Like Constance Flynn, I've never really cared much for rubies—they don't look particularly good with my skin—but I must say, the Vasvar rubies were truly extraordinary. They were richly colored and ranged in size from one to sixty carats. A number of very nice diamonds and pearls completed the collection that made up the parure's tiara, necklace, earclips, bracelets, and brooch. I slid stacks of briefkes into small, self-sealing Bubble Wrap envelopes and then packed them in larger

Bubble Wrap bags. Then I tucked those bags into three overnight envelopes.

The time had come. Before I sealed the bags, I had to make a decision whether or not I was going to involve someone else, have an accomplice to witness, aid, and abet my reverse crime. Aside from Thomas, there wasn't anyone I trusted. And I didn't even trust him 100 percent. But, funnily enough, after some thought, it wasn't as hard as I thought it would be.

I pulled open the desk drawer and found a tidy stack of heavy ecru writing paper and a fountain pen. I withdrew three sheets and composed a brief note for each shipping bag.

"Dear Sister Immaculata," I wrote. "Kindly keep these in a safe place. If you don't hear from me within sixty days, please feel free to sell them. They will more than take care of your long-term needs. Warmest regards, KDK"

I included the name of the person in Zurich who would arrange a discreet sale of the gems, no questions asked.

CHAPTER 29

There are certain five-star hotels around the world that specialize in making sure their single women guests are made to feel particularly welcome and protected. The Berkeley in Kensington is just such a place, a safe, secure haven on a little side street in a popular part of town where, as a woman traveling alone, the moment you step through the front door you know all the employees have their eyes on you.

"Mrs. Hallaby." The doorman opened the door of my sedan. "Welcome to The Berkeley." He helped me out of the car. It was already dark out, and all the shops in Kensington twinkled as though it were Christmas.

My fatigue from earlier in the day was gone, replaced by the familiar, exhilarating adrenaline buzz that puts me on top of the world when I'm about to go to work around beautiful jewelry.

As anticipated, the Royal Courier packages with Constance's jewelry had been placed on the desk in my suite, a wonderful affair with a large blue taffeta swag above the bed and hunting prints on the butter yellow walls. I let Bijou out of her bag and she ripped around the rooms, checking everything out, dragging out her toys. I put her bowls on the bathroom floor and gave her some well-earned dinner. She was such a good dog—ten pounds of brains. She knew when she was in her bag that she had to keep her mouth shut—no one even knew she was there.

Then I picked up the phone and ordered a cheese tray, chocolate-dipped strawberries, cashews, and a bottle of Dom Pérignon, and after that, I very happily took off my clothes. The jewel-packed corset had made the suit tight and uncomfortable and I was glad to be out of it and able to take a deep breath. I laid it on a chair beneath a towel in the bathroom, and then pulled on one of the hotel's thick terry cloth robes. Moments later, the doorbell rang and the butler brought in my tray.

"May I pour you a glass of champagne, madam?" He asked.

"No thank you. I'll open it later."

"Very good. I am at your service." He did a quick bow and was gone.

I put out the DO NOT DISTURB sign, double locked the door, ate one of the strawberries, and opened my suitcase.

It was ludicrous that just blocks away in my flat, I had a fully equipped jeweler's bench with superb lighting, a 65x magnification glass, and a comfortable chair. But I didn't want these pieces of jewelry in my house. What I was going to do was technically extremely easy but the circumstances had made it complicated logistically. If someone by some fluke were to uncover this caper, I could walk out the door and disappear into the night without a trace.

The light was brightest in the bathroom, so that's where I set up shop, on the counter. I laid out my tools on the glass shelf above the sinks, which I had closed and lined with plastic wrap on the slim but potentially totally disastrous chance that I would drop a stone. Just the thought of watching a perfect white diamond bounce itself down the drain made my blood run cold.

I had duplicate photos of each piece, and I laid one stack to the left of my work area and one to the right and then pulled on my headband with its supermagnification lenses, which made me look like a brain surgeon about to attempt a intricate and complicated procedure. As I had done in Zurich, I completed one piece at a time beginning with placing the real stones on the photograph to the right, the piece itself directly in front of me and then once the stone had been replaced, I put the fake stones on the photo to the left, until one side was empty and the other filled. It didn't take long for me to develop a rhythm and by one o'clock in the morning, I was done. I closed up shop, putting the loose synthetics in the appropriate briefkes and repacking the real jewelry in the courier envelope, which I addressed to Kick Keswick at Ballantine & Company Auctioneers. Finally, it was time to celebrate. I started the tub, poured in two bottles of bubble bath and uncorked the champagne with abandon, letting it make a declassé and entirely joyful pop! I don't think I'd ever felt so good. Bath and champagne bubbles were everywhere.

I'd just poured my second glass and re-submerged when the video cell phone on the stool next to the tub began to vibrate, practically giving me a heart attack. I reached out, catching it just before it hit the floor, and watched the secret door in my office open. The strong beam of a high-intensity flashlight cut across the walls. Then a figure moved confidently to the safe, set a soft-looking satchel on the floor next to him and, with the flashlight between his teeth, commenced to spin the locks. He spun them again. And again. All the while muttering a blue streak under his breath. Nothing was clicking. Holding the flashlight in his mouth must have gotten to be too much for his jaw because he took the extraordinary risk of turning on the desk light. He pulled a slip of paper from the pocket of his sport coat, studied it, and spun the locks again. And again. Then, after a couple more unintelligible epithets, he switched off the lamp, picked up his satchel, and departed the way he came. I never could get a proper look at his face.

The number of people it could have been was unknown. It could have been Roman McIver, maybe even Talbot Merrill. But it wasn't. Without being able to see his face clearly, I would have known that voice and that shape and that man anywhere. It was Owen Brace.

What on earth was Owen Brace doing in my office? How would he know anything of value was in the safe? Or was he simply trying to steal whatever was there and cause a commotion and embarrass me and the house? Two things gave me comfort: my intuition that somehow Owen was behind some of Ballantine's problems proved correct. And also, he evidently hadn't learned anything at all. He'd underestimated me before and now he'd done it again. Owen Brace would have to get up a lot earlier in the morning if he wanted to catch me coming around corners. I went to sleep with a happy smile.

Coffee and croissants arrived at six and by seven o'clock, Bijou and I were on our way home, walking through a drizzling rain. At the flat, I changed into comfortable slacks and jacket, happy to resume myself, happy to be out of Mrs. Hallaby's corset and wig. Before I left for the office, I rummaged around in the tool kit in the utility closet off the kitchen. It was a professional collection of power tools, hammers, screwdrivers, pliers, nails, screws, and so forth—everything in perfect condition and everything a handyperson would need to make small or large repairs, and all of the best quality that money could buy. I put the battery-operated drill, drill bits, and a good supply of huge, four-inch screws in my briefcase.

Although it was the weekend, I knew most of the department heads and associates would be working since the season opened on Tuesday with a black-tie evening auction of Impressionists—a collection of paintings I was impressed the head of the department had been able to attract. Tradition had it that no one came in before noon on the last Saturday before opening, because it would be the last quiet Saturday until spring—from then on, sales would be held every weekend. However, when I got to the office about nine, I was amazed to see that the place was already a beehive. The reinvigorated commitment and enthusiasm of the staff were heartening—they were an outstanding crew and I wasn't going to let Bertram's incompetence or a little twerp like Owen Brace and his stupid, immature, little revenge plot hurt them or the company. Honestly, he was such a jerk.

"Appears you're going to be doing some remodeling, Miss Keswick," the security guard said in a chipper, chatty way, as my briefcase passed through the screening machine. "Maybe when you're done in your office, you can make a few repairs in mine." He had a big, gap-toothed grin.

"It would be my pleasure," I answered. "But, in fact, I'm taking the drill in for repairs at lunchtime."

He nodded and turned his attention to the next item on the scanner.

Thankfully, Ruth and Roman hadn't come in yet and the executive floor was still dark and quiet. I let myself into Bertram's office, locked the door behind me, and pulled eight of the big screws and the drill out of my bag and screwed them into the paneling around the secret door, effectively sealing it shut. Then I covered the screws with wood filler and brushed that with fruitwood stain to match the paneling. I did the same in Roman's office and in mine. If Owen wanted to get in again, he'd have to use the front door or a fire axe.

The Royal Courier Service hadn't delivered Constance's jewels yet, and I could feel myself getting anxious, which made the strong hotel coffee boil in my stomach. I fussed around my office for a few minutes, accomplishing little, and then decided to visit the troops, take the temperature, and see how everyone's attitude was about the upcoming week.

I went upstairs to the offices and workrooms and downstairs to the cellars, dropping in on the experts and associates and visiting with them as best I could. The mantle of leadership didn't come easily to me, the concept of "team" had never been part of my makeup or history, so small talk was a foreign tongue. I was not by nature an especially warm person and it had never been in me to inquire about people's children or grandchildren, to ask about their gardens or charitable activities, unless their answers would further my own interests. However, I was so impressed by this staff's dedication to their chosen fields, in particular, and the house's success, in general, that I made an effort and it turned out better than I expected. I even commented on a baby picture or two and sounded as though I meant it. Which, in some ways, I did, although I've never been able to tell one baby from another. Mostly I asked a few pertinent questions here and there about their goods and their sales projections and concluded with a clipped, but heartfelt, "Carry on," and surprisingly, they seemed to appreciate it.

Back in the main lobby, as I was crossing between sale rooms, the messenger, rain dripping from his cap and fogging his glasses, came through the front door. He greeted the guard and placed the package on the X-ray machine. I watched it go through, watched the guard study the screen, and study it more. I'd stopped breathing by the time he picked it up to read the label.

It was minutes before ten. Outside, through the glass front door, I watched Ruth's umbrella, then hat, then face, then whole body appear, coming up the front steps. Oh no. I didn't want her to see I'd accepted a delivery. She would ask questions and I didn't want to have a conversation with her about it. I didn't entirely trust Ruth. Well, in fact, I didn't really trust Ruth at all. She put her hand on the knob.

"It's for you, Miss Keswick," the guard said.

"Perfect timing," I smiled. Ruth put her hand on the door and then stopped. The door man had struck up a conversation. Keep her talking, I silently begged. Just another second or two.

I turned my back to the front door, signed the release, and accepted the package from the guard. "Carry on," I said over my shoulder and headed up the stairs, awash in relief. It's the little foxes that spoil the vine, and all it would take to force me into a messy pile of lies and cover-ups would be a mysterious delivery. I glanced back when I reached the landing. Ruth's purse was on the conveyor belt and she was having a good chat with the guard.

I closed my office door and dashed to the safe, where I removed the jeweled Madonna who had a serene, beatific expression on her porcelain face, as though she were enjoying the whole nerve-wracking affair. She would have fetched millions at auction. I wrapped her in a square of midnight blue velvet and an Hermès scarf and placed her securely in the false bottom of my briefcase. Then, I sliced open the delivery envelope and unpacked Constance Flynn's jewels. Ruth was hanging up her phone when I came out of the office.

"Oh! Miss Keswick." She put her hand on her chest. "You startled me. I wasn't expecting to see you today."

Did she seem surprised as in glad? Or surprised as in foiled?

"Good morning, Ruth. I couldn't miss the Saturday before opening."

"I know," she smiled. "It's very exciting, isn't it? Lots of good energy."

"Indeed. Very special. Would you ask Mr. Merrill to come up? And also, I think I'll break down and have some orange rolls. Just to celebrate and because it's Saturday."

"They're on the way," she winked conspiratorially. "I think I'll have some myself. I think we've earned them this week."

She had no idea.

CHAPTER 31

"Mrs. Edgar Flynn came in yesterday noon," I explained to Talbot, who looked elegant in fawn slacks and a tweed sport coat with a dashing persimmon foulard. "And since you'd gone, Ruth brought her to see me. She's asked us to sell a large portion of her jewel collection for her. As you can see, it's quite remarkable."

The plastic Ziploc bags containing Constance's now fully reconstituted pieces were arrayed on the conference table. Talbot and I went over each one of them in detail.

"Wonderful, wonderful," he said as he examined them and their accompanying paperwork. "I'm impressed you know so much about gems and jewelry, Miss Keswick. Your descriptions are perfect."

"No mystery to that, I'm afraid. I'm far from an expert," I reassured him. "I simply copied off the specifics from the bills of sale."

He seemed pleased.

"So, now they are in your good care, Mr. Merrill."

He nodded quietly. "This is a lovely, lovely collection. Very unusual. Just look at this piece. This is one of the most beautiful necklaces I've ever seen." He held up the Cartier estate necklace with the cabochon sapphires suspended from the diamond collar. The lights made it look as though it were on fire. "The workmanship is extraordinary." He put a loupe in his eye. "The platinum thread in these pendants is so fine, it's basically invisible. I can't imagine the skill it took to tie these off without breaking the thread. It's almost impossible to find talent like this anymore."

I admit, I did feel myself preening a bit. He was right. Working with a length of metallic thread finer than a single skein of silk, passing it through the stone and then tying it into a one-carat diamond bead on the bottom, required a steady hand, years of practice, and powerful visual magnification. I think my efficiency and efficacy had also been improved by the incentive of the Dom Pérignon waiting for me when I was done.

Talbot removed the loupe and I saw his eyes were filled with tears, which he wiped away with the back of his hand. "Forgive me," he laughed sheepishly and laid the piece gently back on the table. "The beauty of some of these things overwhelms me sometimes. They're just inescapably magnificent. Well, I'll get these in the system." Moments later he was back with a metal rolling cart and loaded the sealed bags on the top shelf. "I'm very happy she chose Ballantine and Company," he said. "This will be a major sale. Enormous fun."

"I think the fun hasn't even begun," I said. "She told me she has a story to go with each piece."

"I imagine she does, too. Squabble, squabble, squabble. Aren't they a pair? This will be a circus with all the trimmings." He rubbed his hands together with anticipation. "We will make a pot load of money."

"I told her we'd put out a release this week, but that you probably wouldn't be ready to sell them until spring."

"Perfect. I'll take it from here." He pushed the cart out the door. "And, thank you, Miss Keswick."

"For what?"

"For being here and for giving us a second chance."

"I'm only the stand-in."

"You're much more than that and you know it."

⁓⁓ ⁓⁓

I was too tired to make the pancakes on Sunday. It poured rain and I stayed in bed all day and read the papers and listened to music and hoped Thomas would call, but he didn't. I tried calling him, but he didn't answer.

I stared out the window and laid out my plans for the next two weeks. The opening of Ballantine & Company's auction season was Tuesday night, but I knew Roman McIver and the sales team had things well in hand, so my direct involvement would be minimal.

More importantly, I worked out how to insert myself into the wedding weekend at Lago d'Orta. ("Crash" is such an indelicate word.) According to Constance, the festivities kicked off Thursday next. This would wrap up my grand slam. Somehow or other, I'd replace the rubies and track down the jeweled Madonnas and return them to the nuns, and then I would leave the field of play forever. Blending in with the wedding crowd would provide me with the perfect pretense, but I didn't know any of the Flynns or Vasvars. I needed to get creative and come up with some bullet-proof reason for my presence. After an hour or two of quiet contemplation, I settled on just the right identity and setup.

The next ten days simply shot past. Between Bertram's five-way bypass surgery (which he came through with flying colors), the opening of the season, and assembling my wardrobe for the wedding, every waking second was filled and, thankfully, there were no emergencies.

CHAPTER *32*

Milan, Italy

When I lifted off for Milan in Alitalia's delightful Magnifica Class, where the flight attendants are all beautiful or handsome and dressed in couture Armani uniforms and whip up espressos and cappuccinos on an espresso machine that is larger than many other airlines' entire galleys, it seemed as though London and Londoners had settled in for a rainy autumn—their faces were set, their Burberrys buttoned up, and their black umbrellas unfurled. However, when I landed at Linate, Milan's downtown airport, the sky was perfectly clear in a deepening blue twilight and the temperature perfect. Night had fallen altogether by the time I set out for the city in my rented, *nero carbonio*, Maserati Quattroporte.

The Quattroporte was the first Maserati the Turin-based coachworks, Pininfarina, had designed for the automobile manufacturer in over fifty years, ever since it decided to devote all its energies to Ferrari, Maserati's fiercest competitor. Oh, my. What a machine this was—a high-performance Italian saloon car at the top of its class. I couldn't wait until tomorrow when I would be able to get on the Autostrada to Lago d'Orta and really open up the powerful 4.2 liter, V-8 engine. In the meantime, however, I'd creep along in the evening rush hour and content myself with the classic elegance of the rosewood and fine leather interior. It smelled as well-maintained as the tack room at Buckingham Palace Mews.

The other reason I was happy to not be whizzing along at a hundred miles an hour was because finding your way into and through downtown Milan, whether it's brightest day or darkest night, was always a hit-or-miss proposition. No matter how many times I'd stayed at the Four Seasons Milano, I always just happened to run across it. Inevitably, moments before I decided to pick up the phone to call and ask them to come get me because I was hopelessly lost in the maze of narrow streets, whose names changed from block to block, or the street signs were mounted so high on the buildings they were hard to read, I would turn one more corner and there I would be on Via Gesù at this relatively unmarked oasis, the doorman in his recognizable brown uniform waiting to rescue me at the anonymous entrance. It never failed.

"Buona sera, signora," he said. "Welcome to the Four Seasons."

The hotel was a restored fifteenth-century convent, only steps from the best shopping in Italy on the Via Montenapoleone and the best opera at La Scala, and I felt an elated sense of accomplishment whenever I walked through the doors into the high-ceilinged lobby. As though I'd been admitted to a secret club. As though we'd all somehow stumbled onto the hidden place, passed the test.

"Lady Amanda Bonham," I informed the man at the registration desk.

Lady Amanda Bonham, a Scots noblewoman of a certain age, was a woman who had come into her own—the sort of woman who brooked no nonsense. She was reminiscent of a vital and vigorous Queen Mary, of everyone's terrifying great-aunt, formidable in both physical presence and attitude. She was flame-haired, green-eyed Maureen O'Hara just in from a march on the moors. She would just as soon smack you on your shins with her cane as talk to you if you gave even the slightest hint of impropriety or vulgarity. She was impe-rious. She was a force of nature. She was a battleship that sailed with a mighty prow. She was sturdy as the Rock of Gibraltar. She was, in a word, magnificent.

There was no real Lady Amanda Bonham, of course. I'd made her up out of whole cloth years and years ago and then, with a few well-planned and well-placed news releases that became little blurbs in local Scottish newspapers, I constructed an entire legitimate life and identity for her. She was married to Laird Wynn Bonham who had been injured in a riding accident over twenty years ago. They had had no children or other relatives and she'd devoted her life to caring for her invalid husband. They never left their castle, and over time, they basically disappeared into the Highland mists and were forgotten. I think that before the accident, when she was a bride and life held so much promise, she was a live wire, and with that added to all the hardship she'd known, she'd grown into the indomitable woman I'd created. Indomitable on the surface, but I made sure she had a large streak of vulnerability because I had a feeling it would come in handy.

"Buona sera, Lady Amanda," the man replied.

As always, the lobby bar was filled with an international slice of the world's glitterati—top models, top businessmen, and designers—super sleek, super elegant, and their limelight rubbed off on me, making me feel like a superstar as well.

I loved the look my auburn wig and green eyes gave me—mysterious, glamorous, aloof, and most probably famous. I was look-ing forward to getting my real hair dyed and a professional makeup consultation, custom-made for a redhead, tomorrow morning at Lola on the Via Montenapoleone. But for now, I knew I looked fine—a number of heads turned and gave me appreciative glances when I took a seat at a small cocktail table. I think the cane added to Lady Amanda's mystique—it was smart and commanding. Big league.

There was one man in particular who did not make even a slight effort to conceal his interest in me. Although he was seated, I could tell he was tall, his long legs were crossed comfortably, showing off be-spoke black leather shoes. He wore a charcoal gray suit, blue shirt with white pinstripes, and a yellow club tie emblazoned with coats-of-arms.

He had a tint to his skin—somewhere between natural bronze and a good tan, black hair, and black, thick-lashed eyes, slightly too close together, and straight brows. He looked rich and dangerous. He was with another man, presumably a business associate and while they talked, the man never took his eyes off me. I found his attention unsettling. The bar was filled with famous models. I would have felt better if he had looked at them.

I ordered a vodka martini, straight up—the ideal aperitif for what I knew was going to be a world-class dinner—and spent an enjoyable twenty minutes watching the lobby's comings and goings while I sipped it. When the time came to take care of my check, the waiter told me the man had already paid for my cocktail.

"No," I said. "I cannot accept. Please bring me my tab."

"But, madam," he said. "It's . . ."

"I insist."

The waiter nodded and returned momentarily.

I didn't look at the man again, but felt his eyes on me as I left the bar and went into the dining room. The intensity of his gaze made me shiver, as though I'd walked through a shadow.

A few minutes later I saw him and his colleague come to the captain's stand. After years of eavesdropping on any number of conversations at any given time at cocktail and dinner parties, auction galas, and private exchanges, I had highly attuned hearing and quite dependable lipreading skills. While the entrance was too far away for me to hear over the dining room's muted rustle, I could tell the captain, a small, graying older man in a three-button, gray Armani suit and shiny shoes, was dismayed he couldn't seat them immediately. The man was clearly someone of distinction, a dignitary known to all in the hotel.

"I'll have a table for you in thirty minutes," he said. "But for now," he gestured with defeat. "You can see we're fully booked—it's the truffles. They make people go crazy! Let me bring you an aperitif with my compliments."

The man put his hand on the captain's shoulder, in a way that looked familiar but at the same time, threatening, intentionally intimidating. "Not a problem, Giovanni. I ought to be on my way home. See you soon." Then he turned his back to me so I couldn't see his mouth, but I could tell he was asking who I was, and the captain answered. Before he left, the man turned and looked straight at me and smiled, and then he was gone.

I hadn't realized I'd been fidgeting and drumming my fingers on the table. I stopped them immediately, horrified at the urges I felt inside. What had gotten into me? I had spent my life overruling temptation, keeping a lid on my emotions and pleasures. The only enjoyment I'd allowed myself to give way to completely was the extreme pleasure I received from jewels—they were my worldly comfort, my lovers, my security. My only slip had been the debacle with Owen, and I admit that every now and then the touch of his hands would blow through my mind like a sultry erotic wind, but it would be replaced so quickly by an Arctic gale, it was as though someone had opened a door. Until Thomas, my heart had been a block of ice. Until Thomas, I knew nothing about real love or intimacy.

Maybe the stranger had affected me because he reminded me of Owen, who was now trying to maneuver himself into my life for some reason, making an effort to rattle me by breaking into my office, returning fakes for full credit. And this man, this handsome stranger, exuded the same international, suave animal power as Owen. Why was I thinking about sex and seduction and betrayal? This was so not like me. I took a deep breath and I suddenly knew. It wasn't sex.

It was the truffles. The erotic perfume of white truffles. Some say they're better than sex.

Oh. Dio.

CHAPTER 33

White Truffles.

These rare little nuggets are as precious and as costly as gold, and people either love them or hate them, but there is seldom indifference. Their powerful fragrance strikes one as aphrodisiac, and another as repellant. White truffles are unique to a small area of northern Italy and every autumn, in October and November, special truffle-hunting dogs course through forests of chestnut trees and sniff them out. But it's a one-sided relationship—the success of the search is by the grace of the truffles, which control the harvest by making their presence known via their distinctive fragrance only when they are perfectly ready to be gathered. There could be a row of a dozen truffles on the ground, but if they aren't ready to reap, the dogs don't even notice them.

Unlike black truffles, which can be grown on plantations, white truffles cannot be cultivated. They are wild, unpredictable, manipulative. Practically sinful. A bit like me.

"Olio, signora?" the waiter inquired as he placed a plate with a disk of fresh veal tartare before me. It sat on a bed of mâche sprinkled with capers, minced scallion, and pimentos.

He dressed the tartare with a drizzle of extra virgin olive oil, its color as sensuous as green moss in springtime. He picked up the pepper grinder and I nodded. Then, the moment had arrived. "*Tartufi*, signora?"

"Si," I answered, tingling with anticipation "Per favore."

The waiter gave a nod to the captain, who approached carrying a silver tray arrayed with a selection of perhaps fifteen truffles that ranged in size from slightly smaller than an egg to perhaps as large as a persimmon, and ranged in color from soft ecru to dark brown.

He put down the tray and smiled into my eyes. "Signora," he said. His look was intimate and sensual, as though we were about to make love. But the desire wasn't for me, it was for the imminent satisfaction he was about to experience in preparing the tartufi for me and the satisfaction I was about to experience in eating them. He picked up a truffle, held it close to his nose, closed his eyes, and inhaled deeply. No. Not the right one. He put it back and picked up another. This one passed. "Aah," he said. "Perfetto." He took up his truffle slicer and held it over the plate and began to run the blade back and forth. The fragrance exploded from the paper-thin slices so intensely I wanted to pick them up with my hands and press them into my skin. I closed my eyes and inhaled. There was nothing like this in the world. When he'd finished, he gave me a quick bow. "Prego," he said and swept his tray off my table with a flourish and bore it away.

The sommelier, who had earlier opened a half-bottle of La Spinetta Barolo, reappeared and poured some of the dark cherry red wine into my glass. "Prego," he said and departed, leaving me to enjoy the illicit combination of rare delicacies: chopped veal that was as light as a feather, white truffles, and wine. How I wished Thomas were here to enjoy this with me. When we got home, whenever that was going to be, and he found out where I'd been and what I'd eaten, he'd die from envy.

The veal was just the start—for my *segundi piatti*, I had risotto with asparagus and truffles, followed by roast lamb and truffles, and finally a little tossed salad and cheese. No truffles. And just to ensure I had sweet dreams, my meal ended with a mouth-watering dark molten chocolate cake filled, unexpectedly, with cherries, and drizzled with Grand Marnier chocolate sauce. A curl of sugared orange peel sat on top. A little flute of Palladino Muscato was the finale. There could not have been a more perfect menu to start a few days in Italy.

The dinner cost four hundred euros.

Next morning, instead of putting on the wig, I covered my hair with a scarf, tying it back at the nape of my neck, adding a fedora on top of that and large dark glasses. I walked the three blocks to Lola. I wore no makeup because I didn't want them to know what I normally looked like. I wanted to be a blank canvas. When I left the salon, three hours later, I was transformed. My hair had been cut to just below my jawline, colored a wonderful burnished auburn with a few highlights, and fixed in a structured coiffure that required rollers, ratting, and a great deal of hair spray. It was close to bouffant and swept back, making a glamorous, formal frame for my face. The makeup artist worked wonders, creating a palette to complement both my skin color, my green eyes, and my red hair. With just a few clever strokes of his brush, unbeknownst to him, he had changed my appearance and my personality completely.

By noon, Bijou and I were in the Quattroporte on the A-28, making fast tracks to Orta San Giulio, the little town on the little peninsula at Lago d'Orta. The car was so fun to drive, I wished my destination had been much farther away, but as it was, we arrived in under an hour.

CHAPTER 34

Lago d'Orta, Italy

I almost missed the hotel—the sign for its entrance was buried among banners for a miniature golf course, not an encouraging omen. But, once I turned down the steep, pebbled drive to the main building, I felt much better, especially when I saw all the fancy cars jammed into the tiny lot. I was banking on the custom of all good hotels to keep a sprinkling of rooms and suites available at all times in case of emergency. The sort of emergency I was about to create.

Anyone who has been to out-of-town weddings, or actually any wedding at all, knows there's almost always someone there who nobody seems to know. The bride and her family think the person belongs to the groom's side of the affair, and vice versa, which makes weddings very easy to crash. And if that is compounded by the combination of a disorganized and incompetent wedding coordinator, warring, divorcing parents, and myriad nationalities and languages, it became, from my point of view, a perfect storm of disconnections. Neither side would ask the other for fear of offense.

So it was with Lady Amanda Bonham—the wedding coordinator, Miss Laddie Murphy, would move heaven and earth to make sure I was accommodated without a ripple because, when all was said and done, it would be her fault that she hadn't been expecting me. Edgar Flynn's temper was famous and if he learned that a member of the aristocracy to which he so aspired had been turned away from his son's wedding, things would turn ugly.

The challenge for me would be keeping the families from comparing notes as the days went on, but as Constance had also mentioned, the families hadn't even met or gotten together, so I doubted there would be much, if any, conversation about Alice's or William's great-aunt or godmother or whatever she, I, was.

The terrace outside the hotel lobby was a madhouse, piled with the luggage, accoutrements and wardrobe wedding guests required for a gala three-day affair. An emaciated, nervous-looking woman in large, thick, black-rimmed glasses, who I assumed to be the ersatz organizer hired and paid for by Edgar Flynn, stood at the front door with her clipboard. Poor thing had already eaten off all her lipstick. She smiled at me and seemed to flinch. I could tell she was completely frazzled and would burst into tears at the slightest provocation. I felt terrible about making her day worse, but there was no getting around it.

"Good afternoon," she said in an Irish brogue. Her name tag read: LADDIE MURPHY. "Welcome to the San Rocco. May I have your name, please?"

I drew myself up and frowned down my nose at her. "I beg your pardon."

"Your name?"

I was so intimidating I even scared myself. "Lady Amanda Bonham," I replied.

"Oh," she tweeted and eyed her clipboard. She ran a shaking finger down one page and then the next. "Oh, dear. Oh, dear." She licked her lips. "I can't seem to find your name on my list."

"You can't be serious."

"Oh, I know we're expecting you, Lady Amanda. I've seen your name on everything, I just can't seem to find you here on the room list. Now, please remind me, you are . . ."

"Miss Murphy," I pulled her aside and muttered an unintelligible name that could have been that of the bride, Alice Vasvar, and then added, "great-aunt and godmother."

"Yes. Yes," she said breathlessly and then swallowed. "Of course. If you'll give me just a minute." She dashed into the lobby and had a quick consult with one of the ladies at the front desk. After lots of nodding, pursed lips, subtly flared nostrils, and raised eyebrows, I saw a key handed across the counter and she returned and signaled to a bellman. "Lady Amanda is in suite number twenty in Villa Gippini," she told him and then turned to me. "Please forgive me. It seems everything has gotten confused. I would be ever so grateful if you didn't mention this to Mr. Flynn. He'll, he'll . . ."

I put my hand on her arm. "Don't give it another thought, dear. I know how these things can happen and I know what a difficult man he can be. This will be just between the two of us."

She was so grateful, I thought she was going to throw her arms around me. "Thank you so much, Lady Amanda. I'll have your schedule brought to your room directly and just to remind you, luncheon begins in fifteen minutes on the hotel terrace."

"Thank you, dear Miss Murphy," I said. "I don't envy you your job."

"Oh, I'll be all right once we get everyone comfortably situated."

I wanted to tell her to breathe—everything after me would be easy.

And there I was, in like Flynn. She wouldn't say a word and naturally, neither would I.

The bellman threw open the shutters in the spacious bedroom and bright sunlight poured across the deep balcony and through three sets of French doors. Beyond, the view opened to a small lawn with an apple tree whose leaves had turned bright yellow, orange, and red, and beyond that was the sparkling lake and Isola San Giulio with its Benedictine basilica. On the opposite shore, loomed Castello Vasvar, impenetrable, almost foreboding atop its sheer cliff.

A second bellman delivered a heavy ecru envelope, beribboned with white satin and elegantly inscribed with the bride and groom's names along with mine, just below theirs. In my opinion, Laddie was doing an impressive job. The envelope contained the weekend schedule, with the formal invitation to each event, and a list of the members of the wedding party, a rather nouveau but—from my point of view—extremely considerate touch.

Outside my window, a number of lake cruisers bobbed in the sunlit water at the hotel's small dock. As I started unpacking, I could see guests beginning to gather on the terrace. This would be everyone's first chance to meet and I would take my time. I had to make the proper impression.

After opening my brand new palette of toiletries designed specifically for redheads—skin care products and makeup, all sealed in Lola's beautiful pure white packaging trimmed with yellow velvet ribbons—I arranged them on the glass shelves in the pink marble bath. I unpacked and put myself together. Of all the seasons, I love autumn best, and it had been sheer pleasure assembling an autumn wardrobe for a redhead. I put on a beautiful Chanel coat and dress ensemble of pistachio-colored light wool with cantaloupe fringe, layers of creamy pearls, a cantaloupe pashmina draped over one shoulder, and diamond and pearl earrings. I slid a fifteen-carat, emerald-cut, yellow diamond ring onto my finger and pinned a Van Cleef & Arpels blossom of yellow diamonds onto the lapel of my coat. The cane was the finishing touch.

I studied the list one more time before leaving for lunch.

The Wedding Party

FAMILY OF COUNTESS ALICE VASVAR

Father of the Bride—Prince Georg Friedrich "Freddie" Vasvar
Step-Mother of the Bride—Sylvia, Marchioness of Kennington
Step Grand-Mother of the Bride—Mary Margaret, Duchess of Kennington
Companion to the Duchess—Miss Victoria Forester

FAMILY OF MR. WILLIAM FLYNN

Mother of the Groom—Mrs. Constance Flynn
Her Escort—Mr. Clifton Boatwright

Father of the Groom—Mr. Edgar Flynn
Miss Lauren Cambridge
Sister of the Groom—Miss Katharine "Katie" Flynn
Best Man—Mr. Roman MacIver

The two family contingents could not have been more diverse—if I didn't hit the right notes, I would be out before I'd finished my first glass of bubbly.

I was interested in the Flynns of course, Edgar and particularly his son, William, and in ferreting out where they'd put the Vasvar ruby parure. Once I identified that, this aspect of the caper should be fairly straightforward. But that was the rub, wasn't it? The rubies could be anywhere. In the safe in Edgar's room. Or William's. In the hotel safe. Or in a bank vault in the town. And when was he planning to give them to Alice? At the rehearsal dinner the night before the wedding or the morning of? Or tonight or tomorrow at lunch?

More fascinating to me than any of the Flynns, though, was the father of the bride, Prince Freddie Vasvar.

Sister Immaculata's words echoed in my mind: "Freddie Vasvar murdered the nuns in cold blood. His valet, who conveniently died the next day falling off the cliff at the castello, helped him. Freddie planned to pledge the collection of Madonnas as collateral for a loan to help underwrite a fledgling revolution in Hungary, but the murders and the theft received too much publicity too quickly for him to use them. We believe they're still stored somewhere at the castello. They're no good to him—the slightest murmur of their existence would stir a firestorm of questions and accusations. And, he'd go to jail for the rest of his life."

"How do you know all this?" I'd asked.

"One nun survived, an American, and she made it back to New York. Freddie doesn't know there's an eyewitness. He's a butcher."

If I had even a snowball's chance in hell of finding the Madonnas, it would only be through Freddie, although the thought of it gave me the creeps.

I stopped off at the front desk to deposit a stack of felt jewelry bags, filled with nothing more than cotton and marbles, in the hotel vault, hoping I could catch a quick glimpse of the vault itself. It was a brand new, modern affair, with a number of drawers and an electronic master lock. This would be a complicated safe to break into—not the electronic lock but the safe deposit drawers themselves—the sort of heist that would require the doping of the night desk clerks and a drill. Well, I thought, if the rubies are in there, they are. I'd come prepared for any and everything, including a little gizmo that shot tranquilizer darts.

I took one last look at the luncheon invitation. It was incredibly formal and overwrought for a poolside gathering—a black card with raised gold printing and thick red-and-gold borders. It was the sort of invitation that the self-aggrandized twenty-five-year-old girlfriend, Lauren Cambridge, of the overweight fifty-five-year-old industrialist, Edgar Flynn, would think was appropriate. It looked absolutely ridiculous.

CHAPTER 35

"Signora," said the waiter when I passed through the glass doors to the terrace. I accepted a glass of champagne—Dom Pérignon's impressive 1996—and then stepped over to the receiving line where I was greeted first by the host, Edgar Flynn.

He extended his hand, which was as clammy as I always knew it must be just from seeing him at Ballantine & Company auctions when he appeared to be, if not sweating, then at least damp all the time. He was medium-sized in height and portly, with thinning hair and an artificially tanned, round, rather bloated face. His upper and lower eyelids had the telltale red lines of recent cosmetic surgery—so easy to spot on men because they don't have the luxury of wearing eyeliner to hide the incisions. His eyes themselves were mean and aggressive and he radiated a very self-satisfied, arrogant, piggish attitude. In a word, I found him corrupt.

He was too old to believe he still could get away with everything.

He was a middle-aged man who'd fallen into the honeyed, tender trap of believing that the beautiful woman on his arm was really blind to his sagging belly and pendulous pectorals and loved him for his sexual prowess and personality, not his money. He looked like a fool.

"Welcome," he said. "I'm Edgar Flynn, your host for this bash, and this is my fiancée, Lauren."

As you would expect of one of the world's top supermodels, Lauren was about 6'3" and so striking it took your breath away, but I saw what Constance had meant when she said she was tough. She was tough as nails, in the Julie Newmar school of Valkyrie Tough. Big-boned and brawny, more awe-inspiring in person than in print, she was almost more aggressive and masculine than Edgar. For the last three or four years, she'd appeared continuously on the cover of virtually every fashion and celebrity magazine, and in numerous television and print ads for perfumes, cosmetics, and designer clothes. She was most often posed in a ferocious spread-eagled stance—a living, breathing, man-eating Venus Flytrap. Her hands were large and tan with long French-manicured nails that looked like talons, and there was a stunning engagement ring on her left hand. It looked to be twelve to fourteen carats of very sparkly, heart-shaped pink diamond—probably five or six million dollars' worth if it had come from Graff, which, just judging by its size, I assumed it had. The incongruity of Miss Cambridge and Mr. Flynn reminded me of the old story about the Curse of the Blotnik Diamond—the curse being Mr. Blotnik himself.

Lauren Cambridge had a reputation of being a diva—difficult, bulimic, needy, expeditious, and only marginally intelligent. By the hard and empty look in her eyes, I could tell she'd sold her soul long ago back there in some photographer's studio. She was a known manipulator and user of people, which made her and Edgar more evenly matched in spite of the measurable difference in their heights. They were both comfortable pretending to be in love with someone other than themselves.

In reality, Edgar liked the envy with which other men—and his soon-to-be-former wife Constance—looked at him, and Lauren liked the access. But if the real, real truth were to be told, just based on my knowledge of these May-December affairs, I imagined Edgar was wondering just how much longer he could keep up the physical pace and psychic effort she required, in and out of bed. The phrase "high-maintenance" had been invented for animals like Lauren.

She was as vicious as she was unscrupulous, and she was getting old for her profession; her shelf life was almost used up. This was compounded by the fact that Lauren had spent all the money she'd earned, which was estimable. As a supermodel, she'd gotten a taste of the high life, of how comfortable it was to be rich, and while she hadn't come from a poor background, it was working class, and Lauren (nee Lisa Higgenbotham) had created and cultivated an upper class persona, and she wasn't going back to the jammed outskirts of Birmingham, England. She'd found the way to keep the jewels, furs, and designer clothes coming. She would segue easily into Edgar's jet set world in London, New York City, Gstaad, Santa Fe, and St. Tropez, and become his hostess, his decoration, maybe even have his baby, ride in his private jets. She would do whatever it took. I imagined their lawyers were hard at work hammering out a complicated prenuptial agreement.

"Lady Amanda Bonham," I said, taking her hand, which was as hard and bony as Edgar's was pulpy and damp. The nails wrapped around and dug into the back of my hand like claws. "Delighted to meet you."

At the sound of my title, Edgar's eyebrows went up and he took my upper arm in a decisive grip. "Lady Amanda, I've been looking forward to meeting you."

Was I surprised that he wouldn't admit that he'd never heard of me? That I hadn't been expected? Not in the slightest. He was royalty crazy.

"What do you think of this hotel?" Lauren sniffed. I was shocked at her voice. It was nasal and complaining—the sort of voice that makes you want to slap the person using it—and to make matters worse, her breath reeked of onions, and her skin exuded the unmistakeable aroma common to vitamin abusers.

"I think it's perfectly acceptable," I answered.

She sneered. "It's a total dump—not our kind of place at all."

"Really? What is your kind of place?"

"This is a lake for nobodies—we're usually over at Como, either at Villa d'Este or at George's."

"How very lovely for you."

"Is your room all right?" Edgar ignored his fiancée's fatuous attitude. "Anything we can get for you?"

"No, thank you, Mr. Flynn. I'm quite comfortable."

"Have you been to this place before? This Lago Orta?" He said it,
Leggo.

"Yes, it's quite quaint and charming, isn't it?"

"If quaint and charming are the same as rundown," Lauren cawed.

"Shut your damn yap," Edgar ordered out of the side of his mouth
and then turned back to me. "You know, that's the palace where the
princess bride lives." He indicated the mighty mountaintop castle
across the water.

"Yes. I know the castello well."

"Nice," he said. "So you've been here a lot? Visiting the Vasvars?"

"Often enough."

He turned to Lauren. "You hear that? 'Often enough.' That's real
class talking. You two ought to get to know each other, spend some
time together. My treat. Okay? Sort of a finishing school deal. Okay?
I'll pay you."

"Very lovely to meet you both," I said, trying to get away, trying to
get his sweaty hand off my Chanel-covered bicep. "Thank you for including me."

"No, really," he pressed. "How much do you want to teach her
some class?"

I could feel myself blushing. "Mr. Flynn . . ."

"Just kidding. Just kidding." He grabbed Lauren's rock-hard bowl-
ing ball of a bottom. "She knows all the important things. If you know
what I mean."

I was frankly speechless.

"Is it true that they never let people outside their family and best
friends into the place? That they're letting outsiders in for the first
time in a hundred years? Just for the bridal luncheon and wedding
reception?"

"Yes, that's true," I answered, although it was the first I'd heard of
it. "They're a very low-key group."

" 'Low-key' is code for 'Classy,' " Edgar explained to Lauren.

"'Low-key' is code for 'Boring,'" she shot back, and then, of all things, she muffled a belch, as though she'd been drinking beer.

Edgar ignored her and turned to me. "Back to the grindstone. We're getting a traffic jam in line behind you. William," he said, as he pushed me toward his son as though he were shoving me into a re-volving door, "Say hello to Lady Amanda."

Edgar and his son could not possibly have been more different in appearance. In his mid-thirties, William was tall, well over six feet, sturdily built, broad-shouldered, with sun-streaked chestnut hair and dark-lashed, sandy blue eyes. And surprisingly, a bit of a paunch. I studied him, recalling how Constance had left words hanging when-ever she said his name. While his expression was generally benign and inscrutable, I could see a little darkness there and feel an under-current of toughness and aggression that his charming manners and sunny looks belied. He was a faker, a dissembler, a chameleon. I could tell—it takes one to know one. He was walking out the etiquette to get his hands on the air rights.

His fiancée, Alice, who was very young—she looked to be in her early twenties—was as beautiful as he was handsome. Also tall, she was a classic Hungarian beauty with her long dark hair, held back from her face by a wide bandeau. Her deep blue eyes seemed somewhat glazed, as though she'd been sedated. She was gracious but I could tell she had no more enthusiasm for the affair than he did. I knew she was following her father's orders. I'm sure he'd told her the family's entire future rested on her slim shoulders. Poor thing.

Where William gave the impression of being warm and welcom-ing, Alice appeared cool and reserved, but I'd have been surprised to discover either one of them was either of those things. I think he was angry and she was a neurotic mess.

"This is such a romantic weekend," I said holding their hands in mine as though they were both very dear to me. "And William, how absolutely smashing of you to give Alice the rubies as your wedding gift. So, so thoughtful. So appropriate."

He smiled. "Thank you, Lady Amanda."

"Tell me," I whispered to him, sotto voce, smiling at poor Alice the whole time, "When will you present them? Or is it a surprise?"

"I haven't decided yet," he answered.

"Keeping us all on pins and needles! How divine. Oh, Alice, dear, what a beautiful couple you are. I'm so thrilled for both of you. You remind me of when Wynn and I were first married." My eyes misted. "Well, I'd best move along. I don't want your father yelling at me!"

The party was filling up with a sharp group of young people. Not children, but a mix of young professionals in their thirties. As I looked at Roman, who was William's best man, it suddenly dawned on me that no one was in London running the shop. Auction season had begun and the two principals of the company—Roman and I—were gone. Old Masters were Saturday night—Roman's forté. I'd been so preoccupied with my own plan, the company hadn't even crossed my mind since I left London yesterday afternoon. Well, I couldn't worry about that now, but I did make a mental note to call Ruth later. As far as she knew, I was in bed with a migraine.

The party was split into four distinct camps. Once a guest passed through the receiving line, he or she chose up sides: Edgar's, Constance's, the bride and groom's, or what appeared to be the Eastern European Iron Curtain Mafia—a fierce-looking, down-at-the-heels bunch who looked as though they were plotting sedition.

Sitting off to one side under a tree, not seeming to be allied with any particular faction, were two elderly white-haired ladies sipping champagne, talking at the same time at the tops of their lungs and laughing. Each had her cane propped within easy reach and they were elegantly dressed in light wool knit suits, one baby blue, the other peach. Matching handbags hung in the crooks of their elbows. I recognized both of them: Duchess Mary Margaret Kennington in the blue—it was her daughter, Sylvia, who was married to Freddie—and her cousin/companion, Victoria Forester, in the peach.

On the far side of the garden, Constance and her new sweetheart stood in the center of a group of people. A young woman, more of a girl really, stood next to Constance. That would be her daughter, Katie.

My nemesis, Giovanna MacDougal, moved smoothly between

the contingents with her cameraman, still photographer, and note-book, while two additional videographers mingled in the crowd. Edgar had sold the exclusive rights to Giovanna to cover the wedding weekend for an undisclosed seven-figure sum. In his world, every-thing was for sale.

I'd just taken a fresh glass of champagne from a passing tray and was contemplating my next move, when a deep, richly accented voice spoke behind me.

"Buon giorno," he said. "I was hoping I would see you again."

I turned to see who it was. It was the man from the hotel.

"Prince Freddie Vasvar, at your service." There was a slight curl to his lips. He bowed and took my hand and kissed it. He had hair im-plants on top of his head.

I'd never met a sociopathic murderer face to face before.

CHAPTER 36

I'd prepared myself to meet Freddie, and actually quite looked forward to it, but having him be the mysterious stranger from the Four Seasons in Milan did catch me somewhat off guard. I studied him closely. Yes, he was as handsome as he could be. Mid-to-late sixties, perhaps. Very well-maintained. I knew now that what I had initially taken for danger in his glance at the hotel bar, was accurate. He was a very dangerous man. Lethal in fact.

"Prince Vasvar," I said. "I'm pleased to meet you."

"I've seen how much you love truffles, and I've been told we're having them at lunch." Anyone hearing this statement would have said he was merely making conversation, but looking in his eyes, that had a hard, flat glint, like the cold-blooded eyes of a snake, I knew he meant to be innocuously suggestive. He was subtle, disrespectful, and insinuating.

"You mean you were watching me eat my dinner last night?" I asked.

"I have many spies, and a woman as beautiful as you is never un-observed. I love your perfume. Is it Sublime?"

I forced myself not to shiver at his menacing familiarity. "No. Why? Is Sublime your favorite?"

He nodded. "Few women are able to wear it, it's so assertive, so complicated. Even my wife—who is the most complicated woman I've ever known—is unable to carry it off." He smiled. "That was a little joke."

"I see."

"I checked the seating list and was very pleased to see you're at our table. Tell me, where is Lord Bonham?"

"My husband is an invalid. He doesn't travel."

"Ah. I'm sorry to hear that. We will do our best to see that you have a good time without him. Come, let me introduce you to my family." He offered his arm, which I accepted, and he guided me across the terrace to the surly mob, whose names all began with "C" or "Z" and included a "zyk" and were indistinguishable to my ear. They were all fairly drunk, due to the three open bottles of Polish vodka on the café table from which they kept their shot glasses continuously full.

"Vodka?" Freddie held up the bottle and offered.

"No, thank you. I'll stay with champagne."

"You had enough vodka last night, no doubt," he said, referring to my martini cocktail. After helping himself to the vodka, he took my arm in a proprietary way. "Come, we must pay homage."

He guided me to the two elderly ladies and as we drew closer to them I noticed their jewelry. In addition to layers of pearls, they both had on beautiful diamond brooches, and Duchess Mary Margaret, in the baby blue, had two royal orders pinned to her jacket—one of Queen Mary and one of Elizabeth. Royal orders are very hard to come by. They are brooches that are actually miniature paintings—generally about the size of a silver dollar or smaller—typically framed in diamonds or some other precious gem and attached to stiff taffeta ribbons. They are personal gifts from a monarch to an especially beloved subject.

"Lady Amanda," he said in a loud, succinct voice, "may I present you to my mother-in-law, Duchess Mary Margaret of Kennington."

"Your grace," I curtsied.

A slight frown crossed her face, which still had traces of great beauty. Her bright blue eyes peeked out from beneath heavy lids. "Excuse me," she demanded. "You are?"

"Amanda Bonham. Laird Bonham's wife from Edinburgh."

"Speak up, for God's sake. Don't mumble." She was deaf as a post.

"Amanda Bonham," I repeated louder. "Laird Bonham's wife."

"Of course," she beamed, working to make the connection. "How lovely to meet you. Isn't that funny? I used to know a Laird Bonham, but he was killed in the war."

I nodded. "That was Albright. My husband is Wynn, his cousin. You've doubtless never met, he's been an invalid for years. A riding accident."

"Ah," she nodded. "Of course. I'm so sorry. Well, Albright was as crazy as a bed bug. Did you meet him?"

"No. I'm sorry to say I didn't," I answered, not bothering to point out that the war was over some sixty-plus years ago.

"No one was surprised he was killed—he was crazy as a March hare."

"Yes. So I've heard."

"Oh, my. The fun we used to have over Christmastimes in Balmoral."

"Excuse me, Mary Margaret, dear," Freddie broke in to her reminiscences. "Don't you want to introduce Victoria?"

She shot him a harsh look. "I've told you before not to interrupt me. If I have to tell you again"—each word punctuated with a sharp tap of her cane on the stone terrace—"there will be consequences."

"Forgive me," he replied, unruffled by her threat. "But we're about to sit down and we'll look forward to hearing more over lunch. Lady Amanda is seated at our table."

"Oh, lovely." She smiled up at me, her face serene and clear. "Tell me, dear, what is your name?"

Her friend, Victoria—the woman in peach, who also had on a very smart little luncheon hat—patted her arm. "It's Lady Amanda, dear," she shouted and then looked up at me. "She gets a little confused sometimes."

"Don't we all?" I breathed a huge sigh of relief. I'd been prepared, but not anxious, to pursue the Bonham family line.

"Pardon?" Victoria shouted. They were both deaf as posts.

"I said, 'Don't we all get a little confused sometimes.'"

"Oh, my, yes. I'm Victoria Anne Forester. The Duchess's friend."

"Very pleased to meet you, Miss Forester."

"Shall we, ladies?" Freddie moved to help the two octogenarians to their feet.

It happened so fast, it was as though it didn't happen at all: Duchess Mary Margaret swung her cane up and smacked the side of his head so hard it made me jump. I mean, she just pulled back and let him have it. Hard. "We don't need your help. Bugger off, Bozo."

I had trouble keeping a straight face. A red weal began to form itself across his ear. "Are you all right?" I asked. I could tell he was mad as hell. Knowing what I knew about Freddie, I also saw that the only reason his mother-in-law had survived was because she controlled the purse strings, otherwise, she would have been flung over the cliff months ago.

"Fine. Shall we?" He offered me his arm. "Have you met the mother of the groom?"

"Oh my, yes. She's one of my oldest friends."

As we set out, I searched around for a diversion, a way to sideline Freddie, to keep from arriving in front of Constance with him. The success of my identity scheme depended on either side believing I was close to the other, so I couldn't have members of one family introducing me to members of the other. I quickly found a solution—the waiters were all inside.

"Oh, dear." I stopped dead in my tracks and turned back toward the ladies. "Excuse me a moment. I'm really in such a fuddle. I so seldom go to parties."

"What is it?"

"I forgot my champagne."

Freddie smiled and it made my skin crawl. He was just plain evil. I wouldn't have been a bit surprised if his incisors had been prominent and pointed, and there were reddish glints in his eyes, the way they do with the devil in the movies. "*Quelle horreur!*" He joked. "And I know how much you like your champagne. Let me get it for you."

"Do you mind?"

"Not at all. It is my pleasure to look after you. A woman alone."

"Thank you so much, Your Highness. You can't imagine how I appreciate it. As you've discerned, I'm not used to being out by myself— I'm really quite uncomfortable about it. But I certainly don't want to keep you from your wife—I don't want her to get the impression I've commandeered you."

"No. No. She understands perfectly. I insist you call me Freddie— that's what all my friends call me. And I can tell you and I are going to be very good friends."

"All right, Freddie. And you must call me Mandy."

He did a little bow and headed off for the bar. He was the most controlling person I'd ever met. He had the practice of getting very close to you and towering over you and speaking in assumptions and innuendo. He didn't frighten me—I knew exactly how to handle him—but, I could not have felt colder if I'd been standing on the top of Everest in a hundred-mile-an-hour gale.

CHAPTER *37*

I made a beeline for Constance Flynn. She was dressed in a very smart dark red Calvin Klein dress and coat and wore no jewelry except for a string of pearls, pearl earrings, and the Rolex watch.

"Mrs. Flynn." I offered my hand. "Lady Amanda Bonham."

She responded as I knew she would, with warmth and openness. "I'm pleased to meet you, Lady Amanda. I saw you talking to Duchess Mary Margaret. She and Victoria are such lovely women—we're very fortunate and honored to have them here."

I nodded. "We all love them so. But, as you can imagine, the family's not entirely sure what to do about the Duchess. She has quite a lot of spirit."

Constance laughed. "I know. I saw what happened. She looks like a handful."

"Well said."

"This is my friend, Clifton Boatwright."

Clifton was as she'd described him in my office—rumpled and brainy—not hurtful to look at, but certainly no matinee idol. He was relatively tall and had totally white hair and hazel-brown eyes that peered through thick, smudged, black-rimmed glasses. A well-trimmed white beard covered what looked like a strong jaw. The tip of his nose arched slightly over a white mustache. He looked, in fact, quite like Efrem Zimbalist Jr. gone to seed. He was dressed in tan slacks that were stained with a spot or two of old soup or something similar, a dress shirt with a stay in only one collar, so the other curled up a bit, and a tweed sport coat that was missing a woven leather button on its sleeve and had leather patches on the elbows.

He took my hand and kissed it. "Lady Amanda," he said.

"Mr. Boatwright," I replied. "Lovely to meet you."

I recognized him with no trouble at all. The last time I saw him, his eyes were dark blue, his hair brown, and his name was Owen Brace.

Did he recognize me? No. And he wouldn't.

In those dark hours when I'd realized what a total fool I'd been and sat in my bathtub in London and cried and cried and plotted my revenge, I'd also realized he'd never really looked at me in the first place.

And on seeing him now, did I feel any increase of bitterness? Any more anger or vindictiveness? No. I saw him and our affair for what it was—a joke. On me. I'd moved way past Owen and it looked to me as though he hadn't moved at all. He was still trying to get rich quick.

"Here I am, Mandy, back in the nick of time." Freddie handed me a fresh glass of champagne.

"Oh, Freddie," I smiled. "You're such a prince."

We all had a little amusement at my clever play on words. It was all just too, too.

Suddenly, I had a revelation, as though I'd been struck by lightning. I knew Owen better than he'd ever known himself. I saw as clearly as day what he was up to with Constance: he wanted to queer Edgar's air rights deal. By ripping off Ballantine & Company and getting cash back for fakes—which Roman had said totaled twenty million dollars—he'd scraped together a big enough stake to take a shot at leveraging himself into the lucrative, but risky, wireless business, and Freddie's air rights properties were the last big stakehold. Owen was trying to rob the safe in my office not because he wanted to rattle or embarrass me—I hadn't been a factor at all—but because Constance had told him her jewelry was there and he needed the money.

I wanted to burst out laughing. He was so low, he was subterranean.

A woman appeared at Freddie's side. Her softly graying hair—actually, it was hard to tell if it was light silver or blond or a mixture of the two—was pulled into a bun at the crown of her head and she had the sort of high forehead and fine cheekbones that many women would kill for. Her face and eyes had been lifted very skillfully—not so tightly that she was expressionless but tightly enough that she wasn't overly burdened with extra skin or too many wrinkles. She had on a pale tangerine Yves Saint Laurent suit and the most amazing fire opal necklace and earrings I'd ever seen. She put her hand on Vasvar's arm. This would be Freddie's fourth wife, Sylvia, Marchioness of Kennington. One of the ten richest women in Britain. Correction, one of the ten potentially richest women in Britain. Her mother, the inimitable, cane-wielding Duchess Mary Margaret, currently held the rank.

"Oh, my darling," he said with perfect deference but without a scintilla of ardor. "Let me introduce you."

Once the introductions were complete, she said, "Excuse us, will you?" She put her arm through her husband's and began to turn him away to speak to him privately when, suddenly, a piercing taxi whistle cut the air, followed by the sound of clapping.

We all turned to see Edgar balanced on the corner edge of one of the large tree planters—one foot pointed out in one direction, the other pointed in the other in what could have been a sort of Napoleonesque stance if he hadn't been so unsteady. Silence fell. Lauren handed him his glass and then wrapped her arm around his waist in case he toppled from the three-foot height.

"Welcome," he called out. "Welcome to our special family weekend to celebrate the wedding of Countess Alice to my son, William. He's getting a great girl, and she . . . well, she's getting . . . him." He shrugged and laughed at his own joke, his put-down of his son. "What can I say. He's the only son I've got. He'll have to do. And, in case anyone missed her, I want to introduce my beautiful fiancée and your host-ess, Lauren Cambridge. Isn't she a killer? And let me tell you, I'm not kidding when I call her a killer. She's twenty-five years of nothing but energy. She's making me a young man—but I might die from it." He actually snickered. "Well, let's sit down, because"—he looked at his watch—"we start the next cocktail party in five hours! And I don't know about you, but I'm going to want a nap."

He was even sleazier than he looked.

I glanced at Constance, and her cheeks had turned as red as her dress. She was absolutely horrified. "My God," she said to her daugh-ter, "your father has lost his mind."

The girl, a look of incredulity on her face, coughed out a sound between a sob and a laugh and ran off toward the hotel with Con-stance on her tail.

"This family is absolutely appalling," I overheard Marchioness Sylvia muttering behind me. "How could you encourage your daugh-ter to marry into it? I'll never understand you, Freddie—all for money and those ridiculous rubies."

"What am I supposed to do?" He spat back under his breath. "I have to make a living somehow, you emasculating bitch. And the ru-bies are not ridiculous."

But, by then, she'd turned her back on him and headed toward the table where her mother and Victoria were already seated, leaving him the humiliation of speaking to air amidst curious onlookers.

CHAPTER 38

To say the Vasvars had serious issues in their marriage would be severe understatement—they were at war. And knowing what I knew about Vasvar, he was the last person I'd want to provoke. It didn't take a genius to figure out that the minute Duchess Mary Margaret was gone and Sylvia inherited the bulk of her wealth, Sylvia's days would be numbered, probably in single digits, even hours. I wouldn't be surprised to read someday that she'd tripped and fallen right off the cliff, just like Freddie's late valet/accomplice. She was walking around with a giant bull's eye on her back, and I wondered if I should find a way to warn her.

Freddie had recovered his charm by the time I reached the table. His three male cousins, who spoke little English and looked as though they were trying to figure out how to steal the flatware, made up the rest of our party of eight. They banked Duchess Mary Margaret and Victoria, who bellowed to each other as though they were the only two people in the world, like chattering mynahs sharing a branch. The men simply spoke around and over their little gray heads. According to the placecards, one of the cousins was assigned to sit between Sylvia and me, but he either couldn't read, had no manners, or simply didn't want to sit in his assigned place and sat in my spot next to his cousin, leaving Sylvia and me to sit together.

"Alice is such a beautiful young woman," I said once we were settled and bowls of cream of asparagus soup with shavings of white truffle were being placed and our glasses were filled with Italian Chardonnay. "What a lovely bride she'll make."

As far as Sylvia knew, I was attached to the Flynn clan, so she'd never give me any inkling of her true feelings about the Flynns. "Thank you, Lady Amanda. She is a beautiful girl and is very, very excited about Saturday. William is so attractive. Isn't this a perfect day for a luncheon?" She changed the subject. "The weather is ideal. Mr. Flynn seems to enjoy the luck of the Irish."

"He does. What are these darling little things?" In front of each place setting was a white kid coin purse embossed with a gold heart and the names Alice and William entwined in gold print. I unzipped mine and found disks of chocolate inside wrapped to look like gold florins. "Oh, dear," I said. "This is a bit unfortunate."

Sylvia's nostrils flared a notch and she drew in her breath and sat a little straighter. "Mmm," she said.

I couldn't help it. I started laughing and so did she. I could tell she was biting the inside of her top lip to keep it closed. She picked up her spoon. "Doesn't this soup look delicious? The hotel has such a superb chef."

I put my hand near hers. "Marchioness, you don't have to pretend with me. The fact is, Edgar is a despicable and arrogant fool."

She put down the spoon and took a long sip of wine. "Yes. Despicable, arrogant and fool are a start. He's a perfect example of getting what he's wished for. Isn't he?" She raised her eyebrows and her tone was droll and I fell in love with her on the spot. "He got the trophy girlfriend who I suspect is about to run him into the ground. And now, he's about to get involved with the Vasvar family. And, as we all know too well"—she glanced first at Edgar and then at her husband—"nothing is ever as it seems." Her eyes then fell on William and Alice, and she blinked and looked away from them in a resigned, disinterested sort of way. "And those two? I can't even begin to predict what the future holds for them."

"There's no getting around it," I said. "This marriage is just plain business. What happened to love as a reason?"

Sylvia looked me in the eye. "Love was never even invited to the bargaining table in this situation. And please, call me Sylvia."

"Well, Constance is a treasure," I changed tact. "I'm so happy she's finally getting away from him. He's never been good for her. He's never been good for anyone but himself, actually."

"I agree about Constance. I've just met her for the first time today, but she seems an absolute delight."

"May I ask you a question?"

"Yes." The tenor of her voice meant, perhaps. Depending.

"Where is Alice's mother? Isn't she coming to her daughter's wedding?"

"I have no idea." She scanned the table, her eyes falling first to her husband, who was arguing with one of his cousins, then to her mother and Victoria, then to the table next to ours, where more of Vasvar's brutish clan sat, including three jolly, roly-poly women in their forties—identical triplets—dressed in matching orange dresses, looking for all the world like three pumpkin puddings, then to the other guests, who I could tell she didn't care if she ever saw again, and finally back to me. "Have you ever seen a group of people like this in your life?"

"Truthfully? No."

"I haven't either. I hadn't met any of Freddie's family until they started arriving last night and"—she started laughing—"I'm really just stunned. Oh, waiter"—she signaled—"May I have more wine please? Now, where were we? Oh, yes, Alice's mother. I have no idea who or where she is. She is simply not discussed."

In between Sylvia's trips to the ladies room with her mother, our conversation was lively and convivial. It was during one of those absences that I watched William and Roman in the bar tossing down shots—the classic tableau of the best man girding the groom for the ball and chain.

Bottom-line—it didn't make any difference to me how the bride or groom or members of the wedding party felt about each other, or how they would choose to resolve their lives. Their relationships and baggage were just a simple intrigue, an amusing drama, but I wouldn't let them become a distraction. I was there to find the stolen Madonnas and swap the rubies in the parure, and then I was going home to my farm and I wasn't ever going to leave again.

"Sylvia darling," Duchess Mary Margaret said to her daughter when they returned from one of their trips to the loo, "I'd like a Brandy Alexander."

"Me, too," Victoria beamed. "Or maybe a Grasshopper."

"Oh, a Grasshopper sounds wonderful," the duchess agreed. "Very fresh."

I looked at Sylvia. "You have got a lot going on, don't you?"

She laughed and signaled for more wine. "They aren't always this confused, they've just had a little too much champagne. They'll sleep away the afternoon and be like new tonight."

"You're lucky to have them," I said, thinking I, too, would do whatever it took to keep my mother alive if my husband were a sociopathic maniac who was counting the days until he could kill me. I'd keep my mother alive on life support for a hundred years if I were her.

"I don't believe in luck," she said.

Sylvia and I looked in each other's eyes—hers were the color of ice—and I felt a wonderful kinship with her. I also knew that she knew more about her husband than I had originally thought. She had a hold over him and it wasn't just her money. I wondered if she knew where the Madonnas were. And I further wondered if she'd written down their location along with many other incriminating items in a letter which she'd given to her lawyer to be given to the police if anything irregular should happen to her. Like if she were to end up on the lakeside rocks with a broken neck. But the more I got to know her, I wouldn't be surprised if he were the one to stumble and fall.

Aren't appearances wonderful things? An outsider looking at this group assembled to celebrate a wedding weekend would see a convivial gathering, when nothing could be further from the truth. Frankly, it made me glad I didn't have a family of my own.

Coffee and brandy were served. Sylvia drank her first Courvoisier as through it was water and was now on her second, although she didn't seem any the worse for wear.

I looked across the lake. "I'm looking forward to seeing the castello—I understand it's magnificent."

"Well, it would be with an investment of four or five million pounds. Freddie's been working hard to get it in shape for the wedding, but it's a drop in the bucket when you look at the scope of the project and the extent of the decay. Of course, his family's thrilled to be staying there, since there's indoor plumbing."

I started laughing again.

"I've loved meeting you, Amanda, and will see you this evening," Sylvia said as she got to her feet to leave. "I can't recall at the moment which table I seated you at, but I'm quite sure it's Constance's."

"Wonderful," I replied. "What are you going to wear?"

"Villa Crespi is quite dressy—have you been there before?"

"No. I'm looking forward to it."

"It's so ornate you will be bowled over by the décor, and the food is genius. This is Mother's and my party—I felt this weekend should have at least one occasion done with some touch of class, heaven knows what the rest of them will be like. But everything tonight will be perfect. I've made sure of it." She smiled. "I've brought a wonderful orchestra from New York."

A boatman, uniformed in crisp white duck with navy blue piping, helped the older ladies into the Vasvars' motor launch, followed by Freddie, Sylvia, and Alice. Once they were seated, the craft pulled into the lake and powered away.

I was standing next to Constance, waving good-bye, and out of the corner of my eye, as soon as the boat was well offshore, I watched one of the bridesmaids and William disappear into the hotel together. Constance glanced at me, wondering if I'd seen.

"I don't know you, Mrs. Flynn," I said. "But I see what's happening and you can't do anything about it. They have to make their own lives and their own decisions."

She nodded. "He could save himself so much pain if he'd just . . . oh well. Hell." She gathered her purse and shawl. "Will we see you tonight?"

"Indeed." Behind Constance's head, in the windows of a room on the third floor, I saw a man's figure moving and watched the drapes close.

"I'll look forward to it. It's been wonderful meeting you. Have a good nap."

After all the champagne and wine, I longed for that nap all the other guests were about to enjoy, but there were two errands I had to run first. I went up to my room and put a few items in one of my Hermès travel bags, tucked the dog into her travel case, and walked into the main square, a matter of one or two city blocks through a narrow, medieval corridor. The piazza was almost empty but the parfumeria was still open.

"Signora?" The young woman said from behind a glass counter that held dozens of perfumes.

"Sublime, per favore."

I put the expensive little flacon in my pocket and crossed the square to the dock. Only three water taxi drivers were on duty.

"*Dové*, signora?" The driver asked as he helped me into the cruiser, which was as small and elegant as a vintage Chris-Craft.

"Convento di Santa Maria del Lago," I replied.

CHAPTER 39

The convent's dock needed repair. As a matter of fact, after I gave the boatman a large tip to wait, I stepped out of the launch with trepidation, sure the heel of my shoe would poke through the rotten wood. An overgrown stone path led up the steep hillside and it was hard going in my sling-backed, Chanel pumps. Clearly, the convent had had few visitors over the years. As I ascended, I passed through three little terraced areas with stone benches and was tempted to take a quick break and catch my breath. But, the benches were damp and covered with moss, so I pushed on, the dog eagerly pulling ahead on her leash.

After a few minutes, I arrived, completely out of breath, at an ancient stone wall. The wooden gate was new and looked extremely heavy and sturdy. It had a closed grill at eye level. I glanced around at the trees. There was no security system visible, but why would they need one? That would be closing the barn door after the horse was gone. The gate was flat, with no latch or handle. It was, all-in-all, a most unwelcoming welcome. How did you get into this place? Then I saw an opening to my right in the wall, a little cubby hole, where a brick or a stone had been removed. I leaned down and peered in and saw a thin leather thong curled inside, but the opening was dark and damp and, I was sure, filled with deadly spiders. I drew in my breath—if I was meant to die of a spider bite at an Italian convent, well, so be it. I reached in and took hold of the strap and pulled it as hard and as fast as I could and then jumped back to wait. I thought I heard a little tinkle of a bell somewhere behind the wall, but that could have been just wishful thinking. I checked my watch: three-fifty. Shadows had begun to fall across the lake and it was practically dark where I was standing in the overgrowth. I wrapped my shawl around my shoulders and neck and waited. And waited. Nothing. I screwed up my courage and reached into the black hole and tugged the pull again, faster and harder than before. Then, without any warning, the grille opened and I felt rather than saw a pair of eyes staring out at me.

"Si?" a woman's voice said.

"Is Sister Immaculata in?" I asked.

"Who's calling?"

"Her Aunt Amanda. A very cold Aunt Amanda, by the way," I added to inject a little friendliness and levity into the situation.

I could tell that whoever was behind that gate was not amused.

"What's your name?" She was relentless. I thought nuns were supposed to be kind.

"Lady Amanda Bonham."

"Please wait." The grille closed and the silence descended again.

Sometime later—it had grown too shadowy for me to be able to see my watch—a heavy bolt was drawn and the gate swung open easily. A nun, her face void of expression, stood back and indicated I should enter and follow her. We started up the hill and, thankfully, the pathway on this side of the wall had been cleared a bit. She was wearing what looked like a brand new pair of Merrell hiking boots and it was absolute hell for me to keep up with her. Every time I fell behind too much, she would stop and wait with her back to me—a cold, unfeeling monolith—and as terrible as it sounds, I began to understand how easy it might have been to kill them all, if they'd all been this unfriendly.

We emerged from the trees and the convent towered over us, as welcoming as the Great Wall of China. There were bars on most of the windows. Weak light came from a small number on the first floor and from corner windows on the second. I followed her through the ground floor entrance—it was as cold inside the building as it was outside—and up a flight of stairs, through a small reception room dominated by a large crucifix, and into a well-lit office where a fire burned. Sister Immaculata was seated at the desk, a curious expression on her face.

The other nun put fresh logs on the fire.

"May we have some hot cocoa, please, Sister Terese?" Sister Immaculata said.

Sturdy, surly Sister Terese nodded and left without a word.

"Aunt Amanda?" Sister Immaculata said. "I didn't realize I had an Aunt Amanda." She got up from the desk and came over to where two upholstered wing chairs with small footstools were arranged in front of the fire. "Please," she said. "Let's sit here—it's much warmer. Your dog certainly understands."

Bijou had wasted no time in making herself at home on the hearth rug.

I felt a little out of my element in Immaculata's presence. As though I weren't in control. "That's Bijou," I answered.

"She's darling. Now," she said once we were settled. "How can I help you, whoever you are?"

"Sister Immaculata," I said. "I'm not surprised you don't recognize me, but I'm Kick Keswick, from Ballantine and Company."

She leaned toward me a bit and studied my face and hair, her expression serious.

"Would it help if I took the colored contacts out of my eyes?" I asked.

"Probably."

I did so and she nodded. "Now I see a slight similarity. But why are you dressed like this? Why are you here?"

I put the contacts back in before Sister Terese returned. "I'm attending the Vasvar wedding. Posing as Lady Amanda Bonham."

"You're not serious?"

I nodded. "Completely."

"But why?"

"A number of reasons, one of them being the jeweled Madonnas. I told you I would get them back. But I'm going to need your help."

Immaculata clearly couldn't get her mind around what I was saying. "But how? And why the disguise?"

"It's a long story and I won't bore you with it," I answered.

"I have all the time in the world."

"I'm not sure where to begin."

"Wherever you like."

There was a small tap on the door and Sister Terese came in carrying a wooden tray loaded with a white crockery pot, two cocoa cups, a bowl of whipped cream, a bowl of sugar, and a platter of what looked like fresh, chewy macaroons.

The tranquility and, all right, I'll admit it, the trust I felt with Sister Immaculata was unlike anything I'd ever experienced. Between sips of cocoa and bites of cookie, I told her about my life, my life in Oklahoma, how I learned to steal, my subsequent life as the world's greatest jewel thief, and now my life of rehabilitation. I told her I was at the wedding to replace the Vasvar rubles. I told her everything except my suspicions that I may be her mother.

"You're the Shamrock Burglar?" she said with some admiration.

"I am. Or rather, I used to be."

"Oh, my. And your husband is Inspector Emeritus Sir Thomas Curtis? Who is also the Samaritan Burglar?"

"He is and was. Tell me, Sister, how are you so familiar with the Shamrock and Samaritan Burglars—we operated primarily in London."

"I've always been fascinated by that sort of crime. I used to watch all the mysteries on TV—*Masterpiece Theatre, Poirot, Murder She Wrote.* Your exploits were usually reported in *The New York Times*—you were sort of a cult figure."

"I was? In New York?"

She nodded. "It seems that being a successful jewel thief would take such composure, such confidence. I can't even imagine doing such a thing. Well, face it, Kick," she began to giggle, "I *would* never do it. I'm a nun."

"Sister," I said after we'd stopped laughing. "I've never had a helper— I hesitate to call it an accomplice, because that could put you off—but I need your help."

"You need me to help you *steal* something?"

I shook my head. "No. I'd never ask you to steal anything, but I am going to have to ask you to lie."

She bit the side of her lip and stared into the fire. Her expression became worried. "Lie about what?" she finally said.

CHAPTER 40

The engraved invitation was as formal as it could be and had coats of arms blind embossed at the top of the heavy ecru card.

"Dear Lady Amanda," read the accompanying note slipped under my door. "You will be riding to this evening's party at Villa Crespi in Car No. 1 with Miss Lauren Cambridge and Mr. Edgar Flynn. Please be in the hotel lobby no later than seven-forty-five. Your promptness is appreciated. You are seated at table No. 3 with Mrs. Constance Flynn, Mr. Boatwright . . ." and so on and so forth. Signed, Laddie Murphy. She had accommodated the unexpected guest very gracefully.

I hadn't gotten back to my room until almost six o'clock and was completely exhausted, so once I took off my luncheon suit and slipped into my robe, I lay flat on the marble floor (it was heated!) with my feet up on a chair, my arms straight out from my body, and my eyes closed, breathing deeply. After ten minutes in this position, I was revitalized. I bathed, dressed, and at seven-fifty (I felt confident my tardiness of five minutes would more than fall within Laddie's call for promptness), I crossed into the main hotel and descended to the lobby.

"Well, where in the hell is she?" I heard Edgar berating Laddie as I came down the hall. The lobby was filled with dressy party-goers, including the groom, heading for their assigned limos, all of which were lined up in a bottleneck behind Edgar's.

"I'm sure she's on her way, sir. There was no answer in her room." She looked up and saw me. "Oh, here's Lady Amanda now."

"I'm so sorry to be late." I placed my room key on the counter. "I hope I haven't inconvenienced you."

"Not at all." He struggled to be polite. He took my elbow. "Come on. Let's go. Lauren's already in the car."

I looked in my purse. "Oh, dear. My glasses."

"Forget about your glasses."

"Are you quite mad? I'm blind as a bat without them. I can't see to eat. I'll be just a minute." I returned to the desk for my key. Edgar's round face reddened and he looked to be on the verge of an aneurysm, as though he were about to blow his cork. "Mr. Flynn, please go ahead without me. I'll ride in one of the other cars. I insist. You shouldn't be late."

"You mean *later*," he fumed.

"Precisely. Please. I'll see you at the party."

"If you insist."

"I do."

Laddie almost fainted with relief. "Don't worry, Lady Amanda," she said as soon as Edgar was out the door. "Take your time. I'll arrange a car whenever you're ready."

"Thank you so much, dear. I'll just be a moment or two."

I dashed back down the passageway, but instead of returning to my room, I headed up the stairs to the third floor and went down the hall to William's suite. I removed a slip of plastic, similar to a credit card but much more flexible, from my purse and easily opened the door. The safe was located in the same sort of cabinet as it was in my room and I buzzed it open with my scanner. Empty. Well, I knew it wasn't going to be easy, easy, easy to find the rubies, but I had hoped it would. I closed up the safe and quickly sorted through William's bureau drawers, closet, shoes, empty luggage, minibar, toilet kit, and even under his mattress. Nothing. William kept all his possessions—clothes, papers, toiletries—in precise military order, perfectly squared and lined up. It seemed very impersonal and totally controlled, as though he were taking care of the things for someone else.

I checked my watch. I still had three or four minutes before I'd be rudely late. I went down the hall to Edgar and Lauren's suite—two bedrooms opening onto a common living room. One bedroom was Lauren's dressing room and bath and it looked as if it had been tossed by an amateur burglar who was in a hurry. It was chaos—the burrow of an undisciplined child. The beds had been removed and replaced with four commercial hanging racks of clothes—probably a half-million dollars worth of exquisitely handcrafted haute couture pieces, half of which were on the floor or draped across chairs. A dried-out, half-eaten pizza sat on the mantel and a Coke had been spilled on the floor and had begun to congeal into a sticky puddle. Her bathroom had wet towels tossed here and there and her sink was a mess of spilled, scattered, and smeared makeup.

Now, this is the sort of thing that irritates me enormously—the presumption that someone will come along and clean up behind you. It truly makes me indignant. We all need to carry our own water and treat people who work for us—particularly those who do the menial tasks, such as picking up the wet towels or doing our laundry or just generally tidying up after us—with particular respect. Lauren needed someone to head her in the right direction or she was going to end up with a very unhappy, even emptier life than the one she had now. Well, that wasn't my problem.

I gave her room a thorough, professional search. Her safe was empty because she kept her jewelry on her bathroom counter. So what if it got stolen? There was always more in the pipeline. Easy come. Easy go. The safe in the living room was similarly empty. In the master bedroom dressing room and bath, which were Edgar's purview, I found his passport, a huge stack of credit cards, and close to a hundred-thousand euros tucked inside an ingenious pair of fake shoes. But no ruby parure.

I was back in the lobby ten minutes after I'd left.

"Ready?" asked Laddie.

"Ready." I rode the two minutes to Villa Crespl with Roman and two other groomsmen and we only made party small talk. I wanted to tell Roman that I'd talked to Ruth that afternoon and Sir Bertram was feeling hugely better but very much regretting that he'd given Roman the weekend off because he wasn't so much better that his doctors would give him permission to conduct the Saturday night auction.

"He could be weeks from going back to work," Ruth had said. "I think Roman ought to hie his fanny back to London and forget the wedding."

"I agree completely."

"How is your migraine?" she'd asked. Her voice was indifferent, the question perfunctory for an ailing interloper of a boss.

"No better at all. If it's not gone by tomorrow, the doctor's going to put me in hospital."

"I'm terribly sorry," she'd replied, but I could tell she wasn't sorry at all.

CHAPTER 41

Anyone who knows anything about Lago d'Orta knows about Villa Crespi—an over-the-top affair built in the 1870s by a successful cotton trader who had become enthralled with both Baghdad and Moorish Spain. Situated up the hill from the lake in an enormous private park, the hotel's towering minaret is one of Orta's landmarks and the interior is Byzantium gone wild—the intricacy of the painting and décor is dizzying and the colors vibrant and unexpected. The restaurant, owned and operated by Antonio and Cinzia Primatesta, has two Michelin stars. Although I didn't know the exact schedule of events for the wedding weekend, I knew they would all be fancy and that one of the fanciest of them would be held at Villa Crespi. I had picked the perfect outfit.

I looked quite stunning, in a Carmenesque sort of way, if I do say so myself, although I stayed far from going over the top—I was a subtle Infanta. For instance, I hadn't gathered my red hair up into a curly bun anchored with elaborate onyx combs and a large cascade of stiff black lace flowing from a scrolly diamond tiara. And I didn't have a rose between my teeth, or castanets on my fingers, or black kohl around my flashing eyes, but I did have on a strapless, black Spanish lace cocktail dress with a ballerina skirt. Not all the way to the floor, but ankle-length. Perfect for dancing something dressy such as a tango, or a *paso dobles*. A black lace shawl draped around my shoulders was attached to the center of my décolletage with a silk red rose and an art deco diamond brooch—the shawl could double as a mantilla if we were called to midnight Mass—a five-strand diamond choker and diamond earrings.

Sylvia stood in the Villa Crespi entry hall with her mother to greet the late arrivals, of which I was the latest. They were both so poised and regal, either one of them could have easily assumed the throne and run the country without a moment's hesitation.

Sylvia's mother, Duchess Mary Margaret, had on a silvery gray, beaded chiffon gown that complemented her upswept white hair, and a glorious, Belle Epoque *devant de corsage* of diamonds and sapphires draped across her bodice. The center sapphire looked to be about eighteen carats of flawless Kashmir and it matched her eyes. The other four stones, equally blue and graduated smaller in size, were linked with swags of pavé diamonds. Her tiara, earrings, and bracelet made up the balance of the parure. These were serious pieces of jewelry from the Duchess's famous collection, much of which had come to her from her mother, through her cousins, Queens Victoria and Mary.

Sylvia wore a black satin full-length sheath with silver corded binding and three-quarter sleeves and a rolled silver satin portrait collar that served almost as a mirror reflecting her silvery blond hair, her black-lashed ice-blue eyes—I think they were the most extraordinarily colored eyes I'd ever seen—and a mighty diamond necklace of four *rivières* of cushioned-shaped stones slightly graduated in size from the center, with the largest center stone being approximately ten carats and the smallest center stone being seven. No diamond in the necklace, of which there were over two hundred, was smaller than five carats.

By definition, a rivière is a necklace of diamonds of the same cut, typically cushion-shaped, or round, each of which is set distinctly from the other, yet they are hooked directly together, not linked by a tiny chain or another stone. It is an extremely plain, forthright design. This necklace of four rivières was dazzling. Pieces of this magnitude are rare and seldom seen except at private, and typically regal, occasions — it's not the sort of thing you'd wear at a charity ball, for instance. In all my years at Ballantine & Company, a rivière necklace of this significance had never come up for auction.

We greeted each other as though we were old friends, which we weren't, but if this were an honest relationship (which unfortunately, on my part at least, it wasn't) we would become and remain fast friends forever. At the moment, I didn't have the luxury of being myself. I'd never actually had any friends, especially women friends, but if I did, I'd start with women like Sylvia Kennington Vasvar and Constance Flynn. The three of us were kindred spirits — women of the same age. We'd learned the secret: once you've crossed the Rubicon of years, you have power you cannot even imagine. You are bigger than the Universal Mother — you are the woman only a fool would cross because you control the keys to so many different doors that others want to get through: financial doors, doors of social acceptance, doors of ownership and power. You have a lot of open highway ahead, you will be around for years and years to exert your influence. You can make or break lives with a word delivered in the right ear, and people know it.

Nobody says "No" to a woman-of-a-certain-age because they don't know what she'll do. I'd once watched a young flight attendant tell such a woman, who'd gotten up to go to the loo when the seat belt sign was on, to go back to her seat because it was too rough for her to be walking around. (It wasn't — just a few bumps in the road.) And this woman looked at the flight attendant and very calmly said, "I would prefer not to lose control of my bowels in the middle of your cabin." The girl paled and gasped. She was absolutely horrified by the vision of it all. Horrified. No such thing was going to happen on this girl's watch. She did what any sane person would do when faced with a middle-aged woman: she stepped aside.

Sylvia Vasvar, Constance Flynn, and I were such women. We were fearless and unstoppable, and whatever that meant—and it meant different things to different people—was enough to put terror into the hearts of lesser beings.

"You look stunning," Sylvia said. "You'll steal all the husbands!"

"No thank you," I laughed. "I have my hands full with my own. I'm not interested in anyone else's husband or anyone else's problems."

"Oh, my dear," she said. "Husbands and problems. They are synonymous aren't they? There aren't enough hours in the day for that conversation."

"Sylvia," the Duchess interrupted our conversation. "Do you know that my glass is empty?"

"Come, Mummy." Sylvia took her mother's arm. "Let's go to your table, I think Victoria is there, and we'll find you more champagne on the way."

"What a beautiful party. Did you say there would be dancing to-night?"

"Yes, Mummy," I heard her say as they passed into the dining room. "The orchestra from New York."

"Do you think anyone will want to Cha-Cha with me?"

"I think everyone will."

People could say what they wanted about Sylvia, that she was a dabbler, a dilettante, an iceberg; I hadn't seen any of those sides. What I saw was a woman doing her duty to her aging parent, and doing it with grace, class, and true affection. It made me like her even more.

CHAPTER 42

I went the opposite direction, into the tiny bar which was packed with guests, asked for and received a tumbler of Chivas Regal on the rocks—I was frankly champagned out for the day—and went in search of Constance, who I found in the garden talking to Giovanna MacDougal, who looked her wraithlike self in a black Armani column. I must be fair. She was really very beautiful, with her full blond hair tumbling about her face and down her bare back. Her makeup was perfect, as usual—it had to be, to be on television—but thick.

"You've got to tell me, Constance," she was saying, "when is William going to give her the rubies? The suspense is killing all of us."

"I have no idea," Constance answered. She had on a fabulous shocking pink gown and jacket and soft pink pearls (which would have been rare if they hadn't been fake). "You probably know more than I do—all I know for sure is that the wedding is Saturday afternoon and she will be wearing them then. Do you know Lady Amanda Bonham?"

"My pleasure to meet you, Lady Amanda," Giovanna said and bobbed a curtsey.

"And you are?" I answered.

"This is Giovanna MacDougal, from SkyWord," Constance said.

"Ah. Yes. Television." I said it as though it were a new invention. "I know precisely who you are."

Giovanna gave me a friendly, slightly abashed smile. She was completely unaccustomed to someone not knowing who she was but, I will say in her defense, she handled it quite well. She turned back to Constance and pulled out her notepad. "Tell me about your ensemble and these pink pearls—they're exquisite."

"My gown is just vintage Dior, but the necklace and bracelet are gifts from a friend." Constance beamed.

Giovanna raised her eyebrows. "As in *new* friend?"

Constance didn't answer.

"Well, whoever he is, he certainly has beautiful taste," Giovanna said.

"Yes, he does."

The two of them laughed. Not a real laugh, of course. I had the sense that Constance was scarcely able to tolerate Giovanna, while Giovanna had to maintain her solicitous, ingratiating attitude toward Constance. She needed her for information—not just about her divorce and her son's wedding but as a source for parties and galas that Giovanna wasn't at but wanted to hear about. Constance was no naïf in the matter, of course. She'd made full use of Giovanna to get her message out, seldom passing up an opportunity to fan the fire of her messy divorce from Edgar with little digs here and there that Giovanna passed along to her breathless public, even though it was Edgar who was paying Giovanna and SkyWord.

The guests had been warned with a little note in their arrival packets that SkyWord had bought the rights to the weekend, so if a camera or microphone were present, no off-the-record request would be respected. Of course, in my opinion, I was confident Giovanna did not have the slightest clue what the words "off-the-record" meant in the first place. Giovanna was the common conduit—oh, forgive me, did I say "common?"—and her currency hung on her ability to keep her lines of tabloid communication wide open, which meant making nice even with people she loathed.

"I'm very happy for you," she said to Constance. "You've never looked better. But I still don't understand why you're selling all your other jewelry. You have such a wonderful collection and you surely don't need the money."

"Of course I need the money," Constance lashed out, her anger always just scarcely a small scratch away. "He's trying to take everything, and it's taking food out of his own daughter's mouth."

Giovanna and I both kept our faces completely straight. People say stupid things when they're hurting, but in this instance, even Constance, herself, looked sheepish to have said something so self-serving and patently untrue. It was common knowledge that Edgar had already made a gigantic property settlement on her.

"Besides," she rushed to cover the moment, "I'm glad to sell the jewelry—it just brings back unhappy memories. Edgar's the one who wanted the divorce, he wanted a clean break and now, I'm happy to comply. I want to get on with my new life."

"I understand. Well," Giovanna said as she stepped away, "I'd better circulate. See you later."

"Your pearls really are exquisite," I said. "Did Clifton give them to you?"

She put her hand to her throat and took one of the creamy shell pink eighteen-millimeter spheres in her fingers and caressed it. "He got them at a Ballantine auction. Aren't they fabulous?"

"Positively amazing." I nodded. I didn't have the heart to tell her they were synthetic and they didn't come from Ballantine's, which was the whole point, what got me into all this in the first place: our fakes were so good no one could tell them from the real thing.

Owen, hands in his pockets, dressed in a tuxedo that looked as though it had come from the Oxfam shop, slouched up and kissed the back of Constance's neck. It was languid, lingering, and erotic, and in spite of myself, my skin tingled at the memory of his skillful love-making. What a total bastard.

"Lady Amanda," he took my hand and kissed it. "You're looking beautiful this evening."

"Thank you, Mr. Boatwright."

"Please call me Clifton."

What a pretentious creep. Clifton. Why didn't he just call himself "Cliff," as any normal person named Clifton would. And poor Constance—I could have told her everything she needed to know, everything that was in store for her. Poor, poor thing. Well, she was a big girl, she'd figure it out for herself sooner or later; however, judging by the way she responded to his touch, his kiss, the way she melted and leaned into him, the way her breath caught and her lips parted a bit, she was blind with what she thought was love because her body was on fire every second. Although her eyes appeared to be open, they were still closed. There was always time for reality.

And I knew that the way he acted around her, sexy and attentive, was excruciatingly hard for him. He liked younger flesh, and much less of it. At some point he would get sloppy and flame out, cut and run helter-skelter toward his goal without a backward glance, and I would see to it that he would stumble. Owen was like Lauren, Edgar's superstar model: he didn't have the discipline or self-control to hit the long ball in the big leagues.

CHAPTER 43

"I'd be most appreciative if you'd continue your conversation in the dining room." Sylvia glided into our midst. "Chef has knocked himself out, as usual, and once he starts, he's in charge. We don't want anyone to miss a bite. Constance, your table is in the center room where the orchestra is, and Amanda, that's where you're seated, as well."

Owen, Constance, and I joined the others heading through the doors into the Villa's ornate and brightly painted dining rooms. I was seated on one side of Constance and Owen was on the other. He was on his best behavior, giving Constance's fingers little twists and kisses, putting his hand suggestively on her thigh. It really was too much. I wanted to say, Get a room. Take it upstairs.

The dining room looked magical, with white damask-and-lace-covered tables of eight arced around the dance floor. The padded mahogany chair seats matched the rich turquoise and sea foam green walls and the extravagantly swagged iridescent taffeta drapes. The centerpieces were low round glass containers packed with goldenrod-colored roses, four or five dozen, all cut to the same length, their yellow the same color as the room's paneled accents. Soft light flickered from tall candles onto the gleaming crystal and silver, while additional illumination came from a crystal and gold chandelier and wall sconces that reflected off everything, including the over-the-top gold-trimmed, vaulted ceiling. An earthy, erotic scent emanated from a heaping tray of white truffles that sat next to the door. Their fragrance combined with the colorful, unexpected ambiance made the setting feel wild and ripe. Decadent and exotic.

I suddenly missed Thomas so much—this was an evening for lovers. Next fall, during truffle season, we would come to Villa Crespi for a romantic evening of dinner, dancing, Barolo, Barbaresco and tartufi.

A number of couples were already on the floor, including Edgar who was twirling Lauren around like a feather. She was wearing a flaming red chiffon gown with a halter top and flowing skirt, and had on so many big diamonds—necklace, cuffs, hair combs, I didn't see how she could twirl and not get thrown off-balance.

"Clifton," Constance said brightly. "Let's dance."

Owen snorted out a laugh. "I don't dance." His tone was condescending.

"Not at all?"

He looked at Constance as though he'd never seen her before. "Not at all. Don't be ridiculous. But if you'd like to ask someone else, I wouldn't mind."

She was borderline angry. "You're kidding, aren't you? I mean, everyone dances. That's why we're here."

"I don't dance, Constance."

"I see."

The temperature at our table dropped to sub-zero and I wanted to crack my chair over his head. Owen Brace was a wonderful dancer. He didn't want to dance with her because she was his same age and had twenty extra pounds on her. Owen and his nerdy alter ego,

Clifton Boatwright, certainly had one big personality trait in common, and it had to do with excrement.

Constance's eyes filled with tears. Any idiot could see—just by watching Edgar—that dancing had been a big part of their social life. He was really rubbing it in by showing off all his fancy footwork with Lauren, who'd been well-coached in the steps that Constance and her husband had grown up perfecting together. Lauren's feet were barely touching the ground and every now and then she'd look over at Constance and give her a nasty little grin.

Finally, it registered. "I'm just teasing you, darling. I'd love to dance. But I warn you: I'm not good at it."

She looked him straight in the eye. "Good isn't the point."

"I get it," he replied.

The song came to an end not long after they'd begun to waltz, and on their way back to the table Owen tripped and fell and pretended to have hurt his knee. He sat on the floor and keened over himself until a couple of waiters helped him to his feet and held him steady while he hopped back to the table. Constance ordered up an ice bag and an extra chair for him to prop his injured leg on and just generally fawned over him.

"I'm afraid I've split my kneecap," he moaned.

"Oh, I am so sorry," she said, tending to the ice bag. "It's all my fault. I never should have made you dance."

He put his hand under her chin and turned her face to his and gave her his bravest smile. "You did not *make* me dance—I did it willingly and I'll be fine. Really. But I hope you'll understand if I sit out the next few."

Her expression softened. "You are so wonderful, Clifton. I love you so much."

"You're my sweetheart," he said and drew her face down toward his and kissed her lips.

Okay, I'll say it straight out: Owen Brace was a big shit.

CHAPTER 44

The waiters began to place little *amuse bouches* of Antonio's Insalata Caprese on the table, distracting us from Owen's silly knee, which was no more injured than mine.

I'd heard about this delectable creation but never seen anything like it. A chilled crystal tumbler, about the size of a double shot glass, was filled first with mozzarella mousse, topped with a layer of tomato mousse, topped with a layer of basil purée, and finally a fillip of crème fraîche garnished with a tiny basil leaf. In your mouth, it became an airy surprise of perfectly melded flavors.

At the table next to ours, Freddie got up and, after a deep, courtly bow, gallantly helped Duchess Mary Margaret to her feet. He placed her white kid-gloved left hand atop his right hand, as though they were being presented, and led her onto the dance floor, where he nodded to the orchestra leader, who immediately struck up a bell-ringing cha-cha. The two of them were amazing. They cleared the floor. Everyone watched, agog, while they cha-cha, cha-cha-chaed like professionals, and when it was over, they got a standing ovation. He then led her through a beautiful, elegant, faultless Viennese waltz to Strauss's powerful "Blue Danube." All of us knew we were looking at an age and an era to which we wished we could return—if we'd been on the rich end of things, that is. I'm quite certain it wasn't all that great for those less well-to-do. Mary Margaret's face glowed with happiness as Freddie escorted her back to her table. She looked like a girl, and her smile for him was genuine and coquettish as he held out her chair.

"That was *wonderful*," Constance said. "Her eyes are sparkling more than her diamonds. It looks like she may have let him out of her dog-house."

"Well," I said. "For the moment at any rate. As you know, things have a way of changing quickly with the Duchess."

As the next course was served, a bisque of langoustine with saffron and minced coriander with a shaving of truffle on top, and the white wineglasses were filled with a lean, crisp Italian Chardonnay, Freddie and Sylvia went onto the floor. I couldn't say how much champagne it would take to warm Sylvia up in her husband's arms, but she hadn't gotten there yet. They must have been such a striking couple when they met and fell in love; I can only imagine watching them dance when they wanted to be in each other's arms—they were both tall and slim and beyond handsome and beautiful and as graceful as gazelles. But tonight she stood like a statue as he twirled her around the floor in a technically flawless waltz that lacked even a hint of enthusiasm. I'd overheard her saying she was going to leave him after the wedding, but from my perspective, it didn't look like she was going to make it until the end of dinner.

Freddie had only one obligatory dance remaining: Constance, the mother of the groom. She graciously accepted his invitation and he guided her expertly through a long two-step, one of the most challenging dances on the planet, in my book. It's an archaic dance few people know, popularized in the early twentieth century, and to watch a couple perform it properly gives no indication of the skill and concentration required. Its complexity was evidently too much for Lauren, because she and Edgar left the floor. Constance, however, was more than up to the task. She was an excellent dancer and only made one or two minor missteps, but Freddie, who was quite a lot taller, had a very firm grip on her, and was able to power her through with virtually no discernable interruption. She was happy and breathless as he held her chair.

"You will save another for me?" he asked.

"With pleasure." She smiled into his eyes. She couldn't resist sneaking a look at Edgar, who was peeking at her around Lauren's shoulder, being too short to look over it.

"Now." Freddie turned to me and held out his hand. "Lady Amanda, my Mandy. May I have the pleasure?"

"You may," I replied.

Sir Cramner had been an excellent dancer and he'd taught me everything I needed to know: every dance, every step, every innuendo. Thomas was an adequate dancer, but somewhat self-conscious. He knew enough to get around the floor without embarrassing himself completely, most times. But Prince Freddie Vasvar—the sociopathic murderer with the hair transplants—was the finest dancer I'd ever danced with, and I think he felt the same way about me, which didn't make me exactly comfortable in his arms. I hadn't danced with a good dancer in such a long time, and Lady Amanda hadn't danced with anyone for years. I didn't restrain myself from surrendering to him completely and doing my best. We waltzed—I could feel my dress billow about me like Anna's in *The King and I*—and then tangoed.

"I can tell you need this, Mandy," he whispered as he leaned backward and I wrapped my leg around him. "You are like a rose without sun."

My eyes filled with tears. "Don't say such things to me, Freddie. It's not proper."

"I know what you are. I can see it deep in your eyes. You pretend to be so strong but you are so fragile, so vulnerable."

I turned my face from his and didn't answer. After that we just danced, and I knew I'd positioned myself properly: perhaps a little lonely, perhaps a little insecure. Perhaps a little available? Perhaps. It was a dangerous game to play with a dangerous man, but I'd studied the size of his castle from across the lake and there weren't enough hours in my lifetime to search the entire place for the missing jeweled Madonnas. I needed access.

"That's all," I finally said when the tango ended and a foxtrot began and he seemed intent on keeping me as his partner. "I need to catch my breath."

"Until next time, then." His breath was warm on my cheek. "I know your husband has been ill for a long time, and so if there's anything I can do for you, please don't hesitate to let me know. I am at your service. You need someone to care for you for a change—I can tell you're about to buckle under the burden."

"That is very thoughtful of you, Freddie," I answered. "But, truly, I don't need a thing." I picked up my purse and headed for the powder room. As I passed down the hall, I heard a noise coming from the library and peeked in. The room was in shadows and they didn't hear or see me enter.

"What do you mean, you don't know what you did with them?" Sylvia was asking her mother, who was sitting on a love seat, dissolved in tears.

"I, I just can't remember." Mary Margaret wept.

Sylvia took a deep breath and knelt down next to the Duchess. "Now, Mummy," she said slowly. "Let's go back down to the powder room and I bet we'll find them there right where you left them. Come on." She blotted her mother's cheeks with her handkerchief, helped her to her feet, handed her her cane, and the two of them left the room. As they passed me, I realized that Mary Margaret's devant de corsage and bracelets were gone.

"What would I do without you, Sylvie?" the Duchess said.

Oh, poor Sylvia. Poor Mary Margaret. This was terribly, terribly sad. The saying goes that God is no respecter of persons, and no matter how rich or poor we are, sooner or later, unless we die young, we're all going to become elderly and infirm and forgetful. The Duchess knew how fortunate she was to have such an attentive, loving daughter who she could trust completely, and it suddenly crossed my mind: If something happened to Thomas—which based on actuarial tables it probably would before something happened to me— who would take care of me?

Well, that was far, far too depressing a thought for such a gala evening. I powdered my nose and repaired my lipstick there in the dim library light and returned to the table and took a long, bolstering sip of Prinzi Barbaresco, which was as cheering as eating a bowl of ripe, rich, red, chewy cherries.

CHAPTER 45

Sylvia and her mother didn't return from the ladies room for a long time, not until after the main course had been cleared and the glass-domed cheese carts, as big as incubators, were poised to roll in. When they did come back, Mary Margaret was still minus the jewels. Sylvia ordered Brandy Alexanders for her mother and Victoria (who by then had danced with almost every man in the place), and within minutes the two old friends were laughing and talking as though nothing at all were amiss.

The octogenarians weren't the only ones enjoying themselves to the maximum.

"Mommy?" I heard a voice say behind me. "I don't feel very well."

Constance was on her feet as though she'd been shot out of a cannon. Her fifteen-year-old, Katie, who'd been seated with the younger crowd in the next room, had had far too much to drink. I looked up and her eyes were spinning around and her face was gray and damp, and I thought she was going to throw up right there. On me. Constance had her arm around her daughter and had her moved out of the room so fast it was as though they had on roller skates. William followed close behind.

When she returned—Owen, still in pain, had acquired a cane from somewhere and limped out for a cigar with Freddie—she apologized. "This is Katie's first big formal affair where she's been so unsupervised."

"I daresay it's happened to every person in this room, probably at about the same age."

"That's generous of you, Amanda, but, in fact, I'm terribly worried about her." She spread a swath of butter on a bread crust." "Our divorce has been a blow, she's taken it very hard. She and her father have never been that close to start with and now she hates him. She doesn't eat enough to keep a bird alive. I don't know what to do. And I, unfortunately, am eating everything I can get my hands on."

I didn't know what to say—there was nothing I could do. "I'm sorry."

"Forgive me. I lost track of myself for a moment. You're just so easy for me to talk to—like a stranger on a plane. Things aren't as dreary as I've made them sound. Honestly."

Giovanna walked up and sat down in Owen's chair. "Have you heard?" she said as quietly as she could.

"Heard what?" Constance asked.

"Duchess Mary Margaret's jewelry has been stolen."

"You're not serious?"

Giovanna nodded. "They've searched the entire villa. But Sylvia doesn't want the police called because she doesn't want a scandal."

"Oh, that's just terrible. What happened?"

"The Duchess went to the restroom and apparently someone offered to hold onto her necklace and bracelets while she went to the loo, so being the old muddler she is, she took them off and handed them over. And the robber just waltzed out the front door."

A big smile filled Giovanna's face. "This is like a dream."

"What do you mean?"

"Well, face it, Constance, you and Edgar are always good ink, but you can't keep at it twenty-four hours a day—not that I'd want you to—and the rubies will be a romantic, fairy-tale conclusion to the weekend, but between now and then, it's just a merry-go-round of dressed-up drunks. There aren't even any celebrities here—except for Lauren who doesn't have a brain in her head—which in my business equals a lot of dead time unless something breaks out. Which it just did. This is real news."

Constance frowned. "What do you mean, 'real news'?"

"Well, you know. This is a very big story: the Duchess of Kennington's jewelry is stolen practically right off of her in the middle of a dinner dance hosted by her daughter, Sylvia, Marchioness of Kennington. It doesn't get much bigger than this."

"But you said Sylvia didn't want any to-do about it."

Giovanna shook her head. "That doesn't make any difference," she said. "As a professional journalist, I can't respect her wishes. The public needs to know—besides, if the story's made public, it will make it easier for the police to catch the thief."

"Miss MacDougal," I said. "That is simply a load of self-serving hogwash, and you know it. You should be ashamed of yourself."

She gave me a dirty, dismissive look and turned her attention back to Constance, who said, "And, Giovanna, you also aid Sylvia didn't want the police called."

"She meant the local police. I've taken the liberty of calling for outside help."

"What does that mean?" Constance's expression darkened.

"I've been in touch with Inspector Emeritus Sir Thomas Curtis. He used to be at Scotland Yard but now he's the head of the International Anti-terrorism Task Force."

My heart skipped a little beat.

"What are you talking about?" Constance said. "This doesn't have anything to do with terrorism."

"I know, but he's a good friend of mine and he owes me. He'll be here in the morning."

"I'm disappointed in you, Giovanna."

Giovanna prickled visibly. "I don't see why? I mean, I am a reporter."

"You're going to get yourself in trouble one of these days."

"Don't be silly," she stood up. "It's not that big a deal."

CHAPTER 46

"Can you believe your ears?" Constance said to me when Giovanna was gone.

"Yes." I nodded. "I'm not a bit surprised. I'm sorry for Sylvia, though. She needs this like a hole in the head."

"I think the media is disgusting," Constance said. "I've seen a new side of Giovanna tonight."

I refrained from pointing out that it cuts both ways. If you're going to play their game, you're going to get a little on you.

As I said, I wasn't surprised that Giovanna had disrespected Sylvia's wishes, but I was a bit put out she'd gotten hold of Thomas so quickly since I was under the impression he was incommunicado on some super secret mission. Obviously he was back in London waiting for the next thing to happen in his case, or maybe it was already solved. My Thomas. Although he would never admit it, he never could pass up an opportunity to help out in a high-profile case. Plus, he loved

Italy and, as I've mentioned before, I used to be a little concerned that he loved Giovanna a little bit, too. Now I knew he just loved the visibility. But Giovanna—deluded as she was by the power of her own celebrity—thought it was because he loved her.

Constance reached across me and picked up a bottle of wine and refilled her glass. "I cannot wait until this weekend is over. It's even worse than I thought it would be. I'd just like to kill him."

"I can see what you mean."

Edgar and Lauren were having so much fun, I don't think they'd even sat down to eat. They just danced and danced and danced. And laughed and laughed and laughed. Constance couldn't take her eyes off them, eyes that had brimmed with tears since she'd returned from sending Katie back to the hotel. As for myself, I couldn't see how Lauren stomached it. Edgar had changed his shirt three times, due to extreme perspiration. Now, I know that's better than *not* changing his shirt, but I just couldn't see what Constance saw in him that had kept her married to him for so long. There's no accounting for love.

"Forgive me," Constance said. "I don't mean to be rude about the Vasvars. I know you're close to them. But there're just too many negative things going on—starting with the wedding itself. I'm as fed-up with William as I am with his father."

"I have seen happier brides and grooms."

William and Alice were now on the dance floor and, I'll give them credit for trying, they exchanged a word or two and they smiled, but anyone could tell they both wanted to scream.

"Did you know that Edgar was going to announce his engagement this afternoon?"

Constance shook her head. "No. Did you see that ridiculous ring he gave her? You'd think this party was for them. He's acting like a complete idiot."

Well, she was right about that.

"How long have you been married?" Constance took her eyes—I couldn't tell if they were wistful or calculating—off Edgar.

"My whole life, it seems," I tried to make a joke. "You?"

"Thirty-five years. We met in high school. You know how it is when you know everything about someone?"

"Yes," I answered, although I didn't. I even used to think I knew everything about myself, and what folly that has turned out to be.

"What will I do when he wants to come home?" Constance asked rhetorically. "How are we going to put this all behind us?"

Dessert came and went and the dance floor became increasingly filled and the music got quicker and newer and Constance and I were a couple of wallflowers—no one was the slightest bit interested in dancing with either one of us. We watched Freddie dancing with one of the bridesmaids.

"That guy gives me the willies," Constance said.

"Me, too," I said. "I've never been able to figure out why Sylvia married him."

"Well, obviously their marriage isn't long for this world. What happened to Alice's mother, anyhow? Every time I try to find out, there's a big freeze and it's as though I didn't exist. I don't think William even knows."

"I have no idea," I answered, although I had a pretty good hunch. "It's simply never been discussed."

"You English with your cool reserve and stiff upper lips."

"I'm Scottish," I said. "Big difference."

"Whatever."

Freddie escorted the girl back to her table and went outside. The evening was getting drearier by the second.

"Mary Margaret and Victoria are having such a good time with their Brandy Alexanders," I said. "Let's go get our own. If someone wants to dance with one of us, he'll just have to search us out."

"Excellent idea." Constance's entire countenance lifted. "Let's do it."

We picked up our things and went outdoors to the terrace, where a fireplace sent sparks flying into the cool night air. We could see Freddie and Owen walking in the garden shadows, smoking. Constance and I sat on chaises that had warm lap blankets draped across them, and within seconds, I think we must have looked as though we were on a North Atlantic crossing, settled in for a good, cozy visit. Unfortunately, Sylvia appeared out of nowhere. I had no desire to be in the company of both of these ladies at the same time.

"Do you mind if I join you?" She snuggled under the blanket of another chaise, putting me between her and Constance. She seemed a little tipsy, or maybe it was simply exhaustion.

"Heavens, no," I said. "You know you're welcome. This is where the true power center is."

She laid back, caught sight of her husband and Owen silhouetted in the distance, and closed her eyes. "Do you ever feel like you'd like to jump off the roof?"

"Often," Constance laughed. "Daily. Or shoot someone."

"Be my guest—I'll give you my list."

A waiter stepped over to our little huddle. "Marchioness?" he said. "Signoras?"

"I never know what to do about an after-dinner drink," Sylvia said. "What are you going to have?" she asked me.

"I've had my eye on your mother's Brandy Alexander since it arrived. I haven't had one for years but this seems like the right time."

"I agree."

"Me, too," said Constance.

"Bring us doubles," Sylvia told the waiter. *"Molto forte."*

"Prego."

I wondered who would be the first to speak after he left. It was Constance.

"I'm so sorry about your mother, Sylvia."

"Thank you. At least she and Victoria have gone home—that took some doing because they wanted to help the staff search for the missing jewelry. I think they fancy themselves as the Snoop Sisters— if the pieces don't turn up by the luncheon tomorrow, all the guests best be prepared to be frisked! Honestly, they are so funny."

"So you haven't found them yet?" I asked.

"No. And—please forgive me, Constance, because I suspect she is a friend of yours—but did you know that Giovanna MacDougal, the television announcer, had the audacity to call Scotland Yard to report that they'd been stolen?"

Constance nodded. "She told us. And she's not a friend of mine."

The waiter returned with our drinks in chilled stemmed glasses and set his tray on the cocktail table. He pulled out a miniature grater and grated fresh nutmeg on top of them.

"I was shocked when Giovanna said she'd called the police," Constance said. "Especially right after she told me you'd specifically said they shouldn't be called."

"It just upsets me for Mother," Sylvia said after a long sip. "I don't want her badgered by that girl or her fancy detective. My goodness, these drinks are strong."

"And delicious," Constance said.

"Do you think they were really stolen or simply misplaced?" I asked. They were right—the drinks were strong and very delicious. The powerful brandy was tempered with the deep chocolate flavor of the innocent-tasting, but lethal, crème de cacao, a little cream, and the homey taste of fresh nutmeg.

"As awful as it seems, I have a feeling they were, indeed, stolen. There is not an inch of this villa that hasn't been searched. We'll just have to see what develops when the inspector arrives. How's your daughter? She seemed to be in some distress."

"That's putting it mildly," Constance replied. "She was completely drunk. This has just been one hell of a party, hasn't it?" She raised her glass and we all leaned in, clinked, drank deeply, and signaled for a second round. "Your mother gets robbed. My husband makes a total ass of himself. And my lover is surreptitiously putting moves on the bridesmaids."

"How many times have you been married, Constance?" Sylvia asked.

"Just once. How about you?"

"Twice," Sylvia said. "No, maybe three times. I lose track." She laughed. "This drink is getting the best of me, I think. It just seems like I've been married to Freddie twice, he's such a treacherous bastard. I should have listened to my mother that only an idiot would marry a man who's been divorced four times. It's the power of sex. And Constance, if I may give you a little advice, you seem to be caught in its grips. Do whatever you want with Mr. Boatwright, just don't marry him."

"Don't worry," Constance said. "But I am having a wonderful time."

"I remember that giddy blush of love," Sylvia said. "When I get home, I'm going to change the locks and the alarm code on my house. I've simply had enough. Do you know what I mean?"

We all nodded.

There it was: Constance wanted her husband back and Sylvia wanted hers gone. I felt a growing obligation to warn her about her husband's past, but this was neither the time nor the place. Although we were like three strangers-turned-to-confidantes on an ocean liner, she didn't know me from Adam.

The three of us sat happily by the fire, our blankets wrapped around to keep us warm, and visited like old friends. As much as I didn't want to, as we headed into our second double Brandy Alexander, I stopped drinking, even though I knew anything we talked about from then on wouldn't really make any difference, because after the cocktails, wines, and brandies, my new friends were both totally looped. Constance was telling us about her first time of drinking too much—making absolutely no sense at all—when I looked up and there, across the garden like an angel, came Sister Immaculata. She was dressed in winter white slacks, a white long-sleeved blouse, and a white suede vest embroidered with silver thread and trimmed with white mink. They looked so much better on her than they ever would have looked on me. Bijou lunged ahead of her on her leash.

"Mother," she smiled at me. "I can't believe you're still here—I checked at the hotel and they told me where to find you. It's after midnight. I've come to take you home. Actually, by the looks of it, I think I'll take all of you home."

"Mamie, darling," I laughed. "Come meet my friends."

"Oh," said Constance. "Is this your daughter?"

"It is," I answered.

"Why didn't you tell me she was coming?" Sylvia said.

"She looks exactly like you," said Constance.

I scarcely slept a wink, I was so filled with unfamiliar emotions. She had said and done something that touched me so deeply, I couldn't get it out of my mind. It wasn't that her words were unexpected— we'd planned that she would come to Villa Crespi if I wasn't back at the hotel by the time she got there. It was hearing them come out of her mouth that resonated. "Mother," she'd said. "They told me where to find you. It's after midnight. I've come to take you home." Mother. Mother. Mother. It sounded so natural coming out of her mouth. Did she feel it, too? And she'd come to look after me. Did she have any idea what that meant to me? Or did to me? I curled under the covers and held Bijou close, stroking her soft coat, while hot tears slid onto my pillow.

I couldn't wait to see Thomas.

CHAPTER 47

I finally gave up on sleep and called Immaculata at seven o'clock to see if she was awake and wanted breakfast. She had just gotten back from Mass at the tiny Chiusa San Rocco just a block from the hotel.

"I'll be right there," she said.

"What would you like?"

"Vegetable juice and granola with yoghurt, please."

"Any coffee?"

"Please. With milk and sugar."

Well, there was a good indication she wasn't my daughter—I've never had anything as healthy as granola with yoghurt for breakfast in my life. Maybe today was the time to start—maybe I should skip my fresh grapefruit juice, warm pain au chocolat, or baguette with butter and marmalade. I gave it serious consideration and decided I would try the granola another time. Maybe tomorrow. Maybe not. But not today for sure.

When I opened the door, I was struck that even without her habit, Immaculata looked pure and beautiful, so poised and calm. Her hair was blond and short with lots of natural waves and curl and I was surprised at how well she'd applied her makeup. She looked close to glamorous, and I told her so.

"Do you think nuns are born nuns?" she asked. "I was a completely normal girl living a normal girl life before I was called. I used to own so much makeup my bathroom looked like I was one of the Spice Girls!"

We laughed about how well my clothes fit her even though she was significantly slimmer. "I think it's the shoulders," she said. "We both have very broad ones."

"We need them," I answered.

After breakfast, we agreed to get back together at ten o'clock. That would give us plenty of time to go for a walk up to Sacro Monte and still get dressed before the launches left at twelve-thirty for the bridal luncheon at the castello.

I pulled on my walking clothes: a forest green cashmere warm-up suit with black piping and deep, warm pockets in both the jacket and the pants, gold necklace and earrings, comfortable shoes, and went down to the pool area and dock for some morning air fresh off the lake. It had rained during the predawn hours, and although the sun was trying to break through, the air was still chilly and invigorating. Constance's daughter, Katie, was dead asleep on a chaise by the pool, her terry cloth robe wrapped around her from her neck to her ankles. She was the color of dish water. I looked up at the hotel—all the shades were still drawn except hers. Well, I thought, it's possible she could be storing the rubies for her brother, so I took advantage of the opportunity to take a look.

Her room was as immaculate as William's, not a pencil or shoe out of place. Hair ribbons were wound into tight spools on her dressing table and her brush, comb, and hand mirror were arranged neatly alongside them. She had even made her own bed. It took scarcely a second to buzz my way into her safe.

"Oh, my goodness. Will you look at this. This will not do." I removed Duchess Mary Margaret Kennington's missing devant de corsage and bracelets and watched them sparkle merrily in the hushed morning light. What on earth was Katie thinking? She seemed to have come untethered.

I was by no means an expert on the subject, but just judging by her gauntness, I suspected she was exhibiting the signs of a teenage girl whose secure world had just come to an end, typically due to parents who'd separated, divorced, or were just generally at each other's throats. She was searching for control over something. Anything. Unfortunately, food almost always rose to the top of the list in these instances, either under- or over-indulging, because it was the most immediately controllable element in a world where the carpet had been ripped out from under you and everything had spun beyond your grasp. The idea being, I can't control anybody else, but I can control myself. Other self-destructive symptoms can include promiscuity and drug or alcohol abuse, although I thought the reason for her inebriation last night had more to do with lack of food than her desire to drown her troubles. But stealing?

I made myself comfortable in an armchair to await her return, and before long, I heard her key card slide into the lock and the door click open. She didn't see me at first.

"Oh, God," she said aloud to herself. "What time is it?" She picked up the bed table clock and peered at it. "Oh, God, I think I'm going to die." She pulled her robe more tightly around her and flopped onto the bed and moaned. "I'm never drinking anything again as long as I live." Then she opened her eyes and saw me. After a second of confusion, she jumped to her feet. "What are you doing here?"

"I want to talk to you about something, Katie," I said.

"How did you get in?"

"It doesn't matter how I got in."

"What do you want?" She looked as though she might panic and the last thing I needed was an hysterically screaming fifteen-year-old on my hands. She grabbed the phone.

"Hang up the phone, Katie, and calm down." My tone was firm and

I pointed to the chair facing mine. I had laid the devant de corsage and bracelets on the table between the chairs. She put the phone down and burst into tears.

"Oh, God. Oh, God, I'm so sorry." She sat on the side of the bed, her face in her hands. "It's a mortal sin. Father O'Connell will kill me."

"What's going on here?" I asked.

"Oh, I didn't mean to do it. Oh, I'm so sorry. I knew I'd get caught. Please don't tell her, she'll kill me."

"Don't tell who?"

"My mother."

"Tell me exactly what happened. Why did you do this?"

She continued to weep, getting closer and closer to hysteria as teenage girls are wont to do, the idea being that if they wail hard and long and sorrowfully enough, it will all go away.

"Katharine Flynn," my voice was stern. "Get a hold of yourself. This instant. Tears might work with your father or mother, but they won't work with me. Tell me what is going on here. Why do you have the Duchess's jewels?"

She looked up at me, her eyes red, face splotchy, gulping for air, her mind groping for words.

"Don't even think of lying. You tell me the truth and I'll help you. You lie to me, and you and I will sit here in this room until the world famous inspector arrives and I will have him arrest you. And," I glowered. "I will personally tell Father O'Connell not only that you stole the jewels but that you were also dead drunk."

She swallowed. I didn't think her face could get whiter, but it did.

"I stole them for my mother."

"Why?"

"She needs the money."

"I find that hard to believe."

Katie shook her head. "No. It's the truth. My father's broke. And I don't care if he has enough to live on, but my mother doesn't. So I stole the jewelry because the old Duchess doesn't need them, she won't even remember they're gone. She's one of the richest women in the world."

I let her disclosure of her parents' insolvency sink into my brain for a minute. "Let me be sure I understand. Your mother and father are out of money? Broke?"

Katie nodded, and a fresh flood of tears poured down her cheeks.

CHAPTER 48

I got to my feet and went into the bathroom and returned with an icy cold, damp wash cloth and a box of tissues. "Hold this over your face for a minute and you'll feel much better." Katie did as I instructed and when she removed the cold cloth, a little color had returned to her face and she'd calmed down considerably.

"Now," I said, "tell me exactly what happened."

"I don't know what to do to help mother, and when the old woman and I ended up in the powder room at the same time—and I know how bonkers she is—I just decided to take a chance. I mean the jewelry must be worth millions. So I asked her if she would like me to hold onto her things while she went into the loo, and she said what a lovely idea that was and just handed them to me. And I stuffed them in my purse and waited and when she came out of the stall, it was as though she'd never seen me before. She didn't remember anything about it. So I kept them."

"What did you think you were going to do with them?" I said. "Sell them?"

"I have it all figured out. I've read a lot about jewel thieves—there was this one in London, he was called The Shamrock Burglar, and he stole people's jewelry and gave them a bouquet of shamrocks. And," she paused for dramatic effect, "he's never been caught. Isn't that cool?"

Oh, good heavens. "So you thought you'd do the same thing? Give the Duchess some shamrocks? And then what?"

Katie shook her head. "No. I didn't have any flowers or anything like that—I just thought it would be a cool thing to do."

"What did you think you were going to do with the pieces?"

"I was going to take all the stones out of the settings and then sell them to a pawn shop back in Chicago." She said this to me as though I were an imbecile, as though it would be the easiest thing in the world. "I've seen it done on TV a million times. That's how you do it."

"You were going to break up a devant de corsage as historic and significant and magnificent as this?" I picked up the piece and draped it across my hands. "Are you insane?"

There was so much I could tell her, but of course I couldn't tell her anything at all. "What about the platinum setting? And, what about these swags of diamonds?" I was indignant. "What were you going to do with them? What if the police caught you?"

"I don't know. I guess I hadn't gotten that far yet." She started to cry. "I know it was wrong. I'm so sorry. I just don't know what to do to help my mother. My father is a complete shit. I hate his guts. He took all our money to gamble on the air rights buyout and to put on this stupid farce of a wedding that he's blackmailed my poor brother into."

"What do mean 'blackmailed'?"

"I don't know. It's some big secret that my father's always held over William's head. William won't tell me and neither will my mother, but I know he didn't have any choice. We were happy with the way things were and now my father's wrecked our lives. He took out a short-term, second mortgage on our house just to get some operating cash to get the deal done. And I hate that he's marrying this

Lauren person. She's nothing but a mean bitch, after his money. Oh, I hope I get to see her face when she finds out he doesn't have any. And this man my mother's hanging around with—can you believe him? He's a total sleazoid. I don't care how rich he is, he's gross."

She had no idea.

"Whatever the case, Katie. Stealing the Duchess of Kennington's jewels is not the right approach."

"I know it's not. But now what am I going to do? I just want everything back the way it used to be. Please don't tell my parents what I did—they'll kill me."

"I'll handle it for you," I said.

"How? You don't want people to think you took them."

"Don't worry, they won't. I'll see that they get to Inspector Curtis."

"You know him?"

"No. I've never laid eyes on the man in my life. I'll just see to it that he gets them."

"You won't tell him?"

"No. I won't tell him, but when all this weekend is over, I will see to it that you write a letter to Marchioness Sylvia, tell her the truth and apologize."

Katie's relief was palpable. She closed her eyes and nodded her head. "Okay."

I stood up and dropped the corsage and bracelets into my jacket pockets, one of which contained one of my favorite Columbian chocolate-espresso bars. I pulled it out, unwrapped it, and offered her half. "Listen to me, Katie."

She bit into the chocolate.

"There's nothing you can do to help your mother with her money. She's a savvy woman and she'll look after herself and you. And there's nothing you can do to fix your parents' marriage, which I predict will get back on track before you know it. What you can do, though, is start taking proper care of yourself. Start right now with a little breakfast, a long hot shower, get yourself put together in your prettiest dress for the bridal luncheon, put a smile on your face, and act like the lovely young lady I know you are, which will make your mother very proud. And, keep away from the booze."

"Don't worry. I'm never drinking again as long as I live," She shuddered. "Really, Lady Amanda, do you promise you won't tell?"

"Cross my heart and hope to die."

She got up and put her arms around me. She was so thin I could feel her ribs as though they weren't covered with skin. "Thank you so much."

I couldn't prevent myself from stroking her cheek and her hair and looking in her eyes. It seemed a very natural thing to do, very maternal, or in this instance, almost very grandmaternal, if that's a word. "Don't worry, Katie. You are surrounded by friends you don't even know and I'm one of them. Everything is going to be fine. But you can't interfere. Do you understand?"

She nodded. "I guess."

"There is one way you can help me, though."

"What? I'll do anything."

"You don't happen to know where the rubies are, do you?"

There was a long pause, followed by a noisy swallow.

"Do you?"

"It's a secret," she said.

"You owe me this, and it's important that I locate them."

"They're in the safe at my mother's villa."

"Which safe?"

"Do you want me to show you?"

"I do."

"William and I are going there for breakfast at ten."

"I'll drop in."

Speaking of blackmail.

CHAPTER 49

I returned to my room and sat on the balcony and had another cup of café au lait and considered all the things that Katie had told me about her family and their circumstances. I was awed at how they all were maintaining their composure in the face of ruin. They must have ice water in their veins.

Constance was auctioning off her jewelry because she needed the cash. Fine jewelry was always a good investment—it might not gain hugely in value, but it never diminished, either. And she was mistakenly trying to rescue herself by grabbing onto a new lover and a potential new rich husband, but there would be no future for her there.

And, why would Edgar blackmail his own son? Although the possibility of blackmail did answer a few questions about why William seemed always to be simmering at a low boil. This family was in a mess, desperate straits even. There had been a major disconnect somewhere and they were all floundering around, lost at sea, ship-wrecked, because Edgar, the husband and father, had abandoned them. Surely Edgar knew that Lauren would be out the door the second she found out he was broke. Maybe that was why he seemed so giddy all the time—maybe he was just hysterical. It also explained the dozens of credit cards and huge amount of currency hidden in his shoe—he was tapping all available sources of cash, running it all right to the edge of the cliff on a gamble. He had to make this deal work with Freddie or he would be in bankruptcy, just as Freddie had to make the deal work to get his hands on some capital to save his manhood, his castle, and whatever else was important to him.

What neither Edgar nor Freddie knew was that Owen (Clifton Boatwright) was in the same sinking financial boat, and the three of them—losers all—each hoped the other would bail them out. It was a delicious irony. I personally hoped they would all three sink. I just didn't want them to take anyone down with them, particularly my new friends, Sylvia and Constance, and her children.

I was sick at heart for Katie. How sad for her to be caught in such a tawdry, public squabble, seeing her parents and her life on the world's front pages as a laughingstock. It was as though she were trapped in quicksand and she needed some help before she literally vanished.

Katie had also stirred up a number of hidden feelings in me, made me think about choices we make when we're young that we think are irrevocable, and in fact, some of them are. I thought about my own mother, about why I didn't love her or even have any interest in her, and I realized it was because she'd had no idea how to love me, how to show love for her daughter, because she was only an unloved girl herself. I had no idea where she'd come from. I'd never heard her mention her own parents or grandparents or anything about her own childhood. It was as though she arrived in that oil field trailer fully formed and that I'd somehow simply materialized beside her for a short time—really, only fifteen neglected years—before I'd set out to have my own life. The fact was, those few months I'd lived in the Florence Crittenden Home when I was expecting the baby was the first time in my life I'd been clean, well-fed, well-cared-for, been to a doctor, or had my teeth cleaned; the first time any person had shown the slightest interest in me or my well-being. And for me, there'd been no turning back. I was going to have a good life and I knew that by giving up my child, that he or she was going to have a good life, too, because he or she would end up with a mother and father who truly wanted him or her more than anything in the world. I had chosen not to bring my son or daughter into a world of lack and neglect, just as I had chosen not to live my own life in a world of lack or bitterness or dependency.

In a rare moment of self-examination, I saw that this particular trip had become about much more than the Vasvar rubies or the jeweled Madonnas. It had become some sort of a personal journey, hadn't it? A coming to terms with buried elements of my past.

Suddenly, the sun broke through the clouds and reflected off the lake straight into my eyes, bathing me in its clean light. I felt warm. I felt loved. And I felt happy. I finished my Chocolate Jet and stared across the water at the castello on the hill. Boy, it was big.

I turned on every light in the bedroom, of which there were many, including a number of pinprick spotlights in the ceiling. I removed the real Vasvar rubies from their hiding place and poured all the stones—diamonds, rubies, and pearls—from their soft felt bags and briefkes out onto the bed. They were magnificent. The rubies deep and mysterious, particularly the sixty-carat cabochon centerpiece. It seemed to have a living luster, a firelike glow far in its center that beckoned you to fall into its depths. In itself, it wasn't a dangerous, cursed or evil stone, but if your mind tended to think in that direction, it could easily persuade you of its power to do, or die, or kill for it. The diamonds were excellent. I filled my hand with them and let them fall through my fingers onto the silk coverlet like sparkling water—hard, cold, and heartless. I think I've always had my affinity for diamonds because they have no pretense or allegiance—they're beautiful, valuable poker chips that will sparkle as brightly for a saint as for a sinner. The pearls, six dozen of them, were all the same size, and the same light cream color. They overflowed my hand and tumbled onto the bed like a glossy shower of sugared nuggets, the epitome of elegance.

There was a knock at the door. It was Immaculata.

"Ready?" she said.

"Plans have changed," I answered. "Come and see."

Immaculata gasped when she saw the white silk spread strewn with the jewels—the rubies, pearls, and diamonds. The bright lights had turned my bed into a bonfire on a snowy lake.

She and I smiled at each other and I felt that she understood more about me, about why I was the way I was. I came close to telling her right then that I thought I was her mother. But no matter how fascinated I'd become over my journey to self-awareness, that would be too much honesty, and could easily result in much more commitment and entanglement than I had any interest in. Instead, I put a clamp on my emotions and my mouth and handed her a felt bag. "If you'll put the pearls in here—there are seventy-two of them—I'll gather up the rest."

While she picked the pearls out of the stones, which I was quickly and efficiently matching with their individual briefkes, I explained the categories of diamonds, how to tell some of their more obvious differences, and where rubies came from. I also told her about Katie Flynn, the Duchess's devant de corsage, Edgar's blackmailing of his son William, and Edgar Flynn's insolvency and imminent financial collapse.

"Oh, dear," she said. "Why do people with so much make their lives so complicated?"

"Power, influence, control, hubris."

"I'm so glad I've given up all those things."

Could I give up everything for a promise? Not in a million years. I might have been thawing out a little, but I was a long, long way from warm and fuzzy.

I tucked the major rubies, along with a couple of key jeweler's implements—my needle-nosed pliers, all-purpose pick, and powerful magnification glasses—into my purse. The Duchess's jewels, that I'd rescued from Katie's safe, were still close at hand in my pockets in case I had to dispose of them instantly, throw them in the lake or dump them in a potted plant. I restashed the balance of the Vasvar goods—the smaller rubies and diamonds and the pearls—in their secret hiding place.

"Why aren't you taking all of them?" Immaculata asked.

"There won't be time to replace everything. It will take every bit of my skill just to switch the main rubies, which are all anyone will scrutinize anyway. The rest of the stones are quite good, quite valuable, but most of them are just window dressing."

Instead of circling up through Sacro Monte, as we'd intended, to explore a few of the dozens of tiny chapels scattered throughout the grounds, we headed straight to Constance's villa. A brand-new white limestone wall ran along the road. A button and speaker were embedded in the wall at the gate, a gleaming black wrought-iron opus of Rococo gone wild with birds, flowers, fish, and the ubiquitous San Giulio.

I rang the bell.

CHAPTER 50

A houseman in a green-and-gold-striped work apron led us out to the terrace where William and Katie—who seemed to have recovered, those chocolate bars are amazing—had finished their breakfast and were playing Scrabble. They both stood up when we appeared.

"Good morning, Lady Amanda," they said in unison.

"Good morning. William. Katie," I replied. "This is my daughter, Mamie Bonham."

"Miss Bonham," they said, as Immaculata shook hands with them. I watched William's expression. If there were ever an instance of love at first sight, this was it. He couldn't take his eyes off her.

Constance was lying on a chaise with a thick white gooey mask on her face, cucumber slices on her eyes, and an ice bag wrapped around the top of her head. She lifted up one of the slices and looked at me.

"What were we thinking last night?" She groaned and replaced the cucumber disk.

I laughed. "I don't know but I'm certain we solved a lot of problems."

"As you can see, my children have come to view the body."

"What's on for the men today, William?" I asked. "While the ladies are at the castello?"

"Boar hunting."

"Oh, good heavens," Immaculata said. "Surely you can find a better way to pass your day."

"This was my father's idea," William told her.

Immaculata frowned at him. "Isn't this your wedding?"

"You'd think my father was the one getting married," said Katie.

"That's enough Katharine," warned Constance.

"It is my wedding," William replied, a wry grin on his face and a bit of defensiveness in his tone. "And in fact, I enjoy hunting, although I doubt we'll come home with any wild boar today, just judging by the amount of alcohol consumed last night. I don't imagine anyone can focus his eyes or will even load his weapon. We'll just tramp around in the woods for an hour or two to build up our appetites, and then have some Bloody Marys, a large lunch, several bottles of very good wine, come back to the hotel and pass out."

Immaculata laughed delightedly. "Try not to shoot each other."

"You have my word." William looked at his shoes. His cheeks had turned pink.

"Where's Clifton?" I asked.

"In the shower." Constance sat up, laid the cucumbers on a tray, and took a big sip of water. "What can I offer you? Water? Coffee? Hot tea?"

"Hot tea would be lovely," Immaculata answered.

"Water for me, please," I said. "Do you mind if I use your ladies room?"

"Of course not—but go use mine upstairs, the rest of the house is full of people setting up for tonight. My bedroom is on this end."

"I thought you said Clifton was in the shower."

"His rooms are at the opposite end of the house."

"She wants us to think they aren't lovers," Katie said, cynically.

"Katharine, I'm not going to ask you again."

"Sorry. I'll show you where it is, Lady Amanda." Katie indicated I should follow.

The villa and all its furnishings looked brand new—but not high end. It felt more commercial than residential. Like a place that had been built more to lease out than as a Milanese family's weekend re-treat. Or, maybe this was how the family could afford to build its weekend retreat, by building it as a place that had to pay for itself. The floors were a terrazzo compound of mostly tan and brown tones that would show fewer mars and scuffs than anything lighter, such as the white marble that one would expect to see in a villa as externally grand as this. And every wall had a chair-rail, leaving me with the im-pression they expected events, such as banquets and weddings, with lots of people. The Oriental rugs were acceptable, very cleverly made with nice variable colors to show some wear and sun-damage, but they weren't old, or Persian, or Turkish. I knew without examining their undersides that they were brand new and had been made in China. The furnishings were inexpensive, upholstered with spill and stain-resistant fabrics, the plants and flowers all silk, the paintings all reproductions and the wallpaper all washable vinyl.

Let me put it this way—and I know I sound like a snob, which I may or may not be, but the fact remains is that what I am is trained. And when the house and its furnishings were looked at with a dis-cerning, discriminating, trained thief's eye, such as mine—there was virtually nothing worth stealing.

The master bed-sitting room, Constance's quarters, was a lugubri-ous monochromatic chamber of one of my least favorite colors: dreadful and dreary damask rose—a color that can't decide whether it wants to be blue or purple. It's also a color that's often seen in mass-produced fabrics because the dye is very easy to mix—there's really no way you can wreck it. Just a glug of red and a glug of blue and voila! Damask rose. Skimpy taffeta drapes with matching fringe swagged from the windows, two-toned flocked rose paper covered the walls, and a quilted spread covered the gigantic carved pine (stained to look like mahogany) four-poster bed that would have been more at home in the Brontës' English countryside. Some of the lampshades and throw pillows, of which there were dozens, had beaded fringe. The marble mantel and fireplace were fake. Façades.

In the bath, the towels were damask rose as well, which gave me, to use Constance's word, the "willies." Dark-colored linens—particularly bath towels, hand towels, and table napkins—have always been a problem for me because one can't ever be sure they're really clean, since any lipstick smears, soil, or stains of every possible kind are invisible. The tub, sink, bidet, toilet flush, and shower had swan-shaped fixtures in pressed, brushed satin brass—all made in China as well.

"I've never been in a whorehouse," Katie said. "But this is what I think one must look like."

"I've never been in a whorehouse, either, Katie. But I think you're probably right. This is definitely Early Bordello."

We shared a laugh.

"It's in here." She flipped on a light switch and led me into the closet that had a built-in center island surrounded by drawers and a felt-covered top. Constance's clothes were lost in the cavernous space. She'd packed specifically and carefully for the four-day event. Her suitcases were stacked against the wall opposite her dresses, suits, shoes, and gowns.

"Check this out." Katie pushed a little button on the center island and a false panel of drawers popped free to reveal a good-sized safe with an electronic lock and operating instructions taped next to it. "Cool, isn't it?"

"Very cool. Do you know the combination?" The last thing I wanted to do was open the safe in front of her, or even to let her know I was able to get it open.

"I'm not sure I should be doing this," she said.

"Now is definitely not the time to be getting cold feet, and besides, you don't have a lot of choice," I answered. "I'm not going to steal them—or anything else for that matter—I just need to examine them."

She knelt down and then looked up at me. "You can't look," she said. "This is secret."

"Quite right," I answered and moved to the opposite side of the island.

She punched in four numbers, which were probably the same four numbers her mother used for everything. The locking bar whirred back and the door clicked open with a small whish.

Antique velvet boxes, each holding a piece of the parure were stacked on the bottom of the safe, while the Rolex watch, fake pink pearls, four or five other jewelry bags, and a large stack of euros sat on the shelf.

I turned on additional lights and removed the boxes and placed them on the island's felt top. "Keep an eye out, please, Katie. Let me know if anybody's coming." I removed my loupe from my bag and stuck it in my eye.

"Who are you, anyway?"

"That's not important."

She leaned on the door jamb while I examined the pieces closely. I had done an extraordinarily brilliant job of duplicating the real thing. So good in fact, that the more closely I studied the pieces, the more I realized that unless Vasvar had them reappraised, he would never know. And then, if he did, and they were proclaimed to be fakes, it would be between him and Edgar and that might not be such a bad thing.

"What are you doing?" Katie asked.

"Just making sure they're the real thing."

"Why wouldn't they be?"

"It's complicated."

"They're cursed, you know."

"I know."

"Do you believe it?"

"I do." I replaced them and closed the safe.

"Cool."

"Thank you for showing me. We're almost even."

She gave me a grateful smile.

Just then, we heard yelling from the terrace below.

"Oh, no," Katie's face crumpled and she started to cry.

"What is it?" I asked.

"My father. Why doesn't he just leave her alone. Why doesn't he just leave all of us alone?" And with that, she ran into the bathroom and vomited up her breakfast.

Moments later, Constance flew through the door and went to Katie's side. She stroked her daughter's forehead and got her a cold cloth and laid it across her neck while Katie sobbed. Constance murmured comforting words and looked at me, a stricken expression on her face.

"There, there," she said to her daughter. "It's going to be fine."

"No it isn't. It's never going to be fine. I hate him."

"I understand," Constance said. "So do I." She got up and we went and stood by the bedroom window. "Do you see what I mean?" she whispered.

"I do."

"Sometimes I'd just like to kill him."

Down below, in the garden, Immaculata and William came into view, strolling along, having what looked like a serious discussion. She was carrying a flower and he had his hands deep in his pockets. The sun made the lake look as though it were covered in diamonds and gold.

"Have you ever seen a more beautiful couple in your life?" Constance said. "They could almost be brother and sister."

"No."

"They should be the ones getting married." Constance's voice was scarcely audible. "If he were my real son, I would be able to predict with all certainty that he would drop this wedding like a hot rock and propose to your Mamie right on the spot."

"Your 'real' son?" I said. "What does that mean?"

"William's adopted—we've had him since he was two days old. So's Katie. But even so, with adopted children there's no way to predict what might be around the next corner. In many ways, it's like opening a present every day, sometimes it's a good surprise and sometimes it's a bad one, and at the moment, I'm awfully disappointed in him."

I nodded mutely.

CHAPTER 51

"Did you do it?" Immaculata asked as we headed back down to the hotel, referring to swapping the stones.

"No." I shook my head. I still was reeling from the fact that William was adopted. What if *he* were my son? We certainly looked alike. And he was the right age, the same as Immaculata. Maybe I had twins! The ridiculousness of the thought made me start to laugh.

"What's funny?" She asked.

"Life." I smiled over at her. "Life is very funny. I don't know why I'm laughing, I just feel extraordinarily happy. It must be being with you."

"Good. That means I'm doing my job. Salt and light."

"Excuse me?"

Immaculata shook her head. "Nothing. I'll explain it later. I'm curious why you didn't switch the rubies."

"From a strictly practical point of view, I didn't do it because Katie had her eye on me the whole time, but at least I know where they are. I'll do it tonight during the party. What was the shouting match with Edgar about?"

"He told Constance to call off her stumblebum of a lover-boy."

"That's what he said?" I giggled. I don't know. I know it's small, but it gave me a buzz to hear the great Owen Brace, self-styled playboy of the Western world, described as a stumblebum of a lover-boy.

Immaculata nodded. "Along with a few other choice names for him and Constance that I won't repeat. He said that Freddie had called him this morning and told him that he needed to rethink their deal because someone else was interested and was offering more money, and that someone turned out to be Clifton Boatwright."

"That Owen," I said. "He can wreck anything."

"Edgar told her to get him under control or there would be consequences. She laughed and called him a string of unrepeatable names and then he stormed out."

"What was William doing all this time?"

"Just standing there with his arms crossed over his chest. Not in a defensive way, but relaxed. He seemed about to start laughing. Then she went inside and he asked me to go for a walk."

"He looked smitten with you—as though he'd suffered a *coup de foudre*. What did you talk about?" Then I caught myself. "I'm sorry, darling girl. It's absolutely none of my business what you talked about."

"It's all right, Kick. We talked about marriage. I told him my impression was that he was getting married for all the wrong reasons. That I'd never seen a more dispassionate, detached groom in my life. People should get married to bring each other joy, not things. Not business deals. They should get married because they can't imagine their life without the other."

"What did he say?"

"He said I was right but he was trapped."

"Trapped?"

"That's all he said. Then he asked me what I did and I told him I lived a very quiet life and was in the wine business. He asked me if I was happy and naturally I told him I was very happy. Then he asked me if I was married and I told him I was very happily married as well."

"You're not married," I said.

"Of course, I am."

"You are?"

"Yes, Kick. I'm a nun. I'm married to Christ."

"Right."

"And then I told him that no matter how trapped he was, he should not go through with this marriage. That he should let the truth, whatever it was, come out. He said it would hurt a number of people and I told him it might not hurt them as much as they think."

"I wonder what this 'truth' is," I said, "that's so grave he's willing to let his father blackmail him into doing something as drastic as marriage. Did he tell you?"

Immaculata paused a second before answering. "Katie is his daughter."

"Oh, my God."

"It happened when he was in college. The girl wanted to get rid of it and the Flynns told her they'd pay her some exorbitant sum if she'd have the baby and let them adopt it as their own. William doesn't want Katie to know he's her father, but I think it would be better for her if she did. When I was a child, I would have given anything, anything to have known who one of my parents was."

"And now?"

"Now? I'm content. But this is so sad for Katie—maybe he'll listen. He needs help. They all do."

"Did he tell you he's adopted?"

Immaculata nodded. I could tell that the subject was closed.

We passed through the piazza where the stores and restaurants were starting to open and the smell of freshly baked rosemary foccacia wafted from the bakery. The lakeside park already had a handful of seniors under the trees playing chess and others sitting in the sun. We wandered to the lake's edge and stopped. The tower of Castello Vasvar still had a wisp or two of cloud dancing about it.

"Do you have a plan?" Immaculata asked.

"Of course."

She waited in silence for me to keep going.

"If the Madonnas are there, they've been hidden for over fifty years—behind a secret wall or door or staircase that leads to a secret room. The main part of the castello was built in the seventeen hundreds and in those days, secret chambers, passageways, cubbyholes, closets were always included in the plans as places for the owner to hide from attack by brigands or invaders. The Madonnas are somewhere that only Freddie, as the firstborn son, his ancestors, and his dead valet know, or knew, about."

"Does that mean that Alice knows about it since she's Freddie's only child?"

"I seriously doubt it. He's a man of many, many secrets and, like his ancestors, he still needs a cubbyhole to go to ground if the castello is stormed, by the police in this case."

"The place looks huge."

"It is. I've flown over it."

"This is a needle in a haystack." Immaculata sounded skeptical.

"Yes. But it's also a process of elimination." I laughed. "Don't worry, I won't ask you to do anything dangerous."

"You think I'm afraid?" She looked at me. Her eyes were bright and laughing. "I'm not afraid of anything."

I believed her.

"Well, I am," I said, checking my watch. "I'm afraid of being late and having Laddie pop me over the head with her clipboard."

We set off down the narrow alley and walked up the hotel's back steps into the small parking area where we encountered Giovanna's rented, chrome yellow Ferrari, top down, descending the serpentine driveway so fast its tires screeched on the stones. My Thomas was at the wheel. He had a huge smile on his face.

"Speaking of happily married," Immaculata said. "Isn't that your husband?"

"Yes, that is my husband and believe me, he's smiling because of the car, not the girl."

CHAPTER 52

They came to a stop and Giovanna slipped her long legs out of the very low-slung convertible and got easily to her feet. It was taking Thomas longer.

"Good morning, Giovanna," I said. "Just back from Malpensa?"

She pulled off her scarf and glasses and shook out her bright mane of hair. "Good morning, Lady Amanda. Yes, I've collected Chief Inspector Sir Thomas Curtis."

"Added him to your charm bracelet, have you?"

"Hardly." She could scarcely control her disdain.

"Someone got out of the wrong side of the bed this morning," I said.

Thomas had finally managed to fight his way out of the tight, almost ground-level seat, and was taking a second to stretch his back and reach an upright position. I didn't bother to keep my face straight. In fact, I laughed out loud. He gave me a sheepish grin.

"Inspector, I'd like to introduce you to Lady Amanda Bonham."

He did a smart little bow and took my hand. "Lady Amanda."

"Inspector," I replied. "My daughter, Mamie Bonham."

"Oh, for a moment I thought she was your sister."

Ha. Ha. We all had a little laugh.

"And you're here to locate the Duchess's missing jewelry," I said. Thomas nodded.

"Hopefully it won't vex you too terribly much." I put my dark glasses back on. "Giovanna, will we see you at the luncheon then? Have you decided to play by the rules?"

She put her dark glasses back on as well, to hide her anger at the situation and at me for lecturing her the night before. "The Inspector and I are on our way as soon as he gets settled. I guaranteed the Marchioness I would not get near her mother."

"Good. I hope you will respect her wishes. Lovely to meet you, Inspector."

"And you, Lady Amanda."

As Immaculata and I started up the stairs to the lobby, I heard Giovanna say to Thomas under her breath, "Look out for her. She is a complete bitch."

Immaculata and I smiled at each other. "She has no idea," I said.

"No kidding," Immaculata said. "She's definitely never met anyone like you before in her life."

We collected our keys and as we turned from the reception desk, I accidentally tripped on one of the large potted palms, falling into it and practically knocking it over, causing raised eyebrows and alarmed looks from behind the desk.

"I'm so sorry," I said, as I put my arms around the plant and then made sure the pot was secure and steady. "But it, and I, have survived unscathed."

"Are you sure, signora?" the girl asked.

"Si. Si. Tutto va bene. Grazie. Follow me," I said to Immaculata. "This will be fun."

We went through to the back of the lobby, across the passageway to the other building, down the stairs, back outside, circled around, came back up a separate set of stairs—honestly the main entrance to this hotel was like a rabbit warren there were so many ins and outs—and arrived back on the terrace outside the glass-walled lobby where Thomas was checking in. I pulled my cell phone out of my purse and punched in a number.

Thomas studied his phone and the unfamiliar number for a moment before answering. "Curtis here."

"Inspector Curtis," I said. "If you look in the potted palm to your right, there's a surprise waiting for you."

He first spun around to try to locate who was calling and ended up looking directly at Immaculata and me—very mysterious in our large dark glasses. Then he turned and looked into the palm and removed the purloined devant de corsage and bracelets. By the time he looked back at me, I was gone.

"There," I said. "Not too vexing. Your reputation as the world's greatest detective is still intact." Then I hung up.

CHAPTER 53

"Launches for the bridal luncheon will leave the hotel dock promptly at twelve-thirty," Laddie's note read. "Please make every effort to be prompt."

Immaculata and I had to scramble to change clothes, me into a classic sea green gabardine Louis Féraud suit, a wide gold necklace and earrings, and Immaculata into a Nile blue Chanel dress and coat. And, although we got to the dock right on the dot of twelve-thirty, arriving at the same time as Constance and Katie, the four of us were the last to arrive, and had to suffer Laddie's droopy, disappointed, quivery gaze.

The three launches, each able to carry up to fifteen passengers, were decorated festively with Vasvar pennants and swags of colorful bunting. Two were already full of dressy ladies, many chattering away at full volume, others sat quietly and alone, nursing their aching heads from the party the night before. A uniformed stewardess handed 'round flutes of bubbling Asti Spumante and then our little armada set out across the lake to Castello Vasvar.

Immaculata sipped her sparkling wine and studied the cliff-top castle so intently, it was as though she had developed X-ray vision and was looking straight through the stone walls. Katie stood next to her and copied her every move and gesture, enthralled by Immaculata's grace and beauty. I was glad for her—she needed someone to emulate and, at this time in her life, she couldn't possibly find anyone more suitable than Immaculata. Immaculata smiled over at her and then put her arm around her shoulder and gave her a quick squeeze. I watched that special spark of friendship and understanding pass between them as though they were sisters.

Constance was looking the opposite direction, back at her villa.

"Did the men get underway on their hunting excursion?" I asked.

She nodded. I sensed a change in her and I could tell she was crying.

"Did Edgar come back?"

"No." She brushed tears off her cheek. "Clifton and I had a little squabble—just a misunderstanding. Everything's fine, but frankly, I'm getting sick of crying. I don't think, deep down, he's a very nice person, do you?" She looked at me.

"I'm working very hard to keep my mouth closed," I replied.

"All he does is hurt my feelings. I think Sylvia was right when she said I was in lust, not love, or words to that effect."

I nodded. "She could have a point. I'll admit, I've had a similar experience and barely escaped with my life. I found out just in time and believe me, I was so grateful."

"What happened?"

"You know—just the typical humiliation of a playboy pretending to love a woman his same age when all he wants is access to her connections."

"Well, I'm safe on that count, at least. I don't have any connections, unless he's interested in the Chicago Garden Club."

I didn't answer. Love blinds us to the obvious.

"What did you think of the villa?" she asked.

"I think it's gorgeous," I lied easily.

Constance looked at me over the tops of her glasses. "You're joking, right?"

"Well," I laughed. "What do you expect me to say? That it's a nightmare? A bordello? A banquet hall? That they should be paying you to stay there, not the other way around?"

"Yes," she grinned. "Something like that. I almost died when I walked through the door for the first time. My first thought was, 'I'm paying all this money for this? It's a giant whorehouse.' And that bedroom, dear God. I thought maybe if I moved to a different room I wouldn't feel like I was sleeping in a funeral parlor. But they're all that bad. And they're all the same ghastly color. Well, I have no interest in redecorating the whole place but I hope the rehearsal dinner tonight will be fun, especially with William giving her the rubies. I'll be so glad to get those damned things out of my house. But it should add a little zip to the evening, which, by the way, will be very, very casual. Rehearsal dinners are generally more fun than the wedding, everyone's excited and relaxed and has lots of funny toasts. But I'm not so sure about this one."

"I'm sure it'll be fine."

"I wanted to make it white tie but Clifton balked at wearing tails to two events, so it's just coat-and-tie for the men, cocktail dresses for the ladies."

"What did William want it to be?"

"William wants it to be over."

"Do you think he's going to go through with it?"

"Of course he is. It's business. That's all he cares about."

"Business and his sister, Katie," I added.

Constance kept her eyes on the shore. "Yes," she replied evenly. "And Katie."

CHAPTER 54

The crossing took less than ten minutes, but the castle's dock was only large enough to accommodate one boat at a time, so we waddled around in the water while the first two launches unloaded. There was no visible sign of security or surveillance—video or otherwise—anywhere. An ancient elevator ran up the cliff behind a stone escarpment off to the side, and was for the most part hidden from view of the water. The ornate cage was glassed-in and large enough to carry ten or twelve people. It moved at a stately pace up the rocky face with its first load of bedazzled guests.

"I've never seen anything like that elevator," someone said. "It looks like the one at the Tour Eiffel."

"I heard it was designed by Mr. Eiffel, himself," another person commented.

"I believe it."

As I studied the cliff, steep narrow stairs, carved into the stone, became visible. But, from where I stood, one would have to be very, very sure-footed, practically a mountain goat, and not at all acrophobic, to use them.

I turned my attention to the boathouse, which was set into the base of the cliff and approximately the size of a big and unfriendly barn. Like the castello, it was built completely from hewn blocks of gray granite with walls two feet thick and windows covered with iron bars. Streaks of rust darkened the stone beneath them. The opening for the boats gaped like a black hole, as though everything that entered there would be swallowed up forever. Even the sparkling water turned black and ominous where it disappeared into the grotto.

"What do you think?" Immaculata asked me, our voices obscured by the low rumble of the big diesel engines.

"Let's start there."

Dock hands helped us ashore. I spoke to my helper in Italian, perhaps a hint of desperation in my voice. "Is there a ladies room in the boathouse?"

"Yes, signora."

"Oh, bene. Bene," I sighed. "Immaculata, come with me."

He wouldn't dream of stopping us.

Just as we wouldn't dream of using what he had actually directed us to as a ladies room—nothing more than a hole in the floor that went directly into the lake.

"Stay here." I left Immaculata shivering in the shade in the massive watery room, which had two pristine launches tied in their slips, and ascended to the second floor, where a row of windows looked out on the dark water below. The stairs were slippery and had no railing and when I was halfway up, a bird of some sort—I convinced myself it could not possibly be a bat—picked that moment to fly from the dank eaves, flapping past my face and practically giving me a heart attack. Finally, I reached the solid metal door, which was secured with two fairly new industrial locks. I pulled the lock-picking sticks out of my purse. "Are you all right down there?" I called to Immaculata.

"Fine. Be careful."

It didn't take but a second to jimmy them open. I stepped into the room and closed the door behind me. Weak, wobbly light reflecting off the water below came though windows that had gone opaque from decades of not being washed. I seemed to be in a marine storage room, with spare boat parts, a row boat upside down on a pair of saw-horses, its keel half sanded, and shelves and shelves of paint, and rot-ted and decomposed cardboard boxes of mechanical and electrical supplies, all in a terrific jumble. How anybody could ever find anything in here I couldn't imagine. But maybe that was the point of this musty abandoned place.

I had no way of knowing how deep the room was, how far it went into the bedrock that backed it. I started pushing on the shelves and supports to see if anything clicked, revealing a secret safe or chamber that might possibly be the hiding place for the Madonnas. I switched on my miniflashlight and moved paint cans and boxes to see if I could spot any small telltale electronic glow that would indi-cate a lock. And then I saw it, a slightly larger opening between two slats of wood that could mean they were the edge of a door of some sort. I pushed and heard the soft sound of a small click and a whole section of the wall began to open. My heart pounded in my ears and I listened intently for Immaculata to sound the alarm for me to re-turn. I took a tentative step into the blackness beyond, not wanting to touch the wall to search for a light switch. The air was dank and musty. Icy cold and dead. I put my hand out toward the wall when suddenly a spider skidded down the side of my forehead and I basi-cally jumped out of my skin. I backed out so fast, it was as though I'd been yanked by an elastic band around my waist. Gasping for air, I pushed the shelves back into place and then heard Immaculata's voice from below. I spun toward the window, my hand over my mouth to keep the scream from coming out. It was Constance and Katie.

"Mummy." She rapped on the closed door with the chipped and dirty paint that led into the closet with the hole in the floor. "We'll meet you outside. It's freezing in here."

"Good idea." Constance shivered and out they went into the sun-shine while I made my way as quickly as I safely could down the slick stone steps and out to the dock.

"Are you all right, Amanda?" Constance asked.

I don't think I'd taken a proper breath for at least four minutes. "Yes, why?" I asked weakly.

"You look as though you've seen a ghost. You're white as a sheet."

"Oh, it's the Brandy Alexanders and the boat ride—I'm a bit under the weather, after all." I tried to make a joke, but even so, my heart was pounding so hard I felt it was going to render me deaf.

"Here, Mummy." Immaculata put her arm around me and led me to a bench. "Sit down and catch your breath."

Her simple, loving gesture had the effect of calming me quickly, as though someone had draped a blanket around my shoulders after an accident. Her eyes searched my face with concern and she put her hand on my cheek. "Are you okay?" she whispered.

I nodded and sat up straight and drew in a deep breath. "I'm fine. Just some sort of a small spell." I opened my purse and took out my compact. "A little fresh lipstick and I'll be one-hundred-percent. Oh, good grief, I do look a little shock-y, don't I?" I laughed. What an understatement—I didn't just look as though I'd seen a ghost, I looked like one myself.

Constance and Katie stood a few feet away, concern on their faces, as well.

"Did you find anything?" Immaculata whispered.

"Something. I'm not sure what, but it might be his hiding place," I answered and dusted on a little more blusher. "There!" I said brightly as I got to my feet. "Nothing that a great deal of straight vodka or good champagne won't fix."

As we crossed the dock toward the elevator, the nose of a fast-moving speedboat—driven by a jaunty young man in a captain's hat—suddenly appeared out of nowhere, roaring straight at us. At the last minute, he carved a noisy, showy, arcing turn—showering us in the spray—and came to a skillfully aimed dead halt at the dock. The craft carried only one passenger, who evidently considered herself far too important to ride in the launch with the rest of us.

"Oh, dear," Constance muttered under her breath. "The dreaded Lauren."

We all choked back a laugh.

"Don't go anywhere, amore," Lauren told the boat's captain. "I'll be right back. Oh, hello!" She gushed to the four of us as the mate helped her ashore. "I can't be too terribly late, *if you're* still down here." She looked at Constance. "I've just been so busy helping Edgar with the wedding plans. He really is quite lost without me. Is that the lift?" She dismissed us as her long legs loped across the dock and I could tell she had every intention of leaving us behind and making a grand solo entrance.

I may not have the fitness or the stride of a twenty-five-year-old supermodel, but I am older and wiser. I stuck out my cane and made her trip and fall, and I am further pleased to report that she got a large splinter in her knee and snapped the very high heel off one of her very large Jimmy Choo shoes.

CHAPTER 55

I have no pride in admitting that, left to my own devices, I would have left Lauren there screaming in indignation and pain, but Immaculata's immaculate presence carried a heavy conviction, so, in spite of myself, I said,

"Oh, my dear. I am so terribly sorry. Are you all right?" And I offered my hand to help her up.

"You tripped me, you old bag," she howled, holding her knee. Her face had lost all its beauty and become red and angry—just like all the rest of ours would in the same circumstance.

"Don't be ridiculous. I would never do such a thing. I'm just as clumsy as an ox with this thing." I wielded my cane in her face. "Here, please let me help you."

This time—after removing the splinter—she took my offered hand, got to her feet, and hobbled onto the lift with Immaculata, Constance, Katie, and me—the enemy camp—for a long, silent ride to the top. Lauren kept her back to us and faced the doors. She took out her cell phone and called her agent.

"I don't think I can do the op," she said, choking back tears. "I've fallen and my leg's bleeding quite badly." While she spoke, sniffling continuously in a most unladylike manner, she took off her other sandal and dropped them both by her feet, and then proceeded to fuss with her foundations, her dress, and her bleeding knee. "How did I do it?" she asked. "Well, there are a lot of old people in this group—I tripped over someone's cane." There was a pause. "Yes!" She laughed. "I said cane! There are people here with canes! Oh, God. It's too much. How's Edgar? He's divine. He's as anxious to get the hell out of here as I am."

I watched a slight smile pass between mother and daughter and I knew they were wondering what the scene would be like when she found out that Edgar was broke.

"Got to go. We're at the top."

Lauren picked up her sandals and hung them from one finger and held them in the air as she minced onto the wide, gently sloping lawn. Giovanna and her crew stepped out of the shadows to greet her.

"What happened?" Giovanna asked as the photographers clicked madly away.

"Oh, nothing. I tripped and fell and snapped off my heel. Nothing could make me miss this party!" She flashed her famous smile and twirled for the cameras and displayed her bloody knee.

"Honestly," Giovanna said. "You are such a sport, Lauren. Most girls in your position would have had a tantrum."

"You know, in spite of what everyone says, I'm really not a high-maintenance person."

"Where do I throw up?" Constance said to me.

Thirty seconds later, when the photo op was over, she got back into the lift and returned to the dock. We watched her speedboat pull away.

"Welcome to the family. So, so lovely to see you, too," Katie said in a fake English accent to the vanishing craft. "Bitch."

Now that Lauren was gone, Giovanna approached us. "Constance," she said, signaling her crew to turn off their cameras. "What happened to you? You're soaking wet."

"Just a little boating accident."

"Well, I don't think you want me filming you like this, do you?"

"No. I don't."

"Didn't think so. Come on boys, let's go see what Sir Tom's up to." Without another look at the four of us, she signaled her crew to follow and they traipsed across the grass and vanished through gigantic, rusty wrought-iron gates in the castle wall.

Sir Tom? Sir Tom? Her presumption almost made me choke and I had to remind myself that Kick Keswick might be married to 'Sir Tom,' but Lady Amanda Bonham didn't give two hoots about him. Immaculata looked at me and rolled her eyes.

Constance took out her mirror and examined her hair.

"She's just being mean," I told her. "You look beautiful. Your dress got a little misted, that's all."

"Are you sure?"

"I promise. You look just right. Truly. Honestly, these girls have such a mean streak, I've never seen anything like it."

"It'll catch up with them one day," Immaculata said.

"I hope you're right and I hope I'm there to see it," Constance grumped and looked at me, her eyes still slightly red-rimmed from her earlier cry. "Are you sure I look all right?"

"Yes. Your suit looks fine but you'll want to keep on your dark glasses until you get your makeup properly repaired."

"Thanks," she said, grateful for my candor.

Inside the gates, in a rectangular courtyard almost the size of a soccer green, the guests had gathered beneath a big white tent. At the far end of the courtyard, behind some white screens, was a bank of chemical toilets. Clearly Freddie didn't want anyone in his house overburdening his ancient plumbing. On top of that, two entire sides of the building were hidden behind scaffolding and sheeting, signaling a massive restoration project, paid for, no doubt—for another day or two, if he was lucky—by Sylvia.

I knew Immaculata and I were thinking the same thing: upon seeing the actual scale of the castle, the amount of construction and restoration, and the fact that we were expected to stay outside, this was now, most definitely, a needle in a haystack.

"Oh, dear," I said under my breath. "None of this construction was happening when I flew over two weeks ago. This is not going to be easy."

Freddie stood beneath the edge of the tent to greet the guests, some of whom were dressed to the nines in the latest things, while others were swathed in challis shawls and babushkas. The few men who were there, primarily Freddie's murderous cousins from the old country, had already wiped out the hors d'oeuvre table and were now eyeing the luncheon buffet—two long tables practically sagging under their load of plastic wrap-covered bowls and covered chaffing dishes, a gastronomic medley of every possible incarnation of turnips and potatoes.

"Mandy, Mandy." Freddie took my hand and kissed it. "Welcome to Castello Vasvar. Who is this lovely young lady?"

"Prince Vasvar, may I present my daughter, Mamie Bonham."

"I am honored." He bowed. "Please call me Freddie."

Immaculata smiled guilelessly into his eyes. She was a worthy and able adversary to this man. If Sister Luke—Audrey Hepburn—had stared down the lunatic Arch-Angel with the same cool gaze, it would have saved her a lot of pain and heartache and punishment.

"Freddie," I said. "I was so looking forward to a tour of the castello. Does this," I indicated the tent and scaffolding with my hand, "mean we can't go in?"

He shook his head with disgust. "You cannot imagine how sorry and embarrassed I am by this . . . this eyesore. It was all supposed to be done in time for the wedding and it's just been one disaster after another."

"You mean the wedding will be outside?"

He shook his head. "No. No. It will be in the family chapel and the wedding dinner will be in the great hall, but my household staff needed today to get things in order."

His household staff, my foot. It didn't take a genius to see that the place was falling into the ground—and had been for some time—and it was common knowledge that Freddie didn't have two cents to his name. I would have wagered that his household staff was down to one or two ancient family retainers left over from his parents' time, who needed someone to look after them rather than vice versa.

"You have my complete sympathy," I said. "I've just finished a full restoration of Bonham Hall. It was a nightmare. All one can do is drink and smile and keep signing the checks!"

"Indeed!"

Katie took Immaculata's hand. "Mamie," she said. "Do you want to see something cool?"

"Always."

"Come here, let me show you." She led Immaculata off toward a pile of rocks.

I made a beeline for the bar.

CHAPTER 56

"Signora?" The bartender said.

"Double vodka, please, with a splash of Campari and lemon." I was still feeling a few aftershocks from my encounter with the spider in the secret room and knew the vodka would knock them out once and for all. Although brandy is customarily called for in a situation such as this sort of traumatic shock, a snifter of brandy as a pre-luncheon cocktail seemed a little extreme.

"Si, signora."

"Lady Amanda Abernathy, is it?" Thomas stepped up next to me.

"Bonham. Lady Amanda Bonham."

"I'll have whatever the lady is having," he said to the bartender.

"So, Inspector," I said after a bracing gulp. "Any success?"

"Hmmm," he nodded. "I've made some headway. Tell me," his expression was wry, "which side of the family are you friends with? The bride? The groom?"

"Both, actually," I answered as Sylvia stepped into view.

"Amanda," she beamed. "I'm so glad you're here." We kissed each other's cheeks. "Do you feel as ungodly as I do this morning?"

"I do. It's all your mother's fault, giving us the idea of the Brandy Alexanders."

"I agree. I blame everything possible on my mother. She and Victoria have been up since dawn drawing up a list of suspects. Sir Thomas, you've met Lady Amanda?"

"I have."

Just then, the tip of Duchess Mary Margaret's cane flew into sight, smacking smartly against Thomas's upper arm, followed immediately by the appearance of the two octogenarians, both dressed in pastel with thick white cardigan sweaters secured by jeweled chains draped over their shoulders, and dark glasses over their eyes. "Inspector," she commanded in her booming voice. "I've had another thought."

"Yes, your grace," Thomas said as graciously as he could as he massaged his bruised bicep. "What is it?"

"You aren't having pepper in that drink are you? Well, don't give me a sip. My doctor says no pepper—it irritates my bowels enormously. And Victoria can't have any seeds whatsoever."

"I'm sorry to hear that, your grace."

"Speak up, sir. Don't mumble."

"Forgive me, your grace." Thomas struggled not to burst out laughing. "Would you like one? It has no pepper whatsoever," he bellowed.

"What is it?"

"Vodka and Campari."

"How much vodka?" Mary Margaret asked.

"Well, this one has a double shot, but I know he can make it for you with less, if you like."

"What do you take us for? Ninnies?" Mary Margaret scolded and then looked at Victoria who nodded.

"We'll each have one," she commanded. "Make them doubles and no pepper. And no lemon slices. Lemon irritates Victoria's esophagus and the doctor has taken her off seeds altogether." She leaned toward us and whispered loudly behind her white-gloved hand. "Bowels," she said. "Frightful."

We watched them, drinks in hand, toddle their way across the uneven ground, which may have been lawn at one time in the family's heyday, but was now a lumpy field where what remained of the grass had been mowed to stubble.

"Marchioness," Thomas said to Sylvia. "If I may have a moment of your time. There's something I'd like to discuss with you privately."

"Of course, Inspector. Oh, dear, give me a moment, will you?" She set off to right Victoria, who'd caught her foot in a hole.

I took advantage of our seconds together to pass along a little information to Thomas. "There's much more going on than the jewelry. I wouldn't give it back yet if I were you."

He studied my face and we both worked not to smile at each other. "All right," he said. "I'll look forward to your brief." Sylvia was on her way back. "Incidentally, I like you as a green-eyed redhead."

"Room twenty. Villa Gippini." I tapped his arm with my cane. "Knock three times."

CHAPTER 57

I took my drink and went back through the mighty gates in the castle wall to a circular observation area edged with a stone barrier designed to keep people from tumbling down the cliff, although most of the mortar between the rocks was crumbling and the balance of the rim was completely unsecured. The view was beautiful but that's not why I was there. I was counting on Freddie to appear beside me, particularly now that I'd told him I'd restored Bonham Hall, and he knew his access to Sylvia's checkbook was limited if not already suspended. I also knew he was a man with a romantic, emotional, violent, and ultimately deadly temperament who was drawn to drama. While I waited, I tried to work up a few tears, but they come hard to me. Instead, I took my Sublime perfume-drenched, lacy hankie out of my purse and daubed my eyes.

It didn't take long.

"Women have such a terrible time controlling their emotions, don't they?" he said.

"It's not what you think."

"What is it then, cara?"

"May I speak honestly to you, Freddie? I don't know why, but I feel as though I can trust you."

"I feel the same affinity to you, Mandy. What do they call it when you meet a person you feel instantly close to?"

"Serendipity?" I sniffled a bit and patted my nose, letting the perfume from the hankie waft a bit more.

"Yes? Serendipity with perhaps a little fate, as well. You know you can trust me. Tell me, what's on your mind?"

I turned my back to him and gazed mournfully out over the lake.

Used on the right audience, self-pity is one of the most powerful manipulative tools in the human lexicon, and I was banking on it to help me achieve my ends.

"Sometimes I feel as though I'm going to vanish and my life never will have started at all. I look around at all your wonderful family, your beautiful daughter and her fiancé, and then I look at my life. Sometimes I think if I were to drop dead, no one would even know I was gone."

"What a terrible thing to say. What about your husband? And your daughter?"

"Mamie loves me, of course. But she's making her own life here in Italy—oh, what I'd give to be able to spend more time with her. And my husband?" I shook my head. "My husband hasn't been out of a wheelchair in twenty years. He's wasted and bitter and no longer capable of love. All he has is need. But this . . ." I tilted my face to the sun and turned back to face him. "I feel as though I haven't been in the sun for decades. This is divine. Do you have any idea how lucky you are to live in a place with so much sunshine?"

"You are welcome in my home any time. It must be hard for a woman of your passionate temperament to be hidden away in a dark castle in Scotland—you should be here with someone to care for you. Women are such helpless creatures."

"You mean trade one equally dark castle for another?" I teased. "No thank you."

"Castello Vasvar is anything but dark."

I regarded the looming, gray fortress. "I'm sorry, Freddie. I've been in a lot of castles, and I can tell by looking at yours that it is as dark inside as it is threatening outside."

"That is not true at all—my castle is filled with sunlight."

"If you say so. I'll just have to take your word for it."

"Come," he took my arm. "I'll show you."

"Really?" I said. "I thought you didn't want people inside."

"It's my house; I'll invite in whoever I choose."

"Well, from a practical point, I'd be very interested to see your restoration protocol—there are so many different methods." I freed my arm from his hand. "I'll make my own way, though, thank you. Give me a minute to tell Sylvia where I'm going—I don't want her to think I'm sneaking off with her husband."

"Believe me, she would not care."

"I would care. I'll be right back." I found Sylvia still enmeshed with her mother and Victoria and Thomas. "Freddie has invited me on a tour of the castello," I told her. "Do you mind?"

"Not even slightly. Don't worry, he'll be a complete gentleman. I guarantee it."

"Back shortly," I said, glancing at Thomas.

I crossed the lawn and followed Freddie through a small side door into a mud room and then the kitchen, which was essentially a spectacular museum of late nineteenth- and early twentieth-century appliances. There were three huge stoves, which had been converted from wood or coal to gas, with multiple burners and vast cooktops, and a variety of oven sizes, some small, for just a single batch of rolls, and others with doors wide enough to accommodate a side of beef. There were two kitchen sinks as big and deep as washtubs. Ancient, wooden-door iceboxes had been converted to electric refrigerators, as indicated by thick, scary-looking electrical cords that looked as though they could and would explode into flame at any second. Glass-fronted cabinets jammed with stacks and stacks of plates and

rows and rows of glasses surrounded the room. A modern drip coffeepot, a chrome-sided toaster, a toaster oven, a microwave, and a
television set with rabbit ears sat together on a small part of a counter.
They looked so out-of-place, they could have been dropped from the
moon. Boxes of dry cereal and microwave popcorn were visible in
the cabinet above them.

"The kitchen," Freddie explained.

"Really," I said. "Doesn't look as though it gets used much."

"Sylvia and her mother prefer to go to the hotel for their meals."

"Can't say as I blame them—it would take a modern cook a year
to make a proper dinner with this equipment. If *I* were restoring your
house, I'd start here."

"You like to cook?" His voice was filled with hope.

"Positively thrive on it. If it weren't for cooking for Wynn all these
years, I would have lost my mind, although he can't eat much more
than a little broth now and then. My poor darling, I don't think he's
going to be with me much longer. Oh, and just look at all the sunlight
in here," I enthused. "This could be a wonderful, wonderful kitchen."

He laid his hand on my shoulder and drew his face near mine as
though he were going to kiss me. "My poor, poor Mandy."

I put my hand on his chest and pushed him away. "Don't be presumptuous. If there're two things I will not tolerate, they're kindness
and pity. Now, show me the rest. I want to see everything."

"I've learned never to argue with a woman with a cane," he said
good-naturedly.

We passed through the dining room and into the great hall and it
was true: in spite of its heavy exterior appearance, the castello's interior, while decorated in ancient furnishings—all of which needed to be
thrown into a bonfire—was light and bright, and if the windows had
been cleaned, it would have been downright sun-drenched. I scanned
every room we passed through and so far hadn't seen anything that
looked as though it might conceal the entrance to a secret room or
passageway. Mildew crept along all the walls, marring the plaster and
frescoes. In spite of the sunlight, the place smelled damp and rotted.

He opened a pair of double doors and announced, unnecessarily,
"The Chapel."

"Magnificent."

The chapel was good-sized and in perfect condition—almost as large as the Chapel Royal at St. James's, with which I was well-familiar since that was where I had intended to marry Owen Brace. The air smelled slightly of incense, candle wax, and furniture polish. One side had tall windows bordered with small stained glass panes, leaving ample room for the view of the front lawn, the lake, and the distant peaks, and the opposite wall was paneled in mahogany and hung with carved marble Stations of the Cross. Up a flight of steps, through the intricate and ornate wrought-iron rood screen, and past the choir stalls, the high altar was faced with the Last Supper carved in detailed relief and surmounted with an ancient gold crucifix. Every aspect of the chapel was as though time had stood still—the linens were immaculate white lace, there was an altar rail with brightly colored needle-pointed kneelers, and candles burned in front of a shrine to the Virgin Mary.

"What a beautiful place for the ceremony," I said. "Alice must be very excited."

"How do you say? On cloud nine."

"How much time do you spend here?" I asked when we'd entered the library, which had suffered extensive water damage, probably from a leak in the upstairs plumbing. Many of the books were swollen and the odor was hideous.

"Very little, unfortunately. When I was a child, we spent all summer every summer here, from May to October, with my grandparents, and then the family returned to Budapest for the winter. But during the war we fled to Vienna and then London. When the Iron Curtain fell in the early 1990s and I was able to return to our family estates in Hungary, everything had been destroyed—the houses, the fields. Other families had taken over and laid claim. Everything we had was dead. This castello is the only property remaining out of my family's vast holdings, and"—he held out his hands—"as you can see, it is on the verge of collapse. I so envy your restoration of your family home. I would love more than anything to live here."

"This place is much more interesting than ours. Oh, my, it could be truly magnificent. I'm curious why you started the restoration with the side wings—which I assume are the newer parts—and not the main living spaces and quarters."

"It was not by choice. The term 'newer' is relative. The roofs collapsed."

"Oh, dear. And I imagine you're having to rewire and replumb every square inch of the place."

He nodded. "Nothing significant's been done since before World War One."

"You poor, poor thing," I smiled. "All you can do is watch the money simply fly out the window. What's through that door?"

Vasvar shook his head. "I don't think you'd care for it."

"What do you mean?"

"It's my grandfather's trophy room. Very musty."

"Oh? May I peek inside?"

"Of course." He removed a keychain from his pocket and sorted through five or six keys and then opened the door.

I'm not crazy about trophy rooms. It's not that I'm against hunting—it's not anything I would ever care to do, of course, but I do recognize that if certain species are overly protected and aren't culled, then there's not enough food for them and the whole natural cycle is interrupted. But I'm also not comfortable around hunters and their bloodthirsty conversations, and whenever a show comes on television about Africa and how the species feed on each other to survive because that's the way God intended it, I have to change the channel. I can't bear to watch a cheetah chase down a wounded zebra and rip it to shreds. Can't bear it. But I know it's natural.

Freddie's trophy room was absolutely appaling. I could hardly stand to open my eyes. From the quick glance I took before he pulled me back into the vestibule and closed the door, I believe there was at least one of every animal that had ever walked the earth, and other than the omnipresent mildew from the damp and sagging ceiling, the scent their dust-laden antlers, heads, and necks gave off was that of the long-dead. Nothing.

"Oh, dear Lord," I gasped and leaned against the wall. "I was expecting a boar head or two and perhaps a few sailing or golf or tennis trophies."

He relocked the door and slid the keys back into his pocket. "I keep it locked because I'm ashamed. I don't want anyone to see what butchers my father and grandfather were. When this section of the house is restored, I plan to make this room an extension of the library and dispose of all the trophies. Give them a proper burial."

What a very smooth, believable liar he was. His ability to kill innocent beings far outweighed his father and grandfather's.

"They were very wrong to do this," he continued. "I'm sorry I showed it to you, I can see you're offended. Women really aren't able to take these things very well. Come let me show you upstairs. I'd like you to see my new roof."

CHAPTER 58

Upstairs, Castello Vasvar was in just as poor condition as the ground floor—no wonder Sylvia hadn't visited before and didn't intend to visit again, and no wonder Freddie was looking forward to relieving Edgar Flynn of many of his millions. I estimated it would take as much as five million dollars, maybe more, just to get the most basic infrastructure installed—wiring, plumbing, roof, dry-rot mitigation—before even rudimentary cosmetic, restoration, or reproduction work could begin. From what I'd seen, preservation or conservation of what had probably been unique and valuable centuries-old murals and frescoes, mostly religious and hunting scenes, would not be possible. They were just too far gone.

"I hope you have photographs of all the murals," I said, leaning close to and examining a scene of the Annunciation in the second-floor gallery. "Because it looks to me as though the wall, itself, is crumbling, not just the paint."

Freddie nodded glumly. "I'm afraid I've let it go too long."

"Only by two or three hundred years," I joked.

He grinned but I could tell he was not amused.

Upstairs, a wide loggia looked down on the courtyard with the bedrooms on the opposite side, opening presumably to the view of the lake and the surrounding hillsides. All the doors were closed and the moth-eaten Persian runner muffled our footsteps. The house was silent, it had the feeling of having been abandoned. And, it was larger than it looked from the outside. I realized that short of some sort of a miracle, finding the Madonnas would be impossible.

Suddenly, a sound. Freddie stopped in his tracks and held up his hand for me to do the same. We heard it again. He stepped to a door, put his thumb on the latch and threw it open.

I bit my lip to keep from making any comment, observation, or exclamation.

Alice and Roman were on the bed in all their naked glory. It took Freddie only two giant strides to cross the room. He grabbed Roman by the hair with one hand and around the neck with the other, lifted him off his daughter as though he were a dog, and threw him across the room as though he didn't weigh an ounce. Then he tore the top sheet from the end of the bed and threw it across Alice and slapped her as hard as he could across the face. Then, he slapped her again, bloodying her nose. Roman, meantime, had gotten to his feet and grabbed Freddie's arm to make him stop and that's all it took to make Freddie lose control. He attacked Roman like a wild man, pummeling him unmercifully as though he were a punching bag, while Alice screamed for them to stop. It was terrifying—Freddie had completely lost his mind. There was nothing I could do but pick up a Venetian side chair and smash it down on his head with all my might. A large cut opened in his scalp and he staggered and fell. We all stared at him in stunned silence. After a moment, he began to recoup himself a bit and it looked as though he was going to get back on his feet.

"I wouldn't, if I were you." Roman had a fire poker in his hand. "I won't hesitate to crack open the rest of your head."

Freddie slumped back against the wall and looked at his white-faced daughter. "Alice, Alice," he said. "How could you do this to me?"

After which ensued a fairly typical and predictable family row, which concluded with the bride-to-be and her lover confessing their love for each other, and the father of the bride-to-be ordering the lover—whose nose looked as though it had been broken—off his property and out of his town. He then collapsed back against the wall and sobbed into his hands like a baby.

I slipped out of the room unnoticed and headed for what I hoped would be the master bedroom. It was. Aside from a spectacular view of the lake, it was in unremarkable but habitable condition. I did a quick circle of the chamber tapping my cane gently on the thick plaster walls and found no audible aberration. I flew through Sylvia's closets and bathroom, and then Freddie's bath and dressing room, where nothing seemed to hold any possibility for a passageway. I glanced at my watch. I'd been gone too long to continue my exploration, someone would come looking for me. As I stepped back out into the loggia, Sylvia stepped onto the landing.

"Is everything all right?"

"Not really. I was looking for some bandages."

"Bandages?"

"There's been a sort of a development."

"Development?"

"Your husband found the bride and the best man in bed together."

"What?!"

I nodded. "And, unfortunately, Freddie started beating Roman to a bloody pulp; well, I was afraid he was going to kill him, so I smashed him over the head with a chair."

Sylvia choked back a laugh. "You smashed him with a chair?"

I started laughing, too. "Yes. I know it's not funny but I did. And he's got quite a nasty gash, so I was looking for some bandages."

"Freddie's temper is going to be his undoing one of these days," Sylvia said over her shoulder as she marched down the gallery to Alice's room. "I suppose he's crying now."

"He was when I left."

"Typical. He's either furious or weeping. I don't know why this discovery should surprise him, anyone with a brain in his head can see that his daughter and Roman are in love."

When we arrived back at the scene of the indiscretion, Freddie was sitting in a chair and Alice had wrapped his head in a towel and managed to get the bleeding stopped. I knew Sylvia was wondering why I hadn't thought to do the same thing.

"Oh," I said. "Why didn't I think of that? I've never been any good in an emergency."

Freddie gave me a murderous look.

"I'm so sorry I hit you," I said. "But I was afraid you were going to kill him."

"I would have. He'd be dead by now if you hadn't interfered."

"Daddy!" Alice said. "Don't say such a thing."

"You listen to me." His face was like granite and his eyes glittered like polished jet. "You are going through with this marriage and then once the ink's dry, I don't give a damn what you do or who you sleep with, but you will not interfere with this deal. Your family's entire future depends on you."

"I know, daddy. I understand."

Sylvia had put her arm around Alice. "Freddie," she said. "She's your daughter. It's not worth it."

When he looked at his wife, his eyes turned flat and seemed almost the color of blood. "Get out," he ordered. "Both of you."

We did. Immediately.

I looked over at Sylvia as we moved down the loggia, but kept my mouth closed.

"He is the meanest, most unstable bastard who ever walked on the earth," she finally said. "I'm going to move Mother, Victoria, and me to the hotel right now."

"I would if I were you."

"Do you mind staying with me while I alert my man? It'll just take a moment or two."

"Not at all."

Five minutes later we were back downstairs while Sylvia's and the Duchess's butlers and maids were rapidly filling suitcases. Sylvia's butler had made no attempt to conceal his sheer joy that they would be making a hasty exit from Castello Vasvar. Having seen the family rooms, I hated to think what the staff quarters were like.

I'd been gone for over half an hour and now when I reentered the tent, Thomas looked up. I gave him an imperceptible nod and he turned back to his conversation with Constance.

"I was about to come looking for you," Immaculata said. "Did you find anything?"

"Well. Yes and no. We found the bride and the best man in bed together. But did I find any clues or hints as to what we're looking for?" I shook my head. "Not yet." I didn't want to tell her I thought it was a lost cause.

"You don't think we'll find them, do you?"

"Not without Divine Intervention. And I'll tell you another thing: if I believed in Heaven and Hell? I'd say the devil has the upper hand at the moment, and I'm not so sure I want to mess around with him."

"We'll see. Something will develop." She spoke with such authority, I assumed she was right.

CHAPTER 59

After an in-room massage and facial, followed by a deep and restorative nap, I was ready for the evening. Immaculata and I met to walk to Constance's for the rehearsal dinner. Every window in her villa was filled with light, in stark contrast to the Benedictine monastery that dominated the island in the middle of the lake. A slightly ominous glow came from a few of the monastery's narrow windows.

"What are they doing in there?" I whispered to Immaculata.

"Praying. Contemplating," she answered. "And it does make you feel like whispering, doesn't it?"

I smiled at her and nodded. "It's a bit spooky. Are they allowed to talk?"

"No," she said. "They're allowed to sing. Only the abbot can speak."

"Do you know him?"

"Yes. He came over when we first arrived and introduced himself and we had tea. But I haven't seen him again. The priest who performs our masses comes from the basilica."

As we walked, spotlights came on that lit up the monastery's exterior, softening it and making it much more inviting.

"Is this difficult for you," I asked Immaculata. "Being out in the real world?"

"Not at all. Is this where I want to be? No. But I'm comfortable—I know I'm trying to do something useful that will end up doing some real good. I miss the simplicity of my life. I mean, this jacket"—she held open the pale yellow silk brocade—"is exquisite and the jewelry is unbelievable, but life's trappings don't interest me anymore." She put her hand on my arm. "Please don't misunderstand me, Kick. I'm so grateful for what you're doing, and the risks you're taking, and for letting me wear your clothes and go behind the scenes and see everything firsthand. I'll do whatever it takes to make this happen—well, whatever it takes that's legal by my standards—but I'll be happy to get back home. Happy when all this is over."

"You know?" I said. "I feel exactly the same way—I can't wait to get home. But I must admit, I'm getting excited about switching the rubies—there's something about the danger that energizes me—although in this case, there's little danger and little chance of getting caught."

"Why is that?"

"I'll just take them into Constance's bathroom and lock the door. But, still, it's a personal speed/efficiency/proficiency challenge."

"Do you remember when we had dinner in London," Immaculata said. "And I told you that I'd always been fascinated by the Shamrock Burglar?"

"Of course, I remember. You and Thomas are the only ones who know the truth."

"Well, now that I actually know you, there are so many questions I'd like to ask."

"Such as?"

"How do you keep your fingers nimble enough to work with such exacting little pieces? I'd be dropping things all over the place."

"Exercise," I answered. "Hand and finger exercises are the only ones I do—if I spent as much time keeping my body in shape as I do my fingers, I'd be a goddess."

Immaculata laughed. "You're close enough. What kinds of exercises? Show me."

I demonstrated a couple of my flexibility techniques. "And I squeeze tennis balls for strength and use a nail file to take a couple of layers of skin off my fingertips to make them sensitive if I'm going to be cracking a safe or resetting stones, as I will tonight."

We walked on.

"I know you don't want to go back to the castle, Kick. I wouldn't blame you a bit if you decided to back out."

"That's not an option for me. I'm committed to doing everything I can to get this done. It's important to me. I'm not sure exactly why, since acts of selflessness and placing myself in personal physical jeopardy are not my normal behavior."

"I've also wondered why you're doing it," Immaculata said.

I wasn't about to tell her the truth—to tell her how I felt about her, that I suspected, or maybe just wanted, for her to be my long-lost daughter, that I felt I'd do anything, risk anything for her. "It's complicated," I said. "Far too Freudian for a stroll as short as this. Let's just say I'm not at all looking forward to doing what it may take to find the Madonnas. But, on the other hand, I can't wait to see what they look like. If Freddie just weren't such a scary individual—he's so volatile and unpredictable, so out of control. He's like nitroglycerine."

"If God's in this, it will go like silk. If He's not—step aside—it'll be a big mess. Either way, I'll watch your back."

She and I smiled at each other.

"You and Sir Tom. What a team. Here we are. Time to get to work."

The Vasvar rubies and their cotton muffling gently grazed my thighs from the deep pockets of my silk Cheung Sam.

"What would you like me to do?"

"Nothing. This part comes as naturally to me as breathing. Just enjoy the evening."

CHAPTER 60

Constance had done a very creative job of sprucing up the villa, considering what she had to work with: a pedestrian ballroom and little money. The setting had an elegant, classic, Italian lake country feel. Cocktails were being served on the terrace outside the ballroom, where urns held masses of red flowers and marble statues anchored the balustrade. Inside, round tables of eight with bronze-colored linens and silvery bamboo chairs ringed a large dance floor where a nine-piece band was getting ready to play. Blown-up photographs of William and Alice as children and teenagers were on easels around the room.

"So glad you're here, Amanda. And Mamie." Constance welcomed us. She and Clifton/Owen were on the terrace, mingling with the guests. She had on black silk trousers, a black organdy blouse with a ruffled collar that, in my opinion, was cut too low for a woman her age, and high-heeled sandals. But that was the Owen Effect.

"Clifton, I know you remember Lady Amanda, but I don't think you've had an opportunity to meet her enchanting daughter, Mamie."

"Well, hello, Mamie." Owen looked up at Immaculata, who towered over him. She was much more his cup of tea. "Save me a dance, will you?"

Immaculata returned his gaze. "I know you're just having a joke, sir," she said. "You and I both know you're far too old for me. Lovely to meet you, though." And then she walked off, leaving Owen speechless.

Constance laughed. "Well, she is right. Sir."

"You do seem to have a bit of the Dirty Old Man in you, Clifton," I added.

Owen gave a little good-sportsman laugh. Immaculata had poked a pin in his ego and I knew it hurt and I hoped it would start to worm its way, insidiously, into his confidence until maybe it would cross his mind that if he started hanging out with his peers, and moved his brain above his waist—including his wallet—he might actually get somewhere with his life.

I headed toward the bar, but Immaculata had beaten me to it and now approached through the lively throng with two tumblers of scotch on the rocks with lemon twists. "Sorry," she said. "Dewar's only. No Chivas."

"I'm not surprised, considering the Flynn financial crisis. I'm not going to be drinking for a while anyway until I get my business done. Let's go hear what a hero Thomas is."

Most of the guests had clustered into a semicircle while Giovanna prepared to interview the Chief Inspector Emeritus. An entire outdoor television studio had been set up to broadcast her regular live evening show. There were makeup artists, bright lights, boom microphones, reflectors, and stools for them to sit on. The lake and lighted monastery were the backdrop. Thomas's fan club comprised all the ladies, including the bride, Alice, who had covered her bruised cheeks with makeup. Her eyes were slightly puffy. Sad and hard.

Roman, a bandage across his nose and blackening eyes, stood slightly off from the group, leaning against the balustrade, a tumbler of neat whisky in one hand, the other hand casually tucked in his pocket. I wondered if he had a gun in there. I was also curious what story he'd given to William to explain his condition. Maybe he didn't have to tell him any story at all—William probably already knew. He didn't see this as anything more than the culmination of a business deal—the signing of the contract that would staunch the flow of his company's financial hemorrhage. He didn't care any more about Alice and her feelings than he cared about the man in the moon.

As soon as Immaculata and I joined the group, Katie moved around and took her hand, and William came from the opposite direction and stood as close as he could without taking her other hand. He whispered something to her and she looked at him and smiled.

I withdrew to the edge of the circle and watched Edgar and Freddie—who had a large white bandage where the part in his hair used to be—having an animated conversation while Owen stared at them jealously from Constance's side. She looked at him and then looked at where his eyes were focused and smiled and said something under her breath that appeared to be, "You leave my side right now—just plan to keep on walking." A risk he couldn't take quite yet because Constance still had the power to evict him from her life, and knowing Constance the little I did—but recalling her comments that she knew he wasn't a nice person and she was getting sick of crying—if he didn't start to be a little more attentive, and nicer, she would throw the bum out. And the bum had the brains to know it.

Giovanna and Thomas—who had waved off the makeup girl from anything more than a bit of powder on his nose—were now on the air live and they were off and running, digging into the story for all it was worth, the Duchess's stolen jewels, their mysterious reappearance.

"Inspector," she said. "I'm looking around at this tightly knit crowd of family and friends here to celebrate a wedding, and trying to put myself in your shoes. Are you actually studying each one of us and wondering which one is the thief?"

"Of course, I am," Thomas answered. "That's what I do."

"Any ideas yet?"

"A few."

"How do you begin to crack a case like this? What will be your first step?"

"I'm already on step number five or six, Giovanna." He smiled at her patronizingly. I could almost hear him thinking, You silly, silly thing. "But this is an unusual case, with unusual women ranging in age from fifteen"—he looked at Katie Flynn, who stared back at him, terrified—"to eighty-five." He turned his gaze to Duchess Mary Margaret and Victoria, both of whom beamed. "So it's quite a challenge."

"But you aren't saying that women are the only suspects, are you?"

"For the moment? Yes. The jewels disappeared in the ladies' lounge and someone would have noticed if there were a man lurking about in there."

At that, Thomas began to drone on and on—he, Giovanna, and the audience were all in heaven in the spotlights on live international television with a full hour to run.

This would be the perfect time for me to step upstairs and take care of business. I set my untouched drink on the railing and slipped away as unobtrusively as possible, but as I crossed the ballroom, I felt a hand on my back. It was Constance.

"Amanda," she said. "Do you have a minute?"

"Of course."

"Oh, good. Let's go upstairs."

I followed her to her bedroom where she closed and locked the door. Sylvia was standing at the window and turned around when we entered. Constance joined her and they both faced me. Sylvia was the one to speak.

"Precisely who are you? And what are you up to?"

CHAPTER 61

Who am I?

Well. This was a first. My greatest nightmare come to life. My stomach lurched and a pain shot through my skull and the rubies began to burn my leg like live coals. But I didn't flinch.

"What on earth do you mean?" I asked with a bemused smile.

"You know very well," Sylvia said. "Lady Amanda Bonham, Laird Wynn Bonham, Bonham Hall—none of these people or things exist. You're an impostor."

"That's simply not true."

"My cousin, Sarah, lives in Scotland and knows everyone in the country—every castle, every manor house, every flower show and sheep judge, every word of history. She and I reviewed your dossier on Google and it sounds as phony as a three-pound note."

"I'm sorry, Sylvia, but you're wrong, and I suggest we go back downstairs before someone misses you and comes searching."

The two of them laughed—somewhat cynically, I thought.

"Are you kidding?" Constance said. "Nobody ever knows who the mother of the groom is—usually they don't even know there is one."

"How many people do you think will be missing the estranged stepmother of the bride?" Sylvia asked. "None."

"Your mother?" I proposed.

"She and Victoria are completely entranced with the burglary and the television show—it's the most exciting thing that's happened to them since the bombing of London. Believe me, no one's going to notice we're not there. So"—She took a bracing sip of her martini and then looked me in the eye—"there's no escape. Let's have it. You're up to something."

I glanced at the door, trying to gauge if I could make a run for it. But Sylvia was in very good shape and could out-sprint me in a heart-beat.

"Don't even think about it," she said and slid her hand into her jacket pocket. "I have a pistol." Whereupon she withdrew a lovely shiny little pearl-handled revolver. A true lady's gun.

"Oh, good heavens, Sylvia. You aren't actually thinking to *shoot* me, are you?"

"I certainly hope not. But I do know how to work it."

"I'm sure you do but, please, put it away. You're scaring me to death."

"Katie told me you went through my safe this morning," Constance said.

"What?! I most certainly did no such thing." My insides began to rumble.

"And." Sylvia repocketed the gun, but her hand remained in her pocket and her expression remained unforgiving. "Alice told me that while she and her father and Roman were hashing things about, and they were gushing blood all over themselves, you left. Why didn't you check *her* bathroom for bandages? Or towels? I found that very odd, especially since he and Roman were bleeding so profusely and her bathroom door was standing open, right there. Why did you check my bathroom first? Besides, there was a large tin of bandages in plain sight on my counter and you didn't take them."

"I told you, I'm useless in emergencies."

"Well, now I'm telling you. All of this is just folderol. The bottom line is that Constance and I have put our heads together and discovered that neither one of us knows you or ever knew you. You are not her friend and you're certainly not mine. So either tell us who you are and why you're here posing as a made-up aristocrat, crashing this weekend, or we'll notify Chief Inspector Thomas Curtis immediately."

She and Constance glanced at each other—proud of their assertiveness.

I had to make some decisions. Fast. I studied the two women—I liked them both so much. I'd even come to regard them as friends. Notifying Thomas wouldn't make any difference—he could just pretend to slap me about or rough me up, or whatever one would do in such a circumstance, and then he'd send me on my way. But, I wouldn't have accomplished any of what I'd set out to do.

"Why don't we sit down?" I said, indicating the settee and armchairs arranged cozily around the fake fireplace and mantel. A silver shaker, glistening with icy condensation, and two martini glasses sat on a tray on the coffee table.

They both looked at me reluctantly.

"I assure you. I'm not dangerous. And when it comes to our knowing each other or being friends? I acknowledge that we've never met, but I am your friend. More than you can even imagine." I sat in one of the chairs and waited for them to be seated as well. In spite of a spinning brain, I knew I appeared cool as a cucumber. "May I have one of these?"

Constance nodded and I filled one of the glasses. There was not even a hint of a tremor in my hand as I picked it up and took a fortifying swallow.

They sat on the edges of their seats, backs as straight as broomsticks, and regarded me with angry and suspicious eyes, ready to throttle me if need be.

"Well?" Sylvia said. "Let's hear it."

"Yes, and it had better be good or Sylvia will shoot you."

"I'll do nothing of the sort."

A woman I know says, What difference does it make how deep

the water is if you're already in over your head? And at this point, there was nothing for me to do but hold my breath and jump right off the high-board into the deep end of the pool. "There is no reason to inform Sir Thomas." I placed the icy cocktail back on the tray. "He and I are a team."

This caught them completely off guard.

Sylvia frowned and Constance said, "What?"

"It's true. And another thing that's true is that I'm very glad you're the ones who've approached me, because it was starting to look as though I would need to enlist you."

"Enlist us, how?" Sylvia asked.

By now, in spite of their steely determination, their softening posture indicated their suspicion was in the process of transforming into anticipation.

"It's quite a long story, but let me see if I can make it brief. Sylvia, you remember our conversation at lunch yesterday about the stolen Madonnas and the murdered nuns? And the fact that the statuettes have never been recovered and the killer never brought to justice?"

She nodded.

"What nuns?" Constance asked.

I let Sylvia tell her the story, including the history of Freddie's grandmother giving the order her private, priceless collection of jeweled Madonnas.

"You're kidding? Someone murdered all the nuns?"

Sylvia nodded.

"Well," I interrupted. "As it turns out—all but one. And the one who survived can identify the killer."

"Are you serious?" Sylvia said.

I nodded.

She refilled her glass. "Do you know who the killer is?"

"I do."

"Well?"

"I regret having to tell you," I answered, "because this is so confidential, such perilous knowledge, it will put both of you in danger. This person is a very violent, completely sociopathic individual. He wouldn't hesitate to kill any of us if he felt he were at risk of being exposed. But frankly, we're in a bit of a time crunch and have few options. We'd like your help to find the statues and to make an arrest."

"Who is it?" Sylvia asked, but I had the feeling she'd already figured it out.

"I think you know."

Her clear ice blue eyes studied mine and I could tell her mouth had gone dry. "It's Freddie, isn't it?"

"You're *kidding*," exclaimed Constance, whose brow had furrowed and whose lips had formed a perfect "O." Her eyes darted back and forth between the two of us.

I nodded. "And I don't blame you for carrying a gun, Sylvia. I would too if he were my husband."

"Oh, dear God." Sylvia closed her eyes as tears fell down her cheeks. "Those poor, poor women." Constance and I waited in silence until she'd gathered herself back together. "What do you want me to do?"

After we finished our conversation on the subject of trying to find the hiding place in the castello, about which she had only one suggestion, but a very good one at that, I turned to Constance.

"There's more."

"What do you mean?"

"I'm sorry to have to be the one to tell you this, Constance. But Clifton Boatwright is not who or what he says he is. He is a con man named Owen Brace and he's only interested in using you to gain access to your husband."

"Get out!" she said. "He's ten times richer and more successful than Edgar."

I shook my head, no. "He's a phony. And while we have no jurisdiction over him and no legitimate reason to arrest him, I think you're entitled to have this information for your own self-protection and to use as you see fit."

"Oh, my God." Constance started to laugh. "This whole weekend is absolutely crazy."

"In my opinion," I said. "What this weekend is, is out of control, and to be quite frank, I lay the blame completely on the two of you."

"I beg your pardon," Sylvia said.

"I'm sorry, but I do," I answered. "Constance, I don't mean to lecture you, but you've not only let a twenty-five-year-old nincompoop step in and usurp your rightful position as mother of the groom, but you've also totally lost all your judgment, thanks to Owen Brace's sexual distractions."

She nodded. "I know. It's as though I'm drugged. It's fun but it's pathetic."

"Yes, it is pathetic and you need to change it. My advice to you is to realign the fulcrum, as quickly as possible—you've got the power to do it whether you realize it or not. And Sylvia," I continued. "You're one of the richest women in the world, you have practically unlimited resources and yet I can't think of a single thing you've gotten credit for that's made anyone's life any better, made a difference to humanity, that's improved anybody's lot. How old are you? Fifty-ish?"

"Ish." The color flared in her cheeks but she didn't look as though she were going to shoot me.

I forged ahead. "You're one of the most delightful people I've ever met, but you have an absolutely terrible reputation as a heartless princess with ice water in her veins."

"I find you quite presumptuous."

"I'm being very presumptuous, but it's only because you need to hear these things said out loud. You're a woman of substance. The two of you have let the media, the Giovanna MacDougals of the world, define you and control your public personas. Aren't you sick of it?"

She smiled a little ruefully. "I know what people say about me, and I'd be lying if I said it didn't hurt." She looked straight at me, head held high. "Is there more? You might as well get it all out now."

I shook my head. "No. Other than that, you're perfect."

My attempt at humor seemed to diffuse the situation and soften the sting of my words. I shrugged and held up my hands. "So. Your choice. Sir Thomas and I are going to sort out this situation with Freddie one way or the other, but we'd deeply appreciate your assistance. Do you want to be part of the solution or part of the problem?"

"I'm in," said Constance.

"I am, too," Sylvia agreed.

I smiled and we clinked our glasses. "Thank you. This is going to be very rewarding," I said. "You won't be sorry."

"What do you want us to do?" Sylvia asked.

I refreshed our drinks. "Here's the plan."

Later, as we were leaving the room to go down and join the party, Constance asked me what my real name was.

"It's Amanda Bonham," I said, looking straight into her eyes. "For now."

She nodded. "I understand."

As I stepped into the hall, I could have sworn I saw the top of Duchess Mary Margaret's little gray head disappear down the stairs.

CHAPTER 62

I felt, under the circumstances, it would be imprudent to push my luck and switch the rubies at this time. Immaculata would be disappointed in me but there was nothing I could do about it.

"See what I mean?" Sylvia said when we walked back into the party. "Not a soul has missed us."

She was right. In our absence, the dinner bell had rung and the guests had found their assigned seats, eaten their salads, and were now on the dance floor between courses, which I must say shocked and saddened me. What has happened to people's manners? I could no more imagine sitting down and starting a meal before being invited to do so by the hostess than I could imagine doing I don't know what.

The only person who seemed to have noticed Constance wasn't there was Owen, who knew he was on thin ice. "Where have you been?" he asked.

"Why? Did you miss me?"

"I did."

"Bul-l-l-l—oney."

"Come on, let's dance."

"I don't really feel like it."

"What do you mean? You love to dance."

"I love to dance with Edgar. In fact, excuse me for a moment, will you?" Constance walked out onto the dance floor to Edgar and Lauren, took their arms, and said something to them. They looked surprised and suspicious, but nevertheless, accompanied her out onto the terrace and stopped near where I'd joined a small group talking to—I mean, listening to—Thomas.

"I want to apologize to you both," Constance said. "I can see how deeply you're in love and I've been behaving like a jealous child. I think it's marvelous you're getting married and I wish you all the best."

Edgar started to speak and Constance held up her hand.

"No. Let me finish," she said. "Tonight, I want the three of us to celebrate William and Alice, to be a family, and not have any silly trouble between us distract from the festivities. We're all in this together. Lauren." Constance put her hands on Lauren's shoulders and kissed her on the cheek. "Welcome to the Flynn Family. And I mean that with all my heart."

Lauren gaped.

"And Edgar. I've made a decision to forgive you. I'm not going to fight you any more. And I hope you'll forgive me, too. I've been an absolutely beastly wife so much of the time, I completely understand why you'd want to get away from me and be with someone as young and beautiful and *thoughtful* as Lauren. I think she'll be a wonderful asset to our family."

"Well, Peaches, you old dog," Edgar smiled. "I'll be damned. You never fail to amaze me." From where I stood he looked victorious and vindicated. "You haven't been beastly the whole time. But, I'm glad you've come to your senses."

Lauren frowned. "Peaches? You call her 'Peaches'? Oh. God." She rolled here eyes as though that were the most disgusting thing she'd ever heard. "And what's all this 'family' talk, Edgar? We're starting a new family—you said you were done with your old one."

Edgar was conciliatory because he felt he could be. He was the boss again. Back in control. "Well, I am in one sense. I mean Constance and I are getting divorced and the minute the divorce is final, you and I will be married before you know it. And you'll be my wife, Mrs. Edgar Flynn. But I'll still have my children and we'll still have family occasions like this. Constance and I will still have to have a relationship and it's much better if it can be civil."

"What children? They're *adopted*. They aren't even your children."

"I didn't mean to start an argument between the two of you," Constance said. "I just wanted to apologize."

"Well, mind your own business, you old . . ."

"Careful," said Edgar.

"I'll tell you what," Constance said. "Let's make a deal. Let's pretend, just for the next two days, that we're friends, and then after the wedding's over, we don't have to see or talk to each other again for a very long time."

"Thank God for that."

"Put a lid on it, Lauren," Edgar ordered.

"Listen, Thumper." Constance put her hand familiarly on his cheek. "Once dessert is served, won't you join me in a toast to William and Alice—I mean he is our son, and this is the joining of our two families—and then he's going to give her the rubies."

"Thumper?" said Lauren. "Who in the hell is 'Thumper'?"

Constance and Edgar ignored her. "It's the classy thing to do, and you know it. I really want us to make a good impression on the Vasvars. I know I don't need to tell you how critical it is that we all get started on the right foot."

Edgar flinched a bit at her unnecessary reminder of their highly confidential, highly precarious financial situation. "Let's do it," he said jovially.

"Excuse me," Lauren raised her voice. "Hello? I'm here. Who in the hell is 'Thumper'?"

"Oh, I'm sorry, Lauren, dear." Constance patted her hand. "Don't worry. It's what I've called him for thirty-five years—he used to have the cutest little business—well, I'm sure he still does. I promise I won't call him that anymore."

"Come on, Puss." Edgar put his arm around Lauren's waist and squeezed her close to him. "Let's see that million-dollar smile. Just pretend you're working—sell me some shampoo."

The remark about Edgar's little business would have the same effect on Lauren that Immaculata's comment about age did on Owen. Without being able to help herself, without even being aware of it, Lauren wouldn't be able to focus her thoughts on anything but the current state of Edgar's little Thumper and Constance's intimate thirty-five-year relationship with it.

Dinner moved forward. The seating was much the same as the night before. I was between Constance and a man from Detroit, who was perfectly nice and had as little interest in me as I did in him, but we made the best of it. It was a dreary occasion that lacked the hilarity and joyous anticipation typical of impending nuptials. Everyone was making an effort, but all the toasts fell flat, and the food—which was being prepared by a local restaurant—was indescribably bad, horrendous actually. And, although there were what seemed like hundreds of waiters, none of them seemed to have any experience. It was common knowledge that William was going to give Alice the rubies either tonight or tomorrow and a number of the waiters looked as though they were casing the place. Believe me, I know the look. And Roman, as best man, and therefore, the evening's emcee, understandably had trouble getting his energy and sense of humor moved even into second gear because of his broken nose and black eyes.

The band was good. William danced with Alice, and so did Roman, regardless of Freddie's ominous looks. In fact, at one point, I watched Roman extend his middle finger in Freddie's direction behind Alice's back, but Freddie must have missed it, otherwise he would have gone after him again.

I noticed William and Immaculata on the terrace in a lengthy, and what looked to be serious, discussion. Then, he held out his hand as if inviting her to dance, but she declined. They exchanged a few more words and she smiled at him and he returned to his table. Almost every man in the place had asked her to dance and she turned them all down, except for Thomas. Thomas, on the other hand, had turned down all Giovanna's invitations to dance. She now watched him and Immaculata on the dance floor and drummed her fingers on the table as though she were having a jealous little fit. Finally, she got up and went to the powder room.

Sylvia and Freddie danced. One of the assignments that she'd agreed upon upstairs was to make him think that reconciliation was a possibility. Even likely. He seemed to enter a sort of state of euphoria, brought on not only at the possibility of getting his rich wife back, but also at the fact that soon, in just a matter of minutes, the Vasvar Rubies would be restored to his family after decades on the move, ending what his great-great-grandfather had said was a curse on whoever owned them, but in reality had turned out to be more of a curse on the Vasvar family itself. He was a dancing dervish, flighty with happiness, dancing non-stop with Sylvia, her mother, and Victoria. He tossed off a shot of vodka between each round and was growing increasingly intoxicated. "The only way I'll go back to the castle with him is if he's unconscious," Sylvia had said. He was well on his way.

Edgar danced once with Constance, and they fit together like two peas in a pod. Constance still declined to dance with Owen, which made him more and more insecure.

"I really do know how to dance," he said.

"Yes," she said. "Just not very well."

"May I have the honor, Lady Amanda?" It was Thomas, and I almost burst out laughing at the expression on Constance's face. She was now an insider in what she thought was an official, elaborate Scotland Yard-sponsored undercover operation. She looked as though she'd swallowed a bird and were going to explode. Sylvia, on the other hand, maintained her typical British aristocratic deadpan expression.

"Regarding Clifton Boatwright," Thomas said as we lumbered our way around the floor in his familiar dancing school box-step. "I would know that little weasel anywhere."

I nodded and looked at Owen. "I told Constance the truth about him. I imagine she'll find some way to get even."

"With your help, no doubt."

"I don't know what you're talking about. I just wanted to give her the option."

"Inspector!" The Duchess's cane whipped into sight. "You haven't asked me to dance."

"Your ladyship," he said. "It would be my distinct pleasure."

She handed her cane to me and stepped into Thomas's waiting arms. "I know everything about the operation," she shouted to him in her whisper.

"How wonderful," Thomas answered, clueless as to what she was talking about.

"My lips are sealed."

"Good."

"I'm feeling very discouraged about the dessert," Constance said when I got back to the table. The main course had just been cleared, a frightful veal scallopini that had been deep-fried in what seemed like doughnut batter and topped with what tasted like canned red sauce. "I think this will be a total disaster."

"Why?"

"Based on the dinner? Worst food I've ever had in my life. I don't think this chef has a clue what's he's doing. And have you noticed it sounds like they're breaking five out of ten plates out there?"

"I have." I started laughing. "Do you think that's what they're really doing?"

"Yes," Constance laughed, too. "They're dropping things left and right. I'm sure all the plates are rented and I'll be charged for every single one of them. Oh, what the hell." She signaled a waiter. "Bring me a Cosmopolitan, please."

"I hate to think what the kitchen floor looks like."

"It's perfect, isn't it?"

"It is. What is dessert?"

"It's supposed to be flaming baked apples on a bed of cinnamon gelato with a burnt sugar fan."

"It sounds wonderful. But you're right—it might be too much of a reach for this group."

"We'll see. Oh, good grief. I almost forgot."

"What?"

"I've got to give William a high sign so he can go get the rubies. He's going to give them to her after dessert. Excuse me a minute." She got up and went over and whispered in William's ear and he excused himself, left his table, and went upstairs.

She was right—the dessert was awful.

The flaming brandy had been spooned over the hot apples in the kitchen and had extinguished itself by the time the desserts had gotten to the ballroom, the only dramatic effect being to melt the gelato, which pooled in the plates and slopped over the edges as the inept waiters rushed them out. The burnt sugar fans looked as though they were clinging to the sides of apple lifeboats for dear life.

William reappeared and strode across the ballroom to his mother. He knelt down next to her and whispered in her ear.

"WHAT!?" she yelled.

He whispered again.

"You've got to be kidding."

William shook his head. No.

"Oh. My. God. This is a disaster."

"What?" I asked.

"They're gone," William said. "The Vasvar rubies are gone."

CHAPTER 63

It took only a second for the news to ricochet around the room, and then the buzz became a roar. Giovanna trampled everyone in her path getting to William. Thomas shot a glance at me and I shook my head, and then we both looked at Katie, who had turned white as a sheet. She looked at me and shook her head vigorously and emphatically mouthed the word NO. Thomas covered his face with his hands and rubbed his eyes and then got to his feet and made his official way to William.

"Excuse me." He pushed Giovanna aside. "I'll be asking the questions."

"No!" she said. "I have the rights. Edgar sold them to me."

"This is now a possible criminal situation in a foreign country—you don't have any rights at all." He positioned himself between William and Giovanna, took his phone out of his pocket, punched in a number, and spoke in rapid Italian, presumably to his Italian counterpart, who

I assumed would then relay the call to the local chief of police. I had no idea how competent the Orta San Giulio carbinieri were, but since they were Italian, I knew they must have raised bureaucracy to an art form.

Giovanna sidled up to Constance. "Where were they?" she asked, sotto voce.

"In the safe in my closet," Constance replied.

Giovanna cast a sidelong look at one of her cameramen, who backed away smoothly and headed for the stairs, unaware that Duchess Mary Margaret and Victoria were right on his tail.

"What do you mean, they're gone?" Freddie raged. He headed for William, his fists balled. "What are you trying to pull?"

It took four men to restrain him. It was only when Sylvia brought him a drink and smoothed his hair back off his forehead and spoke to him in a serene, caring voice that he began to quiet down.

"Would you all kindly remain calm and in the room," Thomas said. "Until the police arrive and are able to take charge."

Just then, the distinctive sounds of the carbinieris' sirens pierced the air.

The chief of police and two patrolmen, in smart navy blue uniforms with wide blood stripes on their pants and shiny buttons on their jackets, entered the villa. After consulting with Thomas, and putting up with a tirade from an irate Edgar Flynn—who I knew was fighting hysteria, watching his future swirl down the toilet bowl—it didn't take the police chief long to focus his investigation on a handful of the waiters—one of whom seemed particularly known to him. The interrogations brought the evening's formal festivities effectively to a close.

"When you catch this person"—a sloppy-drunk Freddie wagged his finger over Sylvia's shoulder at the chief, as she maneuvered him toward the terrace door to go down to their launch; he was tilted at almost a 45-degree angle against her and if Sylvia'd stepped aside, he would have fallen flat on his back—"you make sure he knows he's cursed until they return to our family."

"Yes, Prince Vasvar. I am as surprised as you that someone would steal these pieces—they're known to carry with them nothing but despair."

Sylvia glanced at me. "Speaking of despair . . ." she said laconically, before she frog-marched him down the short flight to the dock where their launch waited. It should only take another shot or two of vodka back at the castello to knock him out completely for a few hours.

Immaculata and I were among the last to leave the party, which had adjourned to the bar at the hotel.

An hour later—wearing black trousers and jackets—we skirted the edge of the piazza and returned to Constance's dock, where she told me we'd find a small motor boat that came included with the villa's rental. The villa was dark and the boat was just where she said it would be. A thick fog had settled over the lake.

"Do you know how to work this?" I whispered to Immaculata.

"Of course." She stepped into the boat and peered down at a tiny motor that looked as though it had come from a lawnmower. Then she sat down, made herself comfortable and picked up the oars. "I think we'd best wait to fire up the engine until we get a little ways away from the dock. It looks as though it'll make a terrible racket. Just hand me your duffle and then untie that line and climb aboard." The orders came easily, which made me feel better about our midnight reconnaissance and reconnoiter foray across the lake. She evidently knew exactly what she was doing. Since I didn't grow up around water—Oklahoma has a few big reservoirs here and there where people go waterskiing, or sit on houseboats and get burned to a crisp, but I never visited any of them—I've always been happier on terra firma.

I did as she instructed and shoved us away from the dock with all my might. She slipped the oars smoothly into the water and before long we were about twenty-five yards out. Immaculata ignited the motor and we crossed the lake through the muffling fog and arrived at the pitch black castle in short order.

CHAPTER *64*

As agreed, Sylvia had left the power on to the lift, so when I pushed the call button on the dock, the contraption descended quietly. Immaculata and I climbed in and rode back to the top in silence. I handed her an elasticized headband with a miner's light attached.

"Don't turn this on until I tell you," I whispered.

She nodded.

I then secured a heavier band around my own head that held my infrared night-vision goggles, although I wouldn't pull them into place until I needed them. My heart beat with excitement. Sylvia felt confident that the Madonnas were somewhere in the trophy room because that was the only place that Freddie was protective about, and he was fanatically protective, at that. He kept the only set of keys with him at all times. She'd never even been inside the room, so couldn't give us any clues as to where they may be hidden.

When we reached the top, we crept single file along the wall, through the main gates to the kitchen door where Freddie and I had entered earlier in the day. Sylvia was on the lookout for us. She opened the door and then bolted it shut behind us. "I couldn't get the keys," she whispered.

"It doesn't matter," I said. "Is he out?"

"Like a light."

"Do you have your gun?"

She patted the pocket of her robe. "I keep it in close reach at all times."

I nodded. "Good. You go back to bed. We'll take it from here."

"Good luck," she whispered. She started up the stairs as Immaculata and I turned and went down the hall toward the trophy room.

I pulled my goggles over my eyes and examined the door in great detail, searching for signs of alarms or boobytraps. The door knob, doorjamb, and locks glowed with fingerprints and smudges where Freddie had touched them, but otherwise, the area looked clear. I withdrew the lock picks from my pocket and after about twenty seconds, the first deadbolt was done, then the second, and after another half-minute, I had the main lock open. We stepped into the dead menagerie, locking the door behind us.

"You can turn your light on now," I told Immaculata.

"This is disgusting," she said, as her beam fell on a prowling, growling African lion.

"It's beyond disgusting. It's demented. You start over there." I indicated the right side of the room and focused my own attention on the left side, which had floor-to-ceiling bookcases with a glass-fronted gun cabinet set into them. It held at least twenty big-game hunting rifles—some were antiques, others looked much newer. I'd always heard about the old Martini-Henry four-bore elephant guns but never seen one. It was gigantic, with a long heavy barrel—much bigger than I'd imagined. I looked over at the long-dead elephant, whose head, with its mighty tusks, was thrown back, trunk raised in a typical bugling warning stance, the position he would take just before he would lower his head and flatten his ears and charge. Poor thing. I hoped he never knew what hit him.

The weapons were in meticulous condition—indicating that their maintenance was a passionate hobby of Freddie's. Next to each one was a small brass plaque detailing the game it had been responsible for bringing down. Fingerprints showed up all over the glass front of the case, which was secured with a large key-operated padlock. While Immaculata opened and closed drawers in her wall of bookcases and cabinets, I did a quick lap of the room, looking for any obvious signs of a hiding place or secret door. A large coat closet bulged several rows deep with, presumably, his ancestors' favorite bush jackets and safari gear, and as I began to search it, something made me turn back and regard the gun case from across the room. From that different perspective, the proportion to the bookcases that were on either side of it didn't make sense. My hair stood up on the back of my neck and my skin began to feel as though it were fizzing.

"Psst," I signaled Immaculata as I crossed the room. "Come."

I easily unlocked the padlock and the tall glass doors swung open. I tapped on the paneling on the back of the cabinet—the sound was hollow. I searched around the bottom and in the corners and found what I was looking for: a minuscule keyhole, almost invisible to the naked eye unless you knew what you were looking for. I slid a pick into it and twisted. The panels released and showed the center opening.

Immaculata's hand had my left arm in a vicelike grip. I hooked my right index finger under the edge of the panel and pulled. The doors opened silently and lights winked on automatically. There before us, on five shelves, were the jeweled Madonnas, with the Madonna Illuminata in their center—a dazzling beacon of what should have been beauty, solace, and Divine Comfort, but what looked to me like threatening, ice-cold, angry revenge.

"Oh, thank you, Father." Immaculata fell to her knees and started to cry, while I took out my camera and began photographing the statuettes as fast as I could.

"Freddie!" Sylvia's voice suddenly echoed down the stairwell. "Please come back to bed."

"Leave me alone, goddammit," Freddie boomed back as he approached the trophy room door. "I'll come back to bed when I'm ready. I'm just going to have a nightcap."

"Take the duffle and get in the closet," I said to Immaculata. "And turn off your light." While she crossed the room, I closed the secret doors and made sure they were secure.

Freddie's key slid into the first lock. I closed the glass gun case doors but couldn't find the padlock.

"Immaculata," I whispered as loudly as I could. "Where's the padlock?"

She raced across. "Sorry," she said and thrust it into my hand.

The first deadbolt was unlocked. His key turned in the second and then, after a bit of fumbling, connected in the main lock. I slid the gun case padlock home and ran. The closet door closed just as he turned on the lights. We crept through the racks of the safari wardrobe and sat at the back of the deep closet on the floor amongst a collection of tired, old, mud-caked canvas boots.

CHAPTER 65

Immaculata was practically quaking with excitement as we sat there in the dark and listened to Freddie grow drunker and drunker. It sounded as though visiting the jeweled Madonnas was a nightly ritual, and a curious one at that. Not lewd but maudlin. He cried and cried and continually asked Her for forgiveness. Then he told Her he had a present for Her.

I was shaking a bit as well, but not because I was excited. It was cold in the closet and I realized it was cold because there was a breeze. I put my hand behind me where the wall joined the floor and felt cold air pouring through the space.

"I have a beautiful present for you, Mother," Freddie babbled. "Where is it? Let me think. Jacket pocket."

I heard stumbling and suddenly the closet door opened and he began pawing through the clothes. "Where is it?"

Immaculata and I stopped breathing. Only one row of jackets

now stood between us, Freddie, and two-dozen hunting rifles in tip-top condition. For all I knew, they could have even been loaded. Miraculously, he found whatever it was he was looking for and took it back into the room, but left the closet door open.

"See? See? This is for you. This is my wife's favorite necklace. I stole this for you. When she finds out it's gone, she'll call the police and I could go to jail. But it's worth it for you." Freddie was crying. "Why do you treat me this way?" He sat down heavily in a chair. "Please forgive me, Mother. Please look at me. You are so cold."

Immaculata and I finally took a breath. The bittersweet odor of cognac and male perspiration saturated the air.

It seemed ages before he drank himself into a stupor and slid off the chair. Passed out, possibly. But, he was proving to be like Rasputin, who'd been poisoned, drugged, stabbed, shot, wrapped in a rug and thrown into the river where he finally drowned. Freddie had come to before, when his wife said he was passed out for hours, and who knew how much time we had before he came to again. We needed to move.

"Slide as quietly as you can away from this wall," I told Immaculata.

She did as instructed and I examined where I'd been sitting. I took my screwdriver out of my pocket and ran it down the seam in the corner until it hit a latch. I pushed. A narrow secret door swung open.

Freddie mumbled unintelligibly and something made a large clunk—hopefully it was his head hitting the floor. "Ow," he cried.

"Come on." I grabbed her arm and shoved her through the open-ing. "Let's go."

Immaculata and I stepped into the cold, damp darkness and as I pulled the door closed, I heard his voice again saying something into the closet. Through the eerie green glow of my night-vision goggles, I saw that we were on a small landing at the top of a steep winding stair.

"Don't turn on your lamp, yet. Just hold on to me."

We made our way gingerly down the stairs—they were wet and slippery, and the old iron handrail was covered with slime.

"Where do you think we'll come out?" she whispered, as we raced along a low, narrow passageway.

"I know exactly where," I answered. "This is the ancient escape route that I knew was here somewhere. We'll come out in the boat-house."

Our little motorboat was where we'd left it in the still, foggy lake. As before, when we'd left Constance's villa, Immaculata rowed us out several yards before starting the engine.

I know she was as high on the discovery and as grateful for our clean escape as I was, but we didn't talk until we'd reached Constance's dock, and then we just whispered.

"He's crazier than I thought he was," she said.

"That man is about to come apart at the seams. All it would take is a little push."

It was after three when we told each other good night. I restowed my equipment, making sure any dampness from the fog was wiped off and all was back in good order, before I fell into bed and a deep, deep sleep that was filled with visions of the extraordinary Madonna Illuminata, who now, I hoped, had a smile on her face. Tomorrow was looking much brighter.

CHAPTER 66

When the waiter arrived with my morning coffee at ten, he brought the note Immaculata had slipped under my door.

> Good morning, Kick,
> What a beautiful day it is—I hope you'll take some time to rest. I've gone to early Mass and back to the convent for the day, but don't worry, I'll see you at the wedding. I thank God for all you've done for the sisters and I'm praying for your salvation. See you soon.
>
> With all love in Christ,
Mother Immaculata, Abbess
Little Sisters of the Poor

I called Thomas and invited him over for coffee. I told him we'd found the jeweled Madonnas and I e-mailed the photos to his phone so he would know what he was looking for and would be able to make the arrest.

"When will you do it?"

"I need to consult with my Italian colleagues and make sure all the paperwork is in order. That will probably take right up until the time of the wedding. I'll wait until the service is over before making the arrest, try to do it as unobtrusively as possible."

"Good luck, with Giovanna stuck to you like glue. Unobtrusive is not in her vocabulary. Any progress on the rubies?"

"Not that I'm aware of," he said. "Are you sure you don't know where they are?"

"I promise you I don't. I think it must have been one of the waiters."

"Thanks for the coffee. I'd better get back to work. What are you doing today?"

"This and that."

"You're not going to be seeing Freddie, are you? I don't want you anywhere near that man."

"That makes the two of us. Don't worry about me, Thomas. You just focus on capturing him. I'll be fine."

We kissed good-bye and as soon as the door was closed, I pulled out my canvas Hermès travel bags and started to pack. There was no reason for me to stay around and attend the wedding. I'd done all I could and the rest was up to Thomas and the authorities. I hated not being able to tell Immaculata good-bye, though. But maybe that was better. As I tucked in my essentials, I thought about the magnificent wardrobes I'd had to abandon in my flights from Portofino and Switzerland. At least I'd never left any jewelry behind. I closed the cases. Just one more errand and I'd be wrapped up.

I called Executive Aviation Services at Malpensa and reserved a small jet in the name of Mrs. Lillian Hallaby. "I should be there by three o'clock, but it might be a bit earlier or possibly a bit later. I'm driving down from the lake country."

"Would a twelve-hour hold be more convenient, Mrs. Hallaby?"

"That's an excellent idea."

Our business completed, I clipped on Bijou's leash and went for a last stroll around Orta San Giulio. We climbed up to Sacro Monte.

The day was cool and a number of leaves had fallen on the mossy pathway. When we got to the top of the hill, I took out my binoculars and looked across the lake at the castello. There was nothing different to see, all looked normal. I would be sorry to miss the grand finale—miss Thomas apprehending Freddie red-handed in the trophy room in front of the case of stolen Madonnas. In spite of his attempt to keep it low key, Giovanna had antennae, spies, and tentacles all over the place—she'd get it all on film, so at least I'd be able to watch it later on her evening program.

I headed back down the hill. It was noon when I rang the bell at Constance's villa. The maid showed me upstairs to her bedroom. The masseuse had just left, and Constance was stretched out on her chaise, wrapped in a thick terry towel.

"Amanda, I'm so glad to see you. Tell me, did you find the boat all right? How did it all go?"

"Everything went perfectly—we couldn't have done it without you and Sylvia. Any new developments with 'Clifton'?" I made quotation marks with my fingers.

She shook her head with disgust. "I'm going to keep him in sight until after the wedding, then I'll tell him ta-ta. I can't thank you enough for saving me from what would have been complete public humiliation."

"What about Edgar and Lauren?"

"I think that will self-destruct soon, as well."

"And you'll have him back."

Constance nodded. "I know you probably don't understand, but Edgar and I are in this together. I know he loves me. He's just gone a bit off the rails, but I want him back. And I know he wants me back, too."

"And William?"

"You didn't see him and Katie on your way in?"

I shook my head.

"They're in the garden, I think. He's in good spirits. Did you know he met Mamie for early Mass?"

"No." I was legitimately surprised. "How interesting."

"Maybe she's talking some sense into him. Oh, well. He's been in a good mood ever since he got back. And Katie's like his mirror—if he's happy, she's happy. I wonder if the carbinieri will find the rubies?"

"They will. The parure's been lost and found a number of times before. I know you need to get dressed, but I've brought you a gift," I said.

"Oh?"

I got up and locked the door, then reached into my pockets and pulled out the felt bags and laid them on the coffee table. "When the parure is recovered," I said. "It may or may not be discovered or revealed that the stones in it are fakes."

"What?"

I nodded. "The real stones were replaced several years ago with very good replicas." I unwrapped the large ruby and handed it to her, where it sat in the palm of her hand like a fiery red egg. "These bags contain the real stones. Several million dollars worth."

Constance stared at the ruby and shook her head. Tears filled her eyes and she looked up at me. "You can't imagine what this means to me."

"I think I can. I'll see you at the wedding." I left her still sitting on the chaise, looking speechlessly back and forth between me and the cache of jewels.

⟋⟍ ⟋⟍

As Bijou and I walked back through the piazza, I changed my mind. I wanted to attend the ceremony, to see Thomas's moment of triumph, to see my new friends one more time, and make certain Sylvia and her mother and Victoria were all right. Sylvia had the hardest job at the moment: keeping her eye (and her pocketed gun) on Freddie to make sure he didn't try to leave the property. It didn't feel right to me to be walking out on her, or Constance, just when they may need me the most.

I decided to stay.

I stopped at the town dock and visited with the handsome young captain of the water taxi Lauren had used the day before, and then had a crispy little pizza Margherita and glass of Immaculata's Santa Maria del Lago Nebbiolo for lunch at Café Venus.

At three o'clock, I joined the other guests for the ride across the water to the wedding.

CHAPTER 67

Sunlight winked in and out of the chapel through broken clouds, as the music began and guests were escorted in by ushers dressed in formal morning suits with gray-and-black-striped pants and black, slightly dove-tailed jackets. The chapel filled up quickly, and finally it was time for members of the immediate family to take their places. Immaculata still wasn't there, and I realized with a terrible pang that she might not come. It wouldn't be unreasonable for her to leave the official business end of the caper to Thomas and the authorities, they would restore the Order's possessions to them in due time. She was doing what I had intended to do, but the thought of not seeing her one last time filled me with terrible sadness.

An usher escorted the Duchess, whose ostrich plumes wafted gently as she proceeded up the aisle at a stately pace. She took her seat in front of me and turned her head slightly in my direction, indicating she had something to say. I leaned in.

"I believe we're on to something," she muttered.

"Excellent, your grace."

There was the sound of a ruckus at the rear of the chapel.

"Well, what about me?" Lauren said in a loud voice. "What am I supposed to do? Just stand here all by myself?"

"Shut your yap and wait here," said Edgar.

"I told you, I'm happy to take Constance," said Owen. His voice had taken on a bit of a wheedle.

"Get out of my way," said Edgar. "I'm taking her. It's my son's wedding."

Then Edgar, with Constance and Katie looking triumphant on either arm, rushed up the aisle practically at a dead run. He shoved them into the front pew on the groom's side and then rushed around in front of them, back down the side aisle, and appeared again almost immediately, slightly red and puffing, sweating uncontrollably, making his way back up the center aisle with Lauren. In the meantime, Owen came up the side aisle and planted himself between Constance and Katie, who scooted as far away from him as she could get.

With the mother of the groom settled, it was Sylvia's turn, and she advanced toward the altar with an usher as though she were having a lovely stroll. She wore an ice blue silk suit and a gorgeous array of diamonds. She looked at me and smiled. She appeared calm and relaxed. I knew it was because she would be leaving this place the second the ceremony was over—and would never see it, or Freddie Vasvar, again.

The music changed, and a priest in ornate white satin robes embroidered with gold thread stepped from the side of the altar along with two acolytes. William and Roman appeared. Roman had a slightly smaller bandage across his nose, but his eyes were now completely black. I wondered how he'd explain his appearance at the Old Masters auction tonight, and hoped it wouldn't be off-putting to the buyers. Maybe it would make them sympathetic. I could tell he was scarcely holding it all together, that he wanted to be anywhere but where he was at this moment. I couldn't imagine what-all was going through his mind, having to watch his beloved marry his friend, when it was him she wanted.

Alice's attendant came down the aisle in a lovely burnt siena satin gown. She was carrying a bouquet of pale roses and berries and was followed by a darling little girl in a white lace dress with a ribboned garland of white roses in her hair. The little girl dropped her petals judiciously, arriving at the altar with most still in her basket.

The music changed again, to Mendelssohn's Wedding March. The congregation stood and all eyes turned to see Alice and her father. She looked every inch the princess bride. Her dark hair was pulled into a knot and she wore an elaborate antique diamond and pearl tiara in a lace-and-festoon design. An antique lace veil, falling from the back of the tiara, spread along the long, full train of her strapless pure white satin gown. Other than the tiara, her only jewelry was her engagement ring and pearl earrings, a stark reminder of the missing Vasvar ruby parure. Her bouquet was pure white roses with trailing satin ribbons. Alice's eyes were especially dark and blank. She'd clearly been sedated.

The bandage was gone from Freddie's scalp, showing an angry red line of stitches. His expression was jovial, no one would ever be able to tell he'd been completely inebriated and sobbing his heart out the night before. A rasher of medals and ribbons decorated the breast of his tail coat and he smiled broadly as he escorted his daughter down the aisle. William stepped into her line of vision and drew in a deep breath. She looked at him without any emotion.

When she and her father arrived at the bottom of the steps, William turned and faced the priest as Freddie stood between him and Alice. After the service's customary introductory words, the priest asked,

"Who gives this woman to be married to this man?"

Freddie turned to look at his daughter and opened his mouth to answer, when something outside the windows caught his eye. Then his jaw dropped and he gaped in horror. "NO!" He screamed. "NO!"

We all turned to see what he was looking at. It was Immaculata, in a starched white habit, holding the Madonna Illuminata. The rest of the sisters slowly formed a semicircle behind her, each holding a jeweled statuette.

Freddie bolted.

I ran after him, followed by Thomas and Giovanna. But he was way ahead of all of us—we could hear the locks being turned on the trophy room door from down the hall. I took Thomas's arm.

"Come with me." I pulled him out the front door to the lawn at the top of the cliff.

"Stop!" he said. "You're going the wrong way."

"I'm not. Trust me. You'll never catch him going that way."

He, Giovanna, a cameraman, and I raced to the lift and pushed the button, but the ancient thing was far below at the dock. There was no time to wait for it to grind its way to the top.

"Oh, hell," I said and took off my shoes. "Hold on tight."

We started down the cliff-front steps, which at least had the benefit of being dry and having a solid iron handrail, unlike the slimy steps and ancient handrail I knew Freddie was now negotiating in the dark.

"What's happening?" Giovanna said.

"I'm not entirely sure," Thomas answered.

"You'll see," I said. "You just have to take my word for it."

Finally, we arrived at the bottom and raced across the dock and into the boathouse. I pointed up the steep stairs. "He's going to come through that door any second, Thomas. Get up there and greet him."

He didn't hesitate. He sprinted up the steps to the locked door that led into the small room where the secret passageway ended.

"Don't turn on your lights until he comes through the door, Giovanna," I instructed as I went over to the two family launches, opened their engine covers, and removed a sparkplug from each one of them. "He mustn't know you and Sir Thomas are here until it's too late."

She looked at me, confused that it was I giving her orders, and nodded. "All right." She turned and watched and waited.

I tossed the sparkplugs in the water as I left the boathouse. Neither she nor Thomas noticed I was gone. The elevator had just arrived back at the bottom with a load of very curious wedding guests, all of whom dashed past me to see what was happening. I turned and went in the opposite direction to the end of the dock where my water taxi waited. The captain helped me on board and off we went.

Once we'd gotten some distance away, I looked up. Immaculata and the sisters were at the top of the cliff. Wedding guests and carbinieri crowded around them. She turned and saw my boat. She knew it was me. She stepped away from the throng and stood at the top of the cliff. She waved and waved. Just like a child waving good-bye to her mother.

I waved back. I was glad to be so far away so she couldn't see the tears streaming down my face.

London

I got to my flat in time to catch Giovanna's evening wrap-up and see the expression on Freddie's face when he'd thrown open the upper door in the boathouse and the TV lights came on and Thomas grabbed his arm and expertly twisted it behind his back and then handcuffed him. Freddie, still in shock by the vision of Immaculata and the nuns holding up the Madonnas, burst into tears and fell to his knees on the stairs, almost pulling Thomas down on top of him. All-in-all, as Thomas helped him to his feet and escorted him carefully out to the dock, it was at once both a humiliating and gratifying end to a very sad story.

As I watched, I felt much less pleasure in the scene than I had expected, and I realized it was because it reminded me of just how long the arm of the law is. I was relieved to have been able to clean up at least some of the fake jewelry at Ballantine & Company, but I didn't want to think about how much more of it there was out there.

At seven-thirty Monday morning, I went to my old hairdresser on Sloane Square and by nine o'clock, he'd restored my hair to honey blond and secured my French twist with a thin tortoise-shell comb. Then I went to the office. I'd only been gone five days, but it felt like a lifetime.

I'd no sooner sat down at my desk than Roman appeared.

"Good heavens!" I said. "I certainly wouldn't want to see the other fellow. I hope you won."

"I did." Roman smiled. The bruises around his eyes were the color of eggplant, but at least the bandage was off his nose, which was now even more attractive in its imperfection, giving his handsome face additional ruggedness.

I knew he'd won because when my little jet landed in London, I had to wait onboard while he and Alice, still in her wedding gown, deplaned from Edgar Flynn's Gulfstream V. They must have left in one of the helicopters that was parked in the castle courtyard while all chaos was going on at the dock. Three dark-suited gentlemen waited at the foot of the Gulfstream's steps, and I assumed they were there to repossess the aircraft.

"Congratulations on a fine auction Saturday night. I see that you set some records."

"I think it was the curiosity factor," he laughed. "I know you're busy. I just wanted to stop in and say I'm glad you're feeling better."

"Thank you. Let's catch up later today."

I spent the morning dealing with paperwork with Ruth, who appeared somewhat snooty about my return, as though she had a secret. What she didn't know was that the first thing I'd done upon my return was scan my office for listening and visual surveillance devices, because I knew she was a sneak and a gossip. I'd found a little microphone masquerading as a pencil eraser in my leather pencil cup, and dropped it into a bottle of water, which I then put in the bottom drawer of my desk.

"Mrs. Edgar Flynn to see you, Miss Keswick," she announced shortly after lunch. She shot a quick glance at the pencil cup, trying to see if the mike was still there.

I knew sooner or later Constance would appear at Ballantine &
Company to discuss the planned auction of her jewelry, but she'd
come much sooner than I'd expected. I walked around my desk when
she entered and extended my hand. I was inordinately happy to see
her and resisted the urge to throw my arms around her.

"Mrs. Flynn," I said. "What a great pleasure to see you again. What
may we offer you? Champagne? A cup of tea?"

"Tea would be perfect. I'm not quite ready for any champagne,
although I do have a lot to celebrate."

"Orange rolls?"

She paused for a second. "Why not?!"

Once Ruth had brought the tea and the rolls and closed the
door—soon to discover her surveillance plan had failed—I took my
seat. As Constance opened her purse, I noticed she'd abandoned her
pink gold Rolex for a more conservative watch.

"How may we be of service today?"

"You probably heard about the wedding fiasco?"

I nodded. "It would have been difficult to miss. I'm sorry."

Constance smiled. "Don't be sorry—nothing but good came out of
the occasion." She placed a pile of familiar-looking jewel bags on my
desk. "You probably also heard that the Vasvar ruby parure was stolen."

"I did."

"Whoever ends up with it will have the unhappy experience of
discovering that all the jewels in the parure are fakes."

"No!"

Constance nodded and smiled. "Someone will be very, very sorry."
She pushed the bags toward me. "These are the real stones."

"But how? . . ."

"It's a long story. But I'd like to have these auctioned as soon as
possible."

"You don't want to hold off awhile to see if the parure is recovered?"

Constance looked me in the eye. "Miss Keswick, it would be in no
one's best interests to have these things reunited. I don't even want
you to mention that these are the Vasvar rubies. I just want you to sell

them. I'd also like you to sell this watch." She pulled the Rolex Owen had given her out of her purse. "And these pearls." Out came Owen's fake necklace.

"Very well. If you don't mind waiting, I'll ask our jewelry director, Mr. Merrill, to come in to draw up the inventory."

Once Talbot Merrill had inventoried the Vasvar jewels and Rolex, he picked up the pink pearls and weighed them in his hand and then examined them through his loupe. "These are very beautiful, Mrs. Flynn. But they aren't appropriate for us to auction."

"Why not?"

"I'm sorry to be the one to inform you, but these are synthetic. Very good synthetics, but synthetic nevertheless."

"What do you mean, 'synthetic'?"

"I mean they are fake."

"You're *kidding*." Constance's mouth fell open, and I had to bite my lips to keep from laughing.

"I'm sorry, I'm not kidding."

Constance started to laugh. "That bastard. Well, it'll catch up with him sooner or later, I'm sure."

"I'm not sure who you're referring to," said Talbot. "But I'm sure you're right." He let the pearls slide back into their felt bag and laid it delicately in front of Constance. She removed the pearls from their sac as though they were infected and dropped them into the waste-basket, where they landed with a definitively tinny thud.

"If you'd be kind enough to sign this inventory," Talbot said. "We will get to work immediately on the appraisals."

When he was gone, Constance took a bite of her second orange roll. "Do you worry about your weight?" she asked me.

I shook my head. "Not overly. I'm not completely cavalier about it, but it just is what it is."

"I met a wonderful woman on this ridiculous Italian wedding weekend. You remind me of her."

"Oh?"

"Well, just in some ways. She wasn't fat or anything, but she was a woman with presence. Stature. And she didn't worry about her weight, either. I've never met anyone with so much confidence. So much sangfroid."

"I see. I'll take that as a compliment."

Constance shook her head. "It was bizarre. She said her name was Lady Amanda Bonham and she was from Scotland."

"And she wasn't?"

"Well, she pretended to be Marchioness Sylvia Kennington's oldest friend when she was around me, and my oldest friend when she was around Sylvia. But finally Sylvia and I figured out neither one of us knew her."

"Oh? That's fairly nervy."

"That's nothing!" Constance laughed. "When Sylvia and I confronted her, she said she was an undercover police officer, Sir Thomas Curtis's assistant. She's the one who told us about the dead nuns and that Sylvia's husband was a psychopathic murderer, and she also told me that—do you remember when I told you about the man, Clifton Boatwright, who I was seeing?"

"Yes. Of course."

"Well, Amanda, or whatever her real name is, told me he was actually a con man named Owen Brace."

"No!" I said. "He is a terrific cad—he owned Ballantine and Company for a few months."

"So I understand. She warned me about him, and so I got out of that affair just in the nick of time. And he immediately ran off with Edgar's fiancée, that inane model, Lauren Cambridge."

"So now you have your husband back."

Constance nodded. "I know he's a mess, but he's my mess," she said somewhat shyly. "But it turned out that Lady Amanda not only wasn't an aristocrat, she wasn't an undercover police officer, either. When I asked Sir Thomas where she'd gone—because she simply up and disappeared right in the middle of all the excitement—he didn't know who I was talking about. Isn't that remarkable?"

I nodded. "I wonder who she was?"

"I don't know," Constance said. She took a last sip of her tea. "But I'd love to see her again. She was simply a marvelous person."

"Maybe she'll find you."

Constance stood up. "I hope so. Well, I'm off to meet Sylvia Kennington for lunch. That was another good outcome of the weekend—Sylvia and I have become friends. She's also a remarkable woman, brave as brave can be. Nothing like what the papers make her out to be."

I came around my desk and escorted Constance to the door, where I offered my hand. "Thank you for coming by and giving us another opportunity to be of service to you Mrs. Flynn."

We shook hands and looked in each other's eyes. Did she know it was me? She didn't, but I couldn't help wishing she did. I really would have liked to go to lunch with her and Sylvia.

Constance hadn't mentioned either Katie or William, and I wondered what they'd done when the whole affair collapsed. I supposed one of these days, their names would turn up here and there, and maybe I'd even get to see one of them. But I wasn't counting on it. There was no reason why our paths should cross again, but I hoped Katie would be all right.

CHAPTER 69

Late that afternoon, there was a knock on my office door.

"Come in," I called.

The door opened and there stood Sir Bertram, looking more fit than I'd ever seen him. I jumped to my feet and ran to greet him.

"Bertram! What a wonderful surprise."

We embraced each other quickly.

"Come in. Come in." I closed the door, but not before noticing a certain smugness on Ruth's face. " Sit down. How are you feeling?"

"Never better. It's amazing what a regular blood flow, a reasonable diet, and sobriety can do for you."

"I'm so happy to see you. I hope you've found the house in satisfactory condition. The season has had an excellent start."

Bertram nodded. "I'm so grateful to you, Kick, for stepping in at such a crucial point. I look back on it and I can see that I'd gone off the deep end. If you hadn't come to my rescue, I hate to think where Ballantine and Company would be today."

"Bertram," I said. "It's only been four weeks."

"Four critical weeks. You've seen to it that the season had a successful launch and I understand you've brought in the Flynn jewelry collection, which will make an excellent centerpiece for Magnificent Jewelry in the spring."

"It will. But Bertram, I'm getting a sense from you that that's not why you're here. That something's hanging."

He looked at his hands and then back at me. "There is, Kick. As I said, you stepped in when I desperately needed you, but now I need to ask you to go. I've made so many disastrous decisions and mistakes over the last many months, I need to be the one to correct them. If you're here, it will be too easy for me to backslide, as my counselor puts it, revert to my old ways."

"Are you firing me, Bertram?"

"Well, I had rather hoped you wouldn't see it that way. That you'd take it I was saving you from becoming an enabler." He gave me an encouraging smile.

It took every bit of my self-control not to jump to my feet and toss him in the air with joy. I was overwhelmed with relief. "I understand."

"No hard feelings, I hope."

"No hard feelings, at all," I said. "I'm very happy for you and think this is a good decision. It will keep the lines of authority much cleaner."

He nodded and got to his feet. "Will you come tell me good-bye on your way out?"

"Of course."

Of course, I didn't stop in and tell him good-bye. His door was closed and Ruth must have been in with him because she was nowhere in sight. I simply left and drove back to Eaton Terrace through a lovely London mist.

At the flat, I removed the small jeweled Madonna from my safe and packed it for shipment, but before I sealed it up, I wrote my French cell phone number—a number only Thomas had—on a bit of note paper and tucked it inside the package. I would drop it in the FedEx box at the airport. I didn't know if Immaculata was my daughter—or if William was my son—but just in case Immaculata ever needed anything, I wanted her to have a way to find me.

I picked up my travel cases. I could still make the last flight to Marseilles.

"Come on, Bijou," I said. "Let's go home."

CHAPTER 70

La Petite Pomme, Éygalières

"I never thought I'd be so happy to be home," Thomas said.

We were both collapsed on our chaises on the terrace in the afternoon sun. Bijou was stretched out at my feet sleeping so deeply she could have been dead.

"Neither did I," I sighed. "Tell me," I asked after a few more silent moments, "how did your assignment end up?"

"Everything's back where it belongs. Case closed."

"Did you get to see them?"

Thomas nodded.

"Did you see the Darya-i-Nur?"

"I did."

"And Farah Diba's tiara with the seven egg-sized emeralds?"

"I did."

"And the red Pahlavi crown with the 3,700 diamonds and pearls and the white plume?"

"I did."

"Well, *tell* me, Thomas. Don't just keep saying 'I did.' What are they like?"

"They're all unbelievable, Kick. But frankly, they're a bit wasted on me. You would have appreciated them—I simply wanted to get them off my hands and back in the vault where they belonged. I'll tell you one thing, though."

"What?"

"Those seven giant emeralds aren't as beautiful as I thought they'd be."

"What do you mean?" I turned to look at him, leaning on my elbow.

"They have lots of little black specks and cracks all through them."

"You're not serious."

"I am."

"Mmm," I said drowsily and fell back on my pillow. "That makes me feel better."

"Thought it would." Thomas yawned and fell asleep.

When I wakened, Thomas was still snoozing, so I tiptoed inside to fix my makeup and then attempt to put together a batch of those incredible molten chocolate-cherry cakes I'd had for dessert at the Four Seasons in Milan the night my Italian adventure began.

I didn't have a specific recipe, but I knew my way around chocolate quite well and had made dozens of cakes over the years. How hard could it be? I turned the oven to 425 degrees, cut half a cup of butter into a double-boiler, picked up a big chef's knife and carved ten ounces of semi-sweet Valrhona chocolate into pieces and slid them into the melting butter. As soon as the chocolate began to soften, I removed the pan from the heat and stirred absentmindedly—I couldn't stop thinking about my friends, Constance and Sylvia and Immaculata. What did our friendship hold in store for the future? Certainly something. We hadn't met by chance—I didn't believe in chance.

Once the chocolate and butter were smoothly blended, I opened a tin of dark cherries—they were lovely and plump, like fat deep purple marbles—and poured them into a sieve. Then I mixed up egg, sugar, flour and a little baking soda, added the cooled chocolate, and mixed it all together for about three minutes until it was smooth silky. I was so preoccupied, I wasn't really paying attention, and as I ladled the batter into four buttered, sugared ramekins I made a terrible mess, slopping it all over the counter and even onto the floor.

"Pay attention," I said out loud as I dropped five cherries into each cake.

I'd just opened the oven door when my cell phone rang, but by the time I got to it, I'd missed the call and the caller's phone number was blocked. There was only one person it could be. Immaculata. I set the timer for twenty minutes, which I knew wasn't long enough but it was a good checkpoint, and busied myself cleaning up the mess, praying a message would come in. Finally, it did.

"Thank you, Kick," Immaculata said. "God bless you."

And that was it.

I put my hands on the counter and looked out the window as the sun set in the valley. Maybe that was it. Maybe there was such a thing as luck, after all. Chance. Accidents. A moment in time.

Thomas appeared. "Do you mind if I turn on the TV? I think it's almost time for Giovanna's program."

"Not in the slightest. Oh, there's your girlfriend now," I teased.

He uncorked a bottle of champagne. "She's *not* my girlfriend." He handed me a flute and we touched our glasses. "*You're* my girlfriend."

"We're going to Giovanna MacDougal at the Milan airport," said the anchor, "for some breaking news."

There she was, standing in front of the bank of scanners at the security checkpoint in Malpensa's main international terminal.

"Thank you, Roger," she said. "We've just learned that superstar odel, Lauren Cambridge, and an unidentified traveling companion, been arrested trying to clear security for a British Airways flight to n. The airport authorities tell us that they received an anony- and the two of them were apprehended just here"—she the checkpoint behind her—"with the missing six-piece, var ruby parure, which, as you know, was stolen during a e night before the ill-fated Vasvar/Flynn wedding. Italian taken the two of them into custody—wait, I'm hear- that we have some video—yes, there they are being n." Images of handcuffed Lauren Cambridge and her unidentified traveling companion—Owen Brace—being shoved unceremoniously into a police van filled the screen and I suddenly knew without a doubt that William and Katie Flynn had been the ones to steal the jewels, and while the police rushed around the villa that night, Katie had scooted to Owen's room and tucked half in his suitcase and then gone to the hotel and buried the other half deep in Lauren's fancy Goyard travel tote.

Thomas and I started laughing.

"She'll be out in no time," he said. "But this won't go so easily for him in Italy. Particularly because he's broke and won't be able to make bail and they have the most complicated system of jurisprudence on the planet."

"Good. He deserves it." I turned off the television and handed him a small square box. "Welcome home," I said.

"What's this?"

I gave him a big hug and kissed him. I was so glad to see him. "It's dinner," I said.

He removed the lid and withdrew a Ziploc bag that contained what looked like three golf balls wrapped in tin foil. The second he opened the bag, a huge smile creased his face. "Oh, Kick. You shouldn't have."

By then the aroma of the rare white truffles filled the kitchen. Thomas unwrapped one and held the delicacy to his nose and inhaled. "Oh, my. What are you going to do with this?"

"I thought we'd start with asparagus risotto and then lamb chops. What do you think?"

"Sounds wonderful." He picked up the bottle of champagne. "I have the perfect appetizer in mind. Follow me."

At some point I could hear the kitchen timer buzzing and then could smell the chocolate-cherry cakes burning. Too bad. I didn't care. I was home. I was with my husband. We had white truffles. And each other. It was my lucky day.